D0836916

Kudos for *The R*
Craig Parshall's latest legal-suspense novel

"A captivating novel with mystery, suspense, faith and values. Craig Parshall has
written a book that won't let the reader put it down. A story that mixes the one of
history's great mysteries with gripping legal suspense, it will intrigue every reader.
Bravo!"

—Ted Baehr
Chairman of the Christian Film & Television Commission
and publisher of Movieguide ®

"A powerful novel, with the intriguing detail that is typical of Craig Parshall's fiction...This legal thriller doesn't miss a beat, putting you into the dead center of a
murder case only to find out you're confronted with a spiritual mystery."

—Phil Cooke
founder and creative director, Cooke Pictures, Burbank, California

...And for the novels in the Chambers of Justice series

The Resurrection File

"Powerful...one of the most fascinating books I have read in years."

—Tim LaHaye,
coauthor of the bestselling LEFT BEHIND® series

"A compelling, realistic story...Incorporates...spiritual awakening without ever
being preachy."

—Faithful Reader.com

Custody of the State

"This is not only a great mystery, but also a deeply moving, redemptive book...
Deserves translation to the big screen. Bravo!"

—Ted Baehr,
chairman of the Christian Film & Television Commission
and publisher of *Movieguide*®

"Authentic characters and a believable story line make *Custody of the State* gripping and even unnerving reading."

—*Christian Library Journal*

The Accused

"Grisham and Clancy...move over! Craig Parshall has truly arrived...*The Accused* [is] a super thriller—a masterful tale of suspense as well as romance...it could be a superb motion picture!"

—**Ken Wales,**
executive producer of the CBS television series *Christy*
and veteran Hollywood filmmaker

"I was riveted from the first page. Not only an excellent novel, it is also a highly accurate account of military justice and the covert world of special operations."

—**Lt. Col. Robert "Buzz" Patterson, USAF Retd.,**
former military aide to President Clinton
and author of the bestselling book *Dereliction of Duty*

Missing Witness

"A legal thriller wrapped inside a very poignant love story with a twist...Fresh, compelling storytelling...with enough grit to appeal to a mass secular audience."

—**Chris Carpenter,** producer, CBN.com

"The author has a true gift for storytelling."

—**Teens4Jesus Library**

The Last Judgment

"A fitting finale for [Parshall's] Chambers of Justice series. *The Last Judgment* incorporates all of the elements that made us wish the series would continue indefinitely."

—**Faithful Reader.com**

"Craig Parshall is a master at weaving morality into the narrow, litigious [confines] of the courtroom."

—**CBN.com**

THE ROSE
CONSPIRACY

THE ROSE
CONSPIRACY

CRAIG PARSHALL

HARVEST HOUSE PUBLISHERS

EUGENE, OREGON

THE ROSE CONSPIRACY
Copyright © 2009 by Craig Parshall
Published by Harvest House Publishers
Eugene, Oregon 97402
www.harvesthousepublishers.com

Library of Congress Cataloging-in-Publication Data
Parshall, Craig, 1950-
The rose conspiracy / Craig Parshall.
    p. cm.
ISBN 978-0-7369-1514-4 (pbk.)
    1. Murder—Fiction. 2. Artists—Fiction. 3. Freemasonry—Fiction. 4. Washington (DC)—
Fiction. I. Title.
PS3616.A77R67 2009
813'.6—dc22

                                                                2008032122

"The world is in pain,
our secrets to gain."
—A SONG OF THE CRAFT

This is a work of fiction. As such, all of the characters and situations are fictional, including the character of Horace Langley, Secretary of the Smithsonian Institution, as well as all references to that institution, with the exception only of the physical appearance of its famous "Castle" administration building and the general configuration of those political categories that populate its Board of Regents.

However, the references in this novel to the religious philosophy and mysteries of the esoteric followers of "the Craft" are taken from research and writings on speculative Freemasonry, much of it authored by Freemasons themselves. It is unknown to or ignored by rank-and-file members, who consider the Freemasons to constitute merely a fraternal or social organization. "The secret" revealed here was gleaned from the symbols, ceremonies, and history of Masonry itself, and from the writings of those who have studied it.

CHAPTER 1

The driver behind the steering wheel was sweating like a hunter in the dripping heat of the jungle.

But this was a very different kind of jungle.

It was five minutes before midnight, and the car was cruising along the marble-and-monument-studded streets of the Capitol Hill district of Washington DC. The driver was tugging at a collar edge. Drops of perspiration trickled down back and torso, even with the air conditioning on. Maybe it was the freakish heat wave that had hit the city, causing brownouts and power failures across the city. Maybe it was something else... the nasty assignment that had to be taken care of. When the trigger was pulled, and it was all over, the long-missing pages of John Wilkes Booth's personal diary would then be in the grip of someone else's hand.

Yet the driver knew what was actually at stake that night. And it really wasn't about the Booth diary. Or even the assassination of Abraham Lincoln at the hand of a Confederate radical. The note that was about to be seized contained a message with ramifications far beyond any of that.

Sweltering temperatures had suffocated Washington with a relentless haze of humidity that week. Even though it was only June, temperatures were in the low hundreds during the day and in the nineties at night.

The only thing cool to the touch was the white marble of the statues and monuments. The driver steered past the Lincoln Monument and then slowed the car slightly. As usual, interior lights illuminated the massive likeness of Abraham Lincoln in his great marble chair. Once past the monument, the car picked up speed, entered Constitution Avenue,

and started heading toward the National Mall. The destination was the
Castle, the nineteenth-century red-brick building full of turrets and spires
where the administrative headquarters of the Smithsonian Institution
were housed.

The driver parked the car a block away and walked quickly to the
side entrance of the Castle—then, reaching the door, quickly tapped a
code into the security panel. The lock clicked open.

Upstairs, the lights were still on in the office of Horace Langley,
Secretary of the Smithsonian Institution. He was working late.

But the object of his work that night was not business as usual.

Only moments before, Langley had opened his safe and pulled out
a metal case containing a folder enclosed within a plastic zip bag. Now
he was studying the contents—eighteen pages from the diary of John
Wilkes Booth. They had been missing for nearly one hundred and fifty
years. Their disappearance had occurred suspiciously, about the same time
as the federal investigation into the assassination of President Abraham
Lincoln was taking place. Booth's diary had been taken when the assassin
was captured and killed. But at the time at least one witness swore that
eighteen pages had been removed from it.

That was the point at which those pages seemed to have vanished
forever.

Then, a century and a half later, the granddaughter and sole heir of
a farmer in central Virginia went rummaging through her grandfather's
attic after his death and happened upon some boxes of old letters and
papers. But one sheaf of papers looked different. While much of the
writing on them was faded and undecipherable to the layman's eye, a
reference to Abraham Lincoln was visible. In his will, the farmer had
given everything to his granddaughter—except the papers. Those, he
said, must go to the Smithsonian Institution.

After some wrangling with lawyers, the eighteen pages were transferred to the Smithsonian. Horace Langley had succeeded in keeping the
discovery from being leaked to the press, even though he was thoroughly
convinced that the pages belonged to the Booth diary.

That June evening, as Langley studied the pages in his office, he knew
that some eight hours hence, a council of epigraphers and historians were

scheduled to convene and, for the first time, to study the Booth diary entries in that same office.

But he had to get the first look.

He had a pair of white gloves on as he studied the brittle pages, yellowed from age. A pad of paper lay on the desk in front of him, next to his pen. There was a glass of water off to the side.

Langley then began to slowly, painstakingly, write down something on the notepad.

Just a few lines of writing.

He paused to study carefully what he had written.

Then he heard something. He looked up, half-expecting a late-night visitor. "I wasn't sure I would see you," was all Horace Langley had a chance to say.

The individual who had entered through the side door below was now standing in front of Langley holding a handgun with a silencer—and proceeded to fire two clean shots directly into the left upper quadrant of Langley's chest.

The Secretary started to grope upward with his arm, trying to touch the injured area of his chest, but failing. He fell backward into his chair, slumped, and then fell to the floor, where he collapsed on his back, surrounded by an expanding pool of blood.

The shooter stepped over to the desk, picked up the Booth diary pages, placed them back in the plastic zip bag, and put that into a larger bag. The killer snatched the pad of paper, ripped off the top page that had Langley's writing on it and then another page for good measure, and put them also into the bag. Then the killer placed the pad of paper back on the desk with a clean page exposed as Langley lay dying on the floor, making a final gurgling, gasping sound. Before leaving the room, the shooter paused only for a moment at Langley's desk, gazing down at the empty drinking glass that was resting there.

Then, exiting quickly through the same side door below where entrance had been made a few minutes before, Langley's killer made a perfect getaway.

The security guards didn't notice anything out of the ordinary until twenty-five minutes later, when one of them was making the rounds and stopped to check in on the Secretary. He caught sight of Horace Langley's feet protruding past the edge of the desk. And the feet in Langley's dress shoes were absolutely still.

As still as the marble and bronze statues of the famous men that were frozen in time, scattered as monuments across Washington, and that were illuminated by the halogen street lights that buzzed overhead in the suffocating heat of the night.

CHAPTER 2

Two Weeks Later

"You've been called 'one of Washington's most brilliant yet enigmatic lawyers.' That was from the *Washington Post* article. So, how do you react to that kind of assessment?"

"Enigmatically."

"Clever. Okay, let me try it this way...in an article in *Beltway Magazine* you were called a 'triple threat.' You are a trial lawyer and a law professor, as well as a psychologist. So which one really defines who you are?"

"I try not to define myself. I leave that job to reporters like you. And for the record, I decided not to finish my dissertation in psychology. So I never got my PhD in that discipline."

"Why did you leave the law and pursue a graduate degree in psychology, just to return to teaching and practicing law after all?"

"Personal reasons."

"Which would be..."

"Personal."

The female reporter smiled politely.

J.D. Blackstone smiled back. He was used to press interviews. His meteoric rise as a topflight litigator in Washington DC garnered him some of the most celebrated politicians as clients, and some of the most notorious cases. And Blackstone's position as a professor of criminal and constitutional law at the Capital City College School of Law gave him added gravitas.

The reporter was glancing around Blackstone's cramped law-school office. Then she located the picture of Blackstone's wife, Marilyn, with her arm around their fourteen-year-old daughter, Beth. The girl, grinning exuberantly, was dressed in a formal gown. The photo had been taken a few hours before Blackstone had plopped down on his bed for a nap after some sleepless nights of work on a complicated case. And a few hours before his wife and daughter had climbed into the family car and driven off to Beth's piano recital.

"Well, I know, for instance," the reporter went on, "that you've had to deal with some profound tragedy in your life. That must have impacted you."

Blackstone stopped her there with an overobvious sigh.

They always go for that one, he thought to himself. *The soft underbelly.*

The attorney didn't respond. He took an exaggerated glance at his wristwatch.

The reporter took the hint and changed her focus.

She gazed at Blackstone for a moment and studied him before diving into the next line of questions. She found Blackstone attractive. Most women did. He was in his mid-forties but looked younger. His hair, longish, disheveled, curled around his collar. He had a face with strong, angular features. His body was athletic and in great shape.

"Let me just touch for a minute on some of your off-hours avocations," the reporter continued. "You certainly are a man in perpetual motion—and so many different interests." She began flipping through her notes. "Kayaking through the gorges of South America…driving the Baja road rally in the deserts of Mexico. And I find this one really fascinating—you're an equestrian. How did you feel finishing in the top ten competitors in the eight-hundred-mile Santa Fe Trail endurance horse race last year?"

"Sore."

She was about to do a follow-up question, but Blackstone cut her off.

"I'm sorry, but I have a class I need to teach."

"May I watch? I promise to sit in the back of the room. I'll be very quiet."

"I'm afraid not. You see," Blackstone shot back, "I sort of enjoy humiliating my students. And like any good expert in torture, I work best when there are no witnesses."

She gave a little laugh and nodded. Then she rose, turned off her recorder, and threw it and her pad into her purse. Blackstone shook her hand and then blew past her at a fast clip, grabbing a briefcase by the doorway on the run, and headed down the corridor to the lecture hall.

Most of the seventy-eight students were already in their seats when he hurried in. He strode to the lectern, dropped his briefcase, pulled a yellow notepad out, and slapped it down on the podium. Then J.D. Blackstone began.

"Alright, you minions of Lady Justice, first case—*Hamdi v. Rumsfield.* Here's the question: Did the Supreme Court really grant habeas corpus rights to enemy combatants or not?"

But that is when Blackstone noticed a redheaded male law student standing up and raising his hand.

The professor of modern criminal law and policy spotted him, cleared his throat, and nodded for him to speak.

"Professor Blackstone," the student began. "Today is the last class of the year."

"Congratulations, Mr. Delbert," Blackstone shot back. "You've mastered the mysteries of the Gregorian calendar, I see."

"Well, Professor," the student continued. "You had promised us that on the last class period you would submit yourself to questions from the class. *Personal* questions."

A few students were tittering.

Blackstone's face contorted with an overblown expression of pain.

"Fine. Okay," he said with resignation. "But I control the time. You have five minutes. Mr. Delbert, you have showed some admirable boldness here today. Make note of that, students. When in doubt in the practice of law, when lacking in favorable law or strong facts to successfully plead your case, just rely on *audacity*—it works every time."

Several of the students were laughing.

"So Mr. Delbert, you have the first shot."

"Okay," he began with a smirk. "Well, in that case we were to have read for today, *Hamdi v. Rumsfield,* in the opinion authored by Justice Scalia, he quotes the great eighteenth-century British jurist, Sir

William Blackstone. I have heard that you are related to him. Is that really true?"

"Yes," Blackstone said. "Much to the mortification of the rest of his descendants I'm sure."

More laughter.

A female law student in the first row raised her hand, fighting back a grin.

"What do the 'J' and the 'D' stand for in your name?" she asked and then quickly sat down.

"The 'J' was my father's idea. It stands for Justinian, the emperor of Rome in the 500s. His claim to fame, among others, was the *Corpus Iuris Civilis*. You know it as the Justinian Code. The first codification of the laws of Rome into one unified system. That's the kind of name you're stuck with when your father is the Chief Justice of the Illinois Supreme Court and a former President of the American Bar Association."

"How about the 'D' in your name?" the female student asked.

"That one came from my mother. She was a music lover. It stands for a Hungarian composer whose name even I have a hard time pronouncing."

"Hungarian?" someone in the class repeated out loud.

"Yes," Blackstone continued. "You see, I am certified ninety-five percent English. That's the part that makes me so obsessively and coldly analytical."

Then he took a long, dramatic pause.

"And my other five percent is pure Gypsy."

Then he leaned forward to the microphone at the lectern, until his mouth was right up against it, and cocked his eyebrow dramatically.

"And that's the part that makes me *dangerous.*"

The entire class was laughing now.

While a few corners of the class were still chuckling, the law-school secretary entered the hall and scurried to the podium with a pink note slip in her hand. She quietly apologized for the intrusion, gave Blackstone the note, and whispered, "It's from Frieda, the secretary at your law firm. She said it was urgent."

Blackstone glanced down at the note. It read, *"Please come to the law office as soon as your class is over. It's about a new murder case."*

CHAPTER 3

After class, J.D. Blackstone jumped into his Maserati Spyder convertible and motored over to his law office, a twenty-minute drive away in Georgetown. He walked quickly past the desk of Frieda, his secretary, who was on the phone. Frieda hurriedly put the person on hold, and then snatched up a slip of paper and shoved it at Blackstone.

"J.D.," she said, "urgent message. New client. She is coming in momentarily."

"Maybe you ought to have Julia take her," he said. "I need to get back to the college within the hour. We've got our dreaded faculty meeting for the fall semester, cleverly held at the beginning of summer just to torment us..."

"Can't do that. Julia's in court. You'd better read the note."

Blackstone glanced down at the phone message slip.

It read,

> A woman named Vinnie Archmont called. Says she is "target" of grand jury. Smithsonian Institution criminal case. Wants to meet ASAP.

"It's the investigation," Frieda whispered, "into the murder of the Secretary of the Smithsonian, Langley...and the theft—"

"Of the John Wilkes Booth diary pages," Blackstone interjected, finishing her sentence for her. "Yes, I do read the papers, Frieda."

Then he added, "Vinnie...what kind of name is that for a woman?"

Frieda shrugged.

"Fine," Blackstone said. "I'll see her. When?"

"She should be here any minute."

Blackstone disappeared into his office. He leafed through his mail. Mostly magazines. A few of the legal trade papers, the two Capitol Hill dailies, and the latest issues of *Scientific American, Philosophy Monthly,* several current events publications, *Psychology Today,* and the *Southern Poetry Review.*

His intercom buzzed. It was his new client on the way in, Frieda said.

The door opened.

A woman in her early thirties stepped in. She was uncommonly attractive, with deep, dark eyes and a kind of chiseled beauty that still managed to retain a softness to it. Almost a young, girlish look. She was dressed in an artist's smock, blue jeans, and red cowboy boots.

But her hairstyle was an eyeful. Her hair was jet black and configured in a kind of *Gone with the Wind* motif, complete with cascading ringlets, like Scarlett O'Hara. Blackstone was smart enough not to comment on a woman's hair—unless it was to give a glowing compliment. Which he was not about to do.

She was holding the law firm's standard client information sheet, which she handed to Blackstone. He took it, glanced down at it, and then shook her hand. He took a few seconds to study both of her hands, and then smiled and motioned to the chair where she sat down across from his desk.

Blackstone looked over the form. In the blank for "occupation" it said simply "artist." Her studio was listed at an address in the "Torpedo Factory" in Alexandria, Virginia, a stylishly renovated former armaments warehouse dating back to World War II, now converted to boutique art studios and galleries.

He studied her as she smiled brightly. She was grasping one more piece of paper in her hand, carefully folded, which looked like a letter with an envelope.

"I'm here because of this," she said holding up the letter and envelope. But Blackstone didn't move to take them.

"Clients usually *think* they know why they are here," Blackstone said. "But I find that most of the time they don't. Not really."

Then he continued, tapping the client sheet he was holding, "You say here that you are an artist. By the way, are you an athlete?"

"Dear no," she replied with a little giggle. "Why?"

Blackstone ignored her question and probed further.

"Don't lift weights, do gymnastics, anything like that?"

"No, I don't."

He took in her entire frame with a long glance, then he spoke up.

"In that event, I presume you are a sculptor. Right?"

She laughed.

"That's right," she replied with surprise. "So you must be familiar with some of my work."

"No, not at all," he replied.

"Then how did you know?"

"Observation. You are a petite woman, yet you have powerful, deeply veined hands. The kind of hands that result from kneading clay. You have your makeup done professionally, yet you don't any have nail polish on. And I notice you have what appears to be modeling clay under one of your fingernails. Your artist's smock is a little dingy and worn—it is a working piece of clothing for you. But I don't see any watercolor, acrylic, or oil paints on it. So you're not a painter. All that leads me to say you're a sculptor."

"I'm impressed," she said with another big smile.

Blackstone motioned for the letter, which she quickly gave him. Her countenance changed almost as if on cue. Now she had a frightened, confused look.

The letter was on the letterhead of the Office of the United States Attorney for the District of Columbia. It was announcing that Vinnie was the "target" of an ongoing federal grand-jury investigation into "crimes occurring at and in The Smithsonian Institution, including murder and theft of federal documents."

"This is all a huge mistake," she began.

"I hope for your sake that you're right."

"This is serious, isn't it?"

"Yes. Killing a federal official like Horace Langley is a capital offense."

Vinnie had a puzzled look.

"That means that the prosecuting attorney could ask for the death penalty."

The dark-haired beauty was speechless.

"But let's not get ahead of ourselves," Blackstone replied, trying to be consoling. "This is merely a target letter. It doesn't mean you'll get indicted. And it certainly doesn't mean you are going to get convicted. It may mean absolutely nothing...or it could mean something. Depends on what you tell me about your involvement in this thing."

She paused a moment before she spoke. Then she started to explain.

"I knew Horace Langley," she said.

"How well?"

"Professionally."

"Define that."

"I was with him," she said with a stunned look on her face, as if finally realizing the depth of the trouble she was in, "there in his office...with him in the Smithsonian, at the Castle, the day he was murdered."

CHAPTER 4

J.D. Blackstone wasted no time digging into Vinnie Archmont's relationship with the Secretary of the Smithsonian. She said it was strictly professional. On the surface, it seemed to fit.

She said she had received a commission from a nonprofit foundation to sculpt Horace Langley's likeness. The two of them had had several sittings, all of them in the Castle. She had been working on a clay model of his head and shoulders. The plan was to then complete that, fire it in her kiln, and use it as the prototype for the final bronze version. All of the sittings had been in Langley's ornate personal office. The last one, on the day of the murder, was in that same office.

Blackstone buzzed Jason, his paralegal, and had him pull up the schematics of the building off the Internet. In a few minutes, Jason scurried in with a printout.

"Right here," Vinnie said, pointing to a section of the cutaway diagram of the Castle, "that's where we met the day he was killed."

"In that last session, did anything unusual happen?" Blackstone asked.

Vinnie scrunched her shoulders, pursed her lips, and shook her head "no."

Blackstone saw the body language. It was screaming, *I've got more to tell you but I don't feel comfortable.* He decided not to press it. Not yet.

"So tell me," he asked nonchalantly. "What is the big deal about the John Wilkes Booth diary?"

"What do you mean?"

"Why was it worth murdering someone?"

Vinnie was thinking that one over.

"I don't know what you mean."

"Horace Langley was shot to death. The Booth diary pages were stolen. That's what the newspapers said. So I ask you again, what in the world could have been in that diary?"

More shoulder-scrunching from Vinnie.

"Look," Blackstone said. "Maybe you had better come back when you want to really talk to me about what you know."

"I haven't lied," she said, trying to manage a smile.

"Yeah, that's a good start. But what we need here is complete candor."

After a few more uncomfortable seconds Vinnie spoke up.

"I heard that you had lost your wife and daughter in a car accident."

Blackstone was blank-faced and replied simply, "Yes. That's true. Any reason you bring that up?"

"Just wondering if it ever made you think about things."

"What kind of things?"

"Life. Death. Eternity."

"I think," Blackstone said curtly, "you are trying to dodge the point. I think you are hiding information from me. If I am going to be your lawyer, you have to tell me everything. Treat me like a priest. A father confessor. Nothing held back. Absolutely nothing. We have a cloak of confidentiality here between attorney and client."

"What do you believe in, Mr. Blackstone?" she asked.

There was a kind innocence about the way she asked that. Blackstone could see that. *She really wants to know,* he thought to himself.

"I believe in the power of human intelligence," he began, "at least when it is adequately disciplined and harnessed. I believe people can do bad things. I also am firmly convinced that otherwise good people sometimes get blamed for bad things they really did not do. But I stress the word *sometimes.* The statistics say that the overwhelming majority of people who walk into a lawyer's office because they have been charged with a crime are in fact guilty of some kind of criminal offense."

"I thought you said I hadn't been charged with a crime yet."

Blackstone smiled at that.

"You're right. But I was just talking in generalities."

"Mr. Blackstone?" she asked.

Blackstone waited for the point.

Then she smiled a secret little kind of smile, tilted her head coquettishly, and stood up to leave. "Mr. Blackstone," Vinnie said, extending her hand to him. "I like you very much. Perhaps I shall have you as my lawyer. We'll see. But one thing."

"What's that?"

"I don't think you can be either my priest or my father confessor."

She laughed a little when she said that, and then turned and walked out of his office.

Blackstone was sitting there, staring at the target letter from the U.S. Attorney's Office that she left on his desk.

Vinnie Archmont was beautiful but eccentric. And a little too coy for someone who might be charged with a crime that could send her to the death chamber. On the other hand, Blackstone really didn't think that was in the cards. Not a chance in a million. Most likely, the federal prosecutor had sent her the target letter to shake her up. To get her to come running to him and start talking so the government could find out who the real perpetrators were. And if that were the case, the feds were betting on the fact that Vinnie had a connection with someone who had a connection with the murder.

But as he sat at his desk, J.D. Blackstone was not struggling with any of that. What he really wondered about was the question that Vinnie didn't answer.

The one about the Booth diary.

CHAPTER 5

After Vinnie Archmont left, Blackstone looked at his watch and decided he had missed most of the faculty meeting at the college, anyway. So he dashed down to his black Maserati, gunned his way over to the other side of the Beltway, and turned into a medical complex. He parked and hustled across the lot and through the glass door of a banal-looking medical office.

The receptionist recognized him.

"Good afternoon, Professor Blackstone," she said, then glanced down at her appointment book.

"I'm sorry," she continued, "but I don't think Dr. Koesler has you booked today."

"Just tell Jim that his favorite patient is waiting."

"I'm not sure if I can help you."

"Come on, Ginny," he said. "I know Jim always takes an early dinner break at this time. He is probably sitting in his office right now, eating chicken salad, reading something unnervingly exciting—like the newest *Journal of the American Psychiatric Association*."

Ginny was about to throw up another roadblock, when the psychiatrist, Dr. Jim Koesler, stepped across the hall with a Styrofoam container in his hand and ducked into his office.

Before he could close the door, J.D. Blackstone had sprinted down the hall and wedged his foot into the door.

"Jim, so good to see you," Blackstone said with a grin. "Chicken salad again, right?"

24

"You know, J.D.," Koesler muttered unenthusiastically, "you don't believe in appointments…and don't believe in knocking. Those are basics in human civility. Maybe you could start with those and then slowly work your way up."

Then Koesler paused and looked down at the salad he had placed on his desk.

"And it's not chicken," he said with a wry smile. "It's turkey."

"Turkey! You're so wild and unpredictable, Jim!"

"J.D., you help me out in one lawsuit, and as a result, you must think I will indulge your eccentricities forever."

"Much simpler than that. Just refill my prescription. And by the way, where does our friendship fit in here, anyway? Going all the way back to our fraternity days in college."

"Come on. You know the drill," the psychiatrist said.

"Okay. Here it is," Blackstone began in a rote monotone. "My sleeping habits are minimally controlled with the current medication to the point where I can actually sleep a few hours every night. Without it, I suffer from life-altering insomnia, which also affects my eating habits, my work, and my general attentiveness during the day. I have not experienced any adverse reactions with the drug you prescribed. I am not experiencing any dramatic weight changes or mood swings. I am in touch with supportive people and have not isolated myself in terms of psychosocial interactions. I am not a danger to myself or others. And I deny any suicidal ideation."

Then Blackstone grabbed a piece of paper from Dr. Koesler's desk, scribbled something down on it hastily, and tossed it onto his desk.

Koesler glanced down at it. It was a stick-man drawing, with the stick-man's hands on his hips and a jagged frown on his face.

"There," Blackstone said with a smart-aleck smile. "This is my version of the standard Draw-a-Picture Test."

Then he added, "And that's me in the picture there, frowning because I can't sleep at night ever since my prescription ran out last week."

"I sometimes think," Koesler said, "that when you took time off from the law to pursue a PhD in psychology it was the worst thing that could have happened to you. It hasn't helped you to heal emotionally. Which I presume was the reason you did it. Instead, it has simply made you more clever in dancing around the psychological triggers you still need to address since the death of Marilyn and Beth."

"I need to address? Like what?"

"You're clinically depressed, J.D.," Koesler said bluntly.

"Wrong. I lack several of the key indicators. Most importantly, my energy level and personal interactions are totally inconsistent with a depressive personality."

There was a long pause. Neither man spoke.

Then Koesler grabbed his prescription pad, filled out the top sheet, ripped it off, and held it out to Blackstone, who grabbed it quickly. But after reading it he shook his head and complained.

"Hey, what gives?" Blackstone asked. "Last time you gave me a ninety-day supply."

"You stop playing games and start addressing your issues, and I will rethink that next time," Koesler said with a studied tone.

Blackstone stuffed the prescription into his pocket and walked quickly out to the parking lot.

Eight hours later, at almost three in the morning, Blackstone was standing in his Georgetown condo in his gym shorts and a sleeveless T-shirt, with the television remote in his hand, flipping through the channels. A few magazines were scattered on the couch next to him, half opened to articles he was reading. As usual, his brain was wide-awake even though his body was exhausted.

Then the phone rang.

He stared at the caller ID. It read, *Federal Detention Center.*

He had a bad feeling about that.

After wondering if he really wanted to pick it up, five rings later, he did so.

Vinnie Archmont was on the other end, sobbing, barely understandable. It took him several minutes to calm her down.

"I've been arrested," she said in between sobs. "I was photographed... fingerprinted...you said...you said..."

"Vinnie, I have to admit I'm surprised you were indicted," Blackstone said.

"I can't believe this is happening. All because of the Masonic thing. I don't want to die over something like that."

"Vinnie," he said, raising his voice. "Get a hold on yourself. First of all, I am assuming there is a jail guard near you, right?"

"Yes…two of them…right over there."

"Okay. Then try to limit your answers to short responses. When I meet with you in the jail, you can go into all the detail you want. Right now try to stick with 'yes' or 'no' or 'I don't know.'"

"You said!" Vinnie continued in a broken voice, now going to the source of her angst. "Capital offense—that means the death penalty…"

"Now listen carefully," Blackstone said firmly, "forget about the death penalty stuff. I am never going to let that happen."

Suddenly, Blackstone was surprised at his own breach of protocol. He had represented desperate clients before. It was his strict rule to always give optimism whenever it was due, but never to guarantee results. *Never.*

But then the lawyer reflected on something she had just said. "And did you say 'Masonic thing'—is that the phrase you just used? Just give me a yes or no."

"It's complicated…I don't know where to start."

"Alright, forget I asked you. We'll talk about all that later," Blackstone said, recognizing his client should refrain from saying anything else of substance in the presence of the jailers. Then he changed the subject slightly.

"I hate to talk practicalities," Blackstone continued, "but this is going to be a complicated defense. I am going to require a very large retainer fee…"

"In England," she said, now becoming much more focused, "I have a very good friend. Very famous. His name is Lord Magister Dee. He's very wealthy. He knows all about this. He will pay you anything you need. I have his number with me. Just write it down and call him. It's already mid-morning over there. Here it is."

Vinnie gave Blackstone the number. Before hanging up, he assured her that as soon as the federal courthouse was opened that morning he would be there to check out the court file and start working on getting her released on bail.

"I am relying on you to save my life," Vinnie said in a small voice. "Please help me. *Please.*"

After he hung up the phone, Blackstone immediately dialed the number in England.

The call was answered by a Colin Reading, who with a crisp British accent identified himself as "Lord Dee's personal secretary." Blackstone explained who he was and why he was calling. Reading had been expecting the call. Blackstone quoted the retainer fee. The secretary didn't skip a beat. He asked for Blackstone's account number and the bank routing number and said the entire fee would be wire-transferred to the law firm's bank account by the end of the day.

If he had any initial intentions of trying to buy a few hours of sleep, J.D. Blackstone had now abandoned all hope. He grabbed the remote to turn off the television. An infomercial advertising a new vitamin drink that promised "to improve your overall health and add years to your life" had come on. That is when he clicked it off.

He decided to shower and get dressed to go down to the office. He could do some preliminary research at the firm before heading down to the courthouse and then over to the detention center.

As he stripped off his T-shirt he heard Vinnie's words in his head—*"I am relying on you to save my life."*

Had Blackstone been any other DC lawyer, he would have been relishing the thought of his entrée into the year's most spectacular Capitol Hill murder case. But for him, the case was no longer merely a legal curiosity, with its dusty Civil War overtones and Vinnie's hints about the Freemasons. With Vinnie's indictment, things had just been ratcheted up to a whole new level.

Despite the intriguing legal issues of the case before him, Blackstone was dreading, for his own hidden reasons, the obvious fact that he was now responsible for someone else's survival.

CHAPTER 6

Indictments are documents that merely recite the formal charges of a crime, and the basis for a grand jury's charging a particular defendant. In themselves they are not evidence of guilt, and they should never be taken as such.

That is what J.D. Blackstone would tell the law students in his criminal practice class.

But it was hard for Blackstone to really believe that now as he read the indictment in the case of *United States of America v. Vinnie Archmont.*

As he sat at a table in the clerk's office of the U.S. District Court building for the District of Columbia, he was scanning the court documents filed by the U.S. Attorney's Office that charged Vinnie with conspiracy to commit murder against a federal official and with theft of federal documents. Blackstone was getting the clear sense that the coldly calculated murder and sensational theft outlined in the indictment simply didn't fit the limited information he had about his client. At the same time, the allegations made out a powerful case against her.

The indictment cited the findings of federal investigators that

> the murderer(s) had gained access to The Smithsonian Institution administration building, known as "the Castle," after hours, by accessing a private side entrance. That door was controlled by an electronic keypad system. A review of Horace Langley's computer security registry log indicates that he had given the confidential code to defendant,

Vinnie Archmont, shortly before the date of Mr. Langley's
murder.

The charging document also alleged that Vinnie had had several
meetings with Langley, and had personal knowledge of his schedule
and the fact that he would be working late into the night on the date of
the murder.

But it was the final allegation that supplied the guts of the case.
Blackstone knew that while criminal motive is not an essential legal element of a prosecutor's case, it is always a strategic advantage to prove to
the folks in the jury box the big "why": exactly why one human being
would conspire to have another person killed.

The indictment's theory of motive was unique: that Vinnie was a
member of a shadowy cult group. That the group had sought to obtain
the John Wilkes Booth diary pages, and that the murder of Langley
was accomplished in order to secure those documents before they were
subjected to expert analysis and their contents published. The indictment
alleged that the cult was comprised of radical zealots who proposed to
use the Booth papers to advance their agenda.

As Blackstone read that, he found it almost laughable. Not that there
couldn't be such a group. He was convinced there probably was. But
Vinnie as a member? He had had only one meeting with Vinnie, yet for
Blackstone, that was enough. He relied on his ability to dissect human
personality quickly. Vinnie was a typical artisan: creative, a little whim-
sical, nonanalytical. Not particularly agenda-driven. She didn't fit the
anarchist profile. The federal prosecutor was clearly trying to cook up the
motive factor to bolster what could prove to be a thin criminal case.

As Blackstone was driving over to the federal detention center to meet
with Vinnie, he got off a cell phone call to his office.

First he spoke with Frieda, his secretary. She only had one bit of
news.

"Someone called for you and wanted to know if you were in the
office," she said.

"Who was it?"

"A man. He wouldn't give me his name. I asked, but he said 'Never
mind' and hung up."

After that, Frieda transferred him to Julia Robins, his younger legal associate. Julia had been one of Blackstone's law students several years before. A terrifically bright woman, she had graduated second in her class. After a stint as a worker bee in the Office of Legal Counsel for the CIA, she came knocking on Blackstone's door, saying she didn't like federal agency work and asking if he would consider taking her in as a partner.

Blackstone had begun to accumulate a list of prominent Beltway cases by then. That, coupled with his full-time professorship at Capital City College, created a workload that was more than even he could handle alone. He'd been glad to add her to his law practice. All that was shortly before the tragic deaths of Blackstone's wife and daughter.

Julia was attractive, wore dark horn-rim glasses, and her dishwater-blonde hair was usually left in a tangle of slightly disheveled locks. Julia had managed a master's degree in chemistry at Harvard before deciding to switch to law. She attended Blackstone's law school on an academic scholarship and usually had a no-nonsense approach to the practice of law. Blackstone particularly liked that.

"I heard you are into the Smithsonian murder case," Julia began. "Where do I fit in?"

"I need you to check out a guy over in London. An English Lord. His name is Magister Dee."

"With a name like that, he sounds like a kook."

"Let's hope not," Blackstone replied.

"Why?"

"He's paying our legal fees on this case."

"I'll check him out," Julia said. "Who's the client?"

"Vinnie Archmont. She came in the office the other day."

"Oh, so she's the little tart Frieda was telling me about. Frieda said she came in the office all flushed, and gushing all about how she had read about you and what an 'absolutely fabulous' lawyer you must be."

"Tart? My, aren't we catty," Blackstone said with a chuckle.

"Well, Frieda told that me she had her pegged as either a model or an artist of some kind when she sashayed into the office. Very attractive, as I understand it."

That was the other thing about Julia. She had harbored a law-school crush on him when she was a student. Then, about a year after Black-stone's wife and daughter had died, Blackstone threw himself into a short, torrid, and ill-fated romance with Julia. Just as quickly as the relationship started, Blackstone abruptly broke it off. Since then, Julia had had loads of dates, but she never seemed serious about any of them. He was surprised, though, when she had decided to stay on in the small, two-partner law firm with him.

"You coming back to the office?" she asked.

"No, I'm on the way to see the tart at the detention center."

Julia laughed.

"Okay," she said. "You mentioned our having a working dinner to talk about some administrative issues with the practice."

"That will have to wait."

"Fine," was all that Julia said before she said goodbye and hung up.

As he neared the jail facility, Blackstone glanced a few times in his rearview mirror at the car that was four car lengths behind him.

As he roared into the jammed parking lot at the federal jail facility, he was thinking about Vinnie. *I need to know a lot more about this woman,* was the thought that was rolling around in his head.

That—and also his question about why there was a tan Ford Taurus idling at the other end of the parking ramp, which seemed to have been following him for the last twenty minutes.

CHAPTER 7

So, are you being straight with me? About what you've told me so far?"

"I have to, don't I? You're my lawyer."

"Still, some clients play games. Particularly about background information. Things they are ashamed of, or embarrassed about. They think those things don't matter—or that they won't come out. But in a murder trial everything comes out. And it all matters. Do you understand that, Vinnie?"

Vinnie Archmont nodded to Blackstone across the grey metal table in the jail conference room. She was dressed in a bright yellow prisoner's jump suit. She looked much different now. Her bright, flirtatious affect was gone. She looked somber and tired, and her Scarlett O'Hara curls were droopy and unkempt.

Blackstone had just spent their time together going over her "life biography." Vinnie Archmont had an unusual background.

She was raised in Oklahoma by a mother and father who had a reputation for being eccentric. The mother was a flamboyant art teacher in a community college. Her father was a professor of humanities at the University of Oklahoma. He had written some articles which captured the attention, somehow, of Lord Magister Dee in England. The following year the father was invited by Lord Dee to participate in a conference in Scotland. Vinnie's father accepted, and he took his wife and daughter along. Dee met with the trio, took a liking to them immediately. Later he even invited them to his mansion house outside of London, where they spent the weekend.

There was something vaguely incomplete, though, about the way that Vinnie had described her background with her parents, despite Blackstone's prodding. He made a mental note about that. Perhaps he would pursue that later.

Over the next two years, Lord Dee and her parents kept in contact. Then he invited them over to England again, at his expense. They spent some of the time sightseeing. Vinnie was nineteen at the time. But the trip ended tragically. She was attending a matinee performance in London while her parents were taking a day trip by rail to the north of England. There was a train derailment and both of her parents were killed.

Vinnie explained how Lord Dee "swept me up, in all my grief. It was a terrible time. But he took me in. Treated me like royalty. Then when I returned to the States, he personally paid for me to finish art school. And it was Lord Dee who financed my art studio in Alexandria."

Blackstone found all of that intriguing.

"Was there anything romantic—or sexual—between you and Lord Dee?" he asked bluntly.

Vinnie wasn't surprised at the question. But she seemed assured in her denial that there was anything but deep friendship between her and the twice-divorced Lord Dee. Over the years she was invited to England where she would spend holidays with Lord Dee and his various friends attending sumptuous parties. She also said the two spoke regularly on the phone and connected by e-mail.

Most of Vinnie's personal time in recent years was devoted to expanding her art studio and working on her sculptures. Her social circle was comprised mostly of artists, or former college friends. They were all from the Virginia, DC, or Maryland area.

She was once engaged to be married, but she said she broke that off. She described her former boyfriend, Kevin, as "kind and considerate, but a little possessive, and not very exciting."

At the present, she said she wasn't seeing anyone romantically.

"Are you active in any groups? Church? Civic organizations? Political parties?" Blackstone asked. Vinnie said she was not much of a joiner. The only "group" she was part of, other than a local DC artisans' group that put on joint art exhibitions, was a neighborhood project that was raising money to renovate a neglected park. She said she went to a couple of their meetings, donated some money, and helped clean up the playground area.

When Blackstone raised the allegations in the indictment of her being part of a "cult" group that planned the execution of Langley and the theft of the Booth diary, she laughed out loud and denied any such thing. Vinnie admitted that the indictment was correct about Langley giving her the code to the security door. On the day of the murder, when the two met in the late afternoon or early evening, he told her he would be working late that night, and that "she should pop on by if she was bored and wanted to visit," but should use the private entrance if she did.

Vinnie said that she knew that Horace Langley had some romantic feelings for her. But she never reciprocated. And she noted that his obvious overtures did not affect her professional work in working on his sculpture.

Blackstone was looking over his notes on all of that information, when a question came to mind.

"Just curious about something," he said. "Why did your parents name you Vinnie? That's an unusual name for a girl."

"Actually, it was my mother," Vinnie said. "One of her heroes was a famous female artist from Oklahoma named Vinnie Ream. That's who I was named after."

"I'm familiar with a lot of artists. But I haven't heard of her."

"She lived in the 1800s. She sculpted Abraham Lincoln," Vinnie said, trying to manage a smile.

"Interesting," Blackstone remarked.

The time was right. He needed to go in deeper, toward the heart of the case.

"What did you mean about the 'Masonic thing' when we spoke by telephone?"

She paused. He could tell there was an internal struggle going on inside.

"Just that the way things happened. The interest in the John Wilkes Booth diary and all. Lord Dee is a very high-ranking, thirty-third-degree Freemason himself. He and I talked about a lot of things over the years. In a way, he was a kind of spiritual mentor to me. He had always talked about the importance of finding it. The missing diary pages, I mean."

"Why did he want to find them?"

"I was never really positive. Not specifically."

"Well, how about generally?"

She paused and thought about it, then answered.

"I think it had to do with a secret."

"What kind of secret?"

"He never told me exactly. But he said he would someday."

Blackstone put down his pen and stopped taking notes, and leaned forward on the conference table, looking into the sad face of the dark-haired beauty.

"I want to know," he said firmly, "*what kind* of secret."

Vinnie shifted a little in the plastic chair. And then she said it.

"He called it," and then she took a breath. And exhaled. And finished the sentence.

"The ultimate secret of the Freemasons."

CHAPTER 8

Blackstone sensed that he was homing in on the "motive" piece to the puzzle. So he bore down hard.

"What kind of 'ultimate secret'?"

"I'm just telling you what Lord Dee would say."

"What else did he say about it?"

"That's it, really."

"Vinnie, I don't believe you."

"I am trying to tell you everything I know."

"So he starts talking about the ultimate secrets of the Freemasons and you never questioned it?"

"Of course I questioned it. Like anyone else, I was curious. But he never told me exactly what that was. And it wasn't the ultimate *secrets*—it was the ultimate *secret*."

"Singular. Not plural?"

"Right."

Blackstone had done that deliberately. He knew that Vinnie was still holding back.

"What would he tell you," Blackstone continued, "when you asked him about that?"

"Look, I'm really not sure. Mr. Blackstone, I didn't take notes. Lord Dee has a magnificent mind and a very spiritual side to him. He would talk on and on about a great many things. About religion. The God-force, as he called it. Man's destiny. The trouble with the world. Our capacity to shape the future. I'm sure that he would be more than happy to talk with you about it. But Mr. Blackstone, I'm just not sure how any of this is going to help me."

Blackstone eyed his client.

"I'm not sure either," he admitted, "yet."

Then he softened a little and said, "And you can drop the 'Mr. Blackstone' and call me J.D."

She smiled a little and nodded at that and let out a big sigh.

Blackstone shifted gears.

"Tomorrow we'll appear in front of the federal magistrate. I am going to ask for your release on bail. On the other hand, the prosecutor will probably ask that you be detained without benefit of bail. I think I'm going to win that point. But we'll see."

"Two things I am grateful for," she said, trying a little to buoy herself. "First that you are my lawyer."

"The proof of that will be in the pudding," Blackstone quipped. "What's the other thing?"

"Lord Dee says he has no doubts this whole thing will be dismissed. I hope he's right."

"In addition to a magnificent mind and a great soul, does he also have a crystal ball that can see all the way to U.S. District Court in Washington?" Blackstone quipped.

"I don't think that's very funny, J.D.," Vinnie said. But Blackstone could tell that she was not really upset. Maybe she was playing with him a little, despite her horrible circumstances.

By the time Blackstone left the detention center it was after seven at night.

He called his voice mail, and there was a message from Frieda.

"Hey, J.D., just wanted you to know that I had the depositions for tomorrow rescheduled in light of your bail hearing in the Vinnie Archmont case. Reverend Lamb called and said he was going to be at his office at the college until about eight tonight. Needed you to stop by."

Reverend John Lamb was Blackstone's uncle on his mother's side. A conservative Anglican and former parish priest, he taught in the religion department of Capital City College. Because they were both professors at the same school, Blackstone and his uncle would see each other from time to time at all-faculty meetings. Other times, Blackstone would stop by his office during the school term when he had a few minutes to spare, usually to stir up a debate with his uncle on the religious topic du jour that he had seen on TV or read in the papers.

Blackstone found it all very humorous. He felt that he could usually shred "Uncle John" without much effort. But he enjoyed toying with him the way a bored boy might take a twig and poke at a beetle.

He was tempted to simply head home, but he glanced at his watch. He had time to swing by the college. *Why not humor my uncle, the poor deluded religionist?* he thought to himself.

When Blackstone strode up the steps to the second floor of the religion department building, he saw the light on in Reverend Lamb's office and the door open.

"Evening, Uncle!" Blackstone blurted out, startling Reverend Lamb who was at his desk but had his back turned, fishing for a book in his bookcase.

"Oh, you gave me a start!" Lamb said with a smile. "Good to see you, J.D., have a seat."

Reverend John Lamb was sixty-eight, with fair features, a square, pleasant face, and a balding head. The white tufts of hair on both sides of his head were generally in need of a good combing. His eyesight was still remarkably good, but when he was reading he would pull out a pair of glasses that seemed slightly too large for his face.

"I missed you at the faculty meeting." he said.

"That's because I didn't go," Blackstone said. "I had a last-minute conflict."

"No matter," Lamb said. "I would wager that the law school would never give you a problem with that kind of administrative nonsense. You are undoubtedly one of the school's superstars and celebrities. I, on the other hand, am nearing the age where I feel they will want to get rid of me sooner rather than later."

"Come on," Blackstone said, "you're an institution here."

"In twenty-first century academia that is not necessarily a good thing."

"So, with you gone," Blackstone said casually, "who would possibly teach comparative religion, or the history of ancient esoteric religious systems—that is what they call the class, right?"

Lamb nodded. Then he added, "The question is this: Does this college feel that my area of expertise—the esoteric and mystery religions, and how they have influenced the history of heresy within the Christian church—does this school feel those subjects are still relevant?"

"Well," Blackstone smirked, "I'm the wrong person to ask. You know me. I think the study of all religion is no longer relevant. Nothing against you, Uncle."

Lamb was not fazed by that, but his face showed he had remembered something.

"Oh, before I forget. I have this for you," Lamb said, and reached into his desk drawer and pulled out a thin book and passed it to Blackstone. Then he added, "Hot off the presses."

The lawyer looked at the title: *Christianity, Ancient Gnostic Roots of Current Religious Heresy, and the Freemasons*—by Reverend John H. Lamb.

"You know I won't read this," Blackstone said with a smirk.

"That's not my fault," Lamb said with a twinkle in his eye.

"Well, at least I consider myself in a privileged class of people."

"Oh?"

"Yes," Blackstone continued with another smirk. "If this one sells like the others, I will be in that select group of twenty or so people in the entire world who actually own one of your books."

"Funny thing about absolute truth," Lamb quipped with a smile. "It defies quantitative analysis."

"That sounds suspiciously like an author who wants to explain away why his books don't sell."

"My books don't sell because not enough people care about the subject matter. Not because they are not true. You nearly have your PhD in psychology. You know something about human behavior. People want books to entertain them…excite them…astound them. Not to inform them."

"Oh, my," Blackstone replied. "Now you're talking like a Skinnerian behavioralist rather than a Christian. Where is your God in all this? Couldn't he just mesmerize us all, like drones, into walking into bookstores and buying millions of copies of your books? If he is God he certainly could."

"It doesn't work like that," Lamb said with a smile. "He wants just the right people to be led to open up this book. Those who are truly searching."

Then he added one more thing.

"Which is why, J.D., I think you are going to end up reading it."

Blackstone laughed heartily at that, then got to his feet. They said their goodbyes, and when Blackstone had reached his Maserati parked outside, he opened the door and tossed the book onto the backseat. He would wait until he got home to throw it into the dumpster in the parking lot of the condo.

As he turned on the ignition and heard the familiar, well-engineered rumble, he glanced into his rearview mirror. A block away there was a tan Ford Taurus parked on the curb, but with its parking lights on.

"This is going to end," he muttered at the car that was shadowing him again.

And he knew just how he was going to end it.

CHAPTER 9

In the courtroom in Washington, U.S. District Court Magistrate William Boyer had been listening to the arguments of federal prosecutor Henry Hartz for about a quarter of an hour. Hartz was an Assistant United States Attorney for the District of Columbia. In the legal practice, he was called an "AUSA" for short. The case against Vinnie Archmont was unorthodox, even sensational. But Hartz's pitch for the magistrate to order her held in detention without release on bail, pending trial, was textbook.

Blackstone was seated at the defense table next to Vinnie Archmont, who had to suffer the humiliation of watching the proceedings next to her attorney with her hands manacled. Blackstone still knew very little about his client. But everything in him said that this diminutive beauty of an artist was no threat to anyone.

On the other hand, the more Blackstone studied human nature, the more he was willing to be surprised. Vinnie Archmont could just be the next big surprise.

As Hartz stood at the courtroom lectern, steadying himself by gripping it with both hands, Blackstone was taking him in, not just as the prosecutor but as the man.

He hadn't come up against Hartz in any prior cases, but Blackstone knew a few things about him. Hartz needed a cane to walk, for some unexplained reason. When the prosecutor walked, his gait was out of joint. He wore glasses that had thicker than normal lenses.

Hartz had a handsome face and a winning style of verbal delivery. He had gained a reputation among criminal defense attorneys as a fierce legal opponent. He rarely gave any quarter, never asked for any, and almost always won his cases. He had experienced a quick rise from prosecuting misdemeanor drug offenses in the local District of Columbia prosecutor's office to handling the most complex terrorism and murder cases in the U.S. Attorney's Office. He was now the second-highest-ranking AUSA in the criminal division of that office.

His argument focused on two facts: First, that Vinnie Archmont had a history of extensive international travel, which posed a better-than-average risk of flight out of the territorial United States. And secondly, that the indictment alleged she was a member of a secret cult group, which meant that she had access to an underground network that could help her to flee from the country and then hide, rather than face trial and the possibility of a criminal sentence that could yield a death sentence.

The magistrate seemed intensely engaged in the case, and took quite a few notes, but didn't ask any questions of Hartz. The arguments were the usual stuff from an AUSA. The only thing that Blackstone found oddly missing was the intangible element, namely, the typical prosecutor's passion. Henry Hartz was either so overconfident of winning the motion to detain Vinnie without bail that he was sleepwalking through the argument—or else, and Blackstone doubted this one, Hartz really didn't care, down deep, whether Vinnie got released or not.

When it was Blackstone's turn at the podium, he was concise and to the point.

"Regarding the prosecution's argument," Blackstone began, "about my client's history of extensive international travel, and how that makes her a flight risk—well, there is a simple remedy for that. Your Honor, simply require her to produce her passport to the court clerk for safekeeping. That will ensure her remaining in the jurisdiction of the United States until trial."

Then Blackstone stepped away from the podium to drive home his second point. His arms were crossed over his chest, like a professor ready to lecture his class.

"And as for the absurd allegations about my client's membership is some secret society, I simply draw the Court's attention to the fact that Mr. Hartz has failed to file any evidentiary proof to support that. None whatsoever. I think it was De Tocqueville who once said that, in contrast to Europe, 'In America there are factions, but no conspiracies.' Apparently Mr. Hartz, on behalf of the government, believes that if he cannot prove the conspiracy of a secret society, then he is perfectly free to simply invent them. Let Mr. Hartz try his hand at fiction writing if he wants to do that. But Your Honor, let's save the courtroom for *facts*."

Magistrate Boyer had only one question. And it said it all.

"Professor Blackstone, how quickly can your client produce her passport?"

"If she is released today," he replied with a smile, "we can have it filed with the clerk by tomorrow."

"So ordered," the magistrate said. "Mr. Hartz, your motion for detainer of the defendant is denied. Mr. Blackstone, I will order the U.S. marshal to release your client upon the posting of a 10 percent bond on the bail amount of $1 million."

"It has already been posted," Blackstone said with a smile.

The magistrate nodded and gaveled the proceedings to a close.

Vinnie was so happy she was nearly in tears. She hugged Blackstone clumsily, unable to fully embrace him because of her handcuffs.

As Henry Hartz hobbled past Blackstone and Vinnie, leaning on his cane with one hand and holding his thick brown case folder with the other, the federal prosecutor was harboring a strange smile.

"Enjoy this insignificant little victory today," he said to Blackstone. "It won't last long. There's some bad news coming your way tomorrow."

"Oh?" Blackstone asked. "Like what? That you're enrolling in my criminal law class next fall so you can learn how to be a prosecutor?"

But Hartz's smile was spreading slightly into a grin.

"Tomorrow," he said, "I will be filing my formal notice to the court that I will, in fact, be seeking the death penalty against your client, Vinnie Archmont."

"The AUSAs I've dealt with from your office," Blackstone shot back, "usually give defense counsel the courtesy of a conference before filing the death penalty notice."

"I'm all out of courtesy, Blackstone," he retorted. And then he threw a stony glance at Vinnie, and continued walking to the courtroom door.

Vinnie had heard it all.

She grabbed onto Blackstone's sleeve.

Blackstone held on to her and looked into her face. He could see the look of terror in her eyes.

CHAPTER 10

Vinnie, who had just run the emotional gamut from joy to misery in a matter of minutes, was being led away by the two U.S. marshals.

Blackstone's last words to her in the courtroom were, "I'll file your passport with the court clerk, and you'll be out of here in twelve hours, tops." Then he packed up his file, stuffed it in his brown-leather satchel, and turned to walk to the courtroom doors in the back.

In the second-to-last row there was a man still seated in a courtroom bench, waiting for Blackstone.

"Tully," Blackstone said with a smile as he approached the man. "Great to see you. You got my message, I see?"

"Yeah," the man replied. "Looks like you've got a troublesome tail you now want *me* to tail."

"Tully" Tullinger had been J.D. Blackstone's private investigator for several years, ever since his retirement from the federal government. Sixty-three years old with iron gray hair and a pencil moustache, Tully was dressed in a Hawaiian shirt and was holding a white straw Panama hat in his lap, the kind with a big black band. He looked more like a bookie at a horse-racing track than a man who had previously worked at the National Security Agency.

"This guy who's been following me drives a tan Ford Taurus," Blackstone said. "He's not very suave. I picked up that he was tailing me right away."

"Any ideas about why he's following you?"

"I've got some guesses. But I would rather have you operate on a blank slate. Just track him long enough to find out who he is and who he is working for."

Tully nodded, gave Blackstone a warm handshake, and after popping his Panama hat on his head he headed out of the courtroom.

When Blackstone got back to his office he sequestered himself in the law library with the Vinnie Archmont file spread out in front of him.

Julia, his junior partner, walked in.

"How'd it go?" she asked.

"Got her released on bail," Blackstone said.

"On a capital murder charge? Nice work."

"Henry Hartz was on the other side. I expected more from him. You know, Genghis Khan stuff—slaughtering the livestock, burning the crops."

"Don't underestimate him," Julia said. "I've heard that you never, ever want to turn your back on the guy. He'll kick you in the kidneys—with steel-tipped shoes."

"Yeah, but I can easily outmaneuver him," Blackstone said, with that twisted smile that signaled a cynical attack of dark humor. "He walks with a cane."

Julia shook her head at that one and added, "I know. Some kind of health issue. But he paints a very sympathetic picture to a jury."

"I'm trying to formulate our discovery demands," Blackstone snapped, changing the subject, "now that I've reviewed these," Blackstone said, pointing to the pile of FBI reports that he had already received from the prosecution. "I would appreciate your thoughts on this."

Julia sat down and scanned the FBI "302" reports on the federal investigation into the Smithsonian crime. When she was done, one thing had caught her eye.

"The physical evidence documented at the scene of the murder is interesting," she said.

"You're getting warmer," Blackstone said, always the law professor.

"The drinking glass on the desk left on Langley's desk? I notice it's mentioned in the 302 report—though I don't see a lab report on it anywhere."

"That's one thing, right. For some reason they didn't finish the fingerprint analysis on the glass, I guess. Anything else?"

"The pen on Langley's desk?"

"Oh, no, now you're getting colder," Blackstone said, with a mocking tone. "The pen was analyzed, right here," he said, pointing to a lab report, "and it was found to have only Langley's fingerprints on it."

Julia tossed her hair a little anxiously, took her dark-rimmed glasses off, and wiped her eyes. Then she kept them off, twirling them and resting her chin on her hand.

"Okay," she muttered out loud. "We're talking about physical evidence." Then a light went on.

"The notepad on his desk."

"Excellent thought!" Blackstone shouted. "Of course, on the other hand, it was a blank pad."

"Langley could have written something down," she replied, "and the shooter could have removed those notes, along with the Booth diary pages?"

"I'm pretty certain that's what happened."

"How do you know?"

"It's logical," Blackstone replied. "Langley was the head of America's most prestigious national institution of science and history. He is a scholar himself. He had custody of the missing diary pages from the hand of John Wilkes Booth, arguably the most notorious political assassin in American history. Do you think Langley wasn't poring over those pages? And wouldn't an academic like Horace Langley have taken notes? No, the real question is *not* about his missing notepad pages. The real question is this: Does the government have evidence of exactly what it was that he was writing, just moments before somebody put two bullets into his chest?"

Then Blackstone leaned back, with his hands folded behind his head and answered his own question.

"I am betting they do. And now I am going to force them to share it with me too."

CHAPTER 11

Blackstone and Julia ordered some carry-out Thai food that evening, and then worked late, until almost midnight. When they were finished, Blackstone electronically served their motion for discovery on AUSA Henry Hartz and filed it with the U.S. District Court by e-mail. It was thirty-seven pages long.

Blackstone loaded a lot of unusual information requests into his written demand. Unlike civil cases, where the discovery rules allow almost unlimited inquiry into every conceivably relevant area, in criminal cases defense counsel has to operate in a legal straitjacket. The government has to disclose evidence to the defense only within certain narrow categories. But Blackstone thought he had found some loopholes.

He found that the FBI reports previously produced to him by prosecutor Hartz contained numerous redactions: words and sentences blacked out. Those were the bits of information the prosecution didn't want Blackstone to read, and which Hartz had determined were protected from disclosure. But Blackstone needed as many facts as he could gather to defend his client. He wanted it all.

One of the blacked-out sentences in an FBI report produced to Blackstone seemed as if, in the grammatical context of the unredacted sentences before and after it, it had revealed some personal information about Horace Langley. In his motion, Blackstone argued for the full release of that information because, in his words, "The defense believes that Mr. Langley's possible association with any number of ideological groups, including the Freemasons, is material to the defense of this case."

Blackstone had remembered Vinnie's comment about Lord Dee's interest in the Booth diary pages. All of that overblown stuff about the "ultimate secret of the Freemasons."

But the way that the criminal law professor saw it, the real blockbuster in his motion was his demand, in paragraph 77, for everything the government had, in terms of evidence, investigation, or scientific analysis relating to the notepad that was found lying on Langley's desk after the murder. More than that, Blackstone was demanding the right to have the notepad examined by his own expert.

When Julia asked him what he was looking for, Blackstone smiled one of his know-it-all smiles and then proceeded to explain.

"According to the reports, his pen was a Faber Castell Porsche P3150 ballpoint. One of those heavy, expensive jobs—you know, the kind they don't call just *pens*, but *writing instruments*," Blackstone explained. "That thing would have left a deep imprint on the page as well on as the pages underneath."

"Porsche? I thought they made cars."

"They do. And they also have a line of pens for those who love their cars. Not a bad car, the Porsche. But no Maserati," Blackstone noted with a grin.

"So," Julia continued, her brow furrowed, "the pen impresses a mark—all the way down to several pages underneath. And we get a microscopic examination of those pages still left on the pad of paper—to see if we can decipher what Langley wrote as he was examining the Booth diary?"

"Nice work, Robins," Blackstone said. "I lead you to water, and you drink—we make a terrific team."

Julia paused for a minute and then decided to speak her mind.

"J.D., just once in a while, you can try not to be so condescending."

That is when she got up from the conference table, grabbed her briefcase and her purse, and walked out of the office to go home.

Blackstone, who was still studying the motion he had just e-mailed out to the opposing attorney and the Court, was trying hard to act like Julia's comment didn't bother him.

The next day, early in the morning, Blackstone traveled over to the federal detention center. He was waiting in the drab lobby of that facility to greet Vinnie when she was released on bail.

After she gathered her personal effects, Vinnie ran out into the lobby, threw her arms around her attorney, and kissed him on the cheek.

Blackstone, a bit embarrassed, moved away slightly and took Vinnie's arms off his neck, as a female jailer behind the glass window glared at him.

"Easy," Blackstone said to his client. "This is only step one. We still have a case to win."

"And you will do that, I know it," she gushed. "You are my defender and my deliverer."

Blackstone was uncomfortable with her grandiose accolades. So, as he walked her to his car he changed the subject and quickly launched into a preview of the discovery motion he had filed. He drove her to her apartment in Alexandria, not far from her studio. As they were driving, he glanced several times into his rearview mirror.

"Why do you keep looking back?" Vinnie asked.

"Just curious," was all he said.

Blackstone could see the tan Ford Taurus behind him.

And he knew Tully Tullinger well enough to know that somewhere back there, behind that car, was his private investigator, tailing the Taurus.

CHAPTER 12

B eneath the mammoth seal of the United States of America that took up half the wall in his courtroom, U.S. District Judge Robert Templeton was seated at the bench, rocking back and forth in his black executive chair. He was listening to the prosecution's objections to J.D. Blackstone's discovery motion.

Judge Templeton had already ruled against Blackstone on most of his requests for the government to turn over various documents and items of potential evidence. So AUSA Henry Hartz was growing more energized and aggressive in his arguments.

"I can't begin to understand," Hartz said in bewilderment, "Mr. Blackstone's bizarre request for personal information about Horace Langley—including all of his intimate associations. And Mr. Blackstone even wants to know whether the victim had been *a member of the Freemasons.* I would have thought that a law professor like Mr. Blackstone would have consulted his law books before filing such a frivolous, absurd motion."

Judge Templeton interrupted him, directing his question to Blackstone.

"Counsel, why this business about the Freemasons? Frankly, it strikes me as far-fetched. I have to agree with the government on that one. I don't see the relevance of that issue anywhere in this case."

Blackstone quickly jogged up to the podium where Hartz was standing and shared the microphone with his opponent.

"Your Honor, I believe it is material to the question of motive."

"Whose motive?" the judge shot back. "Your client's motive?"

"No, Your Honor. The motive of the true perpetrator, here, which is not my client. She's innocent."

"*Innocent?*" Judge Templeton retorted. "I wonder if I've ever heard that one before."

With that, the U.S. marshals leaning against the outer wall of the courtroom chuckled to themselves. The court clerk, a middle-aged black woman seated below the judicial bench at a desk, was grinning.

"My mistake, Your Honor," Blackstone fired back, his voice showing a restrained sense of indignation. "I thought we were actually still following that quaint Western tradition of a presumption of innocence."

"Because of your considerable competencies in the practice of criminal law, Professor Blackstone," the judge said, his eyes now narrowed to slits and his torso leaning over the bench, "I will ignore that remark. For now. Suffice it to say that in my courtroom that presumption still holds."

Then Judge Templeton straightened up a little in his chair and continued his statement. "But that doesn't mean," the judge went on, "that I am going to let you use it to bootstrap your argument for discovery of personal information about a murder victim that, at least right now, appears to have absolutely nothing to do with the charges of conspiracy to commit murder and theft. For the time being, I am going to deny that motion. You can renew it later if you can give me some support for its materiality."

"That only leaves us," Henry Hartz cheerfully announced, "with Mr. Blackstone's last demand for discovery—located at paragraph 77 of his motion. The request for all of the government's reports dealing with the blank notepad found at the scene of the crime—and Mr. Blackstone's demand for the defense's expert to examine the notepad."

"Mr. Blackstone," the judge said, again addressing the defense attorney who was still standing next to Henry Hartz at the podium, "today you've already argued your legal point for that request based on very general Rule 16 considerations. But what's the factual relevancy of the notepad?"

"That seems clear," Blackstone replied. "The pen was lying next to the notepad. The pen had Mr. Langley's fingerprints on it. Mr. Langley was examining one of the most controversial and historically significant documents in American history. We can logically infer that he was making notes. Those notes may include vital information about motive—why the *real* culprits wanted those diary pages and why they may have wanted Mr. Langley dead."

"There it is—*motive* again!" Hartz shouted out. "Your Honor, the weakness of Mr. Blackstone's defense is apparent: He is trying to exonerate his client by merely showing that others may have had some motive to steal the Booth diary. That seems to me to be a flimsy defense if Mr. Blackstone wants to rely on it at trial. But I suppose he has a right to try and argue that to the jury. But at this early stage of the case, it is nothing but a fishing expedition into our confidential investigative reports. Mr. Blackstone's argument is an insult to this Court's intelligence."

"Well," the judge replied with a half smile, "I don't take it too personally when the intelligence of this Court is impugned—the *integrity* of this Court, however, is a different matter."

Hartz could see that Judge Templeton was seriously entertaining Blackstone's demand. So he redoubled his efforts.

"But he *is* impugning your integrity, Your Honor," Hartz countered. "Blackstone is implying, ridiculously, that the notepad will somehow prove his client's innocence and that you are blocking that evidence from the defense. I can't think of a more direct assault on this Court's integrity."

The judge was silent on the bench, staring off into space. Blackstone knew he might lose this paragraph 77 demand as he had all the others. He was not going to let that happen.

"I have reason to believe," Blackstone blurted out, "that the underlying note pages on Langley's notepad may contain microscopic tracings of what he wrote. That we may be able to reconstruct exactly what Langley was writing just moments before he was murdered."

"And why do you believe that?" the judge asked.

"Because of the pen he was using," Blackstone said with a sigh, reluctant that he was being forced to divulge his conclusions to the prosecution. "A pen that was capable of making a deep imprint several pages down in the notepad."

Blackstone was able to see out of the corner of his eye that Henry Hartz was standing motionless at the podium next to him, gripping the head of his cane tightly, and staring straight down onto the wooden shelf of the podium, where a few of his papers were lying.

More silence.

"I'll grant your requests dealing with the notepad," the judge ruled. "The government will be required to produce copies of any of its reports dealing with the notepad and must provide an opportunity for your defense expert to scientifically examine it."

"There is a mountain of physical evidence in this case," Hartz shot back. "It may take a while for us to locate the notepad in the FBI inventory."

"Then I would ask the Court," Blackstone replied, "to instruct Mr. Hartz that he had better start looking. I need this information immediately."

"Mr. Hartz," the judge said in a conciliatory tone. "Please try to be as expeditious as you can."

Then he gaveled the hearing to a close.

Blackstone tried to catch Hartz's attention to discuss the timing of when his expert could examine the notepad, but Hartz ignored him.

"Henry," Blackstone called out to the prosecutor as he walked with his cane to the end of the courtroom to exit. "Hey, Henry."

But AUSA Henry Hartz never turned around. He just kept walking.

J.D. Blackstone didn't miss that. And he was already trying to figure out exactly what that meant.

CHAPTER 13

Blackstone retained Dr. Ken Coglin, a professor of materials engineering from the University of Maryland, as his expert examiner on the Langley notepad. Coglin had extensive experience as a forensic examiner of document imprint evidence.

AUSA Hartz immediately threw up roadblocks to the examination, but Blackstone wouldn't be diverted. Finally, he called an emergency conference call with Judge Templeton and AUSA Hartz in order to press hard for an immediate inspection of the notepad.

"I've given you a few days already," Judge Templeton said to the federal prosecutor. "Let's not drag this out. I'm sure you can produce the notepad, Henry. Get it done."

Twenty-four hours later Dr. Coglin and J.D. Blackstone were in a spare room in the complex of the U.S. Attorney's Office. The notepad was lying in front of them, sealed in a plastic evidence bag. FBI Special Agent Ralph Johnson, a veteran African-American FBI agent on the case, was in the room, and after snapping on latex gloves, he carefully unsealed the bag and then stepped a few feet away to observe. By agreement with Hartz, Blackstone had conceded that the government could have an agent present in the room during the document examination.

Coglin set up his high-powered microscope and focused only on the top sheet of the notepad. He set up several angled lights around the base for contrast. His microscope was then linked to a printer.

After several hours of examination, having powered down to a mere 10-4 m, Coglin printed out several versions of his microscopy view.

"Done," he announced casually.

Agent Johnson placed the notepad back in the plastic bag and sealed it, signing off on the label on the exterior of the bag with the date, time, and his initials. Then, after a polite nod to Blackstone and Coglin, Johnson left for the FBI building, where he said he would be placing the bag containing the notepad back into the evidence room.

Coglin seemed satisfied with what he saw and explained to Blackstone that his next step would begin as soon as he returned to his University of Maryland lab.

"I will double-check my field findings," he said, "and then feed the data on the gross outline of the impressions on the notepad into a special lexicon/epigraphy software system. I've used it in other document impression cases. I'll start with the assumption that Horace Langley was writing in English when he made his notes. But if the results are inconclusive, then I will try some other language variants. The software system I designed contains one hundred and five language identifiers. So my hunch is that we will be able to decipher the impression he left on the notepad."

When Blackstone got back to the office later that day he noticed the light on in Julia's office down the hall. After he picked up a fistful of phone message slips from Frieda, he strolled down to Julia's office. He strode in and plunked himself down on the leather chair across from her desk.

Blackstone sat for several minutes silently, until Julia finally put down her pen, pushed her file to the side of her desk, and gave him a cold, hard look.

"Yes?" she asked.

"I just like watching you while you work," he said with a smile.

"And I don't like being watched," she snapped back.

"Well, I did have something to say," he said, clearing his throat.

Julia continued to give him a cold stare.

"I admit I was condescending with you," Blackstone said. "Sorry about that. Personality defect. Probably a defense mechanism as a result of my deep-seated insecurities."

"Oh *please*," she groaned.

"Okay. Apology given. Apology accepted. Moving on," Blackstone said with a smile, "I just got back from our examination of the notepad. Dr. Coglin's going to call me at home tonight with the results. Do you want me to conference you into the call?"

"Not really," Julia said with a look of manufactured boredom. "I have a date tonight."

"That's wonderful," he said. "What's his name?"

"Oh, no. We're not going there," she replied.

"Fine. Let's keep the professional hermetically sealed off from the personal."

"Good," she said. "Anything else?"

"Yes. Where's the results of your investigation into this Lord Magister Dee character?"

"I thought you'd never ask," Julia said. Then she tapped a few times on her keyboard, waited for two seconds, and then turned to him and said, "There—I just e-mailed you my report on Lord Dee."

"Why don't you just boil it down for me right here?" he asked. "I prefer the human touch."

She sighed and then launched in.

"Strange guy. A member of the House of Lords. Mega-rich. Comes from old aristocratic money. Lives in a castle estate. Owns several other castles. He is a direct descendant of a guy named John Dee, who was a sixteenth-century mystic and astrologer in England. John Dee was full-blown occult practitioner and the personal mystic advisor to Queen Elizabeth I of England."

"Why is Lord Dee's pedigree important?" Blackstone asked.

"Because," Julia continued, "he's done a nice job of carrying on the family tradition...occult beliefs, theosophy, really medieval kinds of stuff."

"Why did he want the Booth diary?"

"Really not sure."

"Any wild guesses?"

"Well," she continued, "he lectures in Europe and in the UK on what he describes as the 'esoteric religious philosophy of the ancients.' That was the title of one of his talks. He hasn't published anything. But I notice that in his lectures he occasionally talks about the Freemasons. And also about the religious ideas of a very narrow slice of the Confederate leaders involved in the Civil War, who he describes as the 'Gnostics.' "

After a pause Blackstone asked, "Anything else?"

"Oh, yeah," Julia added. "And this Lord Dee guy...he is a thirty-third-degree Freemason himself. That's as high as you can get in the hierarchy."

Blackstone stood up quickly and announced he was heading home to his condo. He added, "I think I need to do some reading up on the assassination of President Lincoln, John Wilkes Booth, and the War Between the States."

"You mean like this?" Julia asked, and reached down to the floor to the side of her desk and picked up several books and held them out to Blackstone.

He glanced at their covers.

"Yes, exactly," he said with a smile. Julia was waiting for a thank-you, but she didn't get one. Blackstone turned and quickly strode out of her office.

At ten-thirty that night, Blackstone was well into one of the books, when his phone rang. It was Dr. Coglin.

"Are you ready to jot this down?" Coglin asked.

"Sure," Blackstone said, grabbing his pen and legal pad. "Ready."

"Okay," Coglin said. "I have no idea what any of this means. But I've reconstructed the impressions left on the remaining pages of the notepad. Here we go. The first line appears to be Langley's own comment. The remaining four lines I presume are a copy of what he read in the Booth diary pages:

> A strange cipher appears in the Booth diary as follows:
> *To AP and KGC*
> *Rose of 6 is Sir al ik's golden tree*
> *In gospel's Mary first revealed*
> *At Ashli plot reveals the key*

There was a dead silence on the phone.

Then Blackstone spoke up first.

"That's it?"

"Yep," Coglin replied.

More silence.

Then Blackstone grunted.

"Well, happy hunting, J.D.," Dr. Coglin said, and hung up.

Blackstone looked over the cryptic four-line poem that, according to Dr. Coglin, was the last thing communicated in writing by Horace Langley before he was murdered.

Then Blackstone, staring at the four lines of coded nonsense as he sat in his empty living room, spoke out loud into the air.

"Rats!" he yelled out in mock anger. "I *knew* Mom should have never thrown away my secret agent decoder ring."

CHAPTER 14

When J.D. Blackstone got to his office at 8:15 the next morning and opened up his e-mail, the prosecutor had a surprise waiting for him.

AUSA Henry Hartz had electronically filed an emergency motion with Judge Templeton. In it, the AUSA was demanding that "defense counsel, J.D. Blackstone, be ordered *not* to divulge, to any other person, any impression made upon, or notes or other writings contained within, the notepad of Horace Langley found at the scene of the crime." The motion also asked that Dr. Coglin be ordered not to further disclose his findings to anyone else at least until trial. Hartz was further demanding that Blackstone not reveal what Langley wrote on the notepad even to his own client and his own law firm staff, including his partner, Julia Robins.

After reading the motion on his computer screen, Blackstone was stunned. He had been engaged in legal disputes over confidentiality issues before. But nothing like this.

Hartz wants to bar me from disclosing the strange little poem that Langley wrote, clearly a key piece of evidence, even to my own co-counsel, Blackstone thought to himself. *He'd better have some blockbuster arguments for something as mind-boggling as that.*

Unfortunately for the defense, he did.

In a court hearing conducted by telephone that afternoon, Hartz explained that even limited disclosure of the Langley notes "could jeopardize our ongoing criminal investigation into the Langley murder."

"I thought you'd indicted the person you consider to be the culprit here, Henry," Blackstone replied. "You're going after my client, remember?"

But Hartz cut him off.

"You'll note that she is charged with being a *conspirator*. We're still investigating the other conspirators. If Langley's notes get out, the others may flee our jurisdiction."

Then Hartz added, "Your Honor, you will note in the sworn affidavit we filed from Detective Victor Cheski, our chief investigator in this case, that exact allegation is set out in detail."

"I suppose you don't want to give me a teeny-weeny little hint on who those 'other co-conspirators' might be?" Blackstone said sarcastically.

Judge Templeton brought things to a head.

"You know, gentlemen, I know you both enjoy being my special phone-pals on these emergency motions, but I've got a docket full of other cases. Let's cut the squabbling and get to the point. I have to give a great deal of deference to Detective Cheski's affidavit. As a result, I am *not* going to allow an ongoing federal investigation to be interfered with."

"The rights of due process and a fair defense trump that, Your Honor," Blackwell interjected, his voice rising. "I need to share this information with my client—that's a fundamental part of trial preparation. And I need to give it to my law partner who is assisting me on this case."

"Yeah, but there's always one lead counsel, Blackstone, and that's you," Hartz chipped in. "You know what the notepad said—that should be sufficient. And you've shown no compelling need to have your client possess this sensitive information, either. Remember, Judge, Miss Archmont is out on bail, something I objected to. She is out there in the community, where she could share this critical information with others...and if she does, the remaining conspirators could hide or destroy evidence to make themselves unavailable for legal process."

"Mr. Blackstone," the judge finally ruled, "I can appreciate your desire to share this with your client, Miss Archmont. And I realize that my order is highly unusual. But for now, I am going to prohibit further disclosure of the contents of the Langley notes, subject to this: If you can show me a genuine, material need you have to get your client's input on this piece of evidence, then file a motion. Detail it. If you don't want opposing counsel to know your strategies on why your client needs to see what's on that notepad, I can understand that—in that case, request that the Court review your arguments in chambers. There's my ruling. Henry, prepare the order accordingly. And gentlemen, please let me get back to the rest of my docket."

After hanging up the phone, all Blackstone could do was shake his head in disbelief. He was being sandbagged. He didn't mind the typical dash to trial...the frantic search for exculpatory evidence...mounting a defense against the government's unlimited resources and manpower. In fact, J.D. Blackstone usually exulted in that kind of race.

What he didn't like was having to run it in a gunnysack.

But there was another thought he had. And it wasn't about the notepad.

Ever since putting Tully Tullinger on the tail of the tan Taurus that had been following him, he had stopped checking his rearview mirror. But that morning, on the way to the office, he happened to catch a glimpse of the Taurus a few car lengths behind him again.

He dialed Tully, who picked up on the fourth ring. Blackstone wanted a status report.

"I was intending to put this in a written report," Tully said.

"Forget that," Blackstone said. "Give me a verbal. Who's the tail?"

"Guy named Howard Mercer," Tully replied. "He works for G & B Investigations, headquartered in New York. They are a national private-investigation firm. Mercer is the PI who heads up the DC branch. I know him a little. So I found out where he eats breakfast every morning and 'accidentally' on purpose sat next to him at the counter. Did some small talk. Asked him if he had any interesting cases lately—that sort of thing. He clammed up, paid his bill, and scooted out of there so fast you'd think I'd just asked him to pick up my tab."

"You didn't leave it there, did you?"

"Come on, J.D. you know me better than that. Course not. But just don't ask me how I came upon the information I came upon, if you know what I mean."

"So?"

"He made a series of international phone calls after every other tail of you, like clockwork, always to the same number."

"Where?"

"A number in the greater London area."

"Whose number?"

"Last name of Dee…does it ring a bell?"

"Yeah—like the hunchback up in the bell tower."

"I sort of figured you already had a handle on this," Tully said. "See, you take all the fun out. So you want me to keep tracking him?"

"No. I'll take it from here," Blackstone said.

After hanging up, Blackstone located the number Vinnie had given him for Lord Dee. Then he called it. It was early evening over in London.

As before, Dee's personal secretary, Colin Reading, answered.

"I need to speak to Lord Dee," Blackstone insisted. "Right away."

"I'm sorry," Reading replied stiffly, "Lord Dee is rather engaged at the moment. Is there anything I can help you with?"

"You can tell Lord Dee that I know all about Howard Mercer and G & B Investigations, who he hired to shadow me. You tell him that. And then remind him that if he wants me to help Vinnie Archmont he is going to have to deal with me directly. No personal secretaries. No backstairs staff. I want Lord Dee personally."

Less than an hour later, Blackstone's cell phone rang as he was preparing to head home for the night.

"Lord Dee has an opening," Reading announced coldly. "Day after tomorrow."

"Shall I call him, or vice-versa?" Blackstone asked.

"Oh, no—Lord Dee won't be on the telephone. He wants to meet you in person. Fly into Heathrow. Lord Dee's personal driver will pick you up. I'll give you my private e-mail address, and you can e-mail me your itinerary. We'll make all the other arrangements for you for a night's stay at Lord Dee's estate in Wessex."

Blackstone made a quick call to his travel agent to line up the flight. Then Julia poked her head in his office.

"You never told me what Dr. Coglin found out about the notepad," she said.

"No, I didn't," he said with a scowl. "And it looks like I won't."

Julia gave him a puzzled look.

"The Court granted a government motion barring me from divulging Dr. Coglin's findings to anybody."

"That's pretty over the top."

"I'm still stewing over that one. I also found out who hired the guy who's been shadowing me."

"Oh?"

"Yeah. His Strangeness, Lord Dee of Mysticville," Blackstone griped.

"You're kidding. The guy who's footing the legal bill."

"I am flying out tomorrow night to England, for a meeting the following day with Dee. He's putting me up at one of his castles. Then we talk. Which is good, because I've got a burning question for him."

"Like?"

"Simple question," Blackstone said with a wry smile. "Like…how are you with metaphysical riddles, m'Lord?"

CHAPTER 15

J.D. Blackstone was standing in the swarm of international humanity at Heathrow Airport's baggage claim area. Elbowing in around him were hundreds of Europeans, Pakistanis, a South Korean tour group, and pockets of business travelers, backpackers, and students on vacation. After craning his neck, he finally spotted a man in a black suit, tie, and cap holding a sign with his name on it. He grabbed his overnight bag and briefcase and headed over.

"Teddy Darrow," the driver announced with a smile and took Blackstone's bags. Then he added, "I'm the chauffeur for Lord Dee. But I'm picking you up today."

"I hope that doesn't mean that your boss is stuck having to use a bicycle," Blackstone remarked.

Teddy laughed and assured him that Lord Dee had several other drivers on call. He walked Blackstone outside to a double-parked black-and-silver Bentley. It was a special edition limo with a glass partition. In the backseat Blackstone found that day's editions of the London *Times* and *The Scotsman* and a bottle of sparkling water, a glass, a bucket of ice, and a few slices of lime.

On the ride to Lord Dee's manor estate, a several-hour ride from Heathrow, Blackstone was thinking back on his attempt to connect with Vinnie before his flight. He had called her both at her home and her studio but got no answer. He wanted to let her know he would be meeting with Dee, and whether she had any more background on her "mentor" that she needed to tell him. But Vinnie didn't pick up at either number.

During the ride, Blackstone glanced again over the file of clippings
Julia had supplied him on Lord Magister Dee. Clearly, this was a man of
eccentricities. He had sponsored several global conferences on Theosophy,
a religious philosophy officially founded in the late 1800s, but which
claimed to have ties to ancient Eastern mysticism. As a belief system, it
stressed the inner spiritual powers of human potential and the brotherhood of man. Dee had delivered the keynote addresses at some of the
conferences, and had spoken at several conventions of world religions.
But he hadn't published any of his theories. Several of the articles had
mentioned his high-ranking status among the Freemasons, but no details
were given.

For some reason, none of the research Julia had produced contained
a recent photo of Lord Dee. Blackstone regretted that. He often found
that the appearance of a person was a key to some of their most important personality quirks. Blackstone would have to assess Lord Dee on a
first-impression basis when he met him.

It was late afternoon when the Bentley pulled up at the front gates of
Lord Dee's estate. The limo stopped in front of a large, black-iron gate
that had the words *Mortland Manor* inscribed in large letters across the
top. Teddy made a call on his cell phone, and momentarily, the gates
swung open. The sun was lying low and reflected in vibrant colors across
a small lake on the side of the road as the car slowly motored through the
grounds. The main entrance road wound through thick, gloomy woods,
and then up through a rocky incline and finally into a clearing. That is
when he saw the manor house off in the distance.

Mortland Manor, the name of Dee's estate home, was more castle than
mansion house. It was surrounded by vast, winding gardens and precisely
manicured hedges. The structure itself was a huge, tan, stone edifice, with
peaked towers on the right and left, and a mammoth three-story house
connecting them in the middle. Blackstone counted ten chimneys.

The Bentley pulled into a sweeping circular drive and stopped at the
main entrance in front of a massive black oak door with two hoop door
knockers the circumference of volleyballs. Before Blackstone could slide
out of the limo, a butler and a manservant opened both front doors, and
then stepped down to greet their visitor. Then they took his briefcase
and bag.

"Good day, Professor Blackstone," the butler said. "Come this way, everything is prepared for you."

They led him through a large foyer with black-and-white checkered marble floors, and then into a larger great room with a massive stone fireplace. On each side there were two winding staircases. He was led upstairs to a bedroom just off the top floor landing. Blackstone tossed his bag and briefcase onto the canopy bed.

"May I bring you anything before dinner?" the butler asked.

Blackstone said he was fine.

"Dinner is in an hour," the butler announced. "In the conservatory on the first floor. Lord Dee requests formal attire for dining. We've taken the liberty of furnishing some evening wear for you. You will find it in your closet."

When dinner approached, Blackstone donned the black silk evening jacket, bow tie, and striped pants that were in the closet. They fit him perfectly.

He walked down the staircase to the first floor and strolled around on the way to the conservatory. There were several large glass display cases containing collections of various kinds, just outside a huge library with floor-to-ceiling shelves.

He looked into one of the glass cabinets, and found a variety of small stuffed wildlife. In another, he saw a collection of fossils and skeletons of various woodland animals, including what appeared to be a two-headed otter. In yet another, he saw a glass box, with gold gilded corners, that contained a large chunk of crystal.

But his concentration was broken by a voice.

"Good evening, Professor Blackstone," someone behind him announced in a rich, powerful baritone.

He turned, and found himself face-to-face with Lord Magister Dee.

His appearance was remarkable. A man in his early fifties, thick-shouldered and a little stout, Dee had a full, flowing beard that ended at his throat and long hair, rock-star length, that came down to his shoulders. His hands were tucked in the front pockets of his purple velvet jacket. Dee pulled out a hand to shake Blackstone's, and gave a powerful grip that was just short of crushing.

"Admiring my collections, I see," Dee remarked, then led the way down the hall that led to the conservatory. "Though in actuality, they are not mine. Not really," he said as they walked toward the garden room where they would be dining.

As they entered the conservatory where the staff was standing at attention next to the dining table, Lord Dee turned to address Blackstone.

Then Lord Dee pointed back in the direction of the glass museum case in the hallway from which they had just come.

"You should know," he said solemnly, "that those oddities of nature were collected by someone else...someone whose shoes I am hardly worthy to untie."

CHAPTER 16

While dining on roast duck with wild rice, and vegetables that Dee proudly announced had been grown organically on his own estate, the English lord and J.D. Blackstone made small talk.

Blackstone finally decided to home in on another concentric circle of information.

"I notice that you call this estate Mortland Manor," Blackstone pointed out. "Yet Mortland is not very close by—in fact, it is in the southwest, just outside of London."

Lord Dee smiled at that.

"Indeed," he said. "Very observant."

"Which leads me to believe that this manor house was named Mortland not because of where it is situated geographically. But rather," Blackstone continued, "because of *who* once lived in Mortland."

"Very good, Professor," Dee replied. "As you have probably read, my distant ancestor, John Dee, lived his life out in the late 1500s and early 1600s in the village of Mortland. This estate was named in honor of him."

"Ah yes," Blackstone remarked. "The one whose 'shoe you were not worthy to untie'—something similar was once said about another religious figure once, but that one lived in the Middle East. You aren't contending that John Dee was able to walk on water, are you?"

"Not literally," Dee said. "But John Dee did some extraordinary things. Some might even say *paranormal* things."

"While I am conversant with the teachings of most religious systems," Blackstone said, "you won't find me a very willing subject, I'm afraid. I relegate the accounts of spiritual realities and supernatural miracles to the frailties and foibles of the human psyche. All tales of religious experience are nothing more than the substrata of man's psychology, trying to come to grip with things he can't comprehend."

Lord Dee put down his knife and fork, which he had been using nonstop since sitting down. He leaned back, folded his hands in his lap, and gave a knowing stare at Blackstone.

"I know you doubt such things," Dee said. "You see, I know a great deal about you."

"Apparently, not enough," Blackstone said with an edge to his voice. "Otherwise, you wouldn't have had to hire a private investigator to tail me everywhere I went."

"Oh, that," Dee said with an offhand laugh. "Please—Professor Blackstone, that is not why I hired Mr. Mercer to follow you."

"No?"

"Of course not," Dee said. "I hired him to see how long it would take you to detect him and then trace him to me. That, in itself, was my test to determine whether you were every bit as clever as I thought you would be. And you proved me correct, of course. Congratulations."

"I don't like being graded when I don't know I'm taking a test," he retorted. "That's fundamentally unfair."

"Perhaps," Dee said with a smile. "But very effective nonetheless. In any event you passed, sir."

"Then let me give you one of *my* pop quizzes," Blackstone said. "What was in the John Wilkes Booth diary pages? And why was someone willing to commit murder for it?"

Lord Dee's eyes left J.D. Blackstone and drifted to somewhere else, beyond the huge rubber plants, wild orchids, and orange trees that filled up the glass-walled conservatory.

"For me to answer that question," Dee said cautiously, "I would have to know the contents of those diary pages. Which would make me complicit in their theft, perhaps even complicit in the act of murder. But I am no thief. And certainly no murderer. You will notice I did not have my solicitors with me during our little meeting tonight. That is because I have nothing to hide. Thus, Professor, I cannot tell you with any certainty what was in those pages."

"But I bet you had some inkling of what might be in the diary of Lincoln's assassin. You wanted those newly discovered pages. Vinnie Archmont told me that. You must have had a reason. And I am betting it had something to do with your religious philosophy, and your self-aggrandizing notion of discovering the 'ultimate secret' of the Freemasons."

"If that were my motivation," Dee said cautiously, "then it would be rather pointless for me to reveal such a secret to you, wouldn't you agree? The point of secrets is to keep them, not give them away."

"Why all this obsession with secrets?" Blackstone said, his voice rising. "Would you rather keep a secret than protect a woman wrongly accused of murder?"

"I would do anything for dear Vinnie."

"Then tell me the truth. Do you know anything, personally, about the murder of the Secretary of the Smithsonian and the theft of the Booth diary pages?"

There was a long pause. A woman from the staff came in to fill their water glasses, but Lord Dee waved her away. Then Dee finally spoke up.

"I know nothing," he said, "that could help you, or Vinnie."

Then after another pause he added, "Professor, you mock the need for secrecy in my pursuit of transcendent truth. You simply cannot appreciate the risk that those, like myself who adhere to the esoteric religions, have to face in the world."

"Try me," Blackstone replied.

"Those collections in the glass cabinets," Lord Dee responded excitedly, "the fossils...the crystal that John Dee himself used to study the refraction of light...all of them."

But then Dee stopped talking and looked for an instant as if he had swallowed a bite of food too large for his throat. He took a sip of water, and then continued talking.

"These antiquities...antiquities...they...were...they were...gathered by Mr. Dee," Lord Dee continued, now picking up steam again, "to observe the natural world in an effort to break through into the supernatural realm. But the local rabble couldn't understand. In November of 1582, while he was traveling in Europe, the villagers, fearful of his philosophies, stormed his house at Mortland, destroying it and most of his exquisite library. No need for secrets, you say? I beg to differ, sir."

"I have no interest in stories about villagers with pitchforks and torches," Blackstone shot back angrily. "I'm here to keep my client, your dear Vinnie, from the death chamber."

"I will help in any way I can. But there are certain things, certain profound metaphysical truths, that I cannot share with a person like you. A skeptic. Someone who bitterly mocks the esoteric path. At least for the time being."

Lord Dee was about to excuse himself and retire for the night, when Blackstone decided to go in for the kill.

"What do you know," Blackstone said bluntly, "about a four-line code, a coded poem? Something that may have been contained in Booth's diary?"

Dee's face took on the expression of a bystander to an automobile collision.

"Poem...four lines," he stammered. "Is that what you said?"

"Did I?" Blackstone said, trifling with his host.

"You did. What did you mean by that, man—what?"

"Unfortunately for you, I can't elaborate. A federal judge in our case has ordered me not to tell you. Sorry."

Dee leaned forward over the table, his face intense.

"I could make you fabulously wealthy. I can do that," Dee said. "Very easily. All you have to do is give me authentic proof of what you were just talking about."

"Can't do it," Blackstone snapped back. "Besides I make a good living at the law school. And I charge exorbitant but well-earned legal fees in my law practice, as you ought to know. I'm comfortable financially. So all in all I would rather not violate a federal court order and be disbarred."

"You have no idea how very important this is," Lord Dee said, his voice shaking.

"No, there you are wrong," Blackstone shot back. "I know *exactly* how important this is."

There was strained silence between the two men for several minutes.

Blackstone kept eating until he was finished. But Lord Dee just stared at him with a strange smile.

Then, pushing himself away from the table, J.D. Blackstone thanked Lord Dee for the meal, excused himself, and retired to bed.

CHAPTER 17

There was no television for Blackstone to watch in his state room in Mortland Manor during the late-night hours. The only sounds in his bedroom were the ticking of an ancient windup alarm clock on his nightstand and the creaks of a mansion house that was three hundred and fifty years old. As usual, Blackstone was being tormented by sleeplessness.

Blackstone had brought his jogging clothes along and was tempted to take a run down the road, but then, sometime after three in the morning, he felt his eyes finally get heavy, and he tried to lie down on the goosefeather bed to sleep.

The next thing he knew, he was rushing around the room, packing up and trying not to miss his flight. Teddy was there, driving him in the Bentley.

But they didn't go to the airport.

Instead the car pulled up to a nondescript building, then circled around to the back, where he was led down a stark corridor with linoleum tiles and green walls.

"Mr. Blackstone?" a man in a shirtsleeves and a tie said to him. "So very sorry. Please follow me."

They passed through two polished steel doors that swung open, and metal cabinets were to the left and a few aluminum-surface tables to the right.

The man in the white shirt reached to the wall to pull out two of the big cabinet drawers, and as he did, Blackstone noticed that the underarms of his white shirt were stained with circles of sweat.

Then the two drawers slid open.

There was one black zip bag in each drawer.

And the black zip bags were unzipped.

There, with face exposed from within one of the bags, was his wife Marilyn. Her skin was pale and grayish, and her hair was uncombed. That was not like her to leave her hair uncombed, Blackstone thought numbly.

Someone must have stopped the time on the clock on the wall as he looked at the deep, red gash on his wife's forehead. But no blood was coming out of the wound, and he struggled, in the middle of the swirling vacuum of confusion, to process the terrible thing he was seeing.

He was keenly aware there was nowhere for him to grab, nothing to hold onto. It was as if he were about to fall off the edge of the world. Gravity could no longer hold him safely down.

Slowly, excruciatingly, he looked over to the other drawer. It was his daughter, Beth, with her young face discolored in death, framed by the hideous black zip bag.

Then a third drawer opened, seemingly on its own.

Blackstone was moving like a swimmer, walking underwater on the bottom of a swimming pool, over to the drawer. He looked down.

It was Vinnie Archmont. She was laid out in the drawer. On her chest was a single red rose.

And her hands were crossed over her breast, with all five fingers on one hand extended, but only one finger of the other hand pointing while the other four were curled into a fist.

His eyes looked up, and at the end of the morgue there was a window. And through the window he could see a church spire. And there was a sound. Was it the sound of church bells?

"Professor Blackstone!"

Someone was calling. There was a knocking on the door.

Blackstone bolted up in his bed, out of his dream he had been having.

On his nightstand, the clock was still clanging, but barely audible, as it was winding down.

Blackstone threw on a bathrobe and stumbled to the door.

It was Teddy, with his coat and tie and cap, wearing a fixed smile.

"Morning, Professor," he said. "Car leaves in thirty minutes. Would you like some tea or breakfast brought up while you dress?"

Blackstone shook his head no, and then closed the door.

He made his way to the bathroom, and turned on the faucets and splashed some water on his face.

Then he walked into the bedroom and sat down on an upholstered sitting chair. And let his head clear.

He thought about his dream. The unsettling feel of it was still haunting the room like an apparition.

Blackstone struggled to focus. He quickly analyzed all three of the ciphers.

The part about Marilyn and Beth he knew too well. And he knew, also, why they followed him, as they often did, into his subconscious world.

And why he could not escape from the dread about them that haunted him constantly.

The symbolic appearance of Vinnie, too, was clear, and so was the rose and her numerical arrangements of her six fingers.

"Rose of 6," he found himself saying out loud.

As for the third component of the dream, the church bells, he knew that one also. It bore a message he had been suppressing.

And as he started dressing he was thinking about that. About how it was distasteful for him to have to bring his uncle into the Smithsonian murder case. On the other hand, from a strategy standpoint, it would be inexcusable not to. It would be critical for Vinnie's defense to be able to glean some insight from Reverend Lamb's unique knowledge of the Freemasons and the world of esoteric religion, if for no other reason than to calculate how Lord Dee was connected to the Booth diary pages and Langley's notes.

It was decided. When he was stateside, J.D. Blackstone would call his uncle, Reverend John Lamb.

And he would ask him if they could meet and have a talk as quickly as possible.

CHAPTER 18

Somewhere, flying thousands of feet over the limitless Atlantic, J.D. Blackstone believed he had begun to figure out one small piece of the four-line coded poem that had been jotted down by Horace Langley as he studied the Booth diary.

The first line of cryptic note read,

To AP and KGC

Blackstone had been harboring an idea about who "AP" was. But he wanted to be certain. Now he was.

In his seat in first class, he had a stack of books Julia had ferreted out on the Lincoln assassination, on Booth, and on the Confederate resistance movement at the end of the Civil War. There was also a separate book specifically on the Freemasons. After scanning them, Blackstone was beginning to see a connection.

And what lay in the very epicenter of that tangled web was one man: Albert Pike. For Blackstone, here was the "AP" of Booth's diary entry.

Pike was not exactly a household name in the history of the War Between the States. But then, that was probably fitting, considering the nature of the man and the weird, secretive, philosophical bent he had.

Pike had been a lawyer by trade and even served on the pre-war Supreme Court of Arkansas as a justice. During the war he became a Confederate officer and rallied Indian tribes to attack federal outposts. There was much controversy about whether he had generated Indian "atrocities" against the North. But when the Confederate cause failed, he was charged with treason. After the assassination of Abraham Lincoln, who was *not* a Freemason, Vice President Andrew Johnson, a high-ranking Freemason himself and also president by succession, narrowly escaped removal from office after being impeached.

Once safe from the attempted removal from office by the Senate, President Johnson then issued an executive pardon to Albert Pike, a Freemason whose thirty-third-degree status actually trumped that of the president. To Blackstone's mind as he delved into the history of it all, Pike's pardon, and his frequent travels in and out of the federal capital despite his status as a war criminal, seemed to stand as one of the Civil War's quiet little anomalies.

A man who bragged of being conversant in numerous languages, well-read in the world religions and philosophies, and an international leader among the Freemasons, Albert Pike met, and was most certainly captivated by, Vinnie Ream, the pretty, coquettish sculptor who had wooed Washington's high society. During their mysterious relationship, Pike arranged for Ream to ceremonially receive several Masonic degrees, despite the fact that women were generally forbidden from joining the Masons.

And in what was either a twist of extreme irony, or a carefully constructed plot, Vinnie Ream was the very person who had persuaded one particular senator, after the impeachment charges had been issued by the House of Representatives, to vote *against* removing President Andrew Johnson from office. That was in 1868, two years after Vinnie met Albert Pike and Pike had received his presidential pardon. The vote influenced by Vinnie Ream would become the pivotal vote that would keep Johnson in the White House. So the question remained—were Vinnie's political efforts on Johnson's behalf a recompense for Johnson having granted a presidential pardon to his fellow Mason and Vinnie's strange soul-partner, Albert Pike?

But all of that was mere history and politics. In Blackstone's mind, that was simply stage dressing for the real drama that had led to Horace Langley's murder at the Smithsonian Castle. It had to be.

Of course, Blackstone figured it was possible there was a rogue Confederate cult group out there somewhere that still cared about the reputation, or the ideas, of John Wilkes Booth. On the other hand, the meticulous, professional sophistication of the murder and theft that occurred at the Smithsonian did not bear the marks of having been orchestrated by some fringe gang of Southern anarchists.

The more Blackstone read and then integrated his historical research with the facts about the crime, the less this looked like a political operation. Indeed, he thought to himself, it looked almost apolitical. For Blackstone, this was not a political crime. This was something else altogether.

To Blackstone, the murder case clearly had religious elements.

First, there was the wording of the coded poem. Blackstone was assuming that the cipher documented by Langley in his note was connected to the crime, because the note was ripped off the page by the assassin and taken, along with the Booth pages. And the four-line poem did not seem to carry any political connotations. The symbolism was loaded with classic religious archetypes: references to a rose, and a tree, and "gospel's Mary."

Next, there was the eccentric religious philosopher and thirty-third-degree Mason Lord Magister Dee, who expressed an otherworldly interest in the Booth diary. Then there was, as Blackstone learned in his reading, the unmistakable theology of the Freemasons in their worship of the "Great Architect of the Universe," as they would refer to God.

Blackstone had neglected to throw away his uncle's latest book on religious heresy, the one Reverend Lamb handed him at their last meeting. When he parked in the airport parking lot before leaving for England, he noticed it was still in the backseat of his car. So he packed it into his briefcase with the other books.

Now he was glad he did.

As he scanned parts of the book, he found that Reverend Lamb had done a nice job, in one particular chapter, of pointing out the connection between the religious beliefs of the Freemasons and the ancient Gnostics. There was also an appendix in the back with some diagrams and explanations of the symbolism and ceremonies of the Freemasons.

As Blackstone considered Lord Dee's desire to obtain the Booth diary because of its possible link to the "ultimate secret" of the Freemasons, it seemed obvious that whatever that secret was, it had some kind of spiritual significance.

For Blackstone, it all seemed very cultic, even ecclesiastical in an unorthodox kind of way.

Then, as Blackstone read on amid the lazy drone of jet engines, he came upon an intriguing news story that appeared in a newspaper shortly after the Lincoln assassination. On April 16, 1865, the day of Abraham Lincoln's state funeral, a brief mention appeared in an extra edition of the Washington *Star*. The article mentioned "recent developments" in the investigation into the assassination that proved "conclusively, the existence of a deep laid plot of a gang of conspirators, including members of the order of the Knights of the Golden Circle."

"Knights of the Golden Circle," Blackstone said out loud. "*KGC*."

The passenger next to him stirred, opened an eye, and then fell back to sleep.

Blackstone paged back to the indexes of each of his books. Only one had a reference to the "Knights of the Golden Circle." By all appearances, the group originally started a shadowy conspiracy of Confederates and Southern sympathizers bent on creating a slaveholding empire in the Southern states, Mexico, and Cuba, and creating a new republic of immense power and wealth. But when the Civil War broke out, the organization splintered, with many of its members being absorbed into the Confederate army.

What happened next was mired in legend and speculation. By the end of the war, Northerners who held allegiances to the Confederacy had seemed to have transmuted the Knights of the Golden Circle into a new kind of group. It likely planned several scenarios for either the kidnapping and ransom, or the assassination, of Abraham Lincoln, and the overturning of the federal government. Reputedly, the KGC was populated by Freemasons.

As Blackstone saw it then, these were the political anarchists, including John Wilkes Booth, who still held on to wild dreams of a new empire.

But in the person of Albert Pike, there was something else—a religious seer whose philosophical theories added something immensely radical and profoundly transcendent to the Southern sympathizers: a new religious way of looking at the world. A new religion. A new spiritual reality rising up out of the ashes of the terrors and death of war. And Albert Pike was positioning himself to be its new pope.

After several hours of study and note-taking, Blackstone was starting to get the big picture. Blackstone had concluded that his identification of "AP" and "KGC" in the first line of the coded message was probably correct. Strangely, though, there seemed to be no historical connection between Albert Pike and the Knights of the Golden Circle—or with John Wilkes Booth for that matter.

Blackstone wondered whether Booth was carrying a message, noted in his diary, that was destined for Albert Pike and perhaps the elite hierarchy of the KGC. Blackstone even entertained the possibility that Booth did not know the meaning of the message he was supposed to deliver to Pike. But in any event, it appeared that the message never reached its intended destination.

The eighteen pages of the Booth diary were apparently removed shortly after the diary was taken from among Booth's possessions, after he had been killed in an ambush by the federal authorities.

According to Congressional testimony offered by Lafayette Baker, a police detective who headed up the spy network for Lincoln's Secretary of War, Edwin Stanton, the pages of the Booth diary went missing *after* the diary was delivered to Stanton. It was widely believed the diary pages might have shown a connection between Stanton, a Freemason, and Booth. Stanton wanted those pages hidden, not because he wanted to protect some metaphysical secret of the ages, but for much more pragmatic reasons: He didn't want to be implicated in the killing of the president. Secretary of War Stanton's behavior shortly before Lincoln's assassination had raised serious questions about his possible complicity. For instance, Stanton had refused to provide adequate security for the president the night he went to Ford's Theater, even though there had been overwhelming evidence of plots against Lincoln swirling throughout Washington DC.

Blackstone peeked through the small, rectangular plane window and saw the city of Washington spread out below, like a miniature continent of white marble buildings, with the towering spire of the Washington Monument dominating the landscape. He felt certain he had cracked the first line of the coded message. What he didn't know, but had to now frantically find out in order to save his client from the death chamber, was why that strange message might have cost Horace Langley his life.

As the 757 slowly started its descent, Blackstone flipped to the midsection of the Civil War history book, the part with photographs. Abraham

Lincoln. Andrew Johnson. Jefferson Davis. Then he saw another photograph.

And it sent a quick tingle down Blackstone's spine. It was a picture of
Albert Pike, the Masonic philosopher and Confederate officer. A stout
man with a full flowing beard, and long, rock-star-length hair down to
his shoulders. Pike looked like a mirror image of Lord Magister Dee.

But then Blackstone flipped the page to another photo.

And when he did, it made him flinch a little.

It was a photograph of Vinnie Ream, the beguiling nineteenth-century
sculptor.

And she was a dead ringer for his client, Vinnie Archmont.

CHAPTER 19

As he left baggage claim, Blackstone walked over to his Maserati at the Reagan National Airport parking lot. He called Reverend Lamb from his cell phone but got his voice mail.

"Uncle," Blackstone said in his message, "it's J.D. Just got back from the UK. I was wondering if you and I could chat about a new case I'm handling. Call me."

Then he retrieved a voice mail from Frieda his secretary. She said his office had received an "urgent" message.

"A man called," Frieda recounted. "He said it was about the Langley murder case. He wouldn't give me his name or contact information. But he said that you needed to be at the construction site down by the federal courthouse, just off Constitution Avenue, by four p.m. today. That you need to talk to a Mr. Dennis Watkins there. Some kind of supervisor. That this Mr. Watkins has some crucial information, and would fill you in down there."

Blackstone drove out of the parking lot, and through early crosstown rush-hour traffic. It was ten minutes to four when he swung up to the large office building under construction.

He parked his car and quickly made his way over to a makeshift office in a trailer, where he introduced himself to a foreman there.

The foreman grabbed his walkie-talkie and spoke to someone. Then he handed a hard hat to Blackstone and said to follow him. As they crossed the construction site, Blackstone could see that the girders were in place, the floors had already been laid, and now they were raising the walls. There were huge blocks of marble being swung into place around the base with the help of cranes.

When they reached a corner of the building, there was a man in a short-sleeve white shirt and a hard hat looking over drawings on a large work table. The foreman introduced Blackstone to Dennis Watkins, the man in the white shirt.

"Got your message," Blackstone began. "Can we talk in private? I am curious about any information you may have."

"Mr. Blackstone, I appreciate everything you're trying to do on this nasty business," Watkins began. "But if you don't mind, I want to withhold comment until I show you this, and you see it with your own eyes. Frankly, I think this is going to make your whole job a lot easier. You know, easier to defend your position."

Blackstone was puzzled, but obliged by following him into a large construction elevator with metal mesh sides and an open top.

Watkins pushed a green up button and the cage door automatically locked with a loud clang as the elevator slowly shuddered upward.

Suddenly, something up above caught Watkins's attention as he craned his neck straight up to see. Then he slammed his fist into the red stop button and snatched his walkie-talkie off his hip.

"Gerald, this is Watkins," he shouted. "Hey, we've got one of your marble fascia blocks hanging in the air over the northeast corner elevator. It's hanging down from crane number three. Three floors up. The thing's dangling right over our heads! Swing that thing away from here, will you?"

Blackstone looked up at the huge white stone block, suspended directly over them about thirty feet over their heads. It was dangling from a cable connected to a crane arm.

Then Blackstone noticed the title on the hard hat of the man in the elevator with him.

It read, *Dennis Watkins—Chief Architect.*

Then something lit up in Blackstone's mind and he muttered, "The Great Architect."

"That stone block over our heads," Blackstone said in a rushed voice. "Tell me, quick. Is it right-angled?"

Watkins threw him a befuddled look.

"Yeah. Sure. All of them are, I think."

Blackstone quickly looked through the metal mesh down to the ground. The elevator was only about six inches off the ground. Blackstone grabbed the cage door handle and jiggled it, but the safety feature on the cage door had automatically locked it shut on the ascent.

Just then a voice squawked at them from Watkins's walkie-talkie.

"Dennis, this is Gerald. I sent Tony up the ladder to crane number three. There's nobody at the controls. But the control booth door is locked. You guys have to get out of there! He says the tow cable is in the descend position, from what he can see. There's a piece of metal jammed in the gear. That's all that's keeping it from coming down. Get outta there now!"

Watkins hit the yellow down button two times in a row. Nothing happened. Then he reached for the green up button, but Blackstone grabbed his arm to stop him.

"You move us up and we're dead!" Blackstone yelled. "I am the target here."

"Let's climb up the sides," Watkins shouted, and tried to lift himself up using the spaces in the metal mesh as finger holes.

"No time!" Blackstone yelled back.

"The block is coming down!" the voice in the walkie-talkie was screaming.

"Do as I do and we'll both live," Blackstone blurted out and threw himself down on the riveted metal floor of the elevator. Watkins looked up just as the large marble block came hurtling down at them. He threw himself facedown next to Blackstone.

A split second later, the daylight overhead was completely eclipsed by the huge stone block that was now dangling over them, just a few feet over their heads. As it swung from side to side, it banged into the sides of the metal cage, sending vibrations through the elevator. The two men were breathing heavily as they lay on the floor. "Lift it up...lift it out of here," Watkins muttered.

Up at the crane, Tony had broken his way into the crane's operating booth and then pulled the lever, reversing the tow cable. Slowly the huge block of stone was lifted up and out of the elevator cage and away from them, and then lowered safely to the ground.

Watkins yelled for a ladder to climb up to the top of the stone block to examine it. By then, the project engineer showed up and scampered up the ladder to the top of the block with Watkins. Blackstone followed quickly after him.

The three men stared at the place on the stone face where the cable hook was connected to a metal loop imbedded in the marble.

"What in the world…" Watkins said.

"A Lewis grappling assembly," Blackstone announced, nodding as if that meant something important.

"Absolutely right," the engineer chimed in. "Haven't seen one of those since engineering school. Really old-school stuff. Three tapped metal key wedges, two angled ones, one straight one in between them in the middle, all inserted together into the stone face. Connected by a vertical bolt, holding the loop in place for hoisting." Then he added, looking at Watkins, "Dennis, this antiquated thing isn't ours."

When the three of them were on the ground level again, the engineer shook Blackstone's hand and introduced himself.

"You guys at the building inspector's office," the engineer said to Blackstone, "really know your engineering stuff."

"Building inspector's office?" Blackstone said with amazement. "You've got the wrong guy. I'm a lawyer. And a law professor."

There was a stunned silence.

"I was told," Watkins interjected, "that a Mr. Blackstone in the District of Columbia inspector's office was coming over here. I was led to believe you were the guy who was pitching for us at City Hall to help us resolve the permit issue over our girder configuration on the fourth floor."

"Who told you that?" Blackstone asked.

Watkins shook his head. "Can't remember. But I am going to chase this down. This is very weird."

Then Watkins looked at Blackstone. "How exactly did you know that our lying flat on the floor was the only way to survive?"

"Because I knew," Blackstone replied, "that the marble block would stop short of hitting the ground."

"He's right!" a voice shouted out. It was Tony, the crane operator, who had just arrived to join them. He was carrying a metal cable lock in his hand.

"This thing was set on the cable," Tony explained pointing to the lock, "so the block would be reeled down—but not all the way. It was set to stop short."

Watkins turned to Blackstone again.

"You still haven't answered my question. How did you know so much about that marble block, mister? And why was it set so it wouldn't reach the ground?"

Blackstone grinned, cocked his head a little, and then he answered.

"I take your question to indicate two things," Blackstone said. "First, that you don't know anything about me or why I am came here today."

"And the other thing?" Watkins asked.

"That your question is proof to me," Blackstone said, his voice growing a little more somber, "that you, sir, have never been initiated into the mysteries of the Freemasons."

Then, as Watkins and the project engineer tried to make sense out of Blackstone's cryptic response, Blackstone looked around, taking in the vista around him, from his position at the construction site.

From there, he could see straight down the street that was crowded with office buildings, all the way to the intersection of Indiana and C and D streets.

Down where, amid all of the concrete office buildings and glass highrises, he could see a large tree in full leaf, partially covering an often overlooked statue of the Masonic religious seer and Confederate officer Albert Pike.

CHAPTER 20

"So from your research on the Freemasons, you knew the marble block wouldn't ever hit the ground?"

As Reverend Lamb asked that, his voice was quiet and intense.

"That's it," J.D. Blackstone replied. "I had been reading, actually in the appendix of your book, how in the Masonic temples they all have these little models of a stone block hanging from a hoist."

"Yes, of course. But always suspended. Never touching the earth. The stone block represents strength and power to them. But then you already knew that, right?"

"Yes, from my research. Obviously then, whoever gave me that little scare at the building site was sending me a message."

"What kind of message?"

"That they are the ones who have the power. I don't. They can crush me at will. That's pretty elementary."

"So they are trying to intimidate you, scare you off from pursuing the defense of this...what is your client's name again?"

"Vinnie Archmont."

"And you're sure this incident in the construction elevator was no coincidence?" Reverend Lamb asked.

"I'm certain."

As they talked, the two men were strolling across the green lawn of the quad between the college buildings where Lamb was teaching a summer school class.

"I realized," Blackstone continued, "that the person who called my office and sent me scurrying over to the construction site had arranged for me to share the elevator with the *chief architect*—a play on words with the Mason's reference to God as the *Great Architect*. And then I discovered there was a square-cornered marble block hanging over my head—perfectly rigged from the crane—and the way that block was hoisted."

"Someone really took the time to emulate the Masonic symbols," Lamb added. "Complete with the antiquated Lewis grappling hook assembly imbedded into the stone. I've seen diagrams of that in the older Masonic writings."

"Which is why I need your help on this," Blackstone said. "You've spent years trying to figure this Masonic business out. Written extensively on it. So, Uncle, what do you think? You want to join me in this case as my consulting expert?"

Lamb paused and stopped walking. He shifted a few books he had under one arm, regained his grip once again on the tattered briefcase in the other, and then looked at his nephew.

"Any more news on who did this to you?" he asked.

"No. The police are investigating. They dusted for prints in the control booth of the crane. But I'm betting they'll come up with zero. This was too well planned to leave some sloppy evidence behind. The construction supervisors checked it out. It was clear someone sabotaged the crane, but they have no witnesses. No one was seen going in or out of that crane before the mishap. Whoever orchestrated this disappeared like—"

"Magic?" Lamb asked.

"I didn't think you believed in magic, Uncle," Blackstone said with a tinge of sarcasm.

"I don't. But I do believe in the power of the prince of darkness," Lamb replied, his voice so low he could barely be heard. And then he added, "And believe me, it is real. Though you must beware…it often comes in ways you do not recognize."

Then he straightened up and continued talking.

"So—specifically, what is it you need from me?"

Blackstone overcame the temptation to mock his uncle's warnings, which sounded vaguely medieval. He got right to the point.

"I'd like your help in deciphering a poem, which I think is a code for something," Blackstone said, trying to be nonchalant. "It was an entry copied, I think, from a page of the John Wilkes Booth diary. But it may have something to do with Freemasonry."

"I assume you have access to it. Why don't you show it to me?"

"I can't. The judge entered a pretrial order prohibiting me from sharing it directly with anyone else. I've got my partner filing an appeal from that order, hoping to overturn it. But I'm not holding my breath. Appellate courts are generally reluctant to interfere with the way a trial judge handles the pretrial conduct of a criminal case."

"Tell me, why is this poem so important?"

"If I can decipher it, then I can figure out who may have had a motive to steal it—and then I can logically deduce who killed Horace Langley. With that, I hope to exonerate my client."

"Alright," Lamb said. "Then how about some hints about the poem… will that avoid violating the court order?"

"Now we're on the same page," Blackstone said with a smile. Then he thought for a moment.

"Okay," he continued. "Let me put it to you this way—why don't you tell me about the symbolic significance of trees in the metaphysics of the Freemasons."

"That's a tall order."

"Then let me narrow it down," Blackstone added. "As I see it, the Masons deny they are a religious order, and yet their symbols and ceremonies are laced with religious references. Christian and biblical references to be precise."

"Not exactly," Lamb countered. "In my opinion, the Freemasons, for hundreds of years, have incorporated theology all right, but not of biblical Christianity, but rather, of Gnosticism—the third- and fourth-century heresy that set itself up as the chief competitor to the gospel of Christ."

"But the two—Christianity and Gnosticism—are related, aren't they?"

"In a way, yes," Reverend Lamb said. "Like a flower and a weed are both related in proximity when they spring from the same ground. Gnosticism was like a weed that steals the nutrients from the ground and wraps itself around the flower, squeezing the life from it. And it would have ended up strangling the gospel had the factual truth of the historical record of Jesus, contained in the New Testament, not won out in the end, which is exactly what happened."

"Now you've just lost me on that one," Blackstone shot back. "I've got to say that I consider it pure bunk to say that there is any reliable evidence of the historicity of Christianity, dating all the way back two thousand years. Religion is nothing but subjective opinion fashioned into certainty, built on fables conflated and expanded over the centuries—and then people simply call it faith."

"Nephew," Lamb said calmly, "we have better historical verification for the life, teachings, and death, and I might add, even the resurrection, of Jesus, than we do for any other first century figure—all of the Caesars of Rome, included. Would you like to go back to my office so I can show you the historical evidence?"

"No, I really don't have the time for any of that, Uncle," Blackstone shot back abruptly. He wanted his uncle to get to the point.

"So, getting back to the reason I came to you—" Blackstone said, "you know, the tree as a religious symbol and how it plays into Freemasonry."

"Well," Lamb said, thinking on it, "Masons use the acacia tree in their architecture. It is meant to refer, I think, to the wood from which the ark of Noah was built. Then there is the Christian concept of the 'tree,' upon which Jesus was crucified. The Old Testament prophecies talk about Messiah being hung from a tree, an obvious reference to a sacrifice that would be fulfilled hundreds of years later when Jesus was crucified on the cross of Calvary."

"Go on," Blackstone said.

"And the tree of good and evil."

"Garden of Eden," Blackstone said.

"Right, in the Genesis account," Reverend Lamb replied. His voice was starting to take on a professorial tone.

"And then," he continued, "in the first chapter of the book of Psalms, a tree is mentioned. And also a mention in the last book of the Bible, Revelation. Then there are other references in the Old Testament, particularly in the prophets, to certain pagan rituals that were practiced beneath trees. You know, J.D., the possibilities really are endless."

Blackstone was starting to lose patience. "But my *time isn't*," he barked so sharply that it took Reverend Lamb aback. "I am rapidly approaching a jury trial with my client facing the death penalty. I have to tell you that I really need answers, not academic ramblings."

"I can understand the stress a lawyer must feel in that kind of situation," Reverend Lamb remarked quietly, studying his nephew with an understanding look. "Okay, J.D., I will help you any way I can. Let me think on this tree business."

"Thank you," Blackstone replied, now having the sense perhaps that he had treated his uncle too harshly. His voice softened a bit. "By the way, if it helps you at all, I think this 'tree' reference may have something to do with something that the Freemason philosophers have considered to be the quest for the ultimate secret."

Lamb stopped on the steps of the liberal arts building, and turned to Blackstone.

"Ultimate secret, you say?"

Blackstone nodded.

"You know," Lamb said, "the Gnostic heretics based their entire cosmology, the whole fabric of their belief system, on the idea of secret knowledge. He who learns the secrets controls the keys to all spiritual power. Or so they believed. But for the Christian, of course, he already has direct access to the mysteries of God. For the follower of Christ, it has already been clearly revealed."

Blackstone chuckled.

"I suppose I have a certain admiration," he said to his uncle with a smirk, "for your persistence in believing your own brand of the Jesus fairy tale. Particularly when even you had to admit, in that book of yours you gave me, that the history of Christianity is one long tale of theological squabbles between the so-called believers and the 'heretics,' stretching over two millennia."

Lamb didn't answer him at first, but turned to mount the last few steps to deliver the lecture in the religion class for which he was already late. But when he reached the top of the stairs he stopped and turned, looking down at his nephew at the bottom.

There was a grin on his face as the mild breeze blew through his thinning white mane of hair, mussing it a bit.

"You see," Lamb said brightly. "I *told* you you'd end up reading my book."

CHAPTER 21

J.D. Blackstone left Capital City College and cruised off in his Maserati Spyder toward the fashionable Old Town section of Alexandria.

As he drove, he was still ruminating over his conversation with his uncle. Their walk together on the campus quad had left Blackstone with a bad taste in his mouth. He really wondered whether, in order to get Reverend Lamb's help as an expert on Freemasonry, he would be able to endure his endless religious proselytizing.

But there was also something else on Blackstone's mind. He was stewing over his client, Vinnie Archmont. He hadn't heard from her for almost two weeks, despite e-mails, letters, and several phone messages he'd left on her voice mail. He had a bag full of questions for her and few answers. Now he had decided to drop by her Alexandria art studio, unannounced, in an effort to track her down.

He was beginning to get that nagging feeling, that hollow, graveyard echo in the gut that lawyers dread—the awareness of impending disaster brought on by the realization your client has been secretly playing you for a complete sucker. And you've fallen for it. Those cases can end only one way.

The way that Blackstone would often illustrate to his law students.

"When representing criminal defense clients," he would say, "remember the celebrated case of the Wild West lawyer. He agreed to represent a bank robber who sued his compatriot because the other thief refused to split the stolen booty with him, fifty-fifty, as they had agreed. The judge patiently heard the case. Weighed the evidence. Then announced his decision. The judge ordered the client to be promptly hung, and the lawyer permanently disbarred. So, students, try to learn something from this august example. Don't let your zeal for a client's case allow you to be played for a sucker."

The thought of Vinnie's almost psychic, not to mention economic, dependence on Lord Dee kept haunting Blackstone. But when he saw how Lord Dee and his client had apparently assumed the likenesses of Albert Pike and Vinnie Ream, those two nineteenth-century star-crossed almost-lovers, he knew something very weird was going on. Something that could, perhaps, explain why the two of them, or one of them possibly, could have conspired to murder Horace Langley and steal the Booth diary entry before it became public. It was a working hypothesis. One he didn't think was actually probable for a number of reasons, but at least feasible. And if it was feasible, then a smart prosecutor like Henry Hartz would be able to make it look true beyond any reasonable doubt.

Blackstone didn't want to think of the beautiful Vinnie being complicit in the crime, for reasons that were now beginning to plague him and threaten his objectivity. He was beginning to feel like someone being sandwiched into an already crowded elevator. But he was still objective enough to know the things that *might* compromise his usually cold-steel powers of analysis. The fact remained that Vinnie seemed to be nothing but a bit player in her contacts with Horace Langley. Lord Dee, on the other hand, was rich, politically powerful, and had a fourteen-karat-gold motive—his undisputed obsession with the Booth diary.

The facts showed that Dee was an obvious candidate for mastermind of the murder and theft. If Vinnie was involved at all, she might well have been merely an unwitting pawn.

The task for Blackstone was to find the evidence to hit a home run on the *unwitting* part.

The Torpedo Factory building, which housed Vinnie's studio, was just off the Potomac River. It was in a classy, restored area draped with restored history and not far from old brownstones and three-story mansions.

Blackstone wandered around some of the other shops and galleries until he located Vinnie's studio. Her name, together with the phrase *TIMELESS ART AND SCULPTURE,* was etched in the glass.

He walked in the door and a chime sounded. There were tables decoratively filled with pottery, busts, and figurines. There were a few historical personages caught in bronze. One was a bust of Abraham Lincoln.

A few moments later Vinnie poked her head around the corner from a back room. She had an artist's apron on, her sleeves were rolled up, and her hands were stained with gray clay.

"J.D.," she said brightly. "I am so glad to see you. How is my very brilliant lawyer?"

"Not happy," he barked out. "And when I am not happy that makes me feel less than brilliant."

"What's the matter?" she said taking a few steps toward him and tossing a tight curl away from her face coyly.

"You," he said sharply.

"Me?" she said with a little pout on her lips. "Don't be such a big, bad, angry old man. I like you much better when you're happy." Then she put her hands on her hips like she was doing a Shirley Temple impersonation.

"Do me a favor," Blackstone said. "Cut the Betty Boop baby-doll act."

Vinnie flinched a little at that. Then she dropped her hands to her side and closed both of her eyes, and tilted her head slightly to the side and gave out an overblown sigh.

"You can leave now," she said quietly. "I was very peaceful and calm before you came here."

"Peaceful is where you are heading," Blackstone barked back. "Unless you start cooperating with me and responding to my calls and e-mails. Permanently peaceful is the place where the AUSA is trying to put you—if you are convicted, they'll lead you from the death-row section of the prison to a table where they will strap you down and put an IV full of poisons into your veins. Then you'll get real peaceful. Is that what you want?"

"No," she said quietly.

"Alright then, let's talk."

"Let's go into the back, where my studio is," she said.

He followed her into the back room, which had a skylight and several large work tables, and a manually operated pottery wheel for throwing pots. There was a smaller table, higher than the others, with a clay bust on it, with what looked like a work in progress. There was something familiar about the face that was the subject of the bust.

There were two wooden chairs, and Blackstone sat down in one. Vinnie wiped her hands and pulled the other chair up so close that her feet were in between his.

"I am all yours," she said with her hands in her lap.

"First question," he asked. "Why have you been avoiding me?"

"J.D., dear, I haven't. I've been busy with several art shows. Two in the Midwest. One in New Mexico. Besides, that's why I hired you, to manage my case. I trust you completely, J.D. Really. I put myself totally into your hands. Body and soul."

He felt her foot touching his so he scooted his feet under his chair.

"I appreciate your trust—" he began, but she cut him off.

"Not only my trust, but Magister's too."

"Lord Dee?"

"Right. He called me to let me know that the two of you had met in England. He said you were every bit as smart as he had figured. He was quite impressed."

"So," Blackstone said, "you were too busy to return *my* calls, but you took his?"

Vinnie threw him a wounded look and said, "That's not fair. Please, J.D. dear, don't say that."

Suddenly Blackstone had the sinking feeling that their attorney–client conversation was devolving into a minor spat between a couple on a date that was not going well.

"Let's keep this objective," Blackstone shot back. "I ask the questions. You answer. So here goes—first question. Why do you and Lord Dee dress like two long-dead figures from the 1800s? Your hairstyle like a nineteenth-century artist. His beard and hair, his whole look, is patterned after Albert Pike."

"I told you my mother named me after Vinnie Ream."

"So what? Does that mean you have to play her like you're trapped in some permanent Halloween party? Why not change the routine? How about doing Cinderella or Wonder Woman next time you play dress-up?"

"I don't know what you're talking about."

"I think you do."

"All I know is that I believe Magister Dee when he says there is a spiritual link between the four of us—between Albert and Vinnie in the 1800s and Magister and me today—and I can't explain it. But I feel, somehow, very deeply, that it is true. So I do my hair up like Vinnie Ream. Is that so terrible?"

"And Lord Dee pays your bills and pays for this studio. And keeps an eye on you like his own personal trophy. Is that so terrible?" Blackstone said mockingly.

"Why are you being so mean to me, J.D. dear?"

"Why don't you tell me *everything* you know about the Booth diary pages, and Lord Dee's desire to get them?" Blackstone asked.

"I don't know anything more than I've told you already—"

"You're lying."

"And you're being terribly hurtful."

"Did the fact that you were hired to sculpt Horace Langley have something to do with the Booth diary?"

"No...I just don't know. I can't answer those things. You'll have to ask Magister."

"Oh, I intend to. Now, last question—why were you *really* with Horace Langley on the day he was murdered? And don't tell me it had anything to do with your sculpting him. I know, because I've read the FBI reports. They interviewed one of the guards who cleared you to visit Horace Langley the day he was murdered. You weren't carrying any art supplies. Nothing."

"Okay. I'll tell you one thing. You're right, I didn't sculpt him on that very last visit. I was going to see him for something else."

"Something else, like doing a dry run?" Blackstone said harshly. "Maybe checking the keypad security code he had given you before you met with him, just to make sure it worked? So that later that evening you could give the code to the assassin, who then slipped into the building after hours to put some bullets into Langley and take the Booth diary?"

"No, no, don't say that," Vinnie cried out. "Please don't...it's not true. I was there because Magister Dee asked me to go."

"To what?"

"To make an offer to Horace Langley…to buy the diary pages… the missing pages he was about to have examined…or, not really to buy them, but to buy the right to inspect them first, before anyone else. That was why Magister's private foundation paid me to sculpt Horace Langley's bust in the first place. To get close to him so I could help Magister negotiate the Booth diary deal. Lord Dee was willing to pay a huge fee to get access to the pages for just a few months, and then would return them to the Smithsonian and to Langley after he was done."

"Done doing what? What was in those pages that he needed to see?"

Vinnie was just shaking her head back and forth.

"But Langley rejected the offer you conveyed from Lord Dee?" Blackstone said.

"Right," she replied. "That's exactly what happened."

"And so, later that very same night he was murdered," Blackstone said in a tone of somber resignation. "That very thing you wanted to obtain for your mystic soul-friend, Lord Dee, ends up missing. How convenient. And how devastatingly simple for the prosecution to prove motive against you."

Vinnie didn't respond.

"Are you done?" she asked quietly.

"For now," he answered.

"Then come with me," she said, and took him by the hand and led him over to the unfinished clay bust that was on the table.

"Look at this," she said, and pushed him a little toward it. "Very closely. And tell me what you see."

Blackstone stared at the face emerging from the clay.

"The bold, sharp eyes," Vinnie said. "The cheekbones. The angular face. Handsome. Strong."

Then Blackstone saw what she was trying to describe. *She thinks she is sculpting me,* he thought as he studied the face she had been molding out of the clay. He turned around.

But as he did, she was right there waiting, and she wrapped her arms around him and pulled herself into him, kissing him fully on the lips, passionately.

Blackstone smelled her exotic perfume, and for a moment he disappeared into her soft embrace. Then he pulled away.

"This is a dangerous game," he said.

"Can't a woman have both a lawyer and a lover at the same time?" she asked.

"Not unless she wants to lose both," he snapped back.

Blackstone turned and headed through the studio and out into the gallery toward her front door. Then he turned around. Vinnie was standing in the middle of the room.

"It's not just the Civil War hairstyle, Vinnie," he said. "It's gone far beyond that. You've adapted Vinnie Ream's modus operandi. Your Civil War heroine gained her celebrity status by two primary means—first, her artistic brilliance. I believe you have that too. But second, by her beauty, which she used as a tool of manipulation. By all accounts, she was a brilliant flirt. Stealing the hearts of men she came in contact with. Even beguiling a reluctant senator to vote against removing a sitting President Andrew Johnson from office—perhaps as a payback to Johnson for his having given her soul-friend, Albert Pike, a pardon two years before."

Then he put his hand on the door handle to leave but paused to add one more thought.

"So, Vinnie, what is the quid pro quo with me? What is it you are trying to get from me?"

"Manipulation? Do you think that's what this is about?" Vinnie asked, her voice breaking a little.

Then she added, "Your logical, hyperanalytical brain just can't conceive that a woman wants you simply because she feels herself slowly falling in love with you...You just can't compute that one, can you?"

Blackstone didn't answer, but turned and left.

While J.D. Blackstone was motoring home, he didn't bother to click on his radio. Or play CDs. He simply listened to the deep, harmonious drone of the engine under the hood of his Maserati and tried to keep his head clear.

Trying to forget the loneliness and the rush of emotions that was drenching him.

And in the midst of all of it, he could not shake the image of Vinnie. Beautiful. Outlandish. Unashamedly flirtatious. Yet hidden.

He knew that thus far in his representation of Vinnie Archmont, he was unable to mount an effective defense, or even form a convincing theory for her innocence that a jury would likely believe. But beyond that, he felt that he was being pulled, as if by some primordial tug from the planets, out to a deep and very dangerous place. As if he was losing his fight to maintain equilibrium. His will to decide his own fate.

Blackstone was coming to the very private realization that his beautiful client was slowly bewitching him.

And although the top of his convertible was down in the balmy Virginia weather, he thought he could still smell the intoxication of her perfume.

Yet just as powerfully, Blackstone could not master the dread that seemed capable of suffocating him, cutting off his breathing—the dark realization that in his secret longings for Vinnie, he was, in some way, betraying his wife and daughter now nearly as much as he had in their deaths.

CHAPTER 22

At his law office, J.D. Blackstone was on the phone with his investigator, Tully Tullinger. Tully said he had some important news about an assignment the lawyer had given him. Blackstone put him on speakerphone so he could keep working while they talked.

"You wanted me to check out the prosecution's insistence that what was inside that Langley note be kept secret, remember?" Tully said.

"Right," Blackstone replied, half-listening while he sat in front of his computer, answering, one by one, a column of e-mails that had been languishing in his inbox.

"So," Tully continued, "the question is this—what was the *real* reason Henry Hartz was pushing so hard to keep you from reading the Langley note, and then from sharing it with anyone else. I know you didn't buy the reason they gave in their affidavit. Frankly, neither did I."

"Well?"

"So I've got a name for you—Senator Bo Collings. You know him?"

Now he had Blackstone's full attention.

"Senator from Arkansas?" Blackstone said.

"That's him. He's on his fourth term, something like that. Permanent fixture in Congress. Like the statues in the Rotunda. Approval ratings in his home state around 70 percent, so the guy's got permanent job security."

"How is he involved in this thing?"

"I know somebody who knows somebody who works in Hartz's office,"

Tully said. "They tell me that there was a call that came to Henry Hartz from Senator Collings *personally*. Right before Hartz filed his motion to keep you from sharing the contents of the Langley note with anyone else on the face of the earth."

"Wow—that's pretty thin, Tully."

"Hey, stay with me here," Tully blurted out. "It turns out that the good senator sits on the Senate Judiciary Committee. From what I hear, he leaned real heavy on prosecutor Hartz, basically telling him that if Hartz didn't file his motion then Senator Collings would make sure that his legal career would end up like something you'd scrape off the bottom of your shoe."

"Okay, now the fog clears."

"One more thing," Tully announced proudly.

"Let me guess," Blackstone said. "Bo Collings, senator from Arkansas, is a Confederate sympathizer?"

"Oh, way better than that. The guy's a Freemason. Finding that out was the toughest part of the assignment, by the way."

"Any connection between Senator Collings and Lord Dee over in England?" Blackstone asked.

"I checked that—nothing came up yet."

"Can you use your source to get me a meeting with Collings?"

"Sorry," Tully said with a tone of finality. "The well's completely dry on this one."

Blackstone thanked Tully, and after he hung up the phone he buzzed Julia to come in. After they talked over a few of her cases, he got to the point.

"Do you know anybody in Senator Bo Collings' office?"

"J.D., why are you asking me? You're the one with all the connections on the Hill. You've represented how many of them over the years? At least one U.S. senator and two congressmen by my count."

"Yeah, but no one close to Collings. Besides, the senators I know are all on the opposite side of the political aisle, including the ones I know on Judiciary, where Collings is ranking member."

"Well, I do know a woman lawyer on Judiciary. She and I were fairly tight back when I was in the Office of Legal Counsel for the Agency. Not exactly gal-pals, but the two of us worked together on some common issues that came up during Judiciary Committee hearings. Besides that, her dad and mine knew each other while serving in Vietnam."

"Call her ASAP," Blackstone said. "I need a face-to-face with Collings."

"Tall order. Hard to do, as you know."

"Then tell her I'd even settle for a polite ambush. I just need to courteously get into Senator Collings face somehow."

Three hours later, when it was early evening, Julia swept into Blackstone's office.

"Done," she announced with a little tilt to her head, the same way she'd do when she was telling Blackstone about her latest victory in court.

"Great—when, where?"

"Not a regular meeting," she explained. "This is going to be a stand-up deal, on the run. Collings has a vote on the floor tomorrow. You will meet him on his way to the Senate chambers."

"What's the vote on?"

"The farm bill," she said.

"Tell me more."

"Oh, gee, what else did she tell me?" Julia was thinking out loud. "I think there's a nongermane rider some senator attached to the bill, a bill for protecting horses from abuse during rodeos. Somebody's pet issue. But it kicked up a little dust during floor debate, I guess. Anyway, that's all I know."

Julia was still standing in the doorway of his office. She leaned against the door frame, crossing her legs a little nervously, then brushed something off her skirt and glanced down, trying to look nonchalant.

After a few seconds of silence Blackstone smiled and asked her a question.

"How's life?"

"Is that a professional or a personal question?"

"Oh, I don't know. Let's not try to cubbyhole it. Just want to know how you are doing."

"I'm doing fine," she said.

"*Fine.* That's one of those words, a kind of idiom that is perfectly meaningless," Blackstone said. "Spoken by people who don't want to commit to really telling you something."

"Okay, I am *exceptionally* fine. There, how's that?"

"Alright," Blackstone said, "you win. I won't pursue it."

But as Julia stood there, looking at him, she knew she had just been lied to. She hadn't won. Blackstone never just let someone else win. That wasn't part of who he was. He had said enough now to make her struggle over what his intentions really were. And she had told herself that she wouldn't play that game with him anymore.

She was about to leave, but then turned her head, swept some hair from her eyes, and adjusted her designer horn-rim glasses. And she asked him a question of her own.

"And how's life with you?"

Blackstone didn't look up from his computer. But he took a deep breath before he answered.

"Messy," he said.

Julia was tempted to follow up on that. She wanted to, so much so that she had to fight the powerful urge to keep talking. To get J.D. Blackstone to open up. To connect. Like the two of them had once, in the past, deeply. Intimately. But she fought back against the urge.

Instead of talking, she pushed herself off the door frame and quietly walked away.

CHAPTER 23

The next day Blackstone took a cab over to the Hill. He passed through security in the Capitol Building, and then inside, on the lower level, met a staffer from Senator Collings's office who had been given the word from Julia's contact. The staffer had been given the impression that Blackstone was a lobbyist for an agricultural association.

He greeted Blackstone warmly and led him to the underground tram that ran to just below the Senate chambers. As they whizzed through the tunnel connecting the two houses of Congress and the central Capitol building, the staffer asked a few polite questions about agriculture. Blackstone smiled a lot, but pretended not to hear most of his questions over the noise of the speeding tram car.

When they came to a halt, the two of them climbed out, along with a few other senators and congressional aides who had been riding with them. Then Blackstone and the staffer headed up the marble stairs.

At the top of the stairway there was a corridor jammed with middle-aged men in dark suits, pressed white shirts, and moderately pricey silk ties. Most of them had aides standing dutifully by.

The staffer walked Blackstone through the crowd and approached a large, pear-shaped man in his early sixties wearing a dark blue suit. He had a shock of white hair that was carefully combed and moussed. Next to him was a young aide with a folder.

"Senator Collings," the staffer began, "this is—"

"Blackstone—J.D.—so very glad to meet you," Blackstone said warmly and shook his hand.

Senator Collings smiled broadly, but as he did, Blackstone could see something in his eyes that said that he had some vague recognition of the name. And it wasn't good. But that didn't stop Collings from keeping the smile firmly fixed on his face as they began talking.

"Farm bill, important to the USA," Blackstone began.

"Yes, of course," Collings replied. "We'll get it passed as soon as we get rid of this 'horse rider' attached to it…no pun intended."

"None taken," Blackstone said wryly. "Now, I am a horse lover myself."

"And you are with?" Collings's aide chirped out, happy to do the dirty work for his boss by asking the uncomfortable but all too necessary initial questions about constituency and power and lobby connections.

"Oh, I didn't say, did I?" Blackstone responded with a smile. "Now, Senator, I was saying that, myself, I am a horse lover."

"I am not opposed to laws protecting animals from cruelty or abuse," Collings said in a rich baritone voice. "I am real proud of my record on animal experimentation. But this horse and rodeo protection bill simply doesn't belong on this farm legislation. It needs to be voted on as a stand-alone bill."

"And of course, Arkansas, your home state, has its share of rodeos too," Blackstone added. "Now as for me, I own a six-year-old Arabian. Black as night and as strong a horse as I've ever seen. Great endurance-racing animal. You, Senator—I know you are a fan of quarterhorses and thoroughbreds. And you own several of each, I understand."

"Yes. Well," the Senator said looking around and edging himself away. "I've enjoyed this chat with y'all, but we've got a vote coming up."

But Blackstone walked right behind him and kept talking.

"Now if your best thoroughbred and my Arabian were to face off in a race, I'm sure on the short course you'd win hands down. But on the long stretch, a couple miles or more, my Arabian would leave your horse panting and foaming at the mouth. You see, Senator, I'm in this for the long haul—the long race."

Then Blackstone moved up right next to Senator Collings and lowered his voice.

"I want to know why you are meddling in the Smithsonian murder case, Senator. And why you are making calls to the AUSA who is prosecuting that case, pressuring him to make things harder for me to defend my client. And I intend to ride those questions to the very end until I get some answers."

"I don't know who you think you are," Collings snapped back. Then the lights came on.

"Of course, Blackstone," the Senator said. He moved away from his aide and took Blackstone by the arm until the two of them were up against a wall, alone, below an oil painting.

"Now, y'all listen up," Collings said with a deep Southern growl, all the senatorial niceties evaporating. "With this little stunt today, you talking to me like you did here, I could have you before a lawyer ethics panel in no time flat. Intimidation of a witness. Obstruction of justice. I could have your law license in my pocket, boy. Or something even worse. You need to know that."

"You didn't answer my question, Senator," Blackstone replied calmly. "On the other hand, maybe you did. Intimidation of a witness—does that mean that you are a potential witness in the Smithsonian case?"

"Just remember what I just told you," Collings snapped and took a step back from the lawyer.

Blackstone stepped away from the wall and noticed the large oil painting over their heads, one of General George Washington yielding up his sword as he retired from command of the Continental Army after the victory over the British Empire.

"Interesting thing about Mr. Washington," Blackstone said to Collings. "His men wanted to make him a king. But he refused. Some in the first Congress wanted to give him the right to run for president without limitation. But he stopped at two terms."

Then Blackstone added, in an even louder voice.

"There is something to be said about limiting the power of one man—wouldn't you agree, Senator?"

But Collings kept walking until he met up with his aide again and then joined the crush of senators who were making their way into the chambers.

CHAPTER 24

Blackstone came into the office by nine in the morning the next day, which was his custom during the summers when he didn't have a teaching load. But the night before had been rough. He was not sure he had slept more than three or four hours straight. The meds he was taking as a sleep aid didn't seem to be working. But he couldn't afford to go stronger. When he had tried a more powerful medication once, it practically left him drooling.

After tossing and turning in bed for a while, he bolted out of bed and trudged over to the oversized teakwood desk in his condo. Sitting in a pair of gym trunks, he went back to drafting a summary of all of the evidence he had gleaned from the prosecution in their case against Vinnie. As he worked on that he would alternatively switch over to his summary of all of the defense evidence that corroborated Vinnie's theory of innocence. There was also a third summary he had up on his laptop as well. He called that one his "wild card" list. It was a hodgepodge of information, witnesses, and facts that didn't seem to comfortably fit either into the prosecution's case or the defense theory.

While he was working on the three summaries, he resisted the temptation to compare them and then draw some conclusions about his chances of success in getting an acquittal for Vinnie. He didn't want to get mired in the dismal realities quite yet. He wanted to leave some room for the "ah-ha" phenomenon, the gestalt-like mental awakening he could usually pull off in every case before it was too late—the one or two, or maybe three, critical concepts that held the key to unfolding a whole picture to the jury, like a hologram in a museum—a three-dimensional, 360-degree portrait of his client as innocent. A feat that usually required him to show how someone else was guilty.

After working on that for several hours, Blackstone finally crashed around three in the morning. A few hours later he stumbled out of bed with his alarm. Then he downed his own morning concoction: some energy drinks mixed with tomato juice. After dressing he stopped by the gym and worked out for three-quarters of an hour, showered there, and then headed to the office.

Julia was already at the firm and met him in the hallway.

"You look pretty whipped, J.D.," she said. "Did you sleep at all last night?"

"The usual," he remarked.

"Oh well, you're a big boy."

"Yes, Mommy, I am," he retorted.

"You know there's a reason why unmarried men die earlier than women, or than married men for that matter," Julia added. "Statistically, I mean. They don't know anything about balance in life. And there's no one around to nag them into practicing any balance. You know, some limits."

"Hmm," was all Blackstone said to that. But then he shifted the conversation quickly back into law-practice gear.

"I need your help on an important part of this Vinnie Archmont defense."

"What's that?" she asked with a bit of suspicion in her voice. Blackstone knew she didn't like his client. On the other hand, he knew Julia was tough-minded enough to separate her feelings from the work at hand.

"Whether we like it or not," Blackstone continued, "Henry Hartz has ratcheted this up to a death-penalty case. That's where you come in."

"You mean, making sure the dosage they give her is lethal enough?"

"Knock it off," Blackstone barked back. "I'm serious. I don't want to hear you talking trash like that again."

Julia was taken aback by her partner's burst of anger. But she was also surprised at her own macabre joke, which had seemed to come out of nowhere. Under usual circumstances it wouldn't be her style.

"Sorry, J.D.," she said quietly. "That wasn't very professional of me."

"Let's just move on," he replied coldly. "I need you to start preparing the death-penalty phase of the defense case, in the eventuality that Hartz gets a jury conviction. I think there's a strong case we can mount for life imprisonment rather than death."

"What about the appeal of the pretrial order on the Langley note? I thought you wanted me to do that. I've been working on the brief."

"I'm taking you off that. I'll do the appeal myself. I need you on the death phase."

"Is there some reason why?"

Blackstone looked her in the eyes, but not for very long.

"I've got my reasons," he said in a thin voice.

Then he turned, strode into his office, and closed his door loudly behind him.

Blackstone got Tully Tullinger on the line.

"Tully, I think I set the trap with the senator. Now, you said the well was pretty dry with your contact in Collings's office."

"Well, there's no way I can arrange another meeting like that with the guy, if that's what you're thinking."

"It's not. Now that I've lit his fuse I need to get some intelligence about what he does about me from this point on."

"Oh, I think I can get you that kind of intelligence," Tully said.

Blackstone was pleased and stressed that time was of the essence on that task.

Then he went over a few of his voice mails. One was from a press reporter who wanted to talk to him about his chances for success on the pending appeal to the DC Court of Appeals in the Smithsonian murder case.

After calling the reporter back, Blackstone gave him a few minutes. He knew better than to predict results. Instead, Blackstone gave the print journalist some of the high points from the docket statement they had already filed in the appeal.

Then he spent the rest of the day on several other cases that had not been attended to for a while. He had been spending a huge amount of time on Vinnie's defense, and it was starting to show in his law practice.

By the end of the day, he felt like some of his other cases were getting back on track.

He looked at his watch. It was six-thirty.

Blackstone picked up the phone and called Vinnie's studio number.

It rang nine times, and then finally she picked up.

Vinnie sounded a little exasperated.

"Hey, it's J.D. here," he announced.

"Sorry, I was involved in a project," she said. "Not going well. Bad day all the way around. And truthfully, I was doing some thinking."

"About?"

"You, actually. Sorry our last conversation went all...you know... icky."

Blackstone had to chuckle at that.

"Yeah. I'm sort of an expert at 'icky.'"

Vinnie laughed out loud at that.

"So glad you called," she said.

He could tell she was smiling on the other end.

"Do you eat dinner?" he asked.

"Sure, from time to time I do," she said. "How about you?"

"Not regularly."

"Then maybe we should do something about that," she said brightly.

"Yeah, I was thinking that too. How about in fifteen minutes? Can you be ready?"

"You know me. I'm low maintenance."

"There's a place called Ben's Bistro over in Georgetown."

"Sure, I know it. Fifteen minutes—I'll be there."

"Great," Blackstone said. "See you there."

He stuffed some things into his briefcase and hurried out through the lobby. Julia was there, surprised to see him actually heading out of the office before eight at night.

"I took your advice," Blackstone announced to Julia.

"About what?"

"Balance in life. I just got me some."

"How?" she asked.

"I'm going out on a dinner date."

Julia's face was deadpan.

"Congratulations," she said in a professional tone.

He strode out the door. A minute later Julia could hear the deep rumble of the engine of his Maserati, out at the curb, being fired up.

She stood and watched him through the glass window in the front door of the office. Julia kept watching, struggling with deeply mixed emotions, until Blackstone put it into gear, and then roared off.

CHAPTER 25

Ben's Bistro was a popular pub restaurant in Georgetown. At night, its winding corridors full of booths and tables were always crowded, mostly with DC career types, executives, lobbyists, lawyers, and politicos. Blackstone knew the owner and could usually secure his favorite booth, one that was tucked into a corner, with more privacy and quiet than the others, situated under a framed and yellowed article about the Bay of Pigs invasion of Cuba. Some of the initial discussions about attacking Cuba, according to the article, had taken place between a few Kennedy Administration officials during their dinner at Ben's. Next to that article, there was a picture of President Lyndon Johnson, signed personally by Johnson.

And next to that picture on the brown brick wall was another framed article, this one from *Today's Lawyer* magazine, containing an interview with J.D. Blackstone.

"Favorite restaurant?" Blackstone was quoted as saying. "Probably the casual kind, Ben's Bistro, that's certainly one of them." Someone had used a yellow highlighter to underline that part.

Blackstone would sit with friends and sometimes clients in that booth, under that framed article. But he would never point it out. And to his knowledge, no one ever noticed it.

That night, he met with Vinnie in his favorite booth. He was already there when she wandered in, looking for him. She was wearing a fake zebra-skin jacket and cowboy boots. Her dark, antebellum style curls were dancing around her face as she jaunted over to the table.

"Hiya, darling!" she blurted out with a smile, and bent over and kissed him on the cheek.

"Good to see you," Blackstone said.

They both grabbed their menus, got the ordering out of the way, and then started to talk. First about her sculpting and some of the art shows she had been doing. Then more serious topics.

"Tell me something," Blackstone said. "Do you know a senator by the name of Bo Collings, from Arkansas?"

Vinnie thought for a moment. Then she said, "No, I don't know him. Why?"

"I think he may have an interest in your case."

"Oh? Why is that?"

"I was hoping you could answer that," Blackstone replied. "I think he may have injected himself into your prosecution. I thought you could help me figure out his involvement."

"Senator Collings—is he for us or against us?" she asked.

"I think he is trying to help the prosecutor. Why, I'm not sure yet."

Blackstone watched Vinnie. She was thinking that one through. Carefully.

"You know, something rings a bell about him. I wonder…" she said casually. "Maybe he came to one of my art shows here in DC. Do you think that's possible?"

"When was the last show you had in the DC area?"

"Well, three in the last two years. One in DC. One in Vienna. And another in Alexandria at the Torpedo Factory, where my studio is."

"Do you have the names of any attendees?" Blackstone asked.

"I'm positive I don't."

"Don't you have a sign-in book for people attending the art show… something like that?" Blackstone asked.

"No. Never keep those," she answered quickly. "Sorry I'm not much help."

"Nothing specific you can tell me about Senator Collings?"

"No. Just that I have a very strong feeling that maybe he and I met somehow, somewhere. You should pursue this, though, don't you think? Find out why he's involved? Maybe…oh I don't know…just thinking that this may be important, don't you agree?"

Blackstone smiled, but didn't respond to that. He was watching her. Her initial gaiety was disappearing. She was getting somber.

"I wish we didn't have to talk about my case all the time," she said with exasperation.

"Why?"

"Because I know you will do the right thing. Everything will work out. You've said the government doesn't have much of a case."

"I've never said that," Blackstone said interrupting her.

"But you think you can keep me from being convicted. I've heard you say that. Besides, Magister Dee has been following this. His lawyers, he tells me, think the same thing. They've read up on my case. Anyway, you're brilliant, J.D., you really are. I'm sure you will figure out *some* way to convince the jury to acquit me."

"There are no guarantees in a criminal case," he said. "None. I wish there were. Believe me when I say that. As for the government's case, I do have to admit I think it's thin. On the other hand, it is feasible that they could actually get a conviction. I'm just trying to be objective here."

"I know you are," she said, and managed a smile. "Is that hard? Trying to be objective...with me as your client?"

Then she reached out and took his hand in hers, across the table.

The waitress arrived with their food and both of them moved backward in their chairs. When she was gone, Vinnie motioned for him to bring his hand out on the table again, and she sort of giggled as she did.

Blackstone put his hand on the table, and she took it in both of her hands and began stroking it, and then his wrists and forearm.

"I bet you're strong," she said. "I'm sure you're in great shape. I know you do a lot of physical conditioning. Right?"

He smiled. "Do you ever wonder," Blackstone said, changing the subject, "whether something you did in your sessions with Horace Langley may have—even accidentally—I'm not saying you intended this... but that you may have innocently done something to contribute to his murder. Ever wonder about that?"

"Why would you say something like that?" she said with a wounded look.

"Do you ever feel guilty, in the least, that you may have been used as a pawn by someone?"

"I don't let myself feel guilty," she said.

"Ever?"

"I try not to," she said. "I believe in living with total abandon. No regrets. Most people don't live like that. Not me. Life can be so full of pleasure, excitement, and fun—and passion. That's what I want. Which is why I won't let this legal case drag me down. It's really a matter of connecting with the God-force you have available inside. Everyone has it. Just letting yourself go. Magister taught me that."

Then Vinnie paused and thought on something. Then she spoke again.

"Besides," she said. "I don't know who in the world could have used me as a pawn to commit that terrible crime. I just happened to be with Horace several times before he was killed. That's all."

Then Vinnie talked a little about a few movies she had seen lately. The two of them finished their dinners, and Blackstone paid the bill.

"Life without guilt," Blackstone mused out loud. "An interesting proposition."

"You ought to try it some time," she said laughing.

As Blackstone stood up to leave, Vinnie stood up next to him.

"Take me home, please, J.D. dear," she said. "I took the Metro over here. I don't like taking it at night."

He nodded and walked her to the parking ramp where his black Maserati was parked.

"Sexy car," she purred as she climbed in.

Blackstone motored her over to her apartment in Alexandria. When he parked the car on the street, she bent over and kissed him hard.

"Come up with me. I don't want to be alone tonight," she said.

Blackstone locked the car and followed her up to the second level where her apartment was. Outside her door, she turned around and kissed him again, even more passionately. Then she fished around in her purse for her keys.

That is when Blackstone's cell phone started ringing.

He glanced down at the number. It was his uncle, Reverend Lamb, calling.

"You going to take it?" she asked with a smile, unlocking the door.

"It's my uncle."

"You can take it in here," she said. "Come on in, you can talk with him in my apartment."

Vinnie was standing just inside her apartment, in the open doorway. Blackstone was standing in the hallway, looking at the envelope on the screen of his cell phone indicating a voice message.

"By the way," Vinnie said, stretching out her hand to his from the doorway, "I noticed the article about you on the wall of Ben's Bistro. Pretty cool."

Blackstone looked at the beautiful young brunette with the kinky hairdo standing in the doorway of her apartment, beckoning him.

Then he glanced down again at his open cell phone.

"Gotta go," Blackstone said, closing his cell phone and putting it back in his pocket.

He walked down the stairs without looking back at Vinnie, who was standing in the doorway, head tilted in stunned amazement and with her hands cocked on her hips, watching him.

CHAPTER 26

While Blackstone was driving home he dialed into his voice mail. The message from his uncle, Reverend Lamb, was short, and he sounded out of breath.

We need to talk right away about your case. I've put something together. It might be somewhat astounding, actually. Can't go into details now. I'm free tomorrow afternoon. I could come over to your office. That might be better, now that I think about it...I could drop off some things at the dry cleaners on the way...which reminds me, I wonder if they still have my good white shirt down there...well, let me know.

Blackstone punched in his secretary Frieda at her home number.

"Frieda," he announced as if it were in the middle of a workday, rather than nine-fifteen at night, "do you have all the numbers for staff with you there at home?"

There was a pregnant pause.

"Yes. You told me some time ago to always keep the numbers with me wherever I go."

"Smart decision, huh?"

Another long pause.

"I guess so," she said with hesitation.

"I need you," Blackstone said with a sense of rising energy, "right now, to call up Julia, and Jason our trusty paralegal, and Tully Tullinger too. Make sure they are all in my office at 2:30 p.m. tomorrow for a meeting. Then call my uncle at his home number and confirm that time with him.

Also, make a point of reminding him that the meeting is at my office, will you? The guy gets a little spacey sometimes."

Frieda, who had over the years gotten used to J.D. Blackstone's manic disregard for normal workday limits, said she would do it.

By the time Blackstone got back to his condo, he knew it was too late to call his uncle directly. He knew that the elderly religion scholar was a notorious early-to-bed-early-to-rise kind of guy.

Quite different from Blackstone. That evening, fueled by curiosity over his uncle's message, his mind now whirling, it was another late-to-bed-early-to-rise night for him. The gray dawn was just about to break when he finally collapsed into bed.

At two-thirty the next afternoon all of the group, less one, had dutifully arrived. Reverend Lamb was the last to show up, about ten minutes late.

Blackstone circulated a memo that he wanted signed by Tully and Reverend Lamb.

"In this memorandum you two agree," Blackstone explained, "as outside consultants and investigators on this case, not to disclose anything we discuss here today with anyone else, absent my express authorization. These discussions today are protected by attorney's work-product privilege and are to be considered confidential."

Those kinds of legal precautions were not new for Blackstone. In other cases he had his experts and consultants, and even co-counsel, sign similar memoranda of understanding. But this time it was a little different.

The difference was the presence of Reverend John Lamb as his "expert" consultant on a murder case.

The night before, Blackstone had experienced a little exuberance thinking that one of Reverend Lamb's ideas might help to break the case open for him. But now he was in the harsh daylight of reality. As he surveyed the faces of his team and studied Reverend Lamb, with his pile of crumpled papers and notes and his tall stack of books on the conference table in front of him, the word *desperation* came to Blackstone's mind.

Now I know, Blackstone thought to himself silently while glancing over at the white-haired Reverend Lamb, *how the cops feel when they have to use some psychic to try to locate a dead body.*

After Tully and Lamb had signed the memos and Blackstone collected them, he leaned back in his chair and gave the floor to his uncle.

"J.D.," Lamb began, "you wanted me do some thinking about the Freemasons, correct?"

"That was part of it, yes. But not the main point."

"Correct," Lamb countered with a grin on his face. "To be precise, the main point being the symbolic significance of the tree in religious and esoteric thinking. Including Masonic religious philosophy."

"Did you say '*tree*'?" Julia said with bemusement.

"Yes, exactly," Blackstone replied. "And don't ask me why I am pursuing that particular symbol. Look, people, remember that I have a court order restraining me from sharing the verbiage of the Horace Langley note with any of you. At least for the time being."

"You goin' to appeal that court order?" Tully asked.

"Already have," Julia snapped. "Our fearless leader, Professor Blackstone, will be arguing that appeal." She threw a look over at Blackstone with that.

"And for what it's worth," Jason chimed in, "I think Professor Blackstone is going to do a groin kick and a knee-drop to the government's throat in that appeal."

"Now Jason," Blackstone objected sarcastically, "no need to confuse the group with all that complicated legalese."

Then he brought them back to task.

"So what do you have for us?"

"A question."

"Oh?" Blackstone asked.

"Do you believe," Reverend Lamb asked him, "that Freemasonry is involved in the Smithsonian murder?"

"As an evidentiary issue? Oh…possibly."

Reverend Lamb leaned back a little with a wide grin. He was enjoying his role as interrogator of his nephew.

"And do you believe," Reverend Lamb continued, this time his voice rising in intensity, "that Freemasonry had any part to play in the note written by Horace Langley—written while he was examining the John Wilkes Booth diary pages?"

Blackstone had a smirk on his face, and he shot a glance over at the bemused Tully Tullinger.

"Gee, I'm not sure," Blackstone said acerbically, "how much more of this crucible of cross-examination I am going to be able to stand."

Tully burst out laughing.

Jason was holding back a smile.

But Julia was not amused.

"Reverend Lamb," Julia said, picking up the ball, "what if the answer was *yes* to your question. Then what?"

"Then," Blackstone's uncle said, still smiling and undaunted, "I have some groundbreaking news for you."

Now Blackstone was no longer smiling.

"Which is?"

"The centuries-old secret of the Freemasons," Reverend Lamb said. "I've been studying this for years from a theological standpoint. Couldn't put the pieces together. Until your case, that is."

"I thought the whole *point* of Freemasonry was secrets," Tully chimed in. "These people still take this very seriously. I know. I had to weasel some information out of some Masons in this case. I got to tell you— you'd have thought I was asking them for a kidney."

"Yes, Mr. Tullinger, you're right," Lamb continued. "They are built on secrecy. Until recently, their whole fabric of their complicated rituals and ceremonies was a closely held secret. But even the books that are written about them, many by former Masons, and even some by practicing Masons—they're written elusively, like painting in shadows. They only give you partial glimpses. I am convinced that only a handful of some of the mystic members of the Masons have ever really known the core doctrinal mission of Freemasonry. The 'ultimate' secret, I believe, is what your client called it. What is at the core of Freemasonry is actually a radical religious philosophy."

"I thought a number of the Founders, like George Washington, were Masons," Julia remarked.

"Certainly true," Lamb said. "He joined for the same reasons a number of other prominent men did too, because it seemed to be a worthwhile fraternal organization. On the surface, the Masonic code talks about good citizenship and the brotherhood of man. Noble ideals. But when

Washington started hearing about their subversive views, he became less and less involved."

"Subversive?" Blackstone called out. "That's a strong accusation. Look, Uncle, I'm not interested in linking my legal defense to some cockeyed conspiracy theory."

"I'm not talking about UFOs at Roswell, for heaven's sake," Reverend Lamb countered with agitation in his voice. He was extending both of his hands cupped out in front of him, as if trying to grasp some invisible orb as he spoke.

"I'm talking," Lamb explained, "about their ages-old mission of creating a select ruling class of spiritual gurus who would lead the world. First, it begins with the realization that Masonry does not need the orthodoxy of Christianity—no, not at all. In fact I ran across a sermon, delivered in 1798 by Reverend Timothy Dwight, the president of Yale College. He pointed out the 'malignant' ideas of Masonry, including its hostility to the Christian religion, and its continuation of 'mysticism' under a blanket of secrecy."

There was a collective silence in the room. The faces of all of Reverend Lamb's listeners were reflecting the same incredulity.

"I see you folks are going to be a tough audience," Lamb said with a smile. "That's why I've brought my evidence with me."

With that, he pulled a small book off the top of his stack.

"*The Spirit of Masonry*," Lamb announced. "Written back in the 1950s by Foster Bailey, himself a thirty-second-degree Mason over in England—and together with his famous wife, Alice Bailey, co-leaders in the twentieth-century Theosophy and mystic spirituality movement. Now what would have attracted a spiritualist like Bailey to the Masons? We get a clue from him here, at page 140:

> Masonry is of divine origin and was created for the purpose of training a group of members of the human family who would be capable of hastening the triumph of 'God's Plan for man.

"So what?" Blackstone interjected. "Isn't that similar to every religion that ever existed? Just think about it—claiming a 'divine origin,' investing some bogus religious doctrine in a small group of followers, and figuring all of that will somehow result in a God-orchestrated revelation, bringing on some apocalypse, or hastening some grand heavenly 'plan'…It's all basic religious anthropology 101."

"So you're ready to agree with my first major point, then?" Reverend Lamb said with a sly smile.

Blackstone's eyes widened.

"What are you talking about?" he snapped, worried that his uncle was actually besting him.

"Oh, just the very thing," Lamb said with a far-off look in his eye, "that most Masonic initiates are trained to deny. And what the small core of high-ranking Freemason leaders know to be true but rarely admit— except in obscure, privately published writings meant to be read only by fellow members of 'the Craft' as they call themselves. But then they die and their widows put their old Freemasonry books up in the attic. And one day a widow dies too. And the kids auction it off in an estate sale. And it ends up, somehow, on a dusty shelf of a used bookstore in Windsor, England."

Then Reverend Lamb smiled and picked up a small, faded red book with a tattered cover and displayed it to the group.

"And an Anglican college professor getting on in age, with a penchant for the old heresies and mystery religions, happens to be there in that bookstore one day. Looking for more evidence of the origins of today's confused and forsaken worldviews. Trying to figure out what lies have been passing for the truth—what enticing religious systems have been substituted for the saving work of Christ, the Savior, on the cross. And so he buys the little book for twelve pounds. And adds it to his collection of out-of-print Masonic literature. This one is called *Builders of Man—The Doctrine and History of Masonry, or the Story of the Craft*. Published in 1923."

Lamb flipped the book open to a dog-eared page and read from it. "According to the author, himself a Mason and a rector in the Church of England, Freemasonry is 'a theocracy.'"

Lamb continued, "That, my friends, is my point. Masonry is, at bottom, a religious ideology. It is also a philosophy, of course. But more than that, it is a religious system. And while it has tried to masquerade as a complement to Christianity, nothing could be farther from the truth."

"But I thought you just said," Julia said with a puzzled look on her face, "that this old book you just read from was written by a rector of the Church of England who also was a Mason? I mean, personally I think I've heard of members of the clergy belonging to the Freemasons."

"Of course," Lamb countered. "But they either have not understood the deeper heresies of Masonry, or else they have actually embraced them."

"Heresies?" Jason spoke up with a question on his face. "There's that word again."

"*Heresy*," Blackstone announced sarcastically, as if reading his own definition. "Ah yes, a term often used by religious zealots whose obsession with their own dogma excludes the possibility that the ideas of others may actually be correct."

"Well," Lamb replied, "what would any honest physician call the work of snake-oil salesmen? If Christ was who the Bible says He truly was, then all counterfeit pictures of Him, all misrepresentations, are nothing but tragically dangerous detours for the soul."

At the end of the conference table Tully was drumming his fingers impatiently.

"Don't mean to be rude," he said. "But can we get to the point here? Professor Blackstone has given me a dumpster full of work to do on this Smithsonian case. Unless there is something I can use in all of this, J.D., maybe I ought to get going."

Reverend Lamb interrupted him.

"Wouldn't suggest that," the old Anglican clergyman said. "I was just going to get to my second major point."

And he turned to Tully and pointed his finger first at him, and then swept his index finger in a circular movement around the table.

"And what I am about to tell you," said Reverend Lamb, "*all* of you, is a two-thousand-year-old secret. But a secret that actually grew out of an ancient mystery that is even older than that."

CHAPTER 27

With his last comment, Reverend John Lamb had managed to rivet the attention of the small group seated around the conference table. Even J.D. Blackstone, who was trying to look uninterested, had both eyes fixed on the elderly religion professor.

"I've told you first, that Freemasonry is, fundamentally, a secret religious order. But not just any religious order."

Then he looked Blackstone in the eye.

"This goes to your comment, Nephew," Reverend Lamb said, "about Masonry having the same structure as all religions. Maybe you're right in a certain sense. But I would qualify that. Not just like any other religion. Certainly not. In fact, and here is my second point, Masonry adopted religious beliefs, but *not* those of Christianity. Just the opposite. Masonry adopted the doctrines of the chief opponent, the most vicious competitor, of early Christianity."

"Chief competitor of the early Christians," Julia, the lapsed Catholic, said out loud. "That's got to be the Roman government. It persecuted the church. Nero lit the Christians on fire."

"You would think so," Reverend Lamb said, shaking his head, "but no—that's not it at all. Of course, the Roman government used its political might, including the power to arrest and torture and murder, to try to subdue the Christians. Without success. Rome collapsed. Christianity flourished. But no, I'm talking about something a great deal more dangerous than the powerful Roman Empire—I'm referring to Gnosticism."

"Say again?" Tully said loudly.

"It's a sect of Christianity," Blackstone interjected, and then directed his comments to Reverend Lamb. "Wouldn't you agree? Gnosticism, from what I know about it, is related to Christianity because it originated from the early beliefs of the Christians."

"Not really," Lamb said shaking his head. "Gnosticism, at its core, is no more related to Christianity than, say, weeds that grow up in a flower bed are related to the flowers. They both grow from the same soil at the same time of course, but one is a separate growth process altogether—a parasite, really, which threatens to strangle the life out of the other."

Then Lamb thought on it for a few seconds and found the point he wanted to make. "Gnosticism was a crude, pagan counterfeit of Christianity that adopted a few of the Christian ideas here and there, and a few features of Christian terminology—enough to cause confusion in the minds of some of the early Christians. It bandied the name of Christ around, but at its base it was a belief system built on a strange mixture of Greek philosophy and Egyptian mysticism, and other pagan ideas. By the third and fourth centuries, hundreds of years after Christ, some of its heretic leaders were writing phony 'gospels' on the life of Jesus, trying to modify history, portraying Jesus as some kind of pure spirit without humanity—denying the crucifixion of Christ—making it out as if Jesus were the leader of some secret cult full of magic words and mysterious revelations."

"I think I saw a TV documentary on that," Jason said excitedly. "They dug these ancient gospels up out of the desert."

"Yes," Lamb said nodding his head. "Near a village in Egypt called Nag Hammadi, several hundred miles south of Cairo. In 1945 a couple of Bedouins stumbled across it while they were digging. They found human skeletal remains, and also an ancient jar. Inside the jar were document fragments from what scholars are now calling 'the Gnostic gospels.' Experts figure the writings in the jar were buried there around AD 400."

Then Reverend Lamb opened his arms to the group as if the conclusion he was about to share was fully self-evident.

"You see," he said, "that is why the apostles in the New Testament, and then the Church Fathers in the hundreds of years immediately after the death of the apostles, spent so little of their writings focusing on the brutality of the Roman government—but instead, spent much of their time warning of the false doctrines of the false teachers. Those who were presenting nonhistorical versions of the life of Christ and passing them off as truth. Chief among those religious heretics were the Gnostics. You see, a clever half-truth about Christ the Messiah, the Promised One, the Savior, is at its core still a lie, but it is more deceptively dangerous to the souls of true spiritual seekers than all the fires that Nero ever lit."

"So that's it? Your shocking revelation?" Blackstone broke in abruptly. "That Freemasonry is, number one, a religion, and number two, specifically the religion of Gnosticism? That's it? That's all you've got?"

Tully cleared his throat. Jason was wiggling nervously in his chair.

Blackstone said it again.

"That's it?"

"No," Reverend Lamb said calmly. "You're impatient, Nephew. You need to practice the art of listening. An art that brilliant men like you sometimes neglect."

Julia was chuckling.

Blackstone leaned back and spread out his arms to his uncle, beckoning him to bring the discussion to a conclusion.

"Let me introduce my third and final point with a question. Just think about this," Lamb said, wagging his finger as he spoke. "What is the principal problem with any movement that wants to become a permanent and enduring influence in the world, but which is built on human leadership?"

No one answered at first. Then Blackstone, with a controlled smirk, raised his hand like a smart-aleck middle-school student.

"Me, teacher, please call on me!" Blackstone shouted out.

Reverend Lamb was working hard to tolerate his nephew's disrespect and nodded with a smile toward Blackstone.

"You're obviously talking about the problem of successorship," Blackstone said with a tone of boredom. "The Karl-Marx-to-Lenin-to-Stalin thing. The degradation of the original philosophy through successive titular leaders."

"Exactly," Lamb replied with a smile. "So…how does one cure that problem?"

"You make sure," Julia chimed in, "that you exert strict controls over the training of the successive leaders."

"Naw, never works," Tully chimed in. "Not really. Human nature being the way it is, you can attempt any set of controls you want. I saw that at the NSA when I worked there—perfect protocols on paper. But then you put it into the hands of human beings, and you have what they call the 'human behavioral factors.' As something gets passed from hand to hand, there's always degradation of the original content. Control? That's just a relative term."

"I don't think that Reverend Lamb is talking about *quality* control over ideology or doctrine—are you, Uncle?"

"No, I'm not," he said quietly. "Something altogether different."

"Yes," Blackstone said with a smile, and with a look in his eye that reflected an understanding no one else at the table shared with him except his uncle. Blackstone had already grasped Reverend Lamb's point quickly. As usual, before anyone else. But the notion that his uncle was proposing was, to Blackstone, preposterous beyond description.

"You're talking about *quantity* control—control of days…and years… that's what this is all about?" Blackstone said, leaning over the table, staring at Reverend Lamb.

"I've been researching Freemasonry for two decades," Lamb said in a strained, controlled voice. "I knew there was a primary, cultic center to it. If I could just find it—locate the missing center piece. What was the principal secret that the high echelon of Masonic thinkers and leaders were hiding, I would ask myself. What was their ultimate religious agenda? They say, in their writings, 'the brotherhood of man.' Yes, that is what the foot soldiers are told. But what did the architects and the generals really believe?"

"Then," Lamb continued, "you brought me into this case, J.D. And I considered your question—about the significance of the tree as a religious symbol—and there it was…beginning to unfold right in front of me. Remember my reading you from the book called *Builders of Man*? Well, listen to this concluding statement by the English Masonic author. He says that the Freemason will have to continue to wear the Masonic garb, the white apron, and so forth…

…until the final Keystone of Universal Being is discovered
ready, in the Stone by the Builders rejected, but now the
Crown of life, the fulfillment of Hope.

"I recognize some of that," Julia said, "from my old catechism days.
'The stone rejected'—that's a reference in the New Testament to Christ,
isn't it?"

"It's intended that way in the New Testament, certainly," Lamb shot
back. "But in Masonry, which creates a whole substratum of secondary
meanings hidden in their words, I would suggest it means something else.
The key here is the use of the word *stone*. And its linkage to the concept
of life—'universal being' as this Masonic author calls it."

There was a pause around the table. Then Lamb broke the silence.

"Ever hear the term 'philosopher's stone'?" he asked.

Blackstone's face reacted, but he kept his peace. Only Jason spoke
up.

"Man, am I the only one around here who reads the Harry Potter
books?" the young paralegal said with a tinge of embarrassment. "Okay,
call me a dork. But I thought they were interesting."

"Yes, you're onto something, Jason," Lamb said. "Magic potions and
so forth. The philosopher's stone for more than a thousand years has been
the term that refers to a special substance that supposedly could be used
in alchemy with very astounding results."

"Turning base metals into gold, I thought that was the deal," Blackstone shot out.

"Partially," Lamb said. "But the deeply esoteric alchemists were after
something much more powerful than that. They thought it possible to
isolate and then apply a substance that would increase human longevity—
human life—indefinitely. *Immortality.* That was what the alchemists were
really after. And that is exactly what lies at the heart of the greatest secret
of the Freemasons. The desire to find a way to cheat death. And thereby
to continue the Masonic reign of the selected ones indefinitely."

While the group around the table was trying to comprehend what
Reverend Lamb had just said, the old Anglican professor put the period
at the end of it all.

"And that, ladies and gentlemen," he said with a flourish, "is my third, final, and most important point."

Blackstone stood up.

"Alright, folks, shows over," he said. "Let's all get back to work. Do something productive."

Julia stood up and smiled at Blackstone's uncle.

"Thanks for all of that, Reverend Lamb," she said with a smile. "Very interesting." Then she threw her senior partner a look and left the room. Jason scurried after her.

Tully was chuckling and shaking his head as he walked out of the conference room.

"Now if you'll excuse me," Blackstone said to his uncle, "I have to try to keep my client out of the death chamber."

"Don't you have any response to what I just told you?" Lamb said with a sense of pleading in his voice.

"Yes, but I'd rather not insult you with it," Blackstone said. "Look, this was probably my fault, bringing you into this. Criminal law is a tough business. The government doesn't play games. It gets ruthless. And all you've got to offer me are your stories about magic and buried religious documents that are fifteen hundred years old, and...alchemy for heaven's sake. *Alchemy!*"

With that, Blackstone turned and strode out of the conference room, leaving his uncle to gather up his books and papers and then find his own way out.

CHAPTER 28

Blackstone spent the rest of the day working on his oral arguments for his appeal in Vinnie's case before the U.S. Court of Appeals for the District of Columbia Circuit. Julia had done most of the work on the written brief to the Court and, as usual, had done an excellent job. Written arguments by both sides had been filed on an expedited schedule because, for better or worse, Blackstone had filed a demand for speedy trial in Vinnie's case. Now, oral arguments were only two days away.

The file on *United States v. Vinnie Archmont* was spread out on a side table next to Blackstone's desk. On top was a manila envelope with a warning in large bold lettering, taped onto the outside of the envelope. It read,

WARNING!
CONTENTS ARE PROHIBITED FROM BEING VIEWED
BY ANYONE OTHER THAN J.D. BLACKSTONE
PURSUANT TO AN ORDER
OF THE U.S. DISTRICT COURT

This was the central issue in Blackstone's appeal. The defense was arguing that the trial judge had erred when he granted the government's motion to seal off any viewing of the note of Horace Langley, likely the last thing the man ever wrote before his murder, from everyone on the defense side except Blackstone himself.

There were only two chances Blackstone had to win. First, he could try to attack the government's affidavit testimony that the note had to be kept secret because making it public might jeopardize their ongoing criminal investigation into "other conspirators." But Blackstone knew he lacked the proof for that.

Or second, he could show that Vinnie's legal defense would be irreparably hampered by preventing Blackstone from having his assistants or his "expert" read the full contents of the note.

Blackstone picked up the manila envelope, opened the little metal clasp, and pulled back the flap. Then he dug his hand inside and pulled out a piece of paper that contained the note of Horace Langley exactly as it had been deciphered by Dr. Coglin. There it was again. It had been a while since Blackstone had actually studied it in its entirety:

A strange cipher appears in the Booth diary as follows:
To AP and KGC
Rose of 6 is Sir al ik's golden tree
In gospel's Mary first revealed
At Ashli plot reveals the key

As he studied it, he wondered how he could argue that this cryptic note was a critical element of the case and in fact essential to the defense theory of Vinnie's innocence. He couldn't help but think about Reverend Lamb and his extraordinary speculations about Freemasonry, Gnosticism, and alchemy.

Blackstone noted, once again, the reference in the third line to "gospel's Mary," seemingly a New Testament reference. *Okay,* he thought, *there it is, the religious element again.* But he had no idea what the "Rose of 6," or "Sir al ik's golden tree" were. Or, for that matter, what "Ashli plot" meant—was it a place name? A location? Or something else?

And he wondered what "key" it was that was intended in the last line. Of course, it was very possible that what Horace Langley was reading in the John Wilkes Booth diary pages—and then copied down in his note—had absolutely nothing to do with his death. Maybe his murder and the theft of those diary pages of indisputable historical value, were both totally unrelated to that one particular part of the diary that happened to catch Langley's attention just before the crime occurred. And if the three federal appeal judges believed that was the case, then Blackstone knew that his appeal on the Langley note issue would be doomed.

But there was another thought, and it had nothing to do with the legal issues or the evidence. It had to do with what Tully aptly called the "human behavioral factors." More specifically, *J.D. Blackstone's* behavior.

Must be nice for Vinnie to live a guilt-free existence, he thought to himself, feeling awash in regret over the way he had treated his uncle.

He picked up the phone and called Reverend Lamb's office but didn't get an answer. Then he tried his home. He let it ring a number of times, but no one answered. His uncle didn't believe in answering machines, so Blackstone couldn't leave a message.

How does this guy survive in the twenty-first century? he wondered as he returned to his file to work some more on the appeal issues.

Thirty minutes later he called again. This time Reverend Lamb picked up.

"Uncle," Blackstone said, "J.D. here."

"Yes. Good of you to call," Lamb said, a little out of breath. "I was just coming into the house with my dry-cleaning. I had quite a pile to pick up. The woman at the dry cleaners said it's been down there for more than a month. I had forgotten about it until just recently."

"Just wanted…to thank you," Blackstone said slightly ill at ease, "you know, for all the work you put in."

"Don't mention it," Lamb replied.

"You should get paid for your time. Just itemize your hours and send it in to me," Blackstone said. "You deserve to get compensated, just like any other expert on one of my cases."

"I didn't do it for the money," Reverend Lamb said plainly. "Not at all."

"I know," Blackstone replied sheepishly. "But still, I want to pay you. As a gesture of appreciation."

After a pause, Reverend Lamb responded.

"You never asked me any follow-up questions," Lamb said sadly. "I figured that meant you really didn't see much use in what I had to say."

Blackstone was rolling his eyes, feeling worse now than before he called.

"This is not a personal thing," he said. "It's simply a matter of whether your opinions have relevance to the legal issues, that's all. Sometimes an expert's opinions can move the ball forward...and sometimes they can't."

"And in this case?" Reverend Lamb asked.

The question hung out there in the air. Almost tangibly. Blackstone could practically see it floating in front of him, like a dialogue balloon in a comic strip.

"Tell me something," Blackstone said, glancing down at the Horace Langley note on the table in front of him. "About those so-called 'Gnostic gospels' you talked about."

"Yes?"

"How many were there?"

"A number of them. Why?"

Then Blackstone looked down at the note again, at the third line of the coded poem—*In gospel's Mary first revealed.*

"Wasn't one of them," Blackstone said, thinking back to what he had read in his uncle's book, "actually called the Gospel of Mary?"

"Why yes, that's correct. What are you getting at?"

Blackstone was tapping his finger now on the piece of paper that contained the Horace Langley note.

"Nothing I can share with you now. Maybe later. We'll see...depending on how my appeal goes."

But then Blackstone remembered one thing he wanted to ask his uncle.

"One more thing," he said. "About something you said during our conference today."

"Oh?"

"You said you had been trying for many years to put together the pieces about the Freemasons. What the core of their 'secret' was."

"Yes, I said that."

"You said that it didn't click in your head until you started working on this legal case for me."

"That's exactly right."

"Well, what was it about this criminal case that triggered your theory about the Freemasons?"

"Oh, that's easy," Reverend Lamb said brightly. "The business about *trees*. You asked me about the significance of trees as religious symbols. Remember?"

Blackstone looked once again at the note on the table in front of him—*Sir al ik's golden tree,* it said in the second line.

"Yes," Blackstone said distantly, "I remember."

"Well, that was it," Lamb replied. "That started the whole thought process—putting everything together in a whole pattern, so to speak."

"But why...how?" Blackstone asked.

"Simple," Lamb answered. "I went to Genesis, chapter 2, verse 9. Do you recall that one?"

"Gosh no," Blackstone said wryly, "and I must have misplaced my Bible—so why don't you boil it down for me?"

"It says this about the Garden of Eden—'Out of the ground the Lord God caused to grow every tree that is pleasing to the sight and good for food; the tree of life also in the midst of the garden, and the tree of the knowledge of good and evil.'"

Then Reverend Lamb added, "That was it for me."

After a lengthy silence from Blackstone, Lamb spoke up.

"Do you see what I mean?"

Blackstone was staring at the Horace Langley note.

"Possibly," he answered.

"By the way, you never asked me," Lamb said, "about how the secret of the Freemasons might be connected to John Wilkes Booth."

"Maybe some other time," Blackstone said, still glancing down at the Langley note. "We'll catch up on things soon, Uncle."

After they said their goodbyes, Blackstone hung up, took one more look at the cryptic poem, and then put it back into the manila envelope and sealed it shut.

His mind was exploding. The gears were flying. He needed to get out of the office. He needed to get some fresh air and think about anything except what he had been thinking about, obsessing over, in Vinnie's defense. He needed to get out of the city.

And he knew the place where he would go. The place where a creature was waiting, with great eyes and muscular flanks, redolent of sweat and hay and the fields.

CHAPTER 29

He knew he was going to have a bad night. And he was right. Tense, high-strung, like he had just downed a gallon of Turkish espresso, Blackstone stalked around his condo into the late hours like an ill-tempered tiger in a cage that was way too small.

Over and over in his mind he kept seeing the words and phrases in the Horace Langley note. There was no insight going on in that process. Just an obsessive, almost neurotic impulse to experience the words and phrases again and again. Like a ritual chant.

The only thing that calmed him a little and helped him slip into sleep was the thought that the next morning he would leave early and drive into the country with the top down and have reunion of sorts with his jet-black Arabian horse.

When the alarm went off, he was out of bed like a shot. He threw on some blue jeans, his boots, and a cutoff T-shirt and headed down to his car. He cruised out of Georgetown and soon was on his way around the Beltway and then heading west on I-66. It was hot, and the air blowing over his face and through his hair felt good.

After thirty minutes he turned off the interstate, and within minutes he was into the rolling hills of Virginia. The countryside was encircled with black horse fence and dotted with tidy houses and barns. He could smell the hay and the grass in the air.

When he got to a long driveway with a large, ornate white sign that said *High Meadows Equine Center,* he turned in and started slowly rolling down the gravel drive toward the stables.

Then his cell phone started ringing. He was tempted not to answer. He looked down. It was Julia calling from his office. He decided to pick up.

"Are you on your way into the office?" she asked him. Her voice was high and tight, like someone plucking the shortest string on a harp.

"No," he said. "I'm staying clear of the office today. I'm out in the countryside this morning, then back to my condo where I will spend the rest of the day getting ready for the oral arguments in Vinnie's case. Preparing in peace and quiet."

"You may want to rethink that," she said sharply.

"I don't think so," he said firmly.

"Well, just so you know, things are falling apart around here."

"Define 'falling apart,'" Blackstone retorted. "Do you mean a few pictures are tilted on the walls, or that the ceiling is caving in and people are being buried under the rubble?"

"I'm not a structural engineer. My masters was in chemistry before I went to law school, remember?" Julia snapped. "Let's just say it's *not* a good time for you to be out of the office."

"Okay," he said reluctantly, pulling his Maserati over to the side of the driveway and guiding the stick shift into neutral. "Let's hear it."

"You got a call from the clerk of the Court of Appeals. They have some question about the appendix you filed for the appeal. And seeing that your oral argument is tomorrow, I would think you ought to call her back."

"The only part of the file I took with me was the argument section," he said. "I left all the rest of the file, including the appendix, at the office. Ask Frieda, she'll help you locate it before you call the clerk back. I'm sure you can handle it for me."

"The next problem is more serious."

"I'm all ears."

"A lawyer from the Senate Judiciary Committee called. He said he was inquiring about your conversation with Senator Collings. Said that there was a complaint by the senator that you were in a restricted area of the Capitol Building under false pretenses. That you harassed the senator. That sort of thing. He said if he didn't hear from you today they would 'take further action.' Those were his words. He didn't sound like he was kidding."

"Give me his number."

Julia called out the numbers, and Blackstone jotted them down on a notepad in his car.

"What else?" Blackstone asked.

"Oh, I've saved the best for last," Julia said. "Your ditzy client Vinnie Archmont called up all weepy. 'I need to talk to you.' Said she hasn't heard from you since and these are her exact words—'that wonderful dinner we had together'—wants to set up another 'date night' with you."

Blackstone was silent.

"Excuse me for saying it," Julia said, flashing into anger, "and I know you are always the professor and I am always playing the student. But have you entirely lost your mind? You've got a first-degree-murder defendant on trial for her life and you're playing footsy with her."

"Technically, she's the one playing footsy with me."

"Do you even care that the DC Bar Association could try to take away your license to practice if this goes down bad?"

"I know what I'm doing," Blackstone said. But he hadn't mustered enough bravado in his voice to fool either Julia or himself.

"Okay, well," Julia said with exasperation in her voice, "you've been told. Now I guess it's my job to try to clean up after the elephants while you go to the circus."

"Clever metaphor," he said. "But just one question."

"What's that?"

"'Where are the clowns?'" he said half-singing.

"Do you really want me to answer that?" she snapped and then hung up.

Blackstone turned off his phone and eased his car into second gear, heading for the huge building of stables at the end of the road.

"Real glad I took that call," he muttered out loud.

When he got to the end he parked his car alongside a large black barn. He could hear the whinnying of horses inside the stable. As he rounded the corner he saw a short Hispanic man carrying a feed bucket. When the man saw Blackstone he stopped in his tracks.

"Mr. Blackstone!" he said with surprise and a big grin. "Good to see you here, sir. So good. And so long. Been a long time."

"Too long, Manny," he said.

"Blackjack is in his stall," the stablemaster said. "Was out in the big paddock, in the fields all last night."

"Yeah, just like his owner. Up all night."

Manny laughed and said, "Remember where your tack locker is?"

"I think so," Blackstone said, and headed into a corridor in the back of the barn lined with storage doors. He stopped at his, unlatched the door, and swung it open. He could smell the leather of his saddle. He grabbed it and gathered up the blanket, bridle, and reins and carried them through the corridor and then into the main section of the stables.

Manny already had Blackjack out of his stable and had the Arabian cross-tied between two beams in the middle of the barn.

"I'm real glad you at least kept Blackjack, Mr. Blackstone," he said, and then smiled when he said that.

Blackstone knew what he meant. When Marilyn and Beth were alive he had bought a tall, milky-white thoroughbred for his wife and a pony for his daughter that he also kept out at the stables. But after the car accident he had sold them off.

As Blackstone walked up to Blackjack, the horse bobbed his head just a little and then snorted a great puff of air through his nostrils.

The two stood eye to eye for a moment, looking at each other. Blackjack pawed the ground. Blackstone took his right hand and slowly ran it up the horse's long skull and then down his neck and along his glistening black back all the way to the withers.

Blackjack gave a little stomp with his front hoof.

After saddling him up, Blackstone led him out to the gate where Manny was waiting. Manny opened the gate to the big oval training ring.

Blackstone thrust his left foot into the stirrup and swung himself up deftly and toed his right foot into the other stirrup. He was fully in the saddle on the powerful Arabian again, and it felt good.

He spent an hour just warming up and putting Blackjack into a trot and then a canter. Nothing fancy. Just getting to know each other again.

At the end, when he was ready to bring him in, he gave him the cluck and a whistle and a little nudge of his boot and Blackjack exploded into a full gallop that sent Blackstone's hair flying.

When he was done, he swung down and onto the ground. Manny was there waiting by the gate.

"I'll take him in for you, Mr. Blackstone, curry him down. Take care of your tack for you," Manny said. "You got things to do, I bet."

"Thanks, Manny," he said, and handed the lead rope to the stable-master.

As Manny was walking the black Arabian back to the barn he shouted out to Blackstone. "You come back again, okay? Blackjack here's been lonely for his pal."

Blackstone smiled and nodded and then walked over to his car.

After he slid into the soft leather seat he dialed up the number for the Senate Judiciary counsel.

A man answered.

"Judiciary," he said.

"I'm returning a call from one of your counsel," Blackstone said. "This is J.D. Blackstone. Don't have a name for who called me."

"That would be me," the man said. "I'm Billy Baxter, Senior Counsel for Senator Collings on the Judiciary Committee. Uh...you must be on a cell phone. I can't hear you very well, I'm afraid...you'll have to speak up."

"Yeah, I'm out in the countryside leaving a horse stable, just barely in cell-phone range, I guess," Blackstone said.

But Blackstone didn't elaborate beyond that. This was the other guy's move.

"So Mr. Blackstone, I called you," Baxter said, taking the lead, "because I have received a complaint from Senator Collings about an encounter you had with him in the restricted area just outside the Senate chambers."

"Things must really be slow there in Judiciary for you guys," Black-stone barked. "Do they have you issuing jaywalking tickets now too?"

"Professor Blackstone," the man said, "this is very serious. I have instructions to contact the Capitol Hill police and have you charged with trespassing and disorderly conduct, and then to file an ethics charge against you with the bar association for unprofessional conduct, if—"

"If what?" Blackstone said, interrupting. "If I don't do what?"

"If you don't send a written apology to Senator Collings."

"You can take out your little BlackBerry that I'm sure you carry with you," Blackstone said, "and type in today's date and enter a memo right there. And type this into the keypad, Billy boy—'Professor Blackstone says that he will give an apology when there are icebergs in hell'—make a note of that."

"Is that your response?" Baxter said coldly.

"That and one other thing," Blackstone added. "Senator Collings's actions against me will look suspiciously hostile before the jury in my murder case when I subpoena him to testify. He will have a lot of explaining to do—under oath."

There was a tense pause, and then finally Baxter spoke and said he would convey that message to Senator Collings immediately.

Blackstone turned on the ignition to his car and then slowly eased his Maserati down the long gravel road.

Back to reality, he thought to himself.

CHAPTER 30

While driving home from the country, Blackstone dialed Vinnie on the phone but only got her voice mail. He called her cell phone and got the same. After her bubbly voice message he left his own message.

"Sorry we're missing each other. Let's get together. Right now I'm getting ready for oral argument tomorrow. I'll let you know how it goes."

He usually made a point of inviting clients to attend the oral arguments. In this case, though, he figured that Vinnie wouldn't want to come. Besides, the argument would be highly technical and procedural.

Blackstone pulled into his parking spot and trudged up to his condo.

He kicked off his boots, turned the ringer off on his phone, and then spread out the file at his work table—with photocopies of cases, his argument outline, and the rest in front of him.

Blackstone would spend the rest of that day and through the night, preparing. He would take a few breaks to grab microwave food from the freezer or to make some reps on his Nautilus equipment to work up a sweat and refocus his mind.

He wouldn't sleep, or even try to, that night. He would save that for *after* his arguments before the Court of Appeals. He knew all the traditional physiological rules, and how maximizing physical rest and lowering stress increases human performance. But he rationalized his brutal approach to preparation this way: *Those rules,* he would say to himself, *don't apply to a guy with a sleep disorder.*

But just as quickly as he would tell himself that, he would then follow it up with another question: *Sleep disorder—is that really what my problem is?*

By the time the early light started streaming through the shutters of his study the next morning, he felt he had maxed out his preparation on the case. His multidisk CD player was halfway through the Suite in F-sharp by Ernst von Dohnanyi, the Hungarian composer, when he walked over to it and turned it off.

"Why couldn't Mom have named me after a *decent* Hungarian composer?" he asked out loud with a smirk. "Like Liszt? Or Bartok?"

Then he took a shower, donned his dark suit and tie, gathered up his file and argument notebook, and headed out. He drove to the federal courthouse off Constitution Avenue, in the Federal Triangle area of downtown Washington. He parked his car and walked at a fast clip over to the courthouse. His case was scheduled to be the first one to be argued that morning.

At the corner of 3rd and Constitution he stopped, just momentarily, before a bronze statue, now green with tarnished age, of the English jurist Sir William Blackstone. He stared at the image of the man in the long, flowing judge's wig and cape, clasping a law book.

J.D. Blackstone gave the statue a modified salute and then hurried over to the front doors of the courthouse, where he went through the metal detectors, went up to the clerk's office to sign in, and then headed to the courtroom.

Henry Hartz, flanked by one of his Assistant U.S. Attorneys and another man in a suit, was already in the courtroom, standing at the government's table.

The courtroom was already filled with news reporters, some court personnel who were curious, and members of the public.

Blackstone went over to shake Hartz's hand. Hartz shook hands coldly, and then introduced the Junior Assistant U.S. Attorney with him.

Then Blackstone glanced over at the other man in the suit next to Henry Hartz who had not been introduced. He was a handsome man, in his late thirties, and Blackstone thought he carried himself like a police officer, but wasn't sure.

"This is Detective Victor Cheski," Hartz announced casually,

introducing the man to Blackstone. "As you know, he is our lead investigator on this case."

Blackstone reached over and shook hands with him, and Cheski gave
him a firm handshake and a confident smile. Then the lawyer strode
over to the defense table, where he laid down his argument notebook, a
copy of the appendix of materials from the court docket in his case, and
a blank notepad.

Suddenly he was aware of someone standing next to him.

He looked up, and to his surprise it was Vinnie Archmont, smiling.
She was leaning over the defense table with her hand on his file.

"Just wanted to wish you luck—but I really don't think you'll need
it," she purred quietly. "Thanks for being my hero on this."

He smiled back and reminded her that in appeals cases the clients
had to sit in the audience section.

She nodded and then made her way back to her seat in the crowded
courtroom. Blackstone thought it was a little strange that Vinnie had
chosen to attend the oral arguments, particularly because her modus
operandi thus far had been to distance herself as much as possible from
the criminal case against her. But he didn't have time to focus on that.

The bailiff called out for the courtroom to rise. In a loud shuffle of
feet every one stood up quickly.

Three black-robed federal appellate judges entered from behind the
bench and took their seats. On the right was an elderly male judge,
nearly bald, with glasses, and on the left a younger judge, also a man. In
the center, acting as chief judge, was Judge Susan Lowry, in her fifties,
peering over her reading glasses.

"Appearances, please," the clerk called out.

"Henry Hartz, AUSA, for the United States Government," Hartz
said.

"J.D. Blackstone, for the defense," Blackstone said.

"Very well," Judge Lowry said, "are counsel ready to proceed?"

They both indicated they were.

Blackstone strode up to the podium first. The little light on the
podium was green. He had alerted the clerk that morning that he would
be reserving a substantial amount of time for rebuttal, so his opening
would be short and concise.

He began to recite to the three-judge panel the procedural status of the case and then went into the core elements of the written indictment against his client. That is when the older judge interrupted him.

"Counsel," the judge said, "what is the relevance of the Horace Langley note to the criminal elements of this case as outlined in the indictment?"

"As I indicated to the trial judge during motions," Blackstone said, "the note goes to motive for the crime."

"And the trial judge rejected that argument, correct?"

"Yes," Blackstone said with a smile, "an error that I am hoping Your Honors, in your collective wisdom, will soon correct."

The other two judges chuckled, but the older judge did not.

"But why is this note necessarily relevant to motive?" the older judge said, pressing in. "All three of us have looked at the note that was submitted with the record in this case under seal. Frankly, while I will not disclose what is actually in that note, of course—and all the parties have agreed that it bears the handwriting of Horace Langley, the late Secretary of the Smithsonian Institution—nevertheless I will say that it seems to reveal nothing, at least on the surface, that would describe *who* may have killed Secretary Langley, or *why*."

"With all due respect," Blackstone shot back, "while I agree with you, Your Honor, that the note, superficially, does not answer the *who* question, it may well answer the *why* question. And as you know, Your Honor, from your experience yourself as a former prosecutor, once you answer the *why* question, then the 'who' in the 'who-done-it' often follows very quickly."

"But counsel," the younger male judge asked, "that could be said of anything in any file of any federal prosecutor. Is that all it takes? For a defense lawyer to speculate wildly about how this document or that might possibly reveal motive behind a crime and thereby supposedly exonerate the defendant? That would mean that the government would then have to open all of its files, willy-nilly, for every defense lawyer in every federal criminal case—based merely on the speculative fancies of creative defense lawyers. Is that your understanding of what the law is?"

Blackstone had expected that noose to be slipped around his neck during argument. He knew it would come. But somehow, it always surprised him how uncomfortable it felt when a noose started tightening.

"No, Your Honor," Blackstone admitted. "That is certainly not the legal standard. The criminal law of procedure is fairly well established—discovery permitted to defense counsel is carefully restricted and very limited. I concede that. But *this case is different.*"

"Why?" the older judge shot back. "The trial judge has permitted you to see the note—correct? You are lead counsel for the defendant, right? You've had the benefit of looking at it. Surely, if you saw something in this very strange, and to my mind, indecipherable note that bore any relevance to the crime that was committed, I am assuming you would have brought it to the district judge's attention—or brought it to our attention here in the Court of Appeals, right? But you didn't."

"That is correct, Your Honor," Blackstone said, struggling to keep the door open for his point. "But when I said this case is different, you have just made my case for me on that. This case against Vinnie Archmont is different precisely *because* the trial judge let me see the note—and as you yourself indicated, Your Honor, this is one 'strange note.' Frankly, I am unable on my own to fully understand it. That is why I need to be able to have experts evaluate its contents, its meaning, and its relevance to those who obviously not only wanted Horace Langley dead, but also wanted possession of the John Wilkes Booth diary pages. And the note that Mr. Langley wrote that appears to be a transcription of at least one part of that diary."

"So," the younger judge said, "are you saying that if the trial judge had not, in the first place, permitted you to have this expert document examiner of yours, Dr. Coglin, examine the notepad and reconstruct this note that Langley wrote from the indentations on the notepad—if the judge had ruled otherwise, then you wouldn't have known what the note said, and you wouldn't be here arguing for a wider distribution of this note, is that correct?"

"Yes, that's correct," Blackstone said, "and then again, if all the inkwells of all the Founding Fathers had run dry in 1776, then maybe they wouldn't have signed the Declaration of Independence either. Speculation on 'what might have been' litters the books on the shelves of a thousand libraries, Your Honor. But one thing here is *not* speculation—my client is charged with murder, and the government will be seeking the death penalty if Vinnie Archmont is convicted. Those two things are certain. But if I cannot have my experts analyze the wording in that note, then there is a chance that the wrong person may be marched down to the death chamber."

When Blackstone studied the faces of the judges, he saw that he had made no points with the older judge and the younger judge was blank-faced. In the middle, Judge Lowry had a look on her face, but it was one J.D. Blackstone simply could not interpret.

And that did not give him any optimism as the light on the podium turned red and he abdicated it to Henry Hartz, who strode up to it, leaning on his cane, with a self-assured smile on his face.

CHAPTER 31

Henry Hartz was a good trial lawyer. But he was an equally effective appellate advocate.

As he laid out all the reasons why the judges should refuse to overturn the trial judge's decision—why the note was not required by the criminal law to be disclosed to those other than J.D. Blackstone himself—one thing was becoming increasingly clear. Blackstone knew that unless someone walked through the crack in the door he had created during his argument, then his efforts to get the note analyzed by his own uncle or perhaps other scholars would be doomed.

"In support," Hartz argued, "of the severe limitations that the law places on what prosecutors are required to provide to defense attorneys, I need only point to the case of *United States v. Haire,* a 2004 decision from this circuit. There, this Court made clear that all the government needs to do is comply with Rule 16 and the Jencks Act. And that is exactly what we have done in this case.

"The law requires nothing more," Hartz continued. "And as has been suggested today by at least one of Your Honors, the District Court Judge probably gave Mr. Blackstone even more than he was required to receive, at that. The trial court and our office, I think, have been more than generous toward Mr. Blackstone's client in providing information. He is entitled to nothing more."

The two male judges asked Hartz a few questions about the record from the court below, but in Blackstone's estimation, the questions were inconsequential.

But then something happened. Judge Lowry spoke up.

"One question, Mr. Hartz," she said. "The note itself—as has been noted in argument here already, the note has been viewed by all three of us up here at the bench."

Then she continued. "My colleague in this panel," and with that she nodded to the older judge next to her, "has indicated he can't decipher that note's meaning. And defense counsel, Professor Blackstone, has conceded that he can't interpret the note fully either. So where do you stand on all of that?"

Henry Hartz smiled, but his confident expression was hiding a frantic interior calculation he was going through before he answered. A tallying of the risk of winning and losing, of arguments advanced, of where he stood at that moment in the minds of the judges, and how likely his answer was to add or detract from what he had already determined was a position of strength.

"I'm not sure of your meaning, Your Honor," he replied.

"Well," Judge Lowry said, "just this—that everybody seems to be admitting they can't construe or explain what this little note jotted down by Secretary Langley means. So, how do you view that note? Can you explain it to us?"

Hartz continued smiling. Blackstone couldn't see his face from his position at the defense counsel's table, but he was reading his body language. As Hartz leaned on his cane at the podium, Blackstone noted that he was lifting his left foot ever so slightly and tapping it nervously on the floor.

"Your Honor," Hartz said, "I have no position on that, really."

"You've read the note, correct?" the younger judge shot out.

"Yes, of course," Hartz replied.

"So then, do you have some kind of theory on what the words in the note mean?" Judge Lowry asked.

After clearing his throat quietly, Henry Hartz answered. "Not really, no."

"So the words in that note are as much of a mystery to you as to everyone else it seems," Judge Lowry added.

"It appears so," Hartz replied.

While the federal prosecutor knew something down deep in his gut, he had not had the chance to fully assess the extent of the damage to his case.

Not yet.

When J.D. Blackstone walked up to the podium for rebuttal, he was betting on who would grill him first. As usual, he was right.

"Counsel," the older judge asked. "The government prosecutor, in his argument, cited in support of his position the case of *United States v. Haire.*"

"Yes, Your Honor, he did."

"And that case is still good law, right? Hasn't been overturned or modified by any subsequent precedent?"

"No, not at all," Blackstone said with a smile. "As a matter of fact, I think that case is excellent law."

"Good, just checking," the older judge said with a smile and leaned back in his black high-backed judicial chair.

"Counsel," the younger judge asked, "it appears, as Judge Lowry has suggested here, that this note may well present a kind of mystery. Maybe a historical mystery of sorts if it relates to the Booth diary. But as one of the older judges of this circuit, now retired, used to tell me, 'Mysteries are always intriguing, but only rarely relevant.' Mr. Blackstone, other than your speculations about motive, where is the relevance?"

"Right there, implicit in your statement, Judge," Blackstone replied, "is the recognition that a note containing a mysterious code, written just prior to the author's murder and purporting to describe something from the most notorious diary in American history, may or may not be relevant to a charge of murder."

"Well," the younger judge said trying to connect the dots, "alright. But what's your point?"

"I think," Judge Lowry said, interjecting, "that this is Mr. Blackstone's point: None of us knows *how* to interpret this note. Am I correct?"

"Exactly, Your Honor," Blackstone said. "Now Henry Hartz said that the *Haire* case only requires the prosecution to comply with Rule 16 and the Jencks Act."

"And you do concede that the government here, has in fact, complied with those two legal rules, right?" Judge Lowry said.

"I do admit that," Blackstone replied. "But Mr. Hartz missed something."

At the government's table, Henry Hartz's face took on a subtle scowl.

"He didn't mention," Blackstone continued, "something else that was addressed in the *Haire* case. The Court reminded all of us of the familiar rule that the government is required—always required—to provide so-called *Brady* material to the defense. As the court put it, the government has to disclose 'information that is favorable to the accused and that is material—to guilt or innocence.' We all know that rule. But here is my question—how can we know whether the note contains evidence 'favorable' to Vinnie Archmont's innocence? Don't we have to *first* understand the words in the note and what they mean, before we can determine that?"

There was a silence on the bench for a few seconds.

"What if the government had a note in its evidence file written in German?" the younger judge asked. "Wouldn't it be the primary right of the *government* to get a German translator to decipher the note—rather than the defense?"

"I would agree," Blackstone shot back. "But what happens if the government refuses to hire a translator and interpret the note? Which is basically the case here. In the government's brief, they concede that they have not hired an expert to interpret the note and don't plan on using the note as part of their case against Vinnie Archmont. All right, so then what? It then has to be up to the defense to do exactly that. There is a lethal injection chamber on death row that is begging someone, somewhere, to figure out this last note that Horace Langley wrote before he died...so we don't execute the wrong person."

Then Blackstone leaned forward on the podium as he noticed the yellow warning light flicker into red to signal the end of his rebuttal time.

"Untie my hands," Blackstone pleaded. "Let me get an interpretation of this note from my experts. And simply impose a gag order on my experts not to further disclose the contents to anyone else until a further order of the trial judge."

Judge Lowry was going to ask one final question, but noticed the red light on the podium and thought better of it.

"Case is submitted," she announced. "Thank you, gentlemen."

The members of the press scurried out into the hallway and waited there to catch come comments from the lawyers as they left the courtroom.

Hartz, Detective Victor Cheski, and the Assistant U.S. Attorney filed out quickly.

As Blackstone collected his materials from the defense table, he had mixed emotions.

On the one hand, he felt good about the way that oral argument had gone.

But on the other hand, something was bothering him.

It was about Vinnie. The fact that she had showed up unannounced like that for the oral argument, so breaking with her attitude about the case thus far, was startling. He couldn't put his finger on it. But he wondered whether he was being played somehow as a sucker. Did she have another lawyer in the wings ready to take over? Or was this just another part of her pattern of manipulation that he had accused her of before? Always keeping something back—something hidden from him. Playing hide-and-seek games with him. Making herself unavailable for days on end—and then showing up suddenly in the Court of Appeals building.

He looked out into the courtroom, but she had already left. There it was again. The elusive Vinnie.

Blackstone breezed out of the courtroom and into the hallway, where he answered a few questions from reporters and then quickly squeezed his way into an elevator.

When he made his way to his car, Blackstone tossed his file and briefcase onto the front seat next to him.

But then he noticed something.

There was a white envelope sticking out a little from his file. It had his name on it. He recognized Vinnie's handwriting. He pulled it out and opened it.

There was a note inside. It read,

Sorry I didn't tell you I was coming. I wasn't planning on it, but something inside told me you needed to see me there. To let you know I was behind you. To let you know how very much I really appreciate everything you are doing for me. And, also, I just wanted to see you, dear. Truthfully. Sorry I couldn't stay, but that would be just too stressful. Besides, I know you did great. I LUV U

—Vinnie.

Suddenly, Blackstone felt foolish for having overanalyzed her appearance in court that day. The note certainly could dispel his doubts about her motives.

While he drove back to the office he would call her and set up another dinner date with her.

CHAPTER 32

I've got bad news for you," Tully said on the telephone. "And I've got some good news. Which one do you want first?"

Blackstone was back in his office, moving quickly around the room, from one part of Vinnie's file to another, with his wireless headset strapped on.

"Give me the good news," Blackstone said. "I need it."

"Okay, on the Senator Collings deal. He's not going to press charges against you as a result of your interaction with him outside the Senate chambers."

"I suppose that's good news," Blackstone said. "But not that good...I didn't think he had a leg to stand on. So give me the bad news."

"My sources indicate this guy is really going to go to war with you if you try to subpoena him as a witness in Vinnie's criminal trial. He's already getting his legal beagles on the Judiciary staff to write up research briefs on why you can't pull him into this."

"Is that all? I assumed as much," Blackstone said, trying to hold back a yawn. His all-night vigil preparing for oral arguments was catching up to him.

"That, and something else," Tully said. "If you serve him with a subpoena, then he is coming after you personally. He fully plans to complain to the DC Bar Association, seeking to revoke your license before the federal bench and your authority to practice before the Supreme Court, the whole bit. They're already gearing up the smear machine. It sounds like the guy is going to make the criminal trial his beachhead.

His Normandy invasion. He will try to destroy you, J.D., if you try to serve that subpoena on him."

Blackstone was mulling that over.

"Don't take this personally," he said. "But what chance is there that Collings knows you have spies in his office?"

"Oh, I always know there's a chance of that," Tully said matter-of-factly. "But honestly, I don't think this guy knows how close I am to what's going on in his office. I don't think he has any idea he's being monitored."

"Interesting," Blackstone muttered.

Then he stopped in his tracks.

"Wait a minute, wait a minute!" he cried out, and dashed over to his computer. "I can't believe I'm such an idiot," Blackstone muttered.

"What's going on, Chief?" Tully asked.

Blackstone began typing quickly onto his keyboard as he accessed the Web.

"I'm checking the Smithsonian's Web page," Blackstone announced. "Hold on."

After just a handful of clicks, he was staring at the page under the title "Board of Regents."

"I'm still wondering why I didn't check this before," Blackstone said impatiently as he scanned the page, moving his cursor down the listing of the members of the Board of Regents for the Smithsonian.

"The Board of Regents is the governing board for the Institution," Blackstone said. "The head of it is the chief justice of the United States Supreme Court. The other regents are the vice president, who is the president pro tempore of the Senate, along with three members of the House of Representatives, and nine other independent members."

"So?" Tully said.

"I'm not done," Blackstone shot back. "The Smithsonian's Board of Regents also includes three members of the U.S. Senate, who are appointed by the vice president."

Then Blackstone scrolled down the pictures of the sitting members of the board until he landed on the photo of a familiar face.

Underneath the face in the photo was the name of one of the Senate members of the Board of Regents:

Senator Beauregard "Bo" Collings

Blackstone read out the name to Tully.

"So where do we go with that?" Tully asked.

"Not sure," Blackstone said. "Maybe Collings is in this deeper than I thought."

"Great. Well, let me know when you come up with some bright idea about what that means. Meanwhile, I've already got a boatload of other stuff you want me to do on this case."

"Not so fast," Blackstone said interrupting him. "There's one thing I do know."

"Which is…?"

"You need to get down to Bo Collings's hometown in Arkansas," Blackstone said. "Whatever town that is, and find out everything you can about the guy. What church he joined. What clubs he belongs to. Where he would get his hair cut. Who he visits when he's back in Arkansas during election time. You already know he's a Freemason. Who else is in his local Masonic temple."

"I'm going to have to take on an extra detail of investigators on this case," Tully said.

"Fine. Whatever you've got to do," Blackstone said.

After he hung up, he realized how exhausted he was. He wondered whether he should try to connect with Vinnie.

"Why not?" he said out loud and dialed her number. She picked up right away.

"Hey, thanks for showing up this morning at oral argument," Blackstone said. "And for the card too."

"I wanted to be there for my guy," she said brightly. "How'd it go?"

"I see a chance," he said. "More than a good chance actually."

"That you'll win the motion?"

"Right."

"Which means," she said, "what—that they would give you permission to show the Langley note to other people?"

"Right," Blackstone said.

He waited. But Vinnie was quiet on the other end.

"People like, who, your experts?" she finally asked.

"Correct," he said.

"Which just might help me out of this mess I'm in."

"That's the plan," Blackstone said with fatigue in his voice.

"You must be tired, darling," Vinnie said. "Why don't you come on over to my apartment? I'll fix you a nice dinner."

"That sounds *really nice*," he said. "But I think I'll just head home and crash. I'm in heavy-duty need of some sleep."

"Are you sure? You know," Vinnie said, "if you come on over, after dinner you could just fall asleep on the couch. I'll slip your shoes off and tuck you in."

"Yeah, well...I think I'm going to take a rain check on that." Blackstone said. "But I'll be cashing it in some time, okay?"

"What are you doing tomorrow?" she asked.

"Oh, probably head out into the country for an hour or two. I've got a horse stabled out there."

"That's right. You're a champion long-distance rider, I had almost forgot...want some company?"

"I wouldn't be very good company, I'm afraid. I'm pretty much all business with my horse."

"That puts me in the same category as your horse, then," she said with a laugh. "You seem to be all business with me too."

"Sorry," he said. "But your case, and your life—they're in my hands. I'm spending the rest of tomorrow working on your case...and pretty much full-time, around the clock from now until trial."

"Okay," she said. "Take care of yourself, J.D. I need you so desperately. In so many ways."

"Right," he muttered. "Take care, Vinnie."

After taking off his headset, he didn't bother to clean up his office. Or even stuff some of the file into his briefcase as he usually did, just to have work to do in the late watches of the night when he couldn't sleep.

He trudged past Frieda in the lobby, gave her a silent wave as he walked through the front door, and headed to his car.

CHAPTER 33

There was the promise, the enticing hint. But like much of J.D. Blackstone's life, it didn't unfold the way he had planned.

When he lumbered through the door of his condo exhausted, having been up for forty-eight hours, he figured that he would be able to finally get some sleep. It was early evening. But the nature of his insomnia was weirdly unpredictable.

He stripped off his clothes and dumped himself into bed. He didn't remember falling asleep. But soon he was dreaming. Marilyn, his dead wife, was there in the middle of his dream. This time she kept coming in and out of focus, as if he were looking at her through a camera lens that couldn't quite get adjusted right, that kept focusing on the depth of field in the background but not the subject. He wanted to see her face. But he couldn't capture it.

Somewhere a voice said, *Don't forget...*

And then he woke up with a start.

He looked at the clock. It was a little before midnight.

And he was wide awake.

He found himself now very frustrated that he had not brought any of his file on Vinnie's case to work on. He could get dressed and drive down to the office and then fetch some work to do. But that seemed ludicrous.

He clicked on his TV, and while a news program droned on in the background he flipped through several magazines he had stockpiled with the intent of eventually perusing them.

He glanced through a philosophy magazine on postmodernism. And the journal of the American Psychological Association. After that he took in a few of the current poets in an issue of the *Southern Review*. Then a Capitol Hill political newspaper.

And then an outdoor magazine. Halfway through he noticed an announcement for a new long-distance equestrian race set in the Southwest.

Maybe I'll get Blackjack up to speed and then enter it, he thought.

That was when he had the fleeting recognition, as he had before, that in the life he was now leading he was free to do everything, virtually without constraint, but found it difficult to muster the will to want to do anything. So he would force himself ahead in a manic, pile-driving effort to keep busy. To do whatever the task was. Never satisfied, even with victory. Never at rest.

He was now beginning to realize how, when Marilyn and Beth were alive, he would leave them often. Of course, sometimes on legal cases that required some travel. Or a few speaking engagements in connection with his professorship at the law school. But often they were his private treks into the wilds to go rock climbing up the sheer face of a mountain, or kayaking down the rapids of rivers in West Virginia, Colorado, even once in South America. That last one was with a group of experienced adventurers, but the rest were solo. Marilyn resented it and said so. She asked why he had the impulsive need to go on those one-man expeditions.

For a man who prided himself on being able to come up with breathtaking solutions for insoluble legal dilemmas and who was capable of mastering a bewildering number of different intellectual disciplines, Blackstone never could come up with a satisfactory answer for that question from his wife.

Then, after a while, they spoke less and less about it. Until finally the icy acceptance of separate lives had set in.

Blackstone had begun working on solving that a few weeks before the car accident. He figured it was just a matter of coming up with the theoretical solution and then applying it to their lives. He looked at restructuring his schedule so his time and Marilyn's could mesh better. He did the same thing with scheduling time with his daughter, Beth.

But the mechanics of it didn't easily solve the emotional heart of the matter. Marilyn was still coldly resentful. Beth had grown distant and secretive, even if she was able to maintain a friendly exterior in a kind of superficial way.

And then they both were taken away from him.

Turning off the TV a little before four in the morning, he decided to try to crawl back into bed again. But he couldn't click off his mind.

He tossed and flipped around in his bed for several more hours until finally, sometime after dawn, he fell into a deep sleep.

Blackstone had not set his alarm, and he had turned off the ringer on his phones.

When he awoke, it was one in the afternoon.

And now he was feeling mildly refreshed. He climbed out of bed, put on his gym trunks, and worked out on his Nautilus. Ordinarily he would then have raced down to the office. But just then he had the urge to drive out into the country again to give Blackjack a workout. He glanced at his watch. He still had time to put Blackjack through the paces and get back into town and work at his office into the evening. He put on his jeans and a cutoff work shirt.

Blackstone was halfway to the stables in the Virginia countryside when his cell phone started ringing.

"J.D.," Frieda said on the other end, a little breathless. "You got a stack of calls from reporters this morning."

"What's up?" he asked. "Something break on our case?"

"Oh, yeah," she said. "Something broke alright. Wait a minute, Julia wants to tell you." And then she put him on hold.

Blackstone kept driving. He was just getting off onto the county road that led to one other county highway that led finally to the stables. He was trying to figure out what was going on. The obvious answer was that the Court of Appeals had issued its decision, but he couldn't see how that was likely. Although he had asked the Court to issue an expedited ruling, he had never heard of a court giving a decision in twenty-four hours.

Usually the panel of judges would convene in conference after argument while the case was still fresh from the arguments of counsel and then take a quick poll. If there were at least two votes out of three, they would have their decision, but it would usually take a while to draft the opinion and then get it past the other judges.

"J.D.," Julia said coming on. "Where are you?"

"Talk to me," he said. "What's going on?"

"The Court of Appeals issued its ruling. Just a one-page order. We got it electronically this morning. Can you believe that kind of turnaround time? Nothing elaborate. Just the nuts and bolts. Are you on your way in?"

"How'd they rule?" Blackstone asked.

"You won," Julia said energetically. "Here's the bottom line: You can share the Langley note with not more than two defense experts, who have to be sworn to secrecy on the contents of the note. You can also share it with me as co-counsel. But if you want your client to see it, or anyone else for that matter, you have to show cause to the District Court and argue why."

"Alright. Now we've got some momentum," Blackstone said. "Have you looked at the file yet to find the note and take a look at it?"

"Not yet," she said. "You've got stuff piled all over your office. I figured I would wait until you got back."

"Fine," he said. "Look, I'll be out until later this afternoon. I'll talk with you around five-thirty or six today, okay?"

"What do you want me to do about all the reporters?" Julia asked. "They're descending like locusts. *New York Times, National Journal, Washington Post.*"

"*You* talk to them."

"Me?"

"Sure," Blackstone said. "Look, what they are really after is some hint about the contents of a note that may reveal something about the assassination of Abraham Lincoln. Number one, we can't even whisper anything to them about what that note says. And number two, the stuff in that note seems to have nothing to do with that anyway. And if they are trying to figure out how that note will have an impact on our legal case, well, we really have nothing to tell them there either, right?"

"So what do I tell them?"

"That we are gratified and encouraged that the Court gave us such a quick victory. But we are prohibited from sharing anything else with the press at this time."

"Alright," she said. "I guess I'll be seeing you shortly."

"Count on it," he said.

He glanced in his rearview mirror. There was a minivan in back of him. Far behind that vehicle there was a white utility truck.

Blackstone slowed down and then turned onto the county highway.

The minivan didn't turn, but kept going.

When Blackstone was a mile down the tree-lined road he glanced at his rearview mirror again.

He noticed that the white utility truck had turned onto the county highway also and was heading in the same direction he was.

CHAPTER 34

Blackstone had called ahead to Manny and let him know he would be driving out to give Blackjack a workout that day.

Rather than cloister himself in his office, Blackstone was glad he was going to get some fresh air. Things had been starting to jell in his brain. The vague outline of his defense theory was starting to configure itself. Whenever that happened, he liked to get away from the law office and the interruptions and distractions.

By the time he pulled up to the stables he had already constructed a mental checklist of the final details that needed to be done before the trial.

When Blackstone walked up to the barn he could see that Manny already had the Arabian saddled and tacked out. He suggested that Blackstone take the horse out into the big field in back of the stables.

Blackjack was led out to the gate, where Blackstone mounted him and then rode him into the open spaces of the back twenty acres of the property. The land was flat, with some gently rolling hills.

He could tell that Blackjack wanted to break out fast. He was like a surging engine waiting to be loosed. But Blackstone kept him at a slow jog first, then posted with him for a while. All the controls were there. Blackjack was responsive and quick. As Blackstone pressed his thighs into the big barrel chest of the Arabian he could feel the full, muscular power of the horse.

"Good boy!" Blackstone shouted out as he took him around a couple of turns, now faster, at a canter, and Blackjack was following his cues effortlessly.

The horse and rider headed back to the far end of the acreage. Alongside the field there was a private road lined with trees, with a black fence separating it from the field. Blackstone glanced over at the winding fence and noticed something odd about the three gates in the fence which were usually closed.

Today, for some reason, they had all been swung open.

He thought that was a little unusual. Each gate had a short entrance-way to the dirt road that ran along the property. He knew that Manny and the stable owners were fastidious in keeping the fence line locked down so the horses they would turn out into that part of the field wouldn't get out.

I bet Manny doesn't know about those gates being open, Blackstone thought to himself.

When he was ready to head back to the barn, he thought, he would stop at the gates and close them up.

Then something caught his attention out of the corner of his eye.

He reined his horse to a stop, and he turned in the saddle and looked back, down the field from where he had come and along the fenceline rimmed with willow trees. Blackstone thought he had seen something large and white.

But now it was gone.

He turned forward again and gently squeezed the sides of the horse into a trot. But the thought was nagging at him.

As he was trotting forward he twisted around in his saddle again to look back. This time he saw it, now from a different vantage point.

Partially covered by the trees, the white utility truck that had been following him was parked in the dirt road next to the fence.

Maybe an electric company truck—or the telephone company, he thought to himself.

But there were no electric poles there. And no telephone wires.

A vague sense of foreboding and urgency overcame him. There was no logic to it, except for the need to ensure one's own survival. And that was something that Blackstone fully understood.

He gathered the reins in his right hand. He was ready to swing the end of the reins down onto the right shoulder and send Blackjack catapulting forward into a full gallop.

But before he could, he heard a *crack*.

And there was a *ping* just behind him. A small puff of dust was released just to the right of Blackjack's right rear hoof.

The horse reared up wildly on his powerful hind legs. Blackstone could see the terror in the eyes of the Arabian.

As Blackstone struggled to one-rein the horse from the left and bring his front legs down to the ground again, he thrust his head straight into the horse's mane.

Then there was a second crack, and a second bullet whizzed just over his head.

Now Blackjack was bucking and stomping like a crazy horse. Blackstone was fighting to stay on. He knew his only chance now was to ride the horse back to a state of control, and quickly. Then he would ride him like a rocket to the far side of the field, out of danger.

When Blackjack was finally reined down and had all fours on the ground, Blackstone quickly craned his neck around to spot the truck.

Now the white utility truck was barreling down the dirt road toward him, sending a cloud of dust up behind it. Then it slammed on its brakes.

Blackstone rammed both of his feet into the horse's sides, lashed his reins down on his shoulder, and screamed, "*Go!*"

Blackjack sprang forward so fast that Blackstone's head jerked back. The horse, all of him, muscle, sinew, hair, and sweat, was now flying across the field, with the rider clamping his legs tightly around his heaving midsection.

Then a third bullet whizzed.

But this time it found its mark.

J.D. Blackstone felt something rip into the back of his left shoulder. A searing, scorching pain. As he was galloping he glanced over. He saw the front of his shirt was wet with red.

Blackstone screamed out for Blackjack to go. To go faster.

The Arabian was bursting into high gear.

But behind the horse and rider, the white utility truck had entered the field through one of the open gates. And it was roaring toward them across the grassy hills, bouncing madly. Then it slammed on the brakes again.

Blackstone reined his horse to the left, still at a gallop.

He began a turning arc, bringing Blackjack around to head him back to the barn.

A puff of smoke burst just to the horse's left. But now the Arabian was at a full launch speed and was unstoppable.

The white truck gunned its engines and roared after them across the field, closing the gap.

Blackstone looked down and saw the red blood from his sweatshirt now running down onto the glistening shoulder of the horse.

"I hope that's me and not you, boy," Blackstone muttered, looking at the blood as he now grabbed two fistfuls of mane, trying to stay on the horse as they galloped together toward the barn and the stables and the main house. He was getting lightheaded and dizzy from the loss of blood, so he lifted his head almost straight up to keep his airway clear. His was leaning against the horse's mane, bouncing back and forth with each stride like a toy on a string.

He could hear the truck coming up from the rear, but the end of the field and the outbuildings were just in front of him.

Then he spotted Manny, across the driveway at a fast run heading toward him.

That is when the white truck did a quick turn and headed like a dirt-track racer to the open gate. When it reached the gate, the driver slammed on the brakes to get through the fence, then drove at breakneck speed down the dirt road to the county highway, took a fast turn to the left, and then sped out of sight.

By the time Blackstone and his horse had reached the buildings, Manny was already running up to them, yelling.

"Mr. Blackstone! What happened to you?" he was calling out.

That was the last thing J.D. Blackstone remembered.

CHAPTER 35

When Blackstone regained consciousness, he was lying, on his back. He was in a vehicle and it was moving fast.

"How's Blackjack...did he...get shot?" Blackstone asked, still in a daze.

Blackstone was lying on a gurney in the rear of a speeding EMT truck. Manny was bending over him. An EMT worker, also in the back of the vehicle,was monitoring his vital signs.

"No, Mr. Blackstone," Manny said. "Blackjack, he didn't get hurt at all. Did a real good job of bringing you up to the barn."

"Good," Blackstone said. "That's good."

Within fifteen minutes the EMT vehicle was pulling into a regional hospital. The EMTs had already stopped the bleeding. He was given a transfusion and a surgical team took an initial look at his left shoulder. The bullet had made a clean entrance and exit, he was told by the head of the emergency room. But it looked like it might have severed a tendon.

"You're pretty much out of the woods," the doctor said, "as far as blood loss is concerned. But we would feel better if you got transferred over to a hospital equipped for microsurgery. You're going to need some exploratory intervention in that area. See what got torn or damaged, and then go right into surgical repair. You live in Georgetown?"

Blackstone nodded.

"Fine. We'll get you transferred tonight."

Manny came in the critical care room to check on him a few minutes later.

"Hey Manny," Blackstone said. "Do me a favor, will you? Call Julia at my office. Tell her what happened. And let her know which hospital I'm going to tonight."

"Sure thing, Mr. Blackstone."

"And tell her to be sure and watch her step. She needs to be really careful about her own safety."

Manny smiled and assured him that he would tell Julia.

After Manny left, a stocky deputy sheriff strode in the room. He introduced himself and said he needed to get some details on the shooting. Blackstone rattled off the entire incident while the deputy was jotting down notes in his daybook.

Then the deputy looked up from his memo pad.

"We've got some personnel looking over the scene for evidence," he said.

"Make sure—" Blackstone said, trying to lean over on his side to face the deputy. But then wincing in pain, and then thinking better of it, he eased himself down again. "That they check the tire prints from the truck. And there should be several bullets in the dirt."

"We'll do our job—don't worry, Professor," the deputy said. "I know you're a big criminal law expert, but out here—we may be in the country, but we can do physical evidence with the best of them."

"Good to hear that," Blackstone said.

The deputy made a few more notes and then said he had all the information he needed except for one final question.

"Know anybody who wants you dead?"

Blackstone thought on it for a few moments.

"Yeah. The three students I flunked in my constitutional law class last semester."

The deputy looked up from his memo pad.

"And then there is my father the judge, who resents the scandalous kinds of criminal cases I'm constantly taking on."

"Did any of these people make threats?" the deputy started to say.

"No. Listen, I'm just kidding," Blackstone said. "Motive? Oh…let me think on that one and get back to you. But there is one thing more you need to know," Blackstone said.

"What's that?" the deputy asked.

"About the shooter—I think it was just one person in that truck." Blackstone continued.

"Are you sure?"

"Sure I'm sure."

"Did you see who it was?"

"No."

"Then how'd you know?" the deputy asked.

"The driver had to stop the truck each time before shooting. Couldn't drive and shoot at the same time. That tells me it was one person."

The deputy thought on it for a moment then responded.

"Could be. We're still looking for the assailant. Unfortunately no ID on the person, just the truck. We've sent out a 'want' electronically to the other departments around the state. Your description of the truck matches the one we got from that fellow from the horse stables."

"Manuel Rodriguez?"

"Yeah, that's him. We did get a response, though, from a detective with the Capitol Police in DC from our APB."

"Do they know something about the suspect?"

"Not sure. They said they're working on a related case."

"Related?"

"Yes, but that's all I know. After you get transferred to the other hospital tonight, someone from their department will probably be interviewing you."

After the deputy left, a nurse came in and said they would be transferring him by ambulance in a few hours. That he could close his eyes and try to get some rest.

"Got anything really powerful for sleep?" he asked, half jokingly.

"Nothing beyond the pain meds you're already getting," she said in a monotone and then left.

Blackstone was half-drifting off about an hour later, when another nurse came in to check on him.

"Excuse me, Professor," she said. "But there's a Judge William Potter Blackstone on the telephone. I am assuming he's a close relative?"

"That's debatable," he replied with a hint of dark humor. "He's my father."

"Would you like me to put him through to your room?"

"Sure…why not?"

A minute later the phone next to his bed rang. Blackstone picked it up.

"J.D., is that you?"

"Yes. I'm still alive, Dad," he answered.

"Julia from your office called us. Your mother and I are very concerned, of course. How are you doing?"

"As they say in the movies, 'It's just a flesh wound'—sort of," Blackstone snapped back. "It went in and out. A clean hole. Nothing to worry about."

There was a pause in the conversation. Then his father continued.

"So, exactly what kind of situation are you mixed up in this time?"

"It's a long story," he replied.

"Most attempted murders are," the father shot back. "Do you know why it happened?"

"Yes," he said. "But Dad, I don't really think I'm at liberty ·to explain."

"I'm not a judge anymore, remember?" his father said. "I retired. There's no ethical or professional reason now for you to play games with me. I just want to know what kind of trouble you've got yourself into."

"No trouble. Just another strange twist in my own, very peculiar practice of law."

"Speaking of your…well, *strange* legal practice, there's something you should know."

"What's that?"

"I've been reading in the papers about your defending this woman in the murder of Horace Langley."

"Oh?" Blackstone said, closing his eyes, shaking his head, and readying himself for the onslaught.

"Were you aware that I knew Horace Langley?"

"No, I wasn't," Blackstone said.

"Not intimately," his father continued. "But he and I were seated next to each other a few years ago at a dinner in Washington. It was a banquet for the Supreme Court Historical Society. Spent the evening talking together. Seemed like a wonderful person. Fascinating fellow. A

horrible atrocity for a fine man like that to have been killed like that—
shot down like a dog."

"Yes," Blackstone said. "His murder was a terrible crime. But never
fear, Dad, before this case is over, I intend to expose the real killer."

"Oh, really?" his father said with a cold air of incredulity. Then he
added, "It's a rotten shame you came in on the wrong side of this one. I
know all about the legal advocate's ethical duty to represent undesirables,
but this one, J.D.—honestly, this really takes the cake."

After a few seconds of silence his father added two more final
words.

"Be well."

Then he hung up.

CHAPTER 36

"Were you the one who called my father and told him?" Blackstone said in a surly tone.

He was just out of surgery and still a little groggy. But not too groggy to miss the opportunity to spar with Julia, who was in the recovery room with him, standing next to his bed.

"He's your father," Julia shot back. "Come on, J.D. How can you blame me? Besides, you've got no wife. No other close friends. Not even a house pet. I'm the one who has to look after those kinds of things for you."

He moved a few of the tubes out of the way to get a better look at his law partner.

Blackstone managed a half-smile.

"At least my trusty horse stuck by me," he said.

He could see that Julia was smiling now too.

"Your horse and me," she said. "Your only true friends. That says something, huh?"

Then something happened, and her voice quivered a little.

"I should be so angry over this whole thing," she said, and her eyes started filling up with tears. "When I heard you were shot..." she started to say, but she couldn't finish. Julia covered her mouth with her hand. She swiped a swath of blond hair away from her face with her other hand, and then took her horn-rimmed glasses off and wiped her eyes.

J.D. Blackstone was watching her. His smile was fading into an open-mouthed gaze. He was amazed. Surprised at the tenderness he saw peeking out from Julia's usual controlled exterior. But he shouldn't have been.

He was tempted to give a smart-aleck retort, but it left him, and so he simply lay in his bed, looking at Julia's attractive, vulnerable face for a long time.

"I need your help," he finally said. "They want me to stay in the hospital for a couple of days or so, primarily for physical rehab on my shoulder. I can't afford to do that. I'm planning on getting myself out of here tomorrow even if it is against medical advice. I've already shut off the painkillers they've got me on."

With that he pointed to the IV drip next to his bed.

"That particular one," Blackstone said, "has a tendency to cause elevated temperatures in the body. The last nurse in here took my temp, and it was ninety-nine-point-five just after they hooked me up. So I disconnected it. I don't want them charting me as having an elevated temp and then wondering whether I've got a postoperative surgical infection giving me all kinds of grief about getting released tomorrow."

"Wonderful," Julia said with an exasperated tone. "So, you're fresh from surgery and you've already taken yourself off pain meds?"

"I need to get out of here. I can't afford to slow down on Vinnie's case. Trial date is rushing up. And I'm just starting to feel the wind at my back."

"So," Julia said, matter-of-factly, "what do you want me to do?"

"First, now that we've got clearance from the Court of Appeals, send the Langley note to our two defense experts."

"And they are?"

"There's a professor at Harvard. Dr. Richard Cutsworth. He's head of the history department. The guy's the number-one scholar in the nation on nineteenth-century American history, with a particular expertise on the Civil War. Published several books on the Lincoln assassination. I spoke to him earlier and he said if I could get the Langley note released, he would agree to take a look at it. Try to figure out what it means. And then maybe we can figure out the motive behind the Smithsonian crime."

"The guy sounds like a real trophy fish for our side. How'd you manage to get him?"

"Professional jealousy. I think he was peeved," Blackstone said, "that

Horace Langley had passed him over in selecting the panel of experts who were supposed to review the Booth diary pages."

"So, who is the second expert you want me to send the Langley note to?"

Blackstone paused for a moment, then rolled his eyes.

"Oh, my uncle, I suppose."

Julia smiled.

"Good choice," she said.

"Now you're being sentimental."

"No, just logical," she said. "Cutsworth is the natural first choice. He can dissect the note from a purely historical standpoint. But Reverend Lamb will be coming from a totally different perspective. He's like Blackjack—in other words, the dark horse—or should I say, the wild card...excusing the double pun."

Blackstone smiled.

"Yeah. That's exactly why I decided on dear old Uncle as my second choice," he said. "It really won't matter what crazy conclusions he arrives at. The fact that he's using a contrary paradigm totally out of left field for his evaluation, all that Freemason-Gnostic-mumbo-jumbo, will put some pressure on Cutsworth to really sharpen his game—he'll want to make sure that his scholarly, historical approach is the theory that we end up going with."

"Anything else?"

"Check with Tully to see how his investigation is going into the two security guards who were on duty at the Smithsonian that night."

"Will do."

"Also, there's an issue with one of the FBI's 302 reports."

"What do you mean?"

"I've been rolling this around in my head," Blackstone said. "According to the FBI investigation at the scene, there was a drinking glass on Langley's desk at the scene of the crime."

"So?"

"But when I looked at the physical evidence inventory sheet in the records that Henry Hartz turned over to me—there was no mention of the glass being bagged and tagged and put into the evidence closet. As you know, Hartz eventually did produce a copy of the crime lab report on the glass—it showed no fingerprints. But why is the glass not mentioned on the evidence inventory? Find out what the deal is with that."

"Okay. I'll get right on it."

"Finally," Blackstone said, "bring the files on Vinnie's case into my room here. I can't afford to waste time."

Julia nodded, and then came closer to his bed. She bent over Blackstone and planted a single kiss on his forehead, then turned to leave.

As she left she said over her shoulder, "Glad to see you're still alive, Professor Blackstone."

"Thanks, Julia," he said. "Thanks for everything. Really. Oh, and Julia—"

She stopped and cocked her head a little.

"Please be very careful. Whoever came after me—it may have something to do with Vinnie's case. So, just be very cautious about your own safety. I'm thinking about having Tully hire a bodyguard for you, just in case."

"First, someone tries to crush you with a two-ton block of marble—then you take a bullet—and I'm the one who needs security?" she said laughing. "No, thanks. I can take care of myself."

After Julia was gone, a nurse hustled into the room and took his temperature.

Then she looked at the little white thermometer.

"Huh. Ninety-eight-point-seven. Your temperature is right as rain now," the nurse said.

Blackstone smiled.

"Of course it is," he said with a measure of satisfaction.

"A detective with the DC police is on his way in to talk with you," the nurse announced. "I guess about your shooting."

"Yeah, I was told about that," Blackstone said.

"Are you up to it?" the nurse asked.

"Sure. Send him in. What's his name?"

The nurse glanced down at the chart in her hand.

"Ah...here it is...Cheski...Detective Cheski."

Blackstone's eyes widened.

"Detective Victor Cheski?"

"Yes. That's him."

As the nurse scurried out of the room, Blackstone was left to ponder that one—why the chief investigator in the Smithsonian murder was now investigating the attempt on J.D. Blackstone's life.

CHAPTER 37

etective Cheski strode into the hospital room with a smile.
"May I shake your good hand?" he said, and reached out.
The men shook hands. Blackstone managed a courteous smile.
"I'm sure you're wondering," the detective began, "why I'm here."
"That, among other things, yes."
"This is a little unusual, I admit," Cheski continued. "So, maybe I can dive right in."
"Be my guest," Blackstone said, eyeing the detective carefully.

This was a good opportunity, the lawyer thought, to size up one of the chief players on the opposing team. He took in everything about the detective. He was good-looking and in good shape. Had an air of overconfidence about him. Wasn't wearing a wedding ring. Looked Blackstone right in the eye as he talked. Almost aggressively so.

"I had been called in to investigate your incident at that construction site," Detective Cheski began, "involving the elevator and the block of marble. That must have given you quite a scare that day."

"It elevated my blood pressure a little bit," Blackstone said. "I never heard the results of the police investigation."

"Some dead ends, I'm afraid. No question that the construction crane had been tampered with. We did check out a hopeful lead on a former, disgruntled crane operator, who had just been fired a week before the incident for stealing some construction materials and tools. But he had a solid alibi. So, we were back to square one."

"Thus the question," Blackstone replied, "where, exactly, is square one?"

"I had the initial suspicion, Professor, that you might have been targeted in that elevator incident, but there wasn't a lot to go on. Just an idea. On the other hand, perhaps it was just a random act of vandalism. Now, with this shooting, it sure raises the stakes. Which is why I am involved."

"Yes, explain that for me," Blackstone said.

"I have two theories here. First, the perpetrator may be someone who's upset over one of your other cases. Lawyers, particularly controversial ones like yourself, make easy targets for some wacko or an angry opponent who you beat in court, that kind of thing."

"And the second theory?"

"Perhaps you are being targeted by a co-conspirator in the Smithsonian crime. It's no secret that we believe that the murder of Horace Langley, and the theft of the Booth diary pages, was a group effort. Very unlikely that it could have been the work of a lone actor, unless...well..."

"Yes?" Blackstone said, inviting him to finish his sentence.

"I was going to say, unless it was a bad actor who was pretty talented, you know, skilled. And I'm talking about a very, very professional type—someone who can do a pretty complicated burglary."

"And a fairly cold-blooded murder," Blackstone said, looking the detective in the eye.

"No question about that," Cheski said with a smile. "Look, I'm not here to discuss your defense of Ms. Archmont. That's your business. You've got a job to do, just like I do. But I want to find out who else was working with Vinnie, Vinnie Archmont, to do this crime. And if I can do this by tracking who has been coming after you, then I am going to do that. She was a conspirator all right. But I want to know who pulled the trigger. Could have been her. Most likely, though, someone else."

Blackstone nodded, but said nothing, not at first. He was studying Detective Victor Cheski closely.

"So," the detective continued, "you have some options here."

"Options?"

"I understand my role as an investigator in the attack on you overlaps with my role as investigator in the Smithsonian case. There's a good part in that. I can try to put the pieces together to see if there is a connection between the two. But there's also a difficult part."

"Like, creating a possible conflict of interest?"

"Right," Cheski said. "Now if you feel uncomfortable in the least with me investigating your shooting incident while I'm also working with AUSA Hartz on the Smithsonian prosecution against you, just say the word. Then I'll have the department assign another detective to work your shooting."

"I've got no objections," Blackstone said. "I'm convinced you'll do your job."

"Okay," Cheski said. "I've got a form here for you to sign, if you would. It simply indicates that you have no objection to my continuing to investigate the crime committed against you."

Then Cheski pointed to the bottom of the form.

"Just sign here."

Blackstone glanced at the form and then signed on the line.

"Is that it?" Blackstone asked.

"I have the report from the local deputy. That gives me a good start. But there was one area where I'd like some clarification."

"Sure."

"Who knew you were going to be at the horse stable that day?"

"My office. But they don't tell clients, or outsiders, where I am going to be. Especially if I'm involved in personal activities not dealing with my law practice or my teaching."

"Anybody else?" detective Cheski asked, eyeing Blackstone closely.

Blackstone was aware of two others, but he wasn't about to share that with the detective. In a phone call once with Billy Baxter, the lawyer from the Judiciary Committee, he had mentioned he was leaving a horse stable, so someone there might have been able to piece together which stable that was. But there was no way he was going to alert Cheski to his recent dealings with the Judiciary attorney, as that would just lead him to investigate the meeting between Blackstone and Senator Collings and its explosive aftermath.

The other was Vinnie, to whom he had made a vague reference in his telephone call the day before he had driven out to the equine center. But for attorney–client confidentiality reasons, among others, there was no way that he was going to open the door for the chief investigator for AUSA Henry Hartz to gain access to his intimate conversations with his client.

"Let me think on that," Blackstone said casually. "But I have a question of my own," he added. "How about the forensics on my shooting?"

The detective smiled at that.

"We've already retrieved a spent bullet at the scene. I rushed it right over to the FBI lab and told them to check it immediately. They say it was fired from an AK-47. Sad. There's a whole lot of those kinds of weapons out there in the wrong hands. So, as you can see, we are prioritizing your shooting, Professor."

"Yes, thanks for that," Blackstone said.

As the detective turned to leave, Blackstone asked one more question.

"I was also trying to figure something else out," he said, stopping the detective in his tracks.

"Yes?"

"Considering the fact that the Smithsonian is a federal institution, I was just wondering..." Blackstone said, letting his voice trail off.

Detective Cheski was waiting patiently with the signed form in his hand.

"I was wondering why," Blackstone continued, "a District of Columbia police detective would be placed at the head of the Smithsonian investigation, rather than someone from the FBI?"

"Actually," Cheski replied, "Special Agent Johnson from the FBI is working this jointly with me."

"Oh," is all Blackstone said to that.

CHAPTER 38

The following day Blackstone was sent down to the physical rehabilitation unit for a functional evaluation of his shoulder. The results were optimistic. In surgery only one of Blackstone's shoulder tendons had needed any repair, and that was only minor.

So, with his agreement to abide to a schedule of outpatient rehab, Blackstone talked the medical staff into releasing him the following day.

When Blackstone was returned to his hospital room after physical rehabilitation later that morning he found that Julia had come by and dropped off most of his file in Vinnie's case: a pile of brown expandable files each six inches thick and several black notebooks, which were now on the floor next to his bed.

He eased himself into bed along with one of the files and started working his way through the testimony transcripts that were contained there.

Back on the same day that Blackstone had been shot, AUSA Hartz had sent a courier with a package from the U.S. Attorney's Office over to his defense law firm. It was a complete copy of the transcripts from the testimony of the witnesses at the grand jury proceeding in which Vinnie was indicted. Blackstone had made a discovery demand for it, and Hartz had complied by sending copies of the transcripts over to him.

Blackstone knew that there was no guarantee that this would be the same evidence that would ultimately be presented at trial. But it was a good indication of the direction in which Hartz would be heading.

As he reviewed the transcripts, Blackstone discovered that at the grand jury, one of the security guards from the Smithsonian testified that on the night of the murder he had made the rounds a few hours before the estimated time of Langley's death, around 7:45 p.m., and decided to poke his head into Langley's office. He spoke briefly with the Secretary who appeared to be in no danger, and who was working at his desk.

Langley had informed the guard that he would be working late but wasn't expecting anyone.

The head of security for the Smithsonian also testified. He discussed the electronic keypad access to the side door. He described how anyone given the access code had to be logged into the computer security system. Three days before his murder, Horace Langley had logged the fact that he had given the access code to "Ms. Vinnie Archmont."

The Smithsonian security chief also said that when the door was activated after hours, it registered an entry into the central security system indicating the time and also the code identification used to access the door. He said that the night of the murder, six minutes and two seconds before Langley's estimated time of death, the side door was activated by someone using the code number that had been assigned only to Horace Langley.

And then, five minutes, ten seconds after Langley's murder, the same door was activated again, presumably by the killer, also using the same code number.

"So," Henry Hartz asked the witness during the grand jury, "according to your security logs, who would have had access to that door using Horace Langley's personal code?"

"Well," the security chief said, "Horace Langley of course."

"And, who else?"

"The only other person, according to our records, would have been the one person that Mr. Langley was recorded as having given the code."

"And that was, who?"

"Ms. Vinnie Archmont."

Another security guard testified that earlier in the day of the murder, he had logged Vinnie in at the main entrance as having visited Horace Langley.

"Was she carrying any art supplies?"

"Not that I could see," the guard testified.

"Had you seen her carry art supplies to the Castle on previous occasions?"

"Sure. I think they were things she was using in doing some sort of sculpture of Mr. Langley, as I recall."

"But on the day of the murder—no art supplies?"

"No, sir."

FBI special agent Johnson testified about his investigation at the scene of the crime when he arrived the night of the murder.

He was not asked, nor did he answer, any questions about the drinking glass on Langley's desk.

During the grand jury, agent Johnson identified the blank pad of paper left on the top of the desk, which Blackstone later had inspected and from which the Langley note was reconstructed through the imprint evidence.

"Did you," Hartz asked him, "gain access to the locked inside of Mr. Langley's desk?"

"Yes," agent Johnson pointed out. "Detective Victor Cheski, of the DC Police, was with us at the scene—he had gained access and was in the process of personally checking the contents of Secretary Langley's desk, but then he received a call from his headquarters, and he stepped away from the desk for a few minutes. So I took over and inventoried the contents myself."

"Did you find a diary or a journal of some kind?"

"Yes," Johnson replied. "A journal with the preprinted date at the top. It was Mr. Langley's personal diary. There was writing on the page that had the date of the murder at the top."

"What did it say?"

"Well, it contained a list of some meetings and other tasks that Mr. Langley had been engaged in. None that seemed to relate to the crime—except for two."

"Would you describe them for us?"

"Late in the day, which appears to correspond to Vinnie Archmont's visit with Mr. Langley, the Secretary had made a notation."

"What did it say?"

"These words—'Vinnie re: Booth—I said no.' That was all he wrote at that time."

"And after that meeting, but on that same day, was there another significant entry made by Mr. Langley?"

"Yes. Mr. Langley wrote, 'Booth work tonight.'"

Another witness testified that Horace Langley was the only one with access to the locked safe where the Booth diary pages had been kept. At the scene of the crime, the safe was open, and the folder containing the Booth diary pages had been removed, presumably by Langley so he could study the pages in his office that night.

Last, Detective Victor Cheski testified.

He revealed the results of his department's investigation, in cooperation with the FBI, into the international activities of Vinnie Archmont.

Cheski said that Vinnie had attended a seminar of the European Theosophical Society in Scotland, accompanied by "an English member of the House of Lords named Magister Dee, who was one of the speakers at the private conference."

The conclave, the detective explained, was held a year before the discovery of the missing Booth diary pages.

According to the detective, two speakers, one being Lord Dee, linked the pages of the John Wilkes Booth diary that had disappeared to the Freemasons. And according to Cheski, Lord Dee stated that in his opinion, if ever found, the missing diary pages "may prove to contain untold secrets that we Freemasons have been pursuing for centuries—if not millennia."

At the secret conference, the other speaker, a Mr. Radfield Kemper, mentioned the "need for us to take radical steps to realize the Theosophical mission that the formal hierarchy of the Freemasons has, sadly, lacked the courage to pursue. It is now up to us to take all necessary action, including force if necessary, to hasten the rise of the new esoteric elite. By seizing for ourselves our inheritance—including the artifacts that will help us finish the task—the task that those like the Knights of the Golden Circle had left undone. I agree with our brother, Lord Dee—the Booth pages may have been removed and hidden immediately after the Lincoln assassination because of the explosive and monumental secret carried within them."

Cheski testified that one witness who had attended the small conclave heard Vinnie overflowing with praise about the seminar. Even more damaging, Vinnie had been overheard praising specifically what Mr. Radfield Kemper had said.

But Blackstone's review of the transcripts was suddenly interrupted.

He looked up and saw the cheery, wrinkled face of Reverend John Lamb looking at him in the hospital room.

His uncle patted his leg and talked with him about how he was recovering. After some small talk, Reverend Lamb's face grew somber.

"Julia from your office sent me a copy of the full text of the Horace Langley note."

"Yes—you, and one other expert, have gotten copies of that note. You understand the confidentiality requirements?"

"Oh yes," he said. "Julia explained all that. No problem."

Then he said, "J.D., such a terrible thing—you being attacked like this."

"Well, they missed my heart," Blackstone said. "Though I suppose some folks might say that would be the safest place for me to have taken a bullet."

Reverend Lamb chuckled a bit at that, but shook his head.

"No, I wouldn't agree with that," his uncle said. "I think you have a very deep heart. The deeper the heart, the greater the wounds."

Then Lamb added, "I did want you to know that I have been studying that note extensively, almost around the clock, since Julia sent it over to me. But I won't go into that now. You need to get some rest. We should talk soon."

"Yes, let's do that," Blackstone said.

Reverend Lamb placed his hand on the sheet over Blackstone's leg and squeezed his big toe.

"Take care, J.D.," he said. "Watch out, lad. There are dangerous forces at play here."

"Yeah, I've noticed," Blackstone said with a half-grin.

"No," Lamb said. "I don't mean that. Of course, protect yourself, by all means—from those that can kill the body. But even more than that, watch out, J.D. Be on the alert against those that can steal the soul."

Then he gave Blackstone's toe another squeeze and walked out of the hospital room.

CHAPTER 39

Frieda was keeping the caller on hold while she paged Blackstone. It was his first day back to the law firm after his discharge from the hospital. He had dutifully reported to physical therapy early that morning. Now it was mid-morning, and he was in his cluttered office in the thick of trial preparation for Vinnie's case, trying to work effectively around the awkwardness of his shoulder sling.

"J.D.," Frieda announced on the intercom. "I've got Colin Reading on the line."

"From England?"

"Yes."

Blackstone remembered him as the personal secretary for Lord Magister Dee.

This is going to be interesting, the lawyer thought as he punched the button to take the call.

"Professor Blackstone?"

"Yes, Colin. What can I do for you?"

Blackstone looked at his watch. With the time difference, it was evening over in England.

"We have been watching your defense of Ms. Archmont with great interest."

"I am sure you have."

"Do you mind discussing the case rather briefly?"

"No," Blackstone replied. "But I will only do it with Lord Dee personally. No offense, but I don't want any middlemen."

"Absolutely. We fully understand," Reading said. "Please hold, and Lord Dee will be with you directly."

This has got to be important, to interrupt one of Lord Dee's evening séances, Blackstone said, amusing himself.

A few minutes later, Lord Dee was on the line.

"Professor Blackstone, so good to talk with you again," he began in his deep British baritone.

"I'm afraid that I will have to remind you," Blackstone began, skipping the niceties, "of the caveat that I imposed at the beginning of Vinnie's case when you paid my retainer fee. I instructed you then, and I will remind you again, that the mere fact that you are paying my bill as a third party to her case will in no way be allowed to impair my professional judgment as her defense attorney."

"Of course, that is fully understood."

"And further, that I cannot divulge any attorney-client communications that have transpired between Vinnie and me. Nor will I reveal my legal strategies or confidential work product we have uncovered in her defense."

"Agreed."

"Lastly," Blackstone continued, "I still need to belabor the obvious— if it will help Vinnie's defense and assist in proving her innocence, and if I have any credible basis at all, I won't hesitate to point the finger at you. To implicate you personally in the Smithsonian crime. Do you understand that?"

There was a pause before Dee responded.

"You have," Lord Dee said, "rather thrown down the gauntlet with that, haven't you?"

"I prefer to use a slightly more American metaphor," Blackstone countered. "I've just fired off a warning shot. A little like the battles of Lexington and Concord. Consider yourself, Lord Dee, having been put on notice."

Blackstone knew that the government prosecutor was still considering Lord Dee to be the unofficial and unindicted chief suspect, the hidden conspirator behind the murder of Horace Langley. Dee's possible complicity was clear now that Blackstone had read the grand jury testimony of detective Victor Cheski about the meeting in Scotland where Lord Dee was not only a featured speaker, but was also accompanied by Vinnie. Coupling that with Dee's unabashed obsession with the Booth diary pages, Blackstone couldn't deny the logic of such a scenario.

"Notice taken," Lord Dee responded in a chilly tone.

"So, what would you like to talk about?" Blackstone asked.

"The Horace Langley note," Lord Dee replied bluntly. "That is what I want to discuss."

"How fascinating," Blackstone began.

But Dee jumped in to continue.

"I know the judges have now ordered that the note can be distributed from you to others."

"Yes, but I'm afraid that the Court of Appeals gave me a very short list. And you're not on it."

"I would have assumed," Dee said, "that you would have had ample time to think up a creative solution to that dilemma."

"Lately, I've been very short on creativity."

"When can the contents of the Langley note be made available to me?" Dee said, persisting.

"I can't say. Maybe after the trial. Maybe never."

"I'm wondering," Lord Dee said, "how I can effectively persuade you to rethink your answer to that."

"You can't," Blackstone shot back.

"Put some thought into that, I urge you," Lord Dee said, bringing the short conversation to an end.

Then Lord Dee added something that surprised Blackstone with its audacity and clumsiness.

"Certainly hope you will be on the mend soon," Dee said coldly. "Sorry to hear about your hospital stay. Goodbye."

If that had been a threat, then Blackstone questioned why Dee would have uttered it in a telephone conversation that could have been recorded without his knowledge.

He called Frieda and Julia into his office.

"Was there any mention of my shooting incident in the newspapers. Anywhere? Radio? Internet?"

They both shook their heads.

"Which surprised me," Julia said. "I would have expected something to get out, considering the fact that you are involved in a very high-profile case right now."

"You're both sure?" he asked again.

They both nodded.

"So, how would Lord Magister Dee know that I was in the hospital?"

"Uh-oh," Frieda said, a little embarrassed.

"What does that mean?" Blackstone asked.

"I just mean that...well," Frieda began. "I think when Colin Reading called...I may have mentioned that you had just gotten back to the office from the hospital...meaning, you know, your visit to physical therapy."

Suddenly, what had started out as another piece of evidence potentially implicating Lord Dee in dark misdeeds, this time in the attack on Blackstone, fizzled out without drama or fanfare, like a glowing ember in the rain.

"From now on," Blackstone said wearily, "no personal information about me or Julia being given to anyone. *No information.*"

They both nodded.

"Now, did either of you tell anyone outside this office that I might be horseback riding on the day I got shot?"

They both assured him that they hadn't and they were certain about that.

After Frieda left Blackstone's office, he asked Julia to stay and brief him on some things.

"What do we know from Tully about Senator Collings?"

"Here is what he told me," she said looking over his notes. "First he did an inside-the-Beltway investigation into Collings. Talked to staffers, lobbyists, fellow members of Congress. News reporters. Then he headed to the Ozarks. Tully called this report in from a small town in Arkansas. He said this information was gleaned only at great personal risk, namely, and this is a direct quote—'having to endure lunches and dinners in several greasy spoons specializing in pork barbecue while trying to find out from Senator Collings's former neighbors what really makes this guy tick.'"

"Tell him I can recommend a good gastroenterologist," Blackstone cracked. "So, give me the thick on Collings's 'tick.'"

"Well, first, he says that there are no big scandals involving the Senator lurking under the surface down in his hometown."

"Fair enough. What else?"

"He did what he called a '360-degree' check on any connection between Senator Collings and all of the main players in your case, namely—Vinnie, Lord Dee, the primary law enforcement investigators, and Horace Langley. Of course you already know that Collings is on the Board of Regents of the Smithsonian, so he had a passing acquaintance with Langley, but nothing of significance."

"No ties with Lord Dee?"

"Zero," Julia said.

"So," Blackstone said, "we are still trying to find out why Collings has tried to put the heavy hand down on Henry Hartz's prosecution of this case. Why did he insist that Hartz keep the contents of the Langley note secret?"

"How about this?" Julia suggested. "Maybe just trying the preserve the good name and reputation of the Smithsonian, and, of course, all those on the Board, himself included."

"That doesn't follow," Blackstone snapped back. "Unless the Langley note shows something down and dirty was going on within the Smithsonian, and how can that be? You've read that note. Does anything in it implicate the Smithsonian in anything ugly? Furthermore, Langley's note has all the earmarks of his having simply recorded a portion of something he read in the Booth diary pages—pages authored around the time of Lincoln's assassination. How could any of that be an embarrassment to Senator Collings or the Smithsonian Institution more than a hundred and forty years after that event?"

Julia said nothing.

Blackstone's eyes flashed.

"I'm waiting," Blackstone burst out, now with his voice, out of nowhere, almost reaching a shout. "Where are the answers here?"

"Perhaps," Julia replied calmly, "you are upset by the fact that your defense of Vinnie Archmont, thus far, has not seemed to have…well… diminished or defeated the plain facts here."

"Plain facts?" Blackstone said. Now his voice was faltering a little.

"Face it," Julia said, now her voice resolute. "The evidence shows, at least in the field of probabilities, that your dear little Vinnie is probably culpable, in some way, of conspiracy to commit murder and conspiring to steal the Booth diary pages."

"Is this some kind of feminine intuition thing going on?" Blackstone sputtered.

"I'm surprised at you," she spit back. "That with all your brilliance you would resort to a base expression of chauvinism."

"Ha!" he shouted out. "You're a woman. And Vinnie, in case you haven't noticed, is very much a woman. And those two incontrovertible facts are getting in the way of your helping me solve this case. It has clouded your perspective. I desperately need a handle. And right now, I have nothing...nothing..."

"Is that really my responsibility?" she said. "To prove that your slippery, flirtatious, manipulative little sneak of a client is innocent? I don't think so."

"No, you're right," Blackstone said with a dark sense of finality. "It isn't. That's *my* job."

She walked to the door of his office to leave. But she knew there was something else Tully had told her that she had to share with Blackstone.

"One more thing," she said curtly. "Senator Collings is the president of some obscure Confederate history society."

"Does it have a name?"

"Yes. The Albert Pike Memorial Foundation."

CHAPTER 40

Blackstone was standing in front of the statue of Albert Pike in the Judiciary Square district, at 3rd and D Streets in the northwest section of downtown Washington. During the summer the trees had grown to the point of covering the top of the statue, hiding it from view unless one was standing, as Blackstone was, very close to its base.

Julia's last comment in Blackstone's office had sent him scurrying out of the office, grabbing a cab, and then getting to Pike's statue as soon as possible.

The bronze statue stood eleven feet tall, mounted on a white marble pedestal. The Italian sculptor who created the memorial had also sculpted another figure at its base—this one resembling a reclining Grecian female, who was holding the banner of the Scottish Rite of the Freemasons.

In Pike's left hand was a massive book—his monumental life's work, a book he titled *Morals and Dogma*. The huge tome set both the symbolic and philosophical basis for the ascending degrees that a Mason can aspire to. But the book also did something else. It laid out Pike's complex, opaque religious philosophy, incorporating a crazy quilt of pagan religions, Egyptology, and Gnosticism.

In his preparation of Vinnie's case, Blackstone had obtained a copy of Pike's book but had only read small portions here and there. But he was now more convinced than ever that the "AP" in the first line of Langley's note of the cryptic Booth diary entry must be referring to Albert Pike.

As he gazed up at the statue—with Pike dressed, not in the Confederate uniform he wore during the Civil War as an officer for the cause of Southern secession, but in nineteenth-century civilian long coat and trousers—Blackstone realized the anomaly of it all. Here was the only Confederate officer ever memorialized in a statue in Washington DC. And not only a Confederate, but a rebel suspected of treason and war crimes.

But there was another symbolic feature in this monument. One that seemed to reach out to Blackstone like the figures in a 3-D screen grasping directly at the startled audience.

There he was, Albert Pike, in all his philosophical pomposity, the grandiose form of a man who spent his life trying to rethink the nature of the world and the essence of its religions. Below him was the servile female figure, like a doting pagan goddess assigned to serve the great figure above on Mt. Olympus. Who was the female at the base of the statue? Was it actually supposed to represent Vinnie Ream, the beautiful sculptress of President Abraham Lincoln and the object of the much older Albert Pike's frustrated affections?

But Blackstone was thinking about his case. About the grandiose and very rich Lord Magister Dee, who fancied himself a kind of contemporary Albert Pike. Which necessarily made Vinnie Archmont the later-day Vinnie Ream. And he was also considering Senator Bo Collings, who headed up a nonprofit foundation whose mission was to preserve the memory and the reputation of Albert Pike.

Suddenly, as J.D. Blackstone was gazing at the two statues he felt a kind of shiver race down his spinal column.

Maybe, he suddenly thought to himself, *I've had the perspective all wrong. Perhaps everything needs to be reversed here.*

He stood before the statue for several more minutes, pondering his revelation.

Then he flagged down a taxi.

He climbed in the cab clumsily with his one good arm, trying not to bang the shoulder with the sling into the car door. When he was in the backseat he leaned forward and instructed the cabbie to wait a moment before leaving that spot.

Then he pulled his cell phone out and called a number.

Vinnie Archmont answered.

"Hey," he started out. "I'm hoping to cash in my rain check. What do you say?"

"Oh that would be marvelous!" she exclaimed. "So, you're coming over for dinner?"

"If you'll have me," he said. "Your place?"

"Sure…anytime…how about right now?"

He asked Vinnie if she could wait for a second. Then he gave her apartment address to the cab driver.

"Okay. I'll be there in about fifteen, twenty minutes, counting cross-town traffic," he said.

"Oh, I am so looking forward to seeing you," she said happily. "Any requests for dinner?"

"I'm not picky. Most of my meals come out of frozen boxes."

"I think I can do better than that," she said brightly.

Just then Blackstone could hear the call-waiting beep on his cell phone.

"Look," he said, "I think someone is trying to call through—can you hold for a few seconds?"

"Don't worry," Vinnie replied. "Take the call. I want to get started on dinner anyway."

Blackstone clicked on the call. It was Julia.

"Hi, it's me," Julia started out. "I left your office a little abruptly today…I know I told you about Senator Collings's involvement with that Albert Pike foundation."

"Yes, you did."

"Just thought you might want to know that Tully also gave us a copy of the foundation's charter document," Julia continued.

"Good."

"It says," she continued, "that the objective of the foundation is to, and I quote, 'Preserve and protect the name, history, and reputation of Albert Pike, statesman, philosopher, military officer, lawyer, judge, and internationally renowned scholar whose writings and insights influenced the foundations of the Scottish Rite and Freemasonry.'"

Then Julia added, "Sorry I interrupted your call. I could hear the beep and knew you were on the line with someone else."

"That's okay," he said. "I was talking to Vinnie. Just setting up a dinner date with her tonight over at her place."

There was no response from Julia on the other end of the line.

Blackstone broke the silence.

"Does it occur to you that I might really know what I'm doing here?"

"You want me to trust your judgment, is that what you're saying?"

"That's exactly what I'm saying," Blackstone replied.

"I'm sorry, but I don't—not in this case. Not when I see you walking into...oh, I don't know," she said grasping for some way to express it, "professional quicksand or something. Frankly, J.D., I don't think it's my job to try to pull you out. Which puts me in the very awkward position of trying to figure out exactly what my future is as your law partner. I don't like the feeling that I'm sitting around, waiting to watch a train wreck."

Then she added her last thought before hanging up.

"So," Julia said with a dismal sense of resignation in her voice, "maybe it's time to just walk away from the scene of the disaster before it happens."

CHAPTER 41

That night Vinnie made a simple meal of shrimp linguini Alfredo and a tossed salad. She said she made the sauce from scratch. Blackstone was impressed. Her apartment was a little cluttered, but bursting with color and art.

When Blackstone first entered her apartment with his left shoulder in a sling, she fluttered around him with a great deal of sympathy and asked him what had happened.

"Got injured while I was horseback riding," was all he said.

Vinnie nagged him incessantly about it at first, asking her lawyer to fill her in with all the details about the incident. But Blackstone refused.

"I'm embarrassed enough that I have to wear this sling," he said with a smile. "Let me suffer in peace, okay?"

After that, she finally relented. Blackstone was settled in his own mind that he was not going to share the fact that he had been shot.

Seated at the simple, glass-topped table across from Blackstone during the dinner, Vinnie was chattering excitedly and seemed to be enjoying herself.

The dinner was pleasant and relaxed. He asked her to respond to something he had read in a magazine recently, during one of his sleepless nights, about the cultural significance of the Armory Show of 1913. They chatted about that for a while.

Then Blackstone abruptly changed the subject.

"Exactly what did Horace Langley tell you," he asked, "when you met with him on the last day of his life?"

"Same thing," she said, picking up a stray shrimp off her plate with a fork, "that I told you before."

"Well, humor me," Blackstone said. "And tell me again."

She sighed dramatically and ran her fingers through her hair.

"Okay. That Lord Dee—I think I mentioned him by name so he knew I was representing a serious principal," she said. "That Magister Dee was willing to pay a huge amount of money for a preview of the Booth diary pages. He didn't even want to own the rights. Just an exclusive look at them before any of the experts were supposed to review the pages. And Magister only wanted them for a short period of time, then he would give them back to the Smithsonian."

"Did you mention a 'rental fee,' a sum of money that Lord Dee was willing to pay?"

"I said it was in the seven figures. I'm sure that's the phrase I used."

"Who was to receive the money—the Smithsonian, or Horace Lang-. ley personally?"

Vinnie smiled at that.

"That's a little touchy."

"So you were talking about paying Langley directly. Under the table, is that it?" Blackstone asked.

"Not in so many words."

"But that is the essence of what you were proposing?"

"I guess so," she said.

Blackstone thought on that for a moment.

"So, in other words," he continued, "your discussion was about money being paid and money received. If Langley would have negotiated a figure with you or with Dee, then the plan was that no one on the Board of Regents or the administration of the Smithsonian would have to have known about it?"

"I suppose that's right," she said.

"Obviously," Blackstone said, boring in, "if the plan was to pay the money to the Smithsonian Institution, on the other hand, then you—or at least certainly Lord Dee—obviously understood that Langley would have had to clear that with the board, presumably, and that would have complicated the deal exponentially."

"Sure, I guess so," she said.

"Interesting," he said.

"What does this do to my case?"

"It has to do with the Fifth Amendment," Blackstone said.

Vinnie had a puzzled look on her face.

"What I mean is this," Blackstone continued, putting down his silverware and pushing away his plate. "You have a right not to testify under the Fifth Amendment. Deciding whether an indicted defendant will waive that right and choose to testify at trial is probably one of the most important strategic steps in a criminal case."

"Who decides?"

"You and I do, Vinnie. I counsel you. I give my very strong recommendation. But ultimately I have to abide by your decision."

"And your recommendation is, what?"

"We'll reserve that until the very last moment," Blackstone replied. "Sometimes even during the trial itself. We can hold back from deciding until after the prosecution has presented its case, even through your defense case. Up to the point where all of our other defense evidence had been presented. But sometime before the defense rests its case, if you are going to testify, that's the last chance…the last train out of the station."

Vinnie was pondering what she had just been told. Then she asked another question.

"But what problem would there be in my testifying on my own behalf?"

"Several potential problems," Blackstone replied. "When you testify, you have to do it truthfully. All of what you just told me, about your offering Langley under-the-table money to give Lord Dee a preview of the Booth diary pages, that will all come out. That is not going to make you look good in front of the jury. Beyond that, much of what you would say will corroborate the government's case against you. You will admit that Langley gave you the security door code. That you tried to get your hands on the diary. Langley refused. His private journal said that he was planning on reviewing the diary pages that same night. Did Langley tell you that?"

"He said he was working late that night…that I could come by if I wanted to…after hours…I think he may have said something about working on the Booth thing, I'm not sure."

"So, right there," Blackstone snapped, "you put another bullet in the prosecution's gun. The only two things you will really be able to deny are these: You would testify that you were not part of any plan to kill Langley or steal the diary, and that you didn't give the code to anyone else, correct?"

"Right. I didn't. Absolutely not," she said adamantly.

"Do you know how you might have inadvertently let the access code get into someone else's hands?"

"I wouldn't have the faintest idea."

Then she thought of something, and narrowed her eyes and asked Blackstone another question.

"You said there were several problems with my testifying. You explained how I might end up actually helping prove the prosecution's case. What are the other problems?"

"If you testify, but you lie, even if you get acquitted of the Smithsonian crime, the government can come after you again for criminal perjury."

"Why do you think I would lie?" she said, pleading.

"People who face a life sentence, or the death penalty, or even just a few years in prison—they get scared," Blackstone said, almost nonchalantly. "They think they can beat the system with a well-contrived story. Or they panic. Lots of reasons. And sometimes a defendant lies because telling the truth would require a confession—they lie because they are guilty and they know it."

Vinnie fell silent. Blackstone could tell that his client was starting to face up to the tough terrain ahead of her at trial.

"Look," Blackstone said, "there's also a procedural matter we need to talk about."

She gave him a wide-eyed deer-in-the-headlights look.

"Nothing nerve-racking," he said, trying to reassure her. "Just a pre-trial conference with the trial judge. The lawyers are going to discuss some preliminary details about the trial and update the court. I need to have you there."

"I really don't want to go."

"Any good reason for that?"

"Nothing that you would understand, I'm afraid."

"Try me."

"You keep saying that I am the client and you have to do my bidding and all of that—well, here it is—I am instructing you to handle this without me. Just tell me what's discussed at the court hearing."

"I'm still waiting for an explanation as to why you won't show up."

"*Fear*—how about that for a reason?" she blurted out. "J.D., just think about that one for a second. I come in acting all worried and frightened and panicky...the prosecutor takes one look at me and is going to be able to read it all over my face...is that going to help my case? For the government lawyer to know I'm scared to death of this trial?"

"I can understand that," Blackstone said. "But I have two responses. First, you are going to be required to be physically present at your trial. That's not an option. So how are you going to handle that? Second, because of that, you might as well start getting psychologically prepared. One way to do that is by going into the courtroom for the pretrial. Get used to the layout of the place, and some of the court personnel. Getting a comfort level with the exterior stuff of the environment where the trial is going to be conducted. That's a first step. Then you and I can start talking about your fears. Dealing with them directly. If you need a professional counselor to help you with that process, I can recommend someone."

"You mean a shrink?"

"Yes."

"No, thanks," she said with a kind of nervous laugh. "J.D., I've made it clear. I don't want to be at the pretrial...you be there for me. That's why you're my lawyer. Is there something I need to sign to make sure I don't have to be there and you can appear for me?"

"Interesting that you should mention it," Blackstone said. "Yes, there is. Stop by the office tomorrow. I will have a waiver form ready for you to sign."

"Good," she said. "Now, I don't mean to be rude, but I've got to run to the bathroom quick," she said. "Don't bother cleaning up. I want to do that. You just stay put."

Then she rose and disappeared around the corner.

Blackstone got up and started meandering around the room, studying the art on the walls, most of it French impressionist, and scanning the magazines on the table and the books in her bookcase. Then he walked over to a closet that was half open.

It was a coat closet. There were a few jackets hanging there. On the floor was a stack of magazines.

He reached down with his good right arm and picked up the magazine on the top. It was *Architectural Digest*. The next one was *ArtCentric*. The one after that was an issue of *National Geographic* with one of the cover headlines dealing with ancient busts of Assyrian kings. He flipped through the pile of miscellaneous magazines, getting a closer glimpse at Vinnie's interests.

Until he was almost at the bottom of the stack. That is when he came across an anomaly.

It was a several-year-old issue of *Crime Journal*. The cover story was the Virginia-Maryland-DC sniper killings of 2002, involving Lee Boyd Malvo and John Allen Muhammad.

Blackstone flipped the magazine over to check out the mailing label. Then he tossed it down and placed the rest of the stack of magazines on top of it.

As he walked out of the closet he saw Vinnie rounding the corner, heading into the little dining room where they had been eating.

"What are you trying to do, tidy up my messy apartment?" she yelled out as she picked up the dishes from the table.

"No, just snooping around to find out where the dead bodies are buried," he countered with a smile.

"Ooh, that's a little macabre, even for you, J.D."

Blackstone strolled back to the table, where she had laid a clean dessert plate.

"Come on, sit down," she said cajoling. "I'm serving coconut cream pie. Nothing fancy. Just the classic dessert."

While he was waiting to be served he said, "I've got a question for you."

"Yes?"

"What's the most memorable sculpture you ever did?"

"Hmm, that's a tough one," she said. "Why do you ask?"

"Just curious."

"Well, I think that Horace Langley, actually, would have been a great sculpting experience...he had an interesting face...but I never got to finish it, obviously."

Then she thought more on it.

"There was another one."

Blackstone was waiting.

"When those two guys, can't recall their names...the 'Beltway snipers,' they were called. When they gunned down all those poor people like that in Virginia, and Maryland, and some in DC, I think too... anyway, a community group later came to me and suggested maybe I could do a sculpting—a kind of memorial for the victims. But it never got off the ground."

Blackstone smiled and nodded. He had wondered about the magazine in the closet. But once again, Vinnie had the right answer. So why did he keep wrestling with doubts about her?

"Got to ask you something else," he said.

"Shoot."

"I was reading in the grand jury testimony about your attending that Theosophy conference in Scotland with Lord Dee."

"Oh, that," she groaned. "Very weird. And yet interesting, I have to admit. I just found the other presenters were not in the same league as Magister Dee. And a few were quite bizarre. A little like attending a *Star Trek* convention."

She placed a large slice of cream pie on his plate.

"The grand jury evidence," Blackstone said, looking around for a fork or spoon on the table but not finding one, "indicated you were very enthusiastic about the conference. You loved the whole thing. And you praised one speaker in particular—a guy by the name of Radfield Kemper. He was talking about using force and violence if necessary to hasten the—I think he called it the 'esoteric elite.' Does any of that ring a bell?"

"Not really," she said from the kitchen where she was fetching some clean silverware.

In a moment she was back in the dining room, standing next to Blackstone. She placed her fork down at her plate, but kept his fork in her hand.

"Look, you have to know something about me," she said, looking down at him. "I can get enthusiastic about things...over the top even... to please people around me. I wanted to show Magister that I was into this stuff. And in a way I kind of was. I think I may have said some things to make it sound like I was all gung-ho. But that was for Magister's benefit, I think."

Then Vinnie, still standing next to Blackstone, took the fork in her hand, sliced into the pie on his plate, and picked up a piece on the end of the fork. She put it into Blackstone's mouth.

There was a small drop of cream pie that lingered on his lip.

Vinnie bent down and kissed it off his lips with hers.

"I'm sure you realize I want you," she said. "I'm not very good at keeping a secret."

But then she straightened up and with a quick change of attitude and tone of voice, she explained herself.

"But I've decided to be a good girl tonight. I'm not going to ask you to sleep over. I think you still need a little bit of space."

"Oh?" he said taking a bite of his own from the pie on his plate.

"Yes. Maybe it's losing Marilyn, your wife. Even though it's been—what?—two years or more from what I know about it. Anyway, with the trial and everything coming up, I just thought it would be better, you know, if you slept in your own bed tonight...unless...well...unless you really wanted to stay with me tonight."

"I'm really not sure what you're saying," Blackstone said.

"To tell you the truth," Vinnie said, running a hand through her curled locks, "I really don't know what I'm saying."

Blackstone swallowed the bit of pie, wiped his mouth with the napkin, and stood up.

"Then, in that event," he announced with a smile, "I'll take my leave. Until you can figure out what you're saying, or not saying."

Blackstone was at the door when Vinnie spoke to him one last time.

"Darling," she said. "When can we do this again?"

"I'll call you," he said, matter-of-factly. "We have a criminal trial to prepare for."

CHAPTER 42

Two days later, in the chambers of U.S. District Judge Robert Templeton, J.D. Blackstone was seated in one of the large red-leather chairs across from the judge's expansive mahogany desk. Julia, as co-counsel, was seated next to him.

On the other side, also facing the judge, was Henry Hartz, along with another assistant federal prosecutor.

In two chairs in the far corner of the room were FBI special agent Johnson and DC Detective Victor Cheski.

It was Blackstone's first day with his shoulder out of the sling. It was stiff, but he tried not to show it.

"Client not here?" the judge said with a measure of dissatisfaction.

"No, Your Honor," Blackstone replied. "My client has signed a waiver. I've filed it with the clerk."

"Yes, I know," the judge said, still perturbed. "I've read it. But I can't imagine a client in a death penalty case just choosing not to show up. Can you?"

"I'm not in a position, Your Honor, to detail our attorney-client conversations."

"I'm not asking you to," the judge snapped. "But for heaven's sake, Blackstone. Can't you control your client? Tell her she needs to be here. I don't want some post-conviction motion being filed—if she's convicted, I mean—arguing that she should have been advised of this or that in the pretrial conference."

"That's the purpose of a waiver," Blackstone said with a small measure of condescension. "Waiver, being defined as the informed, voluntary, and deliberate relinquishment of a known right."

"Don't play law school with me," the judge snapped.

"Mr. Blackstone," Hartz said, interjecting with disdain in his voice. "Are you sure she is still in the jurisdiction? Has she fled from the country, perhaps? Jumped bail?"

"You'd love that, wouldn't you, Henry?" Blackstone shot back. "That would do a nice job of bolstering your sagging little case."

"Alright, that's enough," Judge Templeton barked. "Let's get on with the business here."

"Henry," the judge said, turning to the prosecutor, "have you provided all the necessary discovery to Professor Blackstone?"

"We have, Your Honor."

"Judge," Blackstone interjected. "I still have two requests outstanding."

"Which are?" Henry Hartz snapped.

"Well, first," Blackstone said, "I asked for discovery relating to the drinking glass that the FBI 302 report of Agent Johnson says was on the victim's desk."

"You have a copy of the crime lab report," Hartz shot back. "There were no fingerprints on that glass. So the glass is obviously irrelevant. What's your complaint?"

"I would like to know where the glass went," Blackstone said.

With that, Blackstone turned and looked behind him. In the far corner of the room, FBI agent Johnson was stone-faced. Next to him, Detective Cheski has a pleasant smile on his face.

"The glass is obviously in the evidence inventory," Hartz said with a twisted smirk.

"Not according to your inventory sheet," Blackstone replied. "It's not listed."

"You must have been looking at the wrong evidence inventory sheet."

"Henry," the judge said. "I want you to give an accounting of this drinking glass issue in forty-eight hours. In writing. To the court, and a copy to defense counsel. Okay, next?"

"My demand for exculpatory evidence," Blackstone announced.

"There is no exculpatory evidence in this case," Hartz announced brazenly. "Your Honor, this is one of the few cases I can remember where I couldn't disclose *any* exculpatory evidence to the defense. The more we dig, the more incriminating evidence we find against the defendant, Vinnie Archmont. Rest assured, Judge, if we come across any evidence that tends to support in any way the innocence of the defendant, we will be sure and produce it to Mr. Blackstone."

"Alright, next?" the judge said.

"The government's witness list," Blackstone continued. "I recognize every one of the witnesses on their list because they all testified in the grand jury—all, that is, except one."

Then he lifted up the government's witness list and tapped a name on the list with his pen.

"Who is this woman Shelly Hollsaker?"

Henry Hartz was silent. Then he explained.

"She is the person who overheard a statement made by your client."

"I know that," Blackstone volleyed back. "It says that right here on your witness list. I want to know *who this gal is*—stop playing games here, Henry."

"She's a prisoner," Henry said. "In the lockup. She shared a cell with your client after her arrest."

"And you don't think the fact that a prosecution witness just happens to be a federal prisoner is exculpatory?" Blackstone said, his voice simmering with anger.

"Gentlemen," the judge interjected. "Please. Actually, Henry, your description of the evidence you intend to elicit from Ms. Hollsaker is a little scant. Please submit a more exhaustive description of what she is going to testify to. In writing. Within forty-eight hours. Okay?"

"Will be glad to," Hartz said with a smile.

"One more thing," the judge said. "The media has now begun to file motions asking that the trial be televised. I don't like cameras in my courtroom. You both know that. And the Court of Appeals has given us guidance on that too. So, before I render my decision on those requests, where do you stand?"

"The government is taking no position on that issue," Hartz announced.

"The defense objects to cameras," Blackstone said. "I think that juries can do strange things when they know they are being filmed. This is a capital murder case, not a TV reality show."

"There, you and I agree," the judge said. "Okay. I'll be releasing my decision on that issue pretty soon. Anything else?"

Both attorneys shook their heads.

Judge Templeton dismissed them all.

Out in the corridor, on the way to the parking lot, Blackstone started bulleting out assignments for Julia.

"First thing," he said, "I want you to do a complete public record check on Vinnie. All her vital statistics. Birth certificate. Verification of schooling. Landlord-tenant leases for her apartment as well as her art studio. Get a criminal background check, any civil lawsuit filing with her name on it, and a credit check. We have to screen her with a fine mesh. Anything negative in her background that we don't know about, the government will, and Henry Hartz will destroy her with it if she testifies. And, of course, there is another reason for getting all of that together."

Blackstone was now rolling at a fast walk, and Julia was having a hard time keeping up in her high heels.

"Yes, I realize," she said, "why else we need it. For the death-penalty phase of the case if the government gets a conviction. I've been accumulating some of that information already. I'll get the rest."

"Second," Blackstone continued, "I want you and Jason to schedule a mock cross-examination of our client," he said. "Set up the video camera in the office. Get Vinnie on a DVD so I can study it. I want you to really lay into her. I have a feeling that won't be hard for you," he said, laughing. "I need to assess how she is going to hold up at trial if we decide to have her testify in her own defense. Then I'll schedule my own additional testimony run-throughs with her after that."

Julia was still walking next to him and giving him a polite but restrained nod as he talked.

Then she slowed down the pace to a halt. Blackstone realized it, and he stopped and turned around in the parking lot to face her.

That's when she spoke up.

"I told you the other day that I was going to be making a decision... about continuing on with your office."

"It's not my office," he blurted out. "It's *our firm*. We're partners."

"Funny," she said. "It never feels that way. Well, the point is this. I will help you through this Vinnie Archmont trial. That's the least I can do for my legal mentor. But that's it. I've pretty well decided that after the trial is over, I'm leaving the firm."

"You're kidding."

"How can you doubt it—that I'm serious on this?" she said in disbelief. "I've spelled it out for you. I'm tired of being stepped on, and walked over, and—"

"Taken for granted?"

"Yes."

"And not given ample professional encouragement?"

"Exactly."

"And romantically jilted?"

Julia gave an open-mouthed gasp of exasperation.

"The truth is," Blackstone said, "you and I had a very…good thing going, at least for a while…and then something happened. And it ended. I'm not sure why."

"You ended it," she said. "That's what happened. And like a fool I stayed on at the firm with you, even after the fires of romance had all died out."

"You're no fool, Julia. You're bright, talented, and beautiful. All that captivated me. But then…well, anyway, that doesn't mean we can't continue on as partners," Blackstone said.

Julia stopped and lowered her head as she decided to select her words carefully.

"My decision is not emotional, J.D. It is purely professional. I am giving you notice."

Julia turned and clip-clopped in her high heels over to her car where she beeped the door open, tossed her briefcase onto the passenger seat, and climbed in the driver's side.

CHAPTER 43

When Blackstone was back at the law firm after the court appearance in Vinnie's case, the first thing he did was to sit down in
front of the computer in his office and log onto the United States Senate
Web site.

He had to check out something that had been nagging him for a
while. About Senator Bo Collings's motivations. He needed to come to
a conclusion, somehow, about the Arkansas senator's involvement in the
background of Vinnie's prosecution, where he had been like a character
in a theatrical play lurking behind a thin, scrim curtain. Was Collings's
meddling in the case through his contacts with Henry Hartz simply a
matter of defending his own self-interests? Or was there something much
more sinister at play?

In Blackstone's criminal practice he had learned to spend a great deal
of time ruminating on the varieties and mysteries of human motivation.
His psychological training came in handy. All crimes, and complicities,
were committed for reasons, he had concluded. Even those that didn't
seem to fit the premeditated mold—the random, senseless acts that probably terrified the public the most—also had their reasons. Just not the
typical ones.

But he had formulated a theory on the senator's heightened interest in
Vinnie's case and in the Langley note. Now he had to determine whether
there was any real data to back it up.

On the Senate Web site he typed in a few key words and did a search of pending legislation. He scrolled down a few entries. And then it was there, right in front of him on his computer screen:

Senate Resolution 217

Suddenly, Blackstone was aware of someone behind him.

He turned around. It was Jason, the paralegal, standing in the doorway of his office.

"Professor Blackstone," he said. "I was working on the list of potential witnesses you gave me for the Vinnie Archmont case. You know, so I could help you get the subpoenas ready. But I had one really big question."

"Yes?"

"You got a name on this list...I don't know exactly what the deal is with this one...but Julia—uh, I mean Ms. Robins—told me there is a real serious problem with him."

"You're talking about Senator Collings?"

"Right. That's the one."

"Don't issue his subpoena yet," Blackstone said. "I was just working on that issue."

Jason nodded and disappeared.

Blackstone knew what he had to do. It was a gambit with a risk. He was virtually certain he was right. But he had to test his hypothesis.

He dialed the number.

"Judiciary Committee," the person at the other end said.

"I'm looking for Billy Baxter," Blackstone said, with a sly smile. "I need to talk with him. This is Professor Blackstone. Tell him I'm calling with the results of his bar exam...and it doesn't look good."

After a few minutes Baxter picked up and announced himself in an unamused monotone. Blackstone jumped into the deep end.

"Billy, this is J.D. Blackstone calling," he started out. "Let's forget the bad blood, shall we? I know you are Senator Collings's guy over there at Judiciary. You've obviously got future career plans. Department of Justice? Office of White House Legal Counsel? Or maybe a big law firm or lobbying shop down on K Street. Whatever it is, I really don't think you want me on your enemies list, do you?"

"What is your point, Professor?"

"I would like to avoid serving the good senator with a subpoena for the trial of Vinnie Archmont," Blackstone began. "Because if I do serve him—well, I recall all your threats about what would happen if I do—and we all know what 'mutually assured destruction' means. Thermonuclear war—I'm speaking metaphorically, of course—ruins everybody's day. So here is what I am proposing. I need to meet with the senator right away. Just a short conversation. Off the record. Then I can refrain from bringing him into the middle of this sordid criminal trial. How about it?"

"I doubt," Baxter said, "that the senator wants to ever see you again. For any purpose."

"Then tell him that I want to discuss Senate Resolution 217. Tell him that."

Then Blackstone added, "And when his office calls me back indicating that the senator will meet with me, you need to know I will only be here in the office for another hour or so."

Less than an hour later, Blackstone received a call from Senator Collings's scheduler.

She said that it was very fortunate that there were no votes on the floor of the Senate that day, and that the senator "had an unexpected opening in his schedule" and would like to meet with him in two hours.

"Where?" Blackstone asked.

The scheduler gave him the address. Then she added, "Very top deck."

Very strange, Blackstone thought to himself when he pieced together the site of the meeting. But then again, he realized that this was a very strange case he was defending.

Two hours later, Blackstone drove his black Maserati cross-town to Union Station, in the heart of the government landscape of Washington. He motored up the winding ramp to the parking area and then headed up a few flights to the very top. Once there, he headed over to the far corner and parked his car. Now that it was rush hour, it was almost barren of any other cars.

He climbed out of the Maserati and surveyed the city. From there he could see, off in the distance, the Capitol dome, with its top light burning, and in another direction, the outline of the Lincoln Monument in the waning light that would soon turn to dusk.

Blackstone glanced at his watch. He was right on time. But Senator Collings wasn't. It didn't surprise him. Now the question was whether Collings was going to show at all.

After strolling around his car for a while, Blackstone called his office from his cell phone. No, Frieda said, there had been no messages from Senator Collings's office regarding a change in the meeting. Then he checked his BlackBerry. No e-mails from Collings's office.

Twenty minutes went by. He checked his cell phone one more time to make sure the ringer was on. But his ringer was on full volume. And no calls.

Five more minutes went by.

Then he heard something. The sound of a car coming up the ramp.

A large black limo appeared, slowly prowling onto the top deck. It made its way over to Blackstone and stopped.

The door swung open.

Senator Bo Collings squeezed his considerable girth out of the limo and strode directly over to Blackstone. He had stripped his coat off, and he was in his shirtsleeves.

"Over here," Collings said, motioning to the concrete guard rail at the perimeter of the upper deck, away from Blackstone's car.

When they positioned themselves there, Collings crossed his arms and raised a questioning eyebrow.

"Nice location," Blackstone remarked. "Very clandestine. So, does this mean you're 'Deep Throat'? Which would make me—let's see—was it Woodward or Bernstein?"

"You can knock off the smart-aleck banter," Collings snapped, "and cut to the chase. You wanted this meeting. So talk."

"I am willing to forgo serving you with a subpoena. But I need some information."

"I'm listening."

"Yes or no—you tried to intervene in the Vinnie Archmont case because you didn't want certain information hitting the newspapers— like the contents of the Horace Langley note. Correct?"

"I would never 'intervene' in an ongoing criminal prosecution,

Professor. That wouldn't be right. You know that." Collings was smiling.

"You talked to Henry Hartz."

"I talk to a lot of people."

"You didn't want the Langley note going public if you could help it because you had been told by Hartz—I am assuming it was him, he probably had his own expert try to decipher that note—that the 'AP' in the first line of the note could well have referred to Albert Pike, your Confederate hero. And if that was right, then Pike might be implicated in the Lincoln assassination because his initials had appeared in the diary pages of John Wilkes Booth. Am I getting warmer now?"

"You spin a nice story."

"Here's the sequel," Blackstone said. "Senate Resolution 217, filed by several members of the Congressional Black Caucus. Asking that the statue of Albert Pike which now sits in Judiciary Square be immediately removed, on the grounds that Pike was a 'founding member of the Ku Klux Klan.'"

"Those allegations are spurious," Collings sputtered. "They come up every now and then. No one has ever proven that connection between Pike and the KKK."

"Perhaps," Blackstone said. "But considering your position as the head of the nonprofit foundation vested with protecting Albert Pike's memory and reputation, you have a lot to lose if that resolution gets passed and the current administration and the Department of the Interior are pressured into removing his statue. After all, your home state of Arkansas has treated the guy like a nineteenth-century rock star for years. So, when the case of Vinnie Archmont threatened to expose the possibility that Pike might not only be a racist, but also a potential conspirator in the assassination of Lincoln—well, in this town, the fact that you've been Albert Pike's biggest cheerleader would not exactly guarantee that you'd get a street named after you."

Senator Collings glanced over at the idling limo, and then he cast his eyes over the city of Washington DC.

After a moment he turned back to Blackstone and asked a question.

"What is it that you want?"

"Let's start with what *you* want," Blackstone said. "You want to keep a lid on the fact that the 'AP' in the Langley note might have been Albert Pike."

"How can you guarantee it won't surface in the trial?"

"I don't think Hartz intends to go into that," Blackstone replied. "It doesn't fit into his theory of the case. You ought to know that."

"And you? Are you willing to jeopardize your own client's defense by staying away from that part of the evidence?" Collings retorted, his voice dripping with cynicism.

"I don't see any advantage to my client's case for us to postulate about who the 'AP' was or wasn't—from the standpoint of the defense, dragging Pike into the case would be a mistake. It creates too many red herrings. Too much possibility of a jury backlash."

"But why would I be interested in keeping that out of the Vinnie Archmont trial," Collings said, "when, after the trial is over, the evidence would eventually be made public anyway?"

"Because," Blackstone said confidently, "the Booth diary is now missing again since Langley's murder. And the diary was the best evidence of whether there really was an 'AP' mentioned by Booth. All we have now is a dead man's note, written as he was reading the Booth diary pages—a note now buried in a prosecutor's file. Eventually, a reporter is going to make a Freedom of Information request. Maybe the note would get released. But that would be long after Senate Resolution 217 blows over and the political heat on you cools off. And as for me, Senator, remember, the Court of Appeals didn't give me permission to share the Langley note with the public at large."

"But, Professor Blackstone," Collings said with a sly grin. "You shared part of the first line of the Langley note with me right here—right now. That violates the court order, doesn't it?"

"Not if you already knew what the first line of that note said—and I am betting that Henry Hartz, deferring to your leadership in the Senate Judiciary Committee and your position on the Smithsonian Board of Regents, had let you read the note back at the beginning of this case. Isn't that right, Senator?"

Collings took a deep breath, then exhaled.

"You still haven't told me what you want," Senator Collings asked.

"I need information," Blackstone said. There was nothing sarcastic or flippant in his voice now. Only a sense of urgency. "You know something about this case. I know you do. You need to let me in. Into what you know. Anything."

Collings glanced at his watch. Then he announced, "Gotta go."

The senator turned to stroll back to the limo. But after he took a few steps, he stopped and turned to face Blackstone.

"Funny thing," Senator Collings said. "About Henry Hartz's choice of his lead investigator in the Smithsonian murder case. By all accounts it should have been FBI agent Johnson. Highly decorated federal agent. Top of his class. Most promising African-American FBI field agent in the country. Plus, the Smithsonian is a federal institution. But Hartz chose a District of Columbia detective to lead the investigation instead. Something about who was, or was not, responsible for a certain piece of evidence at the scene of the crime...a *drinking glass,* as I recall."

Then, as Senator Bo Collings strode back to the limo, he paused at the open door. Over his shoulder he called back to Blackstone.

"I'm so sorry that you and I couldn't meet, and that I didn't have this conversation with you. Good day, Professor Blackstone."

CHAPTER 44

The following day, Vinnie Archmont came in to the law office for her mock cross-examination. Blackstone buried himself in his own office with the door closed while it was going on.

Julia had Vinnie sequestered in the conference room for nearly six hours, interrogating her the way that Henry Hartz was likely to do at the trial. Jason ran the video camera.

When Vinnie finally emerged from the conference room at the end of the day she had a shell-shocked look on her face.

Frieda, under instructions from Blackstone, intercepted her.

"Professor Blackstone would like to meet with you for a few moments in his office."

Then the office secretary led her back to Blackstone's office.

Vinnie plunked down on the chair across from his desk.

"You look frazzled," he said.

"That's an understatement," she said.

Then she added, "I was just thinking, coming into your office just now...how I came in and sat in this very same chair in the very beginning of all of this—when the prosecutor sent me that target letter."

"You didn't plan on this going this far, did you?"

"Well," she said. "Neither did you, as I recall."

Blackstone winced a bit.

"Point taken. Well, it is what it is," Blackstone said. "So, let's deal with it."

Then he picked up the hard copy of an e-mail that Henry Hartz had sent him that day, complying with one of Judge Templeton's directives.

"I received an e-mail," he said in a serious tone, "from the prosecution, about one of the witnesses they are going to call at your trial. Woman named Shelly Hollsaker. Does that ring a bell?"

Vinnie shook her head, but she could tell that Blackstone was concerned about this particular witness.

"She's the woman who shared a cell with you in the detention center right after you were arrested," Blackstone said.

Then the lights went on.

"Oh, yes," she said. "I didn't click with her name."

"Did you make a telephone call when you were with her?"

"We were in this huge room, they called it a 'holding cell.' This woman, Shelly, was there, too."

"What'd she look like?" he asked.

"Middle-aged. Tall."

"Race?"

"White. She had glasses. Frizzy hair."

"Do you know why she was there?" Blackstone asked.

"I don't know what she was being charged with, no. There was a telephone at the far end of the room. They said I could make a call out."

"So you did."

"Right. I did," she said. She saw Blackstone's brow furrowed. Then she added, "Was that wrong for me to do that?"

But Blackstone didn't answer. Instead, he kept following the fox hunt he had started. He glanced down at the e-mail, then asked Vinnie the next question.

"Exactly how many phone calls did they let you make?"

"They said I could make several if I wanted. Which surprised me. I had already heard, you know, on TV and stuff, that you get one phone call when you're arrested. I'd never been arrested before, so I really didn't know."

"It is unusual for the feds to give you that kind of accommodation," he said. "They usually go by the book. Which makes me wonder."

"What?"

"Whether this was a setup," Blackstone said. "After all, they put you in the cell with a repeat offender. Shelly Hollsaker had a prior record. The government just provided me with a copy of her conviction record in their e-mail as part of their discovery disclosure. So, she had something to gain by being a snitch. And the government had a lot to gain by encouraging you to talk in front of her. And Vinnie, you had a lot to lose by making your phone calls under those circumstances."

Vinnie buried her face in her hands for a few seconds, then took her hands away and looked up at Blackstone.

"So, what now?"

"You have to be absolutely clear and honest with me," Blackstone said.

"Of course I will."

"How many phone calls did you make?"

She thought for a moment.

"Two. I made two calls."

"One was to me, to my private, unlisted number at my condo," Blackstone said. "It went to voice mail."

"Right. I was very upset."

"I have always wondered," he said. "How did you get my unlisted number?"

"Well," she said with a smile, "Magister gave it to me."

"How did he get it?"

"Oh, I'm not sure. He says his security people have all kinds of access to information that regular people can't get. And I know he has channels with the British government too, being in the House of Lords, so he can get private information that way. He gave it to me after you and I had our first office conference. He thought I might need it."

"So," Blackstone said, "one call was to my voice mail. Who was the other call to?"

"It was...a call to Magister."

"They let you make an international call to Lord Dee?" Blackstone said incredulously.

"It was an international collect call. But yes, they let me make it."

"Anyone else?" he said.

"No. That's it."

"Are you sure?" Blackstone said. His voice was harsh.

"J.D., darling, yes. I'm telling you the truth. Why?"

"Shelly Hollsaker is telling the government that you made three calls. Not two. But three."

"That's a lie," Vinnie said with a shocked look on her face.

"Shelly is telling the government that one call was when you were crying about being arrested, and she said it sounded like it was a call to your lawyer."

"That's the one I left on your voice mail."

"Hollsaker then says that there was another call that was very involved, that you asked for an international operator, and then you were talking about getting a lawyer, and being arrested, and needing some money, and saying you really appreciated his friendship."

"That was my call to Magister Dee."

"Then there was this call," Blackstone said, pausing and looking down at the e-mail he had received from Henry Hartz.

"This call," Blackstone said, now speaking very slowly and deliberately, "according to Shelly Hollsaker, was made by you first, before the other calls. In that telephone conversation, this is what Hollsaker says in her statement to the feds:

> I heard her call someone first. She was really angry and upset. Not crying. Just really angry. Here is what she said: "I thought you told me I was not going to be a suspect. You promised me I wouldn't be tied-in to this. What happened?" Then there was a pause, like she was listening to someone on the other end talking. Then she said, "Why did he do that? Are you sure it was Langley's computer, and not someone else's?"

Vinnie had her lips parted just slightly, as if frozen in the split second before forming the words to say.

Then she responded.

"That—what you just read—all of that is a pack of lies. You said yourself this Shelly person is a previously convicted woman with a record. She would say anything to get a break from the cops. Right?"

"Did you make three calls?"

"I told you already, no. Absolutely not," Vinnie said, her face now flashing with anger.

"Did you make any of those statements I just read out to you—'I thought you told me I was not going to be a suspect. You promised me I wouldn't be tied in to this. What happened?' Did you say that...or anything even remotely close to that?"

"No!"

"Did you say this—'Why did he do that? Are you sure it was Langley's computer, and not someone else's?' "

"No, I did not!" she said vehemently.

"Well," Blackstone said quietly. "We have our work cut out for us. I'm not going to minimize this. We have major damage control ahead of us. Up to now their case against you was very circumstantial and thin. They've obviously been sitting on this witness from the very beginning. She could be devastating to your case."

"You'll be able to destroy that witness, Shelly Hollsaker. Right?" she said. "You're brilliant, J.D. You will destroy her in court?"

"I need ammunition to do that," he said calmly. "You can provide that."

"How? Just tell me what to do."

"You need to think back very hard to that day in the detention cell. To everything that went on. What you might have said that this Shelly Hollsaker might have misconstrued. And what you talked to Shelly about when the two of you were together."

"I can tell you one thing," she said. "I didn't say a word to her. I was scared to death. Why would I want to talk to another prisoner?"

Blackstone nodded. Then he gave her reassurance that her case was the primary and single focus of his office and that they were going to pull out all the stops to defend her.

After she left, Blackstone dialed the U.S. Attorney's Office and asked to speak to Henry Hartz.

When Hartz answered the call, he asked whether Blackstone had received his e-mail about Shelly Hollsaker.

"I did. That's why I'm calling," Blackstone said. "One thing I need to know. Where's the surveillance audio of Vinnie's telephone conversations?"

"What makes you think that we record phone calls of prisoners?" he barked back.

"Come on, Henry. *Please,*" Blackstone said. "Don't insult my intelligence. You'll say it's purely for jail security. Okay. Fine. I'll buy that. Just tell me when I can get a copy."

"Truth is," Hartz said, "I've already checked into that. They tell me there was no audio for that time."

"Why not?"

"I'm checking into that."

"How convenient!" Blackstone barked back. "So the only evidence to those calls, outside of my client, is this Shelly Hollsaker. What kind of a deal did you cut with her?"

"No deal. Just what I said in the e-mail," Hartz said. "If she testifies truthfully at Vinnie's trial, and if we think she gave us substantial assistance in the case, we'll advise the sentencing judge in her insurance fraud case and the court can take that into consideration. No other promises."

"I'm hoping I don't have to ask the court," Blackstone said, "to order you to produce an explanation about the missing audio of the telephone calls."

"That won't be necessary," Hartz said. "As soon as I find out what the story is, I will let you know in writing. Frankly, I would like to know myself what happened."

"I'm counting on that," Blackstone said.

"Oh, and one other thing," Hartz added. "About Shelly Hollsaker."

"Yes?"

"She passed a polygraph test in our office."

"And some people with severe personality disorders, like sociopaths," Blackstone said, pulling that one out of the hat, "are famous for being able to fool lie detectors."

Hartz, unconvinced by Blackstone's comeback, gave a sardonic chuckle at the other end.

"Have a really good day," he said.

CHAPTER 45

Blackstone was getting ready to leave for the day when he ran into Julia. She looked like she was leaving too. She had something in her hand.

"Hey there," he said, very upbeat. "Going my way? Want to catch dinner?"

"Here's the DVD of my cross-examination of Vinnie," she said and handed it to Blackstone. "You can review it at your leisure. I think it speaks for itself."

"Thanks," he said, taking the DVD. "And as for my question, which you adroitly didn't answer?"

"Did you want to talk about Vinnie's case?"

"Not particularly."

"Do you want to discuss any of my other cases, which I have been struggling to keep up with while also helping you out in the Smithsonian case?" she said in a slightly irritated voice.

"No, not really," Blackstone said.

"So this is *not* a professional conversation you want to engage in tonight then, right?"

Blackstone was getting her drift. He shook his head.

"Then in light of that, I think I'll pass," she said and walked past him and out the front door.

Alone, Blackstone locked up the office, turned off the lights, and headed home in his convertible.

On the way home he kept mulling over Julia's interaction with him.

And assessing his relationship with her over the last year and a half. And then there was Vinnie. Her case. What lay ahead if she was convicted at trial. And his thoughts about her as a woman—thoughts that stretched far beyond the strategies of his criminal defense.

And then there were the inevitable, haunting memories too, about Marilyn. Everything he thought about other women always took him back to her. And then, like a landslide, that gravitational force, the aching for his daughter, Beth, that would immediately follow.

Blackstone took a drive over to his college campus. He parked his car in his faculty parking spot. Then he headed up to his uncle's office. He told himself that he needed to catch up with Reverend Lamb about his expert opinions regarding the Langley note.

That is what he told himself.

Reverend Lamb was in his office with a young man. Blackstone waited in the chair outside. He could hear snatches of their conversation. The student sounded like he was thinking of dropping out of school.

After fifteen minutes, the student left and Blackstone entered his office.

"Got a minute, Uncle?" he asked.

"Always for you, J.D."

Blackstone sat down on the little couch that was in front of a cluttered bookshelf.

"I had told you previously that I've retained you and one other expert, on the Langley note."

"Yes. I remember."

"Frieda will schedule a kind of face-off with both of you in my office."

"Face-off?"

"Well, that's what I'm calling it," Blackstone said. "I figured 'gun-fight at the OK Corral' would be a little melodramatic."

Reverend Lamb laughed.

"Here's the layout," Blackstone said. "I think I can only use one of you—or neither of you, depending on your conclusions. But I won't be able to use both of you under any circumstances. It's fatal to a criminal defense to give alternative, inconsistent theories."

"I think I follow you," Reverend Lamb said. "You want both of us to present our findings on what the Langley note meant—that is, decipher the Booth diary page that he copied—and we are to do that in front of each other and with you. Right?"

"That's the gist," Blackstone said.

"Why the 'face-off' format?" his uncle asked. "Do you want each of us to take potshots at each other's conclusions?"

"Something like that," Blackstone said. "Look, I know scholars like you guys detest this kind of situation. But your expert opinions have to be forensically defensible in the most intensively combative environment imaginable. At trial, your credentials will be challenged. Your methodology will be ridiculed. Every published word you've ever written will be held up to scrutiny. That's the playing field when you testify as an expert witness in a criminal case."

"I understand," Reverend Lamb said. "Don't worry about criticizing my opinions. I've got thick skin."

Lamb paused for a minute to study Blackstone, who was reclining on the couch, gazing out into space.

"So, apart from the case," Lamb said, "how's life, Nephew?"

"Challenging," Blackstone said.

"I've never known you not to enjoy a good challenge."

"Then maybe I'd better pick a different word."

"You're a good communicator. What word would you pick?"

"Struggling."

Then Blackstone thought of something.

"That college kid that you were talking with in your office—let me guess, he was a freshman wondering about continuing on this fall as a sophomore?"

"Yes, he was," Reverend Lamb said. "He's struggling, to borrow your word. Wants to jump ship. Had some bad grades and thinks he wants to give it up. Quit college."

"What did you tell him?"

"Oh, nothing very profound. I just told him that it's never a good idea to make decisions out of desperation. That he needs to get a higher perspective on what he wants to do with his life, his talents, and his opportunities."

"It's hard to be objective," Blackstone said, "when you're drowning."

"Yes. That's true," his uncle said. And then, without fanfare, he walked into a subject matter laden with land mines for his nephew.

"You must be lonely without Marilyn and Beth."

"Yup."

"We never talked, you and I," Reverend Lamb said, "about the two of them, and me, and what you thought about all of that."

"No, we didn't," Blackstone said.

"After the funeral," Lamb said, "I don't think the two of us ever mentioned their names in conversation. I wanted to. But I knew how upset you were that Marilyn and Beth had been attending my chapel services."

"She was a grown woman. Marilyn could make up her own mind about things. I wasn't going to try to stop her from going to church. That would've been moronic."

"But I am sure you wondered why she thought she needed Christianity."

"That did cross my mind."

"What did you finally conclude?"

"Every one of us has a vulnerable point," Blackstone said. "For some, fear. For others, insecurity. An unfinished part of our personality. She must have had some little wound that needed a Band-Aid. Religion… your brand of Christianity obviously provided some soothing salve. It wasn't my right to deny her that."

"Well," Reverend Lamb said with a smile, in a quiet voice. "I don't think that was why she embraced Christ. Why, she accepted Him as her Savior, right here in my office one day. Confessed that Christ died on the cross for her and received Him into her heart by faith."

"Oh?" Blackstone said in a biting tone. "And what is your explanation? What do you think she needed?"

"Forgiveness."

"Forgiveness from *what*?" Blackstone said, irritated.

"Sin."

"Your medieval ecclesiastical mantra is ridiculous. Marilyn was the most loving person I had ever met. Frankly, I didn't deserve her. How can you pass moral judgment on her?"

"I don't pass judgment on anyone," Lamb said. "J.D., you pride yourself on your rational, analytical, objective approach to things. Yet, in a real sense, Marilyn, who I'm sure you thought was the emotive and subjective one, was much more objective than you."

"Oh? This ought to be good," Blackstone snapped. "How, pray tell?"

"She considered, very dispassionately, what the biblical record had to say about who she was. What God desired of her. And what she had to do to connect with God. To be reconciled with a holy Creator. That's it."

"You're doing religion-speak now," Blackstone said. "I don't speak your language. It went out of style, I think, around the time of Henry the Eighth."

"If you mean the King James Bible," Reverend Lamb said, with a calm smile, "actually, that was under James I. Early seventeenth century, sometime after King Henry, I'm afraid."

Blackstone leaned back on the couch and sighed, shaking his head.

"Let me just put the capstone on this," Lamb said, "by putting it this way—Marilyn, and Beth too, decided to become Christians—to walk through that open door of Christianity for the simplest and yet the most valid of all reasons."

"Which would be?" Blackstone asked.

"They discovered that it was true."

CHAPTER 46

That night Blackstone nearly pulled an all-nighter. He was high-strung and bouncing off the walls. He wasn't surprised that the discussion with his uncle about Marilyn and Beth had destined him to a night on the emotional roller coaster. His insomnia had been getting decidedly worse, not better, and his sleep medication was barely helping.

At the same time Blackstone detested the feeling of being weak and helpless. In his view, this was all part of a life issue that should have been fairly easy to diagnose and resolve. But it wasn't working out that way.

When he finally fell asleep, in a short fitful bout with dreaming, there it was again—Marilyn's face—and she was saying the same thing she always did in his dreams.

Don't forget.

When Blackstone dragged into the office in the morning, he called Dr. Cutsworth at Harvard. The history scholar said that he had already formulated some tentative conclusions.

"There are a few more sources I am going to check out to assist me with the meaning of the note," Cutsworth said, but then added confidently, "however, I don't anticipate they will impact my conclusions very much. I'm fairly certain I'm right on this one. I know the general message that Booth was trying to communicate, albeit in a primitive kind of poetic code—a riddle, actually. It really wasn't very difficult to break the crude coded set of references he left in his diary."

Blackstone set a time that afternoon, at 3:30 p.m., with Dr. Cutsworth to be available by phone. Blackstone would set up a speakerphone in the conference room. Reverend Lamb would also be there. He would have Julia sit in too. He knew his uncle's teaching schedule and figured it would work out with him being present. He was right.

At 3:30 p.m. Reverend Lamb was there with his stack of books again, and his pile of notes. Julia sat on the other side of the conference table from Blackstone.

Blackstone pushed the button on the speaker phone and dialed Cutsworth's number. Once he had him on the line, so that everyone in the room could hear him and he could hear them, Blackstone began.

"Dr. Cutsworth," he said, "we are all here."

"Very good," Cutsworth said.

"What I want to do is begin with you, if we can," Blackstone said to the Harvard professor. "You will go first and give us your conclusions about the Langley note. Then I will give Reverend Lamb a chance to respond. And my partner Julia and I may have questions for you also. Then it will be Reverend Lamb's turn, and he will describe his findings, and you will have a chance to respond to him. Now I want both of you gentlemen—Dr. Cutsworth and Reverend Lamb—to remember that your opinions on the meaning of the Langley note, and therefore the Booth diary page, will be helpful to the defense side of this case *only* if those opinions shed light on the issue of motive for the murder of Horace Langley and the theft of the Booth diary pages. You may have brilliant scholarship, but what I am looking for is a way to identify the criminal culprits in this case. So, Dr. Cutsworth, are you ready?"

"I am."

"Go ahead, Dr. Cutsworth."

"I thought," he began in a professorial tone, "it might be good to remind ourselves what the text is that we are about to discuss. So, here it is again—the note written by Horace Langley, which I have assumed, except for the first lead-in sentence, was a verbatim copy he made of some of the text of the Booth diary pages that have recently been stolen and now are unavailable. The Langley note says this:

A strange cipher appears in the Booth diary as follows:
To AP and KGC
Rose of 6 is Sir al ik's golden tree

In gospel's Mary first revealed
At Ashli plot reveals the key

"So," Cutsworth continued, "there it is. Let's begin with the very first line of poetic code. The 'KGC,' is a likely reference to the Knights of the Golden Circle, an obscure but historically substantiated group of anti-Northerners. They were 'copperheads,' the Northern citizens with Southern sympathies. At the end of the Civil War, and afterwards, they most certainly discussed various conspiracies to overthrow the Lincoln administration. One plot involved kidnapping President Lincoln. That gave way to the assassination plan ultimately executed by Booth."

"Dr. Cutsworth," Blackstone interjected, "do you have an opinion based on certainty as to who the 'AP' was who was referenced in that first line?"

"No," he replied. "I don't. Not really. I could speculate, but I don't think that is what you are after. No, I really am not certain. There could have been various conspirators, lost to history, with those initials, or maybe it was just another kind of coded reference to someone Booth preferred to keep anonymous."

"Does your lack of certainty about who 'AP' was affect the validity of your other conclusions about the poem?"

"Not in the least," Cutsworth said.

Blackstone was pleased. He had been banking on that in order to make good his promise to Senator Collings to keep Albert Pike's name out of the case.

"Continue, please," Blackstone said.

"That brings us to the second line," Cutsworth said, "which is this: *Rose of 6 is Sir al ik's golden tree.* Let's start with 'Rose.' I believe that refers to Rose Douglas, widow of the famous Stephen Douglas, who ran against Lincoln. After Lincoln was murdered, Rose tried to gain a pardon for Mary Elizabeth Surratt, who had been convicted as an assassination conspirator. By the way, the pardon effort failed and Mary Surratt was hung. The number '6' probably refers to a subgroup of conspirators whom she was linked to. Now, who 'Sir al ik' is, I don't know. I would guess it's probably another member of the group. But the 'golden tree' reference is significant. It is clearly a cipher for the Confederate financing scheme.

At that time, in the waning months of the war, the Confederates had managed to accumulate a storehouse of gold in Canada, which they were planning on using to fund their continued resistance to Northern domination. When the Confederate insurgency failed, the gold was obviously not used. But 'Rose' probably had knowledge of some clues as to where the gold was being kept."

"So," Blackstone said, "that takes us to the third line."

"Right," Cutsworth said. "*In gospel's Mary first revealed*—that's the next line. 'Mary' here would be Mary Surratt, who I just mentioned a moment ago—another figure linked, historically, to the assassination plot against Lincoln. The 'gospel' reference is simply an identifier that Mary Surratt was widely known to be a very religious woman. 'First revealed' means that the Confederates, after contacting Rose Douglas, would have needed to get the next clue on the location of the gold from Mary Surratt. The use of women as conspirators to be keepers of the secret of the location of the gold was a clever ruse, as women would have been less likely back then to attract suspicion than men."

"Any questions so far?" Blackstone asked Julia and Reverend Lamb. Julia shook her head 'no.' Reverend Lamb was busy scribbling down notes, then raised his head to say, "I'll ask my questions when Dr. Cutsworth is finished."

Cutsworth said he was now going to the final sentence: *At Ashli plot reveals the key.*

"This sentence is, to my way of thinking," he said, "the most difficult to decipher, the most opaque. That is because it reveals either the location of the stored gold itself, or the place where its location would be 'revealed' through a map or some other device."

"Ashli plot," Julia said, "any ideas where that might be? Somewhere in America? Or in Canada? Or somewhere else?"

"Unfortunately, I simply have nothing definitive to say about that," Cutsworth replied. "But no matter. For your purposes, Professor Blackstone, I think my interpretation is correct and historically quite viable. And moreover, as you can see, it certainly presents a motive for some criminally inclined person to get to poor Secretary Langley first, in order to get to the location of the gold before everyone else."

"How much gold are you talking about?" Julia asked.

"Well," Cutsworth said, "about a million dollars worth. I believe that is what my research on the Canadian gold of the Confederates indicates."

"Not very much to justify the sophistication used in this crime, though," Julia noted.

"Except," Blackstone interjected, "Dr. Cutsworth, your estimates are based on the value of gold in the 1860s, correct?"

"That's right," he replied. "In 1863, the value of gold was what it had been for many years—it had stayed relatively stable at twenty dollars per ounce."

"What are the gold rates now?" Blackstone asked. "Aren't they over nine hundred an ounce?"

"Yes, exactly. Actually they've climbed up close to a thousand per ounce," Cutsworth said. "Which means that the Canadian gold deposit, wherever it is, might be worth some forty million at current rates."

"Anything else?" Blackstone asked his expert witness.

"No, I think that covers the main points," Cutsworth replied.

"Julia, any more questions?"

She shook her head 'no.'

"Uncle?" he said, turning to Reverend Lamb.

"Dr. Cutsworth," Lamb began, "you see this coded message as having to do with a way to pass on financial information among Confederate conspirators, correct?"

"Yes, that's right."

"Yet, by my count," Lamb continued, "you've been *unable* to account for nearly half of the most critical words in the poem. You can't say who 'AP' is, you don't know what the '6' refers to, you can't identify 'Sir Al ik,' and you have no opinion on what 'Ashli plot' is. Am I right?"

"Yes, you are," Cutsworth said, "but those are either personal names or place names, which, from the standpoint of my forensic task here, to decipher the basic meaning of the poem, are irrelevant...just not that important."

"Now you say that 'Rose' and 'Mary' are names of Confederate conspirators, and that they were vested with the knowledge of the secret location of the gold because women would be less likely to draw attention or suspicion?"

"That's what I said," Cutsworth replied.

"Yet women were placed under suspicion," Lamb said. "And in one particular case, as you noted, a woman was charged as a conspirator in the assassination of President Lincoln and was hanged. You would agree with that?"

"Well, yes," Cutsworth said. "But all that means is that their plan to use women because they wouldn't draw suspicion ultimately failed. It doesn't mean it wasn't tried."

"All about money," Lamb said. "That's what you think the Langley copy of the Booth diary text is all about?"

"In the end, yes," Cutsworth replied.

"You don't see any metaphysical or religious aspect to any of this?" Lamb asked.

"None whatsoever."

"You would agree, though," Lamb said, "that the Knights of the Golden Circle were populated with Freemasons?"

"That may have been true, though the evidence is scant. But the Masons were a popular social group."

"Booth was a Freemason?"

"Again, he was rumored to have been—whether his name was removed from the member rolls after his notorious murder of Lincoln is open to debate. It is very much an open question."

"And your interpretation of 'gospel's Mary' is intriguing," Lamb said, "but I think very flawed, if I may say."

"Oh? Exactly how?" Cutsworth said a little indignantly.

"Your interpretation ignores the clear syntax of the phrase. You would be correct if it read 'gospel Mary' perhaps, where 'gospel' would be an adjective describing 'Mary.' But it isn't. It reads, 'gospel's Mary.' The word 'gospel's' is possessive. It would be better interpreted as 'Mary of the gospel.' Or perhaps, 'the gospel of Mary.' That's the only way the sentence is meant to be read."

Cutsworth was laughing on the speakerphone.

"You are assuming, Reverend Lamb," Cutsworth said, "that John Wilkes Booth, on the run, being hunted down as a notorious murderer, was calmly sitting down in his study, penning some kind of religious treatise. Ridiculous! He didn't care about syntax, I'm sure. I think your training as a clergyman, Reverend, if I may say so, is showing through. You are reading religion into the Langley extract from the Booth diary… historical artifact that has *nothing* to do with religion, or metaphysics, or any such thing."

Reverend Lamb turned to Blackstone and smiled.

Then the Anglican scholar simply said, "Thank you. Those are all my questions."

CHAPTER 47

Blackstone turned to Reverend Lamb.

"Uncle, it's your turn to give it a shot."

Lamb nodded his head. Then he pushed his pile of books and notes aside and folded his hands in front of him on the table.

He paused for a few moments with his hands folded. But he said nothing. After almost a half a minute of silence, Blackstone was about to interrupt him. Then he realized what was going on.

He's praying, Blackstone thought to himself. *That's what he's doing.*

Then Reverend Lamb cleared his throat and looked up.

"Let's begin," he started out, "at the same place where Dr. Cutsworth started. Here is the text we are to decipher:

To AP and KGC
Rose of 6 is Sir al ik's golden tree
In gospel's Mary first revealed
At Ashli plot reveals the key

"Now," Lamb continued, "I agree with Dr. Cutsworth that the 'KGC' in the first line refers to the Knights of the Golden Circle. On that we are agreed. But as to everything else in his conclusions, I take issue with all of it. My conclusions are distinctly different. And I believe I am right. Furthermore, I am prepared to tell you why."

Lamb was now speaking from memory. Nothing in front of him. His eyes were open wide, and his fingers were now dancing a little on the table in front of him.

"Let's take the 'gospel's Mary' reference in the third line," Lamb continued. "What does that refer to? Even back in the 1860s it would have been known, at least among the students of esoteric religion and followers of the Gnostic tradition, that there had been a reputed 'gospel of Mary' attributed to the Gnostic writers in the centuries following the life of Christ. The so-called 'gospel of Mary' purported to describe the interactions between Mary Magdalene and Jesus of Nazareth. It was totally inauthentic, of course. There is no historical proof that whoever wrote this piece of fiction hundreds of years after Christ used any reliable sources of information to concoct this story. Which is why the early church fathers rejected it, along with numerous other 'Gnostic gospels' written mostly in the third and fourth centuries.

"Remember, now, that the Christian gospels, Matthew, Mark, Luke, and John, contained in our New Testament today had been written shortly after the earthly life of Christ, all in the first century—between AD 60 and 85—why, even the liberal scholars concede that point. But, here is this 'Gospel of Mary' which the ancient church fathers knew about and which was finally unearthed in an Egyptian desert near Nag Hammadi in the 1940s, with the Coptic text dating around the end of the fourth century. One page of the text, which is suspicious because it doesn't seem to fit, may be from as early as the third century. But, let's be liberal and say that the Mary writing is indeed from the third century. That still means that it was created two hundred years after the original Gospels! So—which versions do you think would be a more accurate record of the life of Christ? Well, in any event, here is this heretical, bogus 'gospel' of Mary which says that Mary Magdalene was the recipient of special, 'secret' knowledge from Jesus. The text of that false gospel doesn't say what that 'secret' knowledge was."

"Excuse me, Reverend," Cutsworth said through the speakerphone. "But what in the world does this have to do with John Wilkes Booth or his diary?"

"I'm getting to that," Lamb said. "So, as I was saying, we have this heretical reference to Mary Magdalene in this so-called 'gospel' and her supposedly 'secret' knowledge. That is the meaning of the reference in the Booth diary to 'gospel's Mary.' Notice the next line—'first revealed.' In other words, whatever the core of this coded message is, it was supposedly 'first revealed' in this 'Mary' of the Gnostic gospel."

"And what would that core message be?" Julia asked.

"Oh, that is where it gets good," Lamb said with satisfaction. "According to ancient pagan tradition, Mary Magdalene was mixed up in the practice of alchemy."

"*Alchemy,* did you say?" Cutsworth blurted out.

Blackstone rolled his eyes a little.

"Yes, that's what he said," Blackstone answered.

"Of course, the historical record is clear she was no alchemist and certainly no pagan after her faith encounter with Christ. Just read the true Gospel accounts in the New Testament and you can see that," Lamb said. "But, in any event, that is what the ancient heretics, the perverters of the truth who rejected orthodox Christianity, wanted people to believe."

"Alright, so how does this alchemy theme connect everything?" Julia asked.

"Here's how," Lamb replied. "Most people believe that alchemy has to do with precious metals."

"Converting base metals into gold," Julia said. "Yes, I studied that in my history of chemistry classes when I was pursuing my master's degree."

"Exactly," Lamb said. "But most people don't realize that the purveyors of alchemy—and now I am talking about those practitioners through the ages who were deeply involved in the occult practices and esoteric philosophies—that they were after something much more radical than just accumulating gold, or the chemical transference of metals. They were after the most astounding and egomaniacal pursuit of all."

There was silence in the room as Lamb paused dramatically.

"Are you going to break the suspense here, Reverend?" Cutsworth said, chuckling.

"Why, yes I am," Lamb said with a smile. "But before I do, I am going to show you what I am talking about by taking you all back to the language of the poem that was copied down by Horace Langley. Notice the second line, the last two words."

"Golden tree?" Julia asked.

"Right," Lamb said. "Unlike Dr. Cutsworth, I don't think this is a reference to gold, or money, or any kind of financial deposit of the Confederate rebels. No, not at all. Instead, I would refer you all to the name of a classic book that gives you the same clue—*The Golden Bough*, Sir James George Frazer's famous study on the relationship between magic and religion and the mythical symbols of the world's religions. Instead of the golden 'bough' of a tree, the Booth message talks of a 'golden tree.' But same idea. The writer of this note," Lamb continued, "is talking about the most 'magical' tree, if you will, the most famous, the most powerful tree in the history of all religion."

Blackstone was starting to get the drift.

So was Cutsworth, the scholar.

"You don't really mean—" Cutsworth started to say in a scoffing tone.

But Lamb cut him off.

"I told you I am going to take you through the actual text of this note," he said, "to show you the proof. Now look at the words just before the phrase 'golden tree.' Do you see?"

"*Sir al ik's*—is that what you are referring to?" Cutsworth asked.

"Precisely," Lamb said. "The very phrase, Dr. Cutsworth, that you couldn't interpret. Because you started with the wrong presupposition. You were looking at this from a nineteenth-century historical viewpoint based on traditional Civil War and post–Civil War data. As Confucius said, a thousand-mile journey begins with the first step. But in your case, Dr. Cutsworth, despite your considerable historical brilliance regarding nineteenth-century America, in your very first step you headed off in the wrong direction."

"And exactly what *do* you think that phrase means?" Cutsworth asked in considerable affront.

"I believe the phrase 'Sir al ik' was meant to be read and interpreted," Lamb said calmly, "by someone who understood the essence of alchemy, but who was also versatile and learned in other languages."

"Languages like what?" Blackstone asked.

"Like Arabic," Lamb explained. "Interesting thing...the ancient Arabs were very involved in alchemy. Which, of course, explains what that phrase means."

"Which is?" Julia asked.

"It is a word puzzle," Lamb said. "Take the first part, 'Sir,' which seems to be a title of an English lord at first blush. Very clever, I must admit. But it isn't a title at all. It's the last part of a word. Put it at the end of the phrase, and what do you get?"

"Al ik sir," Blackstone muttered. "The 'al' being a common prefix in Arabic."

"You're absolutely right," Lamb said, his voice mounting in excitement. "Now...what does that phrase—'Al ik sir'—really mean?"

"I think I see where you are going with this," Blackstone said.

"*Aliksir* is the anglicized version," Lamb explained, "of the Arabic word that became the English word *elixir*."

"So what we are talking about," Julia said slowly, putting the pieces together, "is an 'elixir of the golden tree.' Is that it?"

"That is exactly it," Lamb said.

"But *what* golden tree?" Julia asked.

"I presume he is referring to the 'tree of life,'" Cutsworth interjected from the speakerphone in a lofty tone.

"The tree mentioned in the Garden of Eden story in the book of Genesis," Blackstone added, tapping his pen now on the conference table.

"The Bible story of the tree of life, in the Garden of Eden, before the Fall of man into sin," Lamb said, "has spawned countless myths and legends about a secret elixir of life supposedly derived from that tree. The secrets of that tree allegedly being passed down through the millennia, according to pagan occultists. There are countless writings of the Gnostic alchemists talking about trying to discover this supposed magical element."

There was a lull for a moment before Reverend Lamb spelled it out.

"This note from Booth, copied down by Langley," Lamb said, "is telling us about the belief that someone had actually found the location of a botanical remnant, some specimen of that tree. The substance that could extend human longevity indefinitely." He glanced around the table at his audience.

"Don't you see?" Lamb cried out. "The location of a botanical element that could, when ingested, actually produce human immortality," he concluded with a flourish.

"What in the world does any of this have to do with the assassination of Abraham Lincoln?" Cutsworth yelled.

"Oh, I will get to that," Lamb said with a smile. "All in due time. Now, look at the last line—here is where the note is saying that the 'key' to the location of the elixir can be found. 'Ashli' is not a name of a person at all. Another clever ruse. Look at the phrase again—*'at Ashli plot reveals the key.'* First, the grammatical structure doesn't make sense, at least at first. Until you realize, as I did, that it *wasn't* saying that some 'plot' of ground belonging to a person named 'Ashli' was going to 'reveal' the location of the elixir. The use of the word 'at' seems out of place grammatically. *Unless* you conclude that the 'plot' mentioned was not a *place* but a *person.* Understood that way, then, that person, Mr. Plot, would 'reveal' the 'key' to the elixir 'at' a place called...Ashli."

"Who is Mr. Plot?" Blackstone asked.

"We don't discover that," Lamb said, "until we first answer this— what is *Ashli?* And we can't find that out until we separate 'Ash' from 'li.' Don't you see?"

More silence in the room.

"Let me give you a hint," Lamb said. "The 'li' is shorthand for the word 'library.' I'll give you another hint—the library is a famous library in England—and the 'Ash' is shorthand for the founder of that library."

"The Ashmolean Library at Oxford," Cutsworth blurted out.

"Excellent, Dr. Cutsworth!" Lamb exclaimed. "Yes, the Library of Elias Ashmole."

"One of the founding members of the Royal Society in England?" Blackstone asked.

"The same," Lamb said. "But he was more than that—he was also a renowned English occultist, astrologer, and alchemist of the early sixteenth century. In fact, Ashmole was tutored by William Blackhouse, the famous alchemist and practitioner of the dark arts, who was dubbed the 'elixir man' because he was in constant pursuit of the 'elixir of life.' Now Elias Ashmole, his student, once penned a poem in Blackhouse's honor, and in that poem he refers to the 'leaves of Hermes' tree,' a direct expression of the belief that the leaves of an ancient tree contain the power of immortality.

"Ashmole became one of the founding members of that branch of

Freemasons known as the 'Speculative' Masons—those whose agenda embraced a worldview and a religious philosophy that borrowed, among other sources, from Egyptian paganism, the Jewish Old Testament, and Gnosticism. 'Speculative' Freemasonry blossomed under Elias Ashmole and his Gnostic compatriots, but all the while keeping a tight rein on who would be made privy to their 'secret' philosophical pursuits. This dark, occult strain of speculative Freemasonry has survived in the shadows for centuries, even up to this very day."

"Reverend Lamb," Dr. Cutsworth bellowed, "you said you would explain that 'plot' reference—you're still not explaining that."

"Oh, yes," Lamb said, "the 'plot' connection. Of course. Well, it so happens that Elias Ashmole's protégé was a sixteenth-century physician by the name of Dr. Robert Plot. He became the curator of the Ashmolean collection of museum oddities and the librarian of the first Ashmolean library at Oxford. Dr. Plot shared Ashmole's belief in the 'esoteric' secrets of nature. He believed that man could deduce and extract the mysteries of the universe and obtain transcendent spiritual powers through deep investigations of the natural world. He obviously shared Ashmole's penchant for the 'ultimate' pursuit of all— alchemy. Dr. Plot wrote extensively on these matters. And his writings are located in the Ashmolean library. This myth of the eternal 'rose' of immortality, the 'philosopher's stone' of alchemy, the pursuit for the 'elixir of life' was so common in the early seventeenth century in England that Ben Jonson lampooned it in his famous satirical play *The Alchemist,* which debuted in...oh, let me see...what was the date?"

"If I recall my Elizabethan literature, I believe that would have been the year of 1610," Blackstone said. His uncle's face lit up with a smile as Reverend Lamb nodded in agreement.

Blackstone, who had been tracking Reverend Lamb's lengthy exposé, now wanted to bring the lecture to an end.

"So," Blackstone said, "that brings us to something that you and I had talked about previously, Uncle. Something that may be an element of this criminal case—something mentioned by someone who may, or may not, be involved in the Smithsonian crimes—namely, the so-called 'ultimate secret' of the Freemasons...I need you to elaborate on that, if I may ask."

"Well, J.D.," Lamb replied, "that is exactly what I have just shared with you. Take that poem Horace Langley wrote down and with my interpretation, you've got it right in front of you."

"Would you indulge us," Julia said, "and just give us your deciphering of the Langley note, in a single overview? It might make it easier to follow."

"I would be delighted to," Lamb replied. "Just pretend that the note says the following, and then you will have distilled its true meaning:

> To AP and the Knights of the Golden Circle,
> The Rose of 6 (that is, the flower from the tree of
>   immortality),
> Which was first revealed in the Gospel of Mary (that is,
>   the "secret" of alchemy),
> Can be located in the writing (that is, the "key") of Dr.
>   Plot in the Ashmolean Library.

Dr. Cutsworth was the first one to break the silence.

"I still see two glaring gaps in your presentation," he said. "First, you haven't explained why you think the 'Rose of 6' reference is a botanical reference to the Genesis tree."

"Oh, that's simple," Reverend Lamb responded. "Two reasons really. First, it makes perfect sense just looking at the sentence structure of the second line. Second, the 'rose' has been used by mystics and alchemists throughout the centuries as a symbol of immortality. It is also implicit in the name of a group called the Rosicrucians, who greatly influenced the early Gnostic, alchemical bent of the speculative Freemasons and were known as the followers of the 'Rose' cross."

Reverend Lamb stopped for a moment, trying to remember the point he was going to make. His index finger was poised in the air. But he had a perplexed look on his face for only an instant. Then, when he found the lost thought, he continued.

"Yes, of course...so then, there is also a third possibility," Lamb said. "It's conceivable that the alchemists within the Freemasons really did believe that some blossom or leaf from the Genesis tree of life existed and that it had a reddish color, or roselike appearance."

"You haven't explained the '6' reference—it says the 'rose of 6,'" Cutsworth shot back.

"No, I haven't explained that," Lamb said candidly. "I haven't come up with a suitable answer for that yet, I'm afraid. I do have one thought on that, though. You see, the Bible, in 2 Chronicles 3:17, gives names to the two main pillars of the Temple of Solomon—a temple which, by the way, figures prominently in the symbols and ceremonies…well, actually in the whole fabric of Freemasonry…in any event, the two pillars are called 'Jachin' and 'Boaz.' And the Masons use these names in their literature.

"But like everything else, the Masons use names and symbols that, for them, also have deeper, hidden, secondary meanings. The actual 'two pillars' of Masonic philosophy, according to some of the oldest written records of the Masonic orders, are two ancient persons: Hermes, the originator of alchemy, and Pythagoras, one of the founders of geometry. All of this is my way of saying that, while the 'rose' has to do with *alchemy*, I think the '6' reference has to do with some facet of natural *geometry*. By that I mean, some geometric feature found in the natural world."

"You also haven't explained the 'AP' reference in the first line, Uncle," Blackstone said. "Why don't you give that a try?"

Remembering his conversation with Senator Collings, Blackstone now had a vested interest in his uncle's opinion on the Albert Pike issue. He was studying the Anglican scholar, waiting for his opinion.

"That I am relatively sure of," Reverend Lamb said confidently. "It refers to Albert Pike, Civil War Confederate officer, Gnostic philosopher, and an internationally renowned commander of the Freemasons. He also prided himself on knowing multiple languages—that goes to the Arabic style of the 'al—ik—sir' reference—or 'Sir al ik' phrase, as the Booth diary coyly writes it. Pike would have been able to transliterate that phrase easily. If you read his life's work, a huge volume titled *Morals and Dogma,* you see Pike speaking explicitly on alchemy. Now, Dr. Cutsworth, you asked what all this had to do with John Wilkes Booth. Well, there was possibility he was a Freemason himself. So were many in the Knights of the Golden Circle. It seems to me that they must have been part of a small band who were interested not only in overthrowing the Lincoln administration, but also in establishing a permanent ruling elite—those possessed of the 'secret' wisdom of the Gnostics, but also who wanted to possess the key to immortality to ensure the permanence of their power."

At that point Blackstone cast a glance over at his uncle that was easy to read. Reverend Lamb was getting the clear message that his interpretation of the Langley note was losing ground quickly. Though he didn't understand why.

"J.D.," Reverend Lamb said to his nephew in an urgent voice. "This is not pride of scholarship talking. I don't want you to accept my version of this note because it will advance my reputation or line my pockets—instead, I want you to believe it for the simple fact that it is *true*. When you study the ceremonies and symbols of Freemasonry, as I have, you see this secret pursuit of immortality. In the initiation ritual the new member is hooded and bound, like a criminal heretic being readied for execution. A noose is placed around his neck. He is symbolically placed in a coffin. But then, suddenly, he is magically spared from death.

"Then there's the fact that the third degree of Masonry, which is the degree that holds the other Masonic degrees together, is called the *resurrection* degree. And the use of biblical acacia plants in the arcana of the Masons is a clear substantiation of everything I've told you, because the acacia leaf is used by the Freemasons as a symbol of immortality.

"In the writings of the Freemason philosophers, it's there to read. When you even go back to the very basis of the Masonic myth—the life and mythic death of 'Hiram'—the 'first Freemason,' so to speak, according to Masonic thought—you see that according to Masonic myth this master builder of the Israelite's Temple of Solomon supposedly possessed secrets from Egypt. In the Masonic legend, when he refused to divulge those secrets, he was murdered. But then, as the myth goes, there is the clear implication that he was resuscitated from death! On that note, it is essential we realize that, according to some of the old manuscripts of the legend, a sprig of the acacia tree had been placed on his grave. It's all there, folks, if you just have eyes to see."

Reverend Lamb took a deep breath and cast a glance over the faces of Blackstone and Julia, and then fixed his gaze on the speakerphone, where, on the other end, Dr. Cutsworth was listening in silence.

"As a Christian scholar," Lamb said, wrapping up his conclusions, "I see all of this as the sad obsession with 'secret' knowledge and the discovery of the key to the infinite extension of earthly life. Which is so tragic when you realize that eternal life, that gracious gift of God, is available to everyone who puts their faith in Jesus Christ—without the necessity of hidden ceremonies, without the occult practices of the alchemist, and without the 'secret' searches of the Gnostics for some special knowledge that belongs just to the esoteric elite.

"Jesus said if you seek Him you will find Him. I often wonder to myself why this marvelous gift of eternal life through Christ is often the *last* option of people rather than the first. Which is precisely the danger of Gnosticism, Theosophy, and the mystic religion of the speculative Freemasons—because they all lead spiritually undiscerning folks into an endless hall of mirrors rather than the simple way of Christ—which leads you first to the cross and then to the empty tomb."

Once more, the room was silent.

"Can't you see?" Lamb exclaimed, his voice now passionate. "The apostle Peter commands us to beware—just read it yourselves, in the New Testament, in his second epistle, chapter two, verse one—'But false prophets also arose among the people, just as there will also be false teachers among you, who will secretly introduce destructive heresies, even denying the Master who bought them, bringing swift destruction upon themselves.' There it is—in Peter's own words, as inspired by the Spirit of God."

After another moment of silence, Blackstone finally spoke up to his uncle and to Dr. Cutsworth.

"I can only use one of you two gentlemen in this case," he said. "There isn't room in my criminal defense strategy for two different theories what the Langley note really means. And so, keeping that in mind, gentlemen…I am now ready to decide."

CHAPTER 48

With that, J.D. Blackstone turned toward the speakerphone that was resting on the middle of the conference table.

"Dr. Cutsworth," Blackstone announced, "welcome to the defense team. I will be using you as our expert witness."

"Wonderful," Cutsworth said energetically. "Do you want me, Professor Blackstone, to reduce my opinions to a written report?"

"Not yet," Blackstone said. "Hold off on that until I give you the green light. Thanks for your time and your expertise."

Then they could hear the click as the Harvard professor hung up.

Blackstone turned to Reverend Lamb.

"Sorry that we had to vote you off the island, Uncle," Blackstone said. "Interesting theory. But I am looking for something that explains the Smithsonian crime, and my client's innocence. Dr. Cutsworth's conclusions accomplish that. Yours don't. Sorry."

"I don't take it personally," Reverend Lamb said. Then he glanced at his watch. "I have a summer school class coming up. Have to rush."

He reached out his hand and shook Julia's hand warmly, then collected his books and papers and headed to the door.

As he passed by Blackstone, who was standing, he said, "J.D., let's be sure and stay in touch. I know this criminal case is taking up all your time. But when the dust settles a little, stop by and see me some time, won't you?"

After Reverend Lamb left the conference room, Blackstone sat back down and looked over the conference table at Julia, who was still in her chair.

"Do you think I made the right call?" he said to Julia. "Going with Cutsworth, I mean?"

She knew it was merely a rhetorical question. Blackstone was already convinced he was right. But the question was meant to be a peace offering. A goodwill gesture.

"If you had to choose," Julia said. "Then sure, I think it makes sense. It's a theory that a jury is going to understand. I'm just not sure how his theory is going to exonerate Vinnie Archmont, though. If the Langley note is all about gold or money, then wouldn't Vinnie be just as likely to want to find the hidden Confederate gold as anyone else?"

"That's our job," Blackstone replied. "To prove that she wasn't after money. And that she wasn't part of a plan to kill for it. At the same time we also have to prove that someone else was."

"It would have to have been someone who knew something about the contents of the Booth diary already," Julia said. "Someone versed in Civil War history—who knew that the Confederates had hidden some gold and that Booth might have known where it could be located."

"Horace Langley was a scholar in seventeenth-century English history, that was what he was known for," Blackstone said, fishing out Langley's biography amidst the files on the Smithsonian case in front of him. "But I think he was also an avid student of American Civil War history."

"Didn't he do some writing on Civil War subjects?" Julia asked.

"Yes," Blackstone said, looking at the bio in front of him, "his curriculum vitae included one article he authored in *American History* magazine about the assassination of Lincoln."

Blackstone buzzed Jason to come into the conference room.

When their paralegal arrived, Blackstone had an assignment for him.

"Contact Tully," he said. "Have him do an in-depth investigation on Horace Langley's background."

"Professor," Jason said with a perplexed look, "he already did. Remember? At the very beginning of the case. He said he didn't come up with anything useful on Langley."

"Tell him to go deeper," Blackstone said. "I want to know everything about Langley's personal life. There's got to be something there."

Then Blackstone added, "Have a seat, Jason. I may have a few more tasks for you."

Jason dutifully sat down with his notepad at the conference table. For a few moments, Blackstone was silent. But Julia and Jason could see the wheels turning in his mind.

"Alright," Blackstone announced, breaking the quiet. "Here's the scenario thus far—going with Cutsworth's conclusions, the motive for the crime may have been filthy lucre. That always plays well in Peoria. Most common folk on a jury can understand crimes seeking money, treasure, gold...But then the prosecution is simply going to counter with this: 'That's right, ladies and gentlemen of the jury. Money was the motive here. And little Miss Vinnie Archmont, struggling artist, loved the idea of getting her hands on forty million dollars worth of gold as much as anyone else.' So, how do we rebut that?"

"Simple," Julia replied. "The money-as-motive argument doesn't correspond to the theory of the prosecution's case."

"You mean the indictment which alleges her involvement with a 'cult'? That one?"

"Right," Julia answered. "Cults are generally driven by twisted ideology, not money. So, when did this one particular group that is vaguely mentioned in the indictment suddenly become so materialistic?"

"Fair enough. Although cults need money to continue their convoluted activities," Blackstone said. "But some of them have other ways besides murder and theft to obtain funding. Bilking their members, to name one. But there's something else. You're forgetting—the grand jury testimony of Detective Victor Cheski. He testified that his investigation indicated that Vinnie was at a conference in Scotland populated by leading European Theosophists. While one speaker did talk ambiguously about using 'force' to put the Gnostic 'elite' into power—none of those conference speakers, including Magister Dee, expressed any belief that the Booth diary had anything to do with Confederate gold. To the contrary, they seemed to have believed, from what I read of Cheski's testimony, that the Booth diary pages might contain some great spiritual secret, hidden through the ages but now revealed."

"Which sounds, now that you mention it," Julia said, thinking on the matter further, "strangely similar to Reverend Lamb's hypothesis rather than Dr. Cutsworth's theory. Wouldn't you agree?"

"Absolutely," Blackstone said. "Which is why we can't go with dear old Uncle John's idea."

Julia was thinking that one through. Before she could connect the dots, her former law professor finished it for her.

"The government's case," Blackstone explained, "is wedded to the testimony of Detective Cheski, based on the transcript of the grand jury. And all that his testimony established was that Vinnie might be involved in a group of esoteric crazies, only one of whom mentioned offhandedly the use of 'force.' When you look at the conference speakers as a whole, they look more like a bunch of kooky librarians or palm readers than revolutionaries or assassins. With this 'European Theosophical Society' you're not exactly dealing with Hamas or the Aryan Brotherhood."

"Okay," Julia said. "So you want to use Cutsworth to show that the government's case, which is trying to prove that the motive for the crime was ideological, was all wrong. That the actual motive was greed. Thus, the basis for the prosecution's case is entirely misguided."

"Bingo," Blackstone said. "Now, the question is this—will the Confederate gold theory exonerate—or incriminate—our client, Vinnie Archmont?"

"That gets back to your point just a minute ago," Julia said. "About Vinnie being just as likely to want to get rich as anyone else. Of course she has a wealthy benefactor, Magister Dee. That tends to diminish the motive somewhat."

"It does indeed," Blackstone added. "And there's another element too. It's a subtle one. Easy to miss. But important. How would Vinnie have known that the Booth diary may have contained some reference to millions in gold being hidden somewhere in Canada? She had no direct access to the Booth diary pages. And she had no scholarly expertise on matters of Civil War history, did she?"

"No, but she had regular contact with someone who probably did," Julia shot back. "Namely, Horace Langley."

"Which is why we need to do some more spadework on Secretary Langley," Blackstone said, turning to Jason and smiling.

Jason smiled back.

Then Blackstone turned to Julia with a surprising question, one that suddenly seemed to change the subject.

"So, honestly," he said. "What did you really think of Reverend Lamb's theory?"

Julia's face broke into a look that seemed to be teetering on the line between a smile and a stunned smirk.

"Is that a serious question?" she asked.

"Yes," he said. "It is."

"Well," Julia continued, "as a woman who was raised Catholic as a kid—to me it had a certain religious appeal. A kind of spiritual bent that strikes a chord. The Genesis tree. The thirst for immortality and all of that. Is that what you're after?"

"Let's get more specific," Blackstone said. "And more scientific. What was your reaction to the 'rose of 6' business? Let's start with the reference to 'rose' in Reverend Lamb's concept being a reference to a botanical substance—a plant, or flower, of ancient origin, capable of prolonging human life. Something that could extend life expectancy almost indefinitely. Let's talk about that. You have a master's degree in chemistry. What do you think—is it totally nutty?"

Jason, who had been sitting idly by at the conference table, was now leaning in, his eyes as wide as silver dollars.

Julia was laughing and shrugging. But she was also nodding her head in a strange acknowledgment.

"Well," she said, "we did read about some studies done at Harvard. I think at the medical school. Experiments on a botanical extract called *resveritrol*. You can find it in the skins of grapes and, oh, I don't know, maybe sixty or seventy other different kinds of plants. They found it had the potential of radically extending human life. Presumably, the presence of resveritrol in plants tells us something about it being present in more ancient plants, probably in greater concentrations. But there was only one problem."

"And what was that?" Jason blurted out.

"It seems that under current atmospheric conditions," Julia explained, "particularly the oxygen in the air, when coupled with light...the O_2 would massively start to limit the effectiveness of the resveritrol."

"What would happen if an ancient plant," Blackstone suggested, "that had high concentrations of resveritrol were placed in a vacuum?"

"You mean dug up in some kind of archaeological dig? There wouldn't be anything left," Julia said. "And if it were found in some kind of molten petrified rock or something like that, the chemical integrity of the resveritrol would not have been preserved."

"I wasn't thinking about that kind of scenario," Blackstone said. "More like this—what if the ancient flower or plant from an ancient tree was frozen in time in some kind of natural vacuum?"

"What are you thinking of?" Julia asked.

At the other end of the table, Jason, wide-eyed, was immobile.

"Actually," Blackstone said, "I was reflecting on what my uncle said about the 'philosopher's stone.' Remember?"

"Yes," Julia said. "I noticed that in Reverend Lamb's little lecture. Haven't heard any reference to that since my graduate school days."

"Yeah. The philosopher's stone!" Jason cried out. "Like I told you guys before, you know, like in the Harry Potter books? The magic stone of the alchemist."

"Yeah, something like that," Blackstone said with smile. "But did you ever wonder why the key to the ultimate pursuit of all alchemy— which Reverend Lamb says is the discovery of a botanical substance that could grant endless human life…Why would that key be symbolized by a 'stone'? That seems odd, doesn't it?"

Jason was now nodding his head. But Julia's eyes were fixed on the law professor.

"Unless…" Blackstone said. Then his voice trailed off.

"Unless," he began again. Then fell silent, and finally continued. "Recall that Reverend Lamb said the 'twin pillars' of speculative Freemasonry were, first, Hermes, the man of alchemy. The second was Pythagoras, the man of geometry. What do we get when we combine geometry with the 'philosopher's stone'?"

Julia and Jason were staring at Blackstone.

"A geometric stone," Blackstone muttered. "Would mean…a crystal… And a perfect crystal," he said, "has *six* sides. Isn't that right?"

"Six sides, yes, that's right," Julia said. "I should have remembered that from my chemistry classes."

"Rose of 6…" Blackstone said. "Meaning an ancient, rose-type flower, somehow imbedded through a freak natural process inside a crystal. And preserving, as you have said, Julia, the super-concentration of resveritrol."

"That would explain it, wouldn't it?" Julia said. "So, does this mean you will be changing horses and using your uncle's opinions at trial after all?"

"No," Blackstone shot back. "I don't think it does. But it has given me some new questions that need answering."

"Like what?" Julia asked.

Blackstone turned to Jason.

"Jason, after you talk to Tully Tullinger about getting more intel on Horace Langley's personal life, also tell him I want to talk with him privately. Ask him to call me."

Jason nodded, scribbled it on his notepad, and left the room.

Julia was still waiting for an answer to her question.

"Let's summarize," Blackstone said. He was now standing up and pacing around the conference room.

"Going with Dr. Cutsworth's conclusions, here is what we have: Langley has an inkling that the Booth diary might contain some data on where the Confederate stash of gold is located," Blackstone said. "So, Langley wants to read the diary pages before the other 'experts' have a chance to read it. Now Vinnie Archmont, who has access to Langley, has no idea that the diary pages may refer to some hidden treasure worth millions. Instead, she is sent on an errand from Lord Dee to try to get a preview of the diary because he is convinced that it may refer to some weird metaphysical prize—the location of the 'rose in the crystal'—the dream-come-true for the alchemists and the upper elite of the Freemasons.

"Because Langley finds that the diary pages in fact do refer to the location of the gold he refuses to give Vinnie, or Lord Dee, or anyone else for that matter, an advance look at the diary pages. Instead, he copies down the coded poem that gives the clues. Only one problem, though. Someone else discovers what Langley has discovered, enters the Smithsonian building, walks in his office in the Castle, kills Langley, and takes the diary and the page of his notepad with his written copy of the poetic ciphers. Vinnie is innocent. But someone else isn't. Someone who knew what Langley knew. Someone with a connection, obviously, to Horace Langley. That's the real killer. That's the conspirator."

Julia thought on his explanation for a while. Then she weighed in.

"Sounds like a solid defense theory."

But she asked further, "Do you believe every bit of it?"

Blackstone stopped pacing. He thrust his hands in his pockets and rocked a little on his tiptoes. Then he responded.

"Maybe not," he replied.

CHAPTER 49

Tully Tullinger was on the line. He had called Blackstone's unlisted home phone number. It was after eleven at night. In the background, where Tully was, there were the familiar sounds of an airport terminal.

"I just landed at BWI airport, and I got Jason's message. If you were anyone else," Tully said to the law professor, "I would apologize for the lateness of the hour. But knowing you, it's probably midday on your freaky internal clock, I suppose."

"You're close," Blackstone said. He was in his gym trunks. He had just finished exercising and was wiping his face off with a towel.

"Sounds like you're huffing," Tully said. "You doing more of that late-night workout stuff?"

"Yep."

"I know you've got a bigger brain sitting up there on top of your spinal column than I do," Tully remarked with a chuckle. "But I had always heard that when you get your physical motor running hard at night, it may be tougher to get to sleep."

"For normal people that's true," Blackstone said. "But when you're already an insomniac, it doesn't really matter."

"Well," Tully said, "I know you didn't want to chat with me about issues of personal health and fitness. So, what's up? I already have the assignment from Jason about going back over Langley."

"Yeah," Blackstone said. "That's the first part."

"You know that I do my job well," Tully said. "I went over this Horace Langley guy pretty closely on the first go-round on this case. Didn't find anything very enlightening. I sent you my report. Included his biography. The whole bit."

"I know that," Blackstone said. "But we're missing something. I can see the hole in the middle of this. It's like a puncture in the skin of a jet airplane sucking all the air out. But we don't know where it is. You need to find the hole. Somewhere in this case there is a space that we haven't looked into. And it has to do with Horace Langley. We need to find the hole before the whole plane goes down."

"Nice word picture," Tully said. "Given the amount of flying I have to do with my job. Yeah, thanks a lot for that. Okay. I'll turn the ground over one more time. Maybe...well, I can try a few things. Don't worry about it. If there is something out there involving Horace Langley, I'll find it for you. I know the trial date is coming up. I'll put a rush on this."

"Then there's another matter," Blackstone said.

"Please continue," Tully said, with a tinge of cynicism. "You have my undivided attention. Is there some other part of my investigation on this case you also want me to redo?"

"No, this part is going to be strictly unplowed ground," Blackstone said. "You remember the FBI agent working the Smithsonian case?"

"Special Agent Ralph Johnson," Tully said.

"I need you to find out where he is right now," Blackstone said. "So I can 'just happen' to run into him. Hopefully he is on assignment where Henry Hartz and his team won't be watching, somewhere outside the District of Columbia."

"You want me to trace an active FBI agent and tell you where he is currently located in his field activities?" Tully asked, with a measure of skepticism in his voice.

"Yeah," Blackstone said. "That's part of it, yes. But more than that."

"This should be good," Tully said. "Don't stop now, I can hardly wait."

"You need to leak to Agent Johnson the fact that I am trying to locate where he currently is being assigned."

"Gee," Tully said. "This is like one of those TV reality shows. Okay. And after I do this daunting task, then are you going to have me ingest a plate full of worms?"

"And your intel about Agent Johnson in particular," Blackstone said. "I really need that pronto—ASAP—overnight delivery."

"I get the drift here," Tully said with a groan. "Oh man. You know, I took up this PI work as a kind of semiretirement after I left the NSA. You're killing me, J.D. There are things besides work, you know...stuff like rest, recreation, seeing my grandkids. Human relationships. Going to the beach. Normal stuff."

"You can do all of that," Blackstone said, "after Vinnie Archmont's trial."

Tully said he would do what he could.

"You're the best," Blackstone told his private investigator.

After the phone call, he showered. His mind was racing, but not about the criminal case.

After dressing in some sweat pants and a T-shirt, Blackstone went into the kitchen of his condo to get something to eat. Then he noticed his pile of keys lying on the kitchen counter. He picked up the key ring and fished through them until he came to a silver key a little smaller than the others.

After staring at it for a while, he stuffed his keys into his pockets. Then he walked downstairs to the parking area. He climbed into his Maserati and fired it up.

After twenty minutes he was in Alexandria.

He knew he was only about a half a mile from Vinnie's apartment. Cruising by the cross street where she lived, he turned off the main drag of Old Town Alexandria and onto Vinnie's street.

Blackstone stopped for a moment in front of her apartment building. He looked up at her window. The light was on, but the drapes were pulled.

He sat there, with the motor running for several minutes. His head was back against the headrest.

But this was not the place where he had intended to visit.

So he put his convertible into first gear and motored off.

Ten minutes later he was pulling up to a sign and an electric metal gate that read *Potomac River Storage*.

He looked beyond the gate to the row-upon-row storage units with locks on them. The entire area was lit by yellow lights on high poles that cast a strange aura over everything.

Blackstone remembered the access code to the electric gate. All he had to do was punch in the numbers and the gate would automatically swing open.

And he also remembered the storage unit number. He had been paying the rent every month for two years. But he had refused to visit it.

Blackstone reached out toward the ignition of the car and isolated the smaller silver key hanging from the key chain. He fingered it.

I told myself I wasn't going to do this, he thought.

And he wouldn't.

Instead, he backed his car away from the gate and drove back to his condo.

CHAPTER 50

The next day, Blackstone was in his office. Shortly after his arrival, he noticed that an e-mail had come in.

It was from Henry Hartz. It was also being simultaneously filed, electronically, with Judge Templeton. Hartz explained, at the outset of the e-mail, that he had obtained a short extension of time from the District Court to furnish the final discovery information to the defense as a follow-up from the pretrial conference with the judge. Hartz had already provided, as required, an expanded explanation of the anticipated testimony of Shelly Hollsaker. Now the prosecutor was providing the last bit of information demanded by Blackstone: an explanation about the drinking glass at the scene of the crime.

In the e-mail, what Hartz had to say about that piece of physical evidence was not about to satisfy Blackstone.

> Your Honor:
>
> Pursuant to the verbal order of the District Court at our last pretrial conference in the above-styled case, the Government has conducted a thorough search of the evidence room utilized by the Federal Bureau of Investigation in connection with this case. The purpose of the search was to attempt to locate a drinking glass which had been identified by Special Agent Ralph Johnson in his 302 report, investigative report #2009456BDC. In that report, Agent Johnson identified a drinking glass on the desk of Horace

Langley, in the office of Secretary Langley at the scene of the crime. Agent Johnson was first on the scene, along with a member of the crime lab and several forensic agents whose duties included the sweep of the room for forensic evidence and preservation of that evidence.

Special Agent Johnson indicates in his report that he used latex gloves to initially inspect the glass, and then he placed it carefully in a clear plastic evidence bag and marked the legend of the bag with an indelible marker along with his name, the date, and the investigation case number.

Several other items of physical evidence were also retrieved, bagged, and tagged in a similar manner, including Secretary Langley's writing pen, a blank notepad, and a personal journal retrieved by Agent Johnson from Secretary Langley's desk. The desk was initially opened by Detective Victor Cheski of the District of Columbia P.D., who arrived about 50 minutes after Agent Johnson arrived at the scene.

In speaking personally with Agent Johnson about the drinking glass, he indicates that his report was accurate and fairly describes the process he used in securing the physical evidence, including the drinking glass. That glass, according to Agent Johnson, was clear, not colored, and was without any logo or design. His visual inspection did not detect any fingerprints. The glass, once bagged in the evidence baggie, was placed with all other physical evidence in a corner of the office floor. At the end of the forensic sweep of the crime scene, all of the physical evidence collected at the scene was gathered up by the crime lab team. In interviewing each of them, there was unanimity that, according to their memories, the glass was among the various items gathered up, transported to the forensic truck, and then taken to the crime lab. However, no one could recall which agent actually carried the bagged drinking glass to the truck.

The physical evidence inventory sheet was filled out at

the crime lab. It appears that the drinking glass was inadvertently omitted from the inventory list for some reason.

Because Agent Johnson had the drinking glass under his investigatory control, he would have been the person responsible to make sure that it was part of an unbroken chain of custody that ultimately led to the crime lab.

Despite our best efforts and a diligent search, we have been unable to locate the subject drinking glass. However, we do believe, Your Honor, that the absence of the glass is an immaterial aspect of this case from an evidentiary standpoint. The lab report describes a full panel of tests that were done on a clear drinking glass matching the description of the subject glass, with the same case identification number on the baggie containing it. The crime lab report, which has already been furnished to defense counsel, J.D. Blackstone, indicates that no fingerprints and no detectable DNA were present in or on the glass.

While we cannot locate where the glass went after its lab analysis, nor do we know where it is presently located, the absence of any discernible evidence in or on the glass makes its absence a moot point in this prosecution.

Furthermore, defense counsel Blackstone apparently never doubted the crime lab findings showing no fingerprints and no DNA evidence on the glass, because he never asked this Court for permission to have his own experts analyze the glass independently.

Lastly, the deadline set by this Court for the defense to have requested its own analysis of the drinking glass has long passed.

Accordingly, while we cannot explain the missing drinking glass, it is entirely irrelevant to this case.

As soon as Blackstone finished reading the lengthy e-mail from the prosecution, he called Henry Hartz.

His secretary said he was in a conference, but as soon as he was available he would call back.

Fifteen minutes later he did.

"Henry, this whole drinking glass incident is outrageous," Blackstone sputtered into the phone.

"Blackstone," the prosecutor replied calmly, "I know how you defense lawyers operate. You will do anything possible to take the focus off your client. You scour the record, the FBI reports, the evidence, looking for the smallest irregularities in law enforcement protocol. And, inevitably, you will find something. There is almost always some minor goof-up that occurs in a complicated crime investigation. And you bellow and holler about how the goof-up is 'outrageous,' it's a 'miscarriage of justice.' It's a police conspiracy to cover up the truth, blah, blah, blah. Frankly, if this drinking glass deal is your biggest and best argument—well, let me just give you a little free advice."

"I'd love to hear some," Blackstone said.

"You'd better focus on the death penalty phase," Hartz said, "because after your client is convicted, there just may still be a slim chance you can convince the jury not to sentence her to execution."

"I'm filing a motion to dismiss, based on the missing evidence, which was lost due to the negligence of the government," Blackstone said. "And I'm also going to argue for a spoliation-of-evidence instruction for the jury if my dismissal motion is denied."

"Be my guest," Hartz said confidently. "The Court won't grant your dismissal motion because the evidence is *not exculpatory*. More than that, the drinking glass is absolutely irrelevant. And on your spoliation jury instruction, I'm not much worried about that either. The most the judge will do is instruct the jury that because the glass was in government custody, if there is any inference to be drawn, it can draw a negative inference about the glass against the government because the glass is now lost. So what? What negative inference is there about the glass? It's a zero sum game on that, Blackstone. You know it and I know it. The jury's not going to care about a missing glass that didn't have fingerprints or DNA on it, but for some reason got misplaced.

"What they are *really* going to care about," Hartz continued with a steely edge to his voice, "is a dead Secretary of the Smithsonian Institution. An honored scholar, shot down in cold blood. And the fact that your client is personally connected to Horace Langley, and connected to the access code to the door used by the murderer, and tied to a motive to get the Booth diary pages. And in a telephone conversation after her arrest, expressed shock and surprise because she had been promised, by her co-conspirator, whoever that might be, that she wouldn't be a 'suspect' in the murder and theft."

"Thanks for a preview of your opening statement for the trial," Blackstone said. "That's going to be helpful for my preparation."

Then Blackstone added, "But one more thing, Henry. This missing glass is not the *only* thing missing here. Or don't you remember? You were going to inform me about why the federal detention people mysteriously failed to tap the phone in Vinnie Archmont's holding cell the day she was arrested and starting making unlimited calls, courtesy of her jailers."

"Actually, Blackstone I was going to explain that for you," Hartz said brightly. "I found out that the Department of Justice contacted the Detention Center early that day to make sure that there was no phone eavsedropping going on. There was a court order on the subject that had been handed down. Obviously, we obey court orders."

"And you will put that in writing?" Blackstone asked.

"I already have. In a hard-copy letter to the court and an e-mail attachment version coming to you. You should have it later today."

"Fine," Blackstone said.

"Always willing to be of service," Hartz said in a sugary-sweet reply.

After hanging up from the telephone conversation with Hartz, Blackstone walked over to Julia's office. He didn't sit down, but leaned against the opening of her door.

"Henry Hartz says they don't have an audio of the Vinnie Archmont telephone calls from the detention center," Blackstone explained, "because the DOJ called them and warned them not to allow it—a court decision had come down, I guess, ordering them to cease recording phone calls. I'm supposed to get an e-mail from Hartz explaining it all. I'll forward it to you when I get it today. If you could check with the DOJ to verify what Hartz said, I would appreciate it."

"Sure," Julia said. "Anything else?"

"I was also wondering how you are coming on the death penalty phase of the defense."

"I'm wrapping up the background data on Vinnie," Julia said. "As you will recall, I put her through a preliminary examination by one of our forensic psychologists."

"Yes, I remember. In my humble opinion, they weren't likely to find anything. Maybe some delayed adolescence issues, some minor personality features."

"That's about all he found," Julia said. "Obviously nothing of any real substance that's going to be very persuasive—very little to go on in order to argue mental or emotional mitigation at the penalty part of the case. Sorry, J.D."

"It is what it is," he replied.

Then he turned and trudged back to his office.

It was mid-afternoon when Tully called him.

"Do I get my bonus now or later?" Tully said. "That's all I want to know."

"Give me some good news, my friend," Blackstone said. "Perk me up."

"Okay," Tully said. "About Agent Johnson. Here's the scoop. It appears that he filed an internal race discrimination claim against one of the lawyers in Henry Hartz's prosecution office, and it kicked up some dust. They've assigned him out to the field."

"Keep going," Blackstone said. "This is intriguing."

"So that may have been the reason that Henry Hartz passed him over for Detective Cheski in terms of who was leading the investigation team."

"That, plus a piece of evidence that Agent Johnson had been responsible for and is now missing," Blackstone shot back.

"Right," Tully said. "Anyway, Agent Ralph Johnson is currently pursuing some phase of the Smithsonian case investigation. And I heard that this is sort of on his own initiative, if you gather my meaning... He is currently down in the Old-Town of Savannah, Georgia. Down by the river."

"He's there now?"

"Right."

"And the other part of your assignment with Johnson."

"Well, there's no guarantees," Tully said. "But I am pretty sure that Agent Johnson is now very aware that you are tracking him. I planted that big fat hint with one of my cronies in the Bureau."

"Good," Blackstone said.

"You're sure that's what you wanted?"

"Oh, yes, "Blackstone said. "I'm sure. Now how about the other job—digging into Horace Langley?"

"I'm flying to Jersey tonight," Tully said. "I've got a contact who may know something. I'll find out soon enough."

"Great. Oh, and one more thing," Blackstone said. "Can you e-mail me quick a photo of Johnson?"

"I think so, give me an hour or so," Tully said.

"That should work," Blackstone said.

After Tully hung up, Blackstone checked his e-mail again. Now Hartz's e-mail about the DOJ and the federal detention center was coming in. He quickly forwarded it to Julia. Then he called Frieda on the intercom.

"Get me a flight out tonight, Frieda," he said quickly. "Out of Reagan National Airport."

"Where to?" she asked.

"Savannah, Georgia," Blackstone replied.

CHAPTER 51

Blackstone flew into the Hilton Head International Airport a little after ten that evening. Frieda booked him a rental car and a room at one of the Hilton Head resorts. The hotels in the city of Savannah were already booked out and he couldn't get anything on short notice.

After climbing into the rental car, Blackstone decided to catch some late dinner along the coast. Blackstone trolled along the beach roads until he saw the lights of a sprawling fish market restaurant perched along the sandy beach, adjacent to a long pier that extended out into the ocean inlet.

It was the type of place that Blackstone and Marilyn had enjoyed frequenting in their early days of marriage. An informal beach eatery right on the edge of the water, with colored, lighted Chinese lanterns swinging in the breeze—music playing—and lots of people and noise.

Blackstone got a small table for himself outside on the big weathered wooden deck overlooking the ocean. The moon was almost full, and it cast a long, glimmering path over the waves. The night was calm, except for the breeze and the sound of the surf slowly rushing up against the shore, and the music of a band playing somewhere.

He ordered a bucket of lobster and shrimp, but didn't eat most of it. A friendly waitress tried to strike up a conversation, but he was in no mood to make small talk.

Like the rolling tide, it often came over him. The memories. The woman he could no longer hold or touch. Or share a pillow with. And then he would try to figure out what grade Beth would be in just then.

What sports she would have gone out for. How she might have changed so much in just the past two and a half years…if everything had been different.

But it wasn't different. It was exactly as it was.

Blackstone tossed down a healthy tip, left his bucket still half full of seafood, and walked through the sand back to his rental car. And then drove back to his resort hotel room.

After an unsatisfactory night's sleep, Blackstone got up early. He drove from Hilton Head into Savannah so he could arrive at the historic downtown tourist area along the river by nine in the morning. Blackstone drove through the streets lined with moss-laden trees, stately old houses, and circular roundabouts at the intersections. He parked his car and headed down to the shops and businesses along the Savannah River.

Then he began.

At each shop he stopped in and met with the proprietor. He would pull out the photo of Agent Johnson that Tully had e-mailed him. Then he asked the same question:

"I am looking for a man named Ralph Johnson. He is with the FBI. Here is his picture. Have you seen him?"

When they would give him a concerned look and shake their heads, then Blackstone would add, "If you do see him, just let him know that I will be walking along the river here, or else up by the little park at the end of Drayton Street. Will you tell him that if you see him?"

By two in the afternoon, he had canvassed most of the shops in the Old Town along the river.

He grabbed a sandwich and then sat down on a park bench on the edge of a small park. Blackstone clicked open his cell phone and called his office for his messages.

By three o'clock, he was still seated on the park bench, watching passersby and horse-drawn carriages. He was beginning to wonder whether he had just wasted a plane ticket and an entire workday.

Then he turned and saw someone standing next to him. Blackstone looked up and saw a broad-shouldered black man, dressed in a dark suit and tie, eating an ice cream cone.

"Agent Johnson," Blackstone said with mock surprise. "How strange we should run into each other like this. And in old Savannah, no less."

Johnson didn't speak at first, but sat down on the bench next to him. Then, when he had nearly finished the ice-cream cone, he began to speak. But when he did, he never turned his head. He kept looking straight ahead.

"You know as well as I do that there are limitations," Johnson said quietly, "on a defense attorney's right to speak to an investigating federal agent without first getting permission from the AUSA prosecuting the case."

"But that is assuming that I would have intentions to question you about the Smithsonian case," Blackstone said.

"You announced your intentions to half the tourist shops in Savannah," Johnson said. "You even waved a printout around with my picture on it. I would have pegged you to be more sophisticated than that."

"Time's short," Blackstone said. "Trial date's fast approaching. I'm down to the slapstick shtick. The vaudeville routine. Really broad stuff. It's not my first choice of methods…but then, what's a guy to do?"

"I'm really not sure why I ought to be talking with you, Blackstone," Johnson said.

"I am," Blackstone shot back. "First, I know that you have been dealt a rotten hand by someone in Henry Hartz's prosecution team. Second, and this is the important part—I think that you know something important about the Smithsonian crimes, and you'd like to tell somebody. Maybe you've already tried, and it was all in vain. Anyway, you would like to share what you know, but you can't quite figure out how you can make that happen."

"You understand I can't talk to you about your client's case," Johnson said.

"Of course."

After some silence Blackstone spoke up.

"Nice picturesque river town, Savannah," Blackstone said. "Only bad thing about a river, though, is that you get rats."

"Rats?" Johnson asked.

"Sure, rats," Blackstone said. "I've seen rats—seen how they scamper up a rope onto a ship. They're quiet. Blend into the corners. Hide in the shadows. The point is this—if you're trying to find out who the rat is, and where he is, where do you start looking?"

Johnson paused for a moment.

"I think it can be a matter of timing," he said.

"Oh?"

"Yeah, timing," Johnson reiterated. "Sailors are supposed to be on the ship. But the rat isn't. I'll tell you something pretty amazing, too. Sometimes a rat can fool you and even blend in like a sailor. So, you have to figure out *when* the sailors arrived—and *when* the rat got there—and you compare the two. That's how you find the rat."

"How would a person go about doing that?" Blackstone asked, thinking hard on the FBI agent's metaphor.

"Oh, you start with paperwork, I suppose," Johnson said. "You look at the obvious, the records you looked at a dozen times before, but this time with a different eye. See if you can see the tracks...a rat leaves tracks, you know."

Then he added, with a bitter smirk on his face, "Little rat tracks. And rat droppings."

Special Agent Ralph Johnson had finished his ice-cream cone. So he stood up from the park bench, wiped his hands on a little paper napkin, and tossed it in an outdoor wastepaper basket.

Then he reached inside his coat pocket and pulled something out. Blackstone stood up next to him.

Johnson held out a little colored brochure of the historical spots in Savannah.

"Too bad," Johnson said, handing the brochure to Blackstone, "that I won't have time to see more of the historical sites in this city. Some of them have real significance."

With that, Agent Johnson looked around and then walked away, with Blackstone still holding the brochure.

Blackstone opened it up. One historical spot had been circled with a pen.

It was the location called "The Cotton Exchange."

Blackstone looked at the map to figure out where the Cotton Exchange was located. Then he realized that it was about one hundred feet directly in front of him, toward the river. Blackstone crossed the little park and strode up to the old, red stone building. The front door was locked and bolted shut. The windows were shuttered tight. At the top were the words *Savannah Cotton Exchange* etched in the stone.

But something else caught his attention. In an aged, arched sign stretching over the doorway of that same building there was another sign.

It read, FREEMASONS' HALL.

CHAPTER 52

A fter landing back in Washington, while he was driving back to the law office from the airport, Blackstone used his cell phone to call Jason.

"I've got some more work for you," he told his paralegal. "Go into my office and grab the black notebook marked '*U.S.A. v. Vinnie Archmont—Gov't Report Summaries.*' Then go to the big black notebook in Vinnie's case where I have indexed all the FBI reports, crime lab reports. When you have both of them in front of you, check my summaries of the crime scene investigation and match it with the actual FBI 302 report of the initial evaluation of Langley's office. I want to make sure that my summaries are absolutely accurate in condensing the activities of the crime scene team."

"Gotcha," Jason said.

"Second," Blackstone said, "and this is critical—go through the whole FBI crime scene report, as well as all my summaries, and create a timeline chart for me. I want you to list each person who had access to Langley's office for the twelve-hour period before the murder, and then the twelve-hour period after he was killed, including the crime lab team members, the agents, and the District of Columbia police. I want to see who they were, and what time they would have entered and exited his office."

"I can do that, sure," Jason said.

"But before you do that," Blackstone said, "check the Internet. Do a Google, then hit the local library if you have to. Check into the history of Savannah, Georgia, and the history of the early Freemasons in that city."

"Will do," Jason said. "Anything in particular?"

Blackstone pondered that, as he started going over in his mind Reverend Lamb's dissertation in his office.

"Check for anything," Blackstone said, "that mentions 'speculative Freemasonry.' Look for that."

"By the way there is a phone call that just came in for you. Wait a minute while I grab it from Frieda."

After a few minutes Jason returned to the phone.

"Here it is," Jason said. "A guy from the U.S. marshal's office called. Said it's important that you call him right away."

Blackstone scribbled down the number.

Then he called the federal marshals service. He waited on the line while his caller was located.

"Mr. Blackstone," the caller said. "I'm one of the agents here with the United States Marshal Service."

"What can I do for you?" Blackstone asked.

"I wanted you to know that we now have custody of your client, Vinnie Archmont."

"I don't understand," Blackstone said.

"Counselor," the U.S. marshal said, "she was caught trying to abscond across the United States border into Canada."

For just an instant, Blackstone's brilliant, polymath mind went numb. All he could do was fixate on the marshal's use of the criminal justice nomenclature, the pejorative loaded with sinister innuendos—*abscond.*

But then, a second later, Blackstone was already calculating the devastating damage that Vinnie had done to her own legal defense.

"Where is she now?" Blackstone asked, trying not to sound frantic.

"Here at the marshal's office, at the Federal Building," he answered. "She will be here for the rest of the day before they decide what facility they will ship her to. I think the AUSA will be filing something with the judge right away."

Yes. I bet he will, Blackstone thought to himself. And he knew exactly what Henry Hartz's next move was going to be.

But he didn't have to wait long to find out for sure.

His call-waiting beeped on his cell phone. Blackstone cut the call short, told the marshal he was on his way over to see his client, and then clicked onto the call-through.

It was Henry Hartz.

"Did the U.S. Marshal's Service give you the bad news?" he asked.

"I just got off the phone with them," Blackstone said, trying not to sound shaken.

"Just filed an emergency motion with Judge Templeton," Hartz said.

"Let me guess," Blackstone shot back. "Asking for jail detention for Vinnie without bail."

"This is exactly why I thought when this case began—that she couldn't be trusted being out on bail, facing a death penalty charge," Hartz said. "The hearing is set for 5:30 p.m., today. After the end of the judge's regular docket. You know now, after she pulled this stunt, he's going to lock her up until trial. No question about that."

"I'll be there at 5:30," Blackstone said.

"One other matter," Hartz said. "I'm also filing a motion with the court asking that, at trial, I be allowed to introduce evidence to the jury of Vinnie's attempted escape out of the country as evidence of implied guilt."

"You don't have any idea what she was trying to do up there at the Canadian border or why she did it."

"Do you?" Hartz barked back.

"I'm on my way to talk to her right now," Blackstone shot back.

"Well, I know one thing," Hartz said. "The judge's clear terms of bail required that she not leave the borders of the continental United States while her case was pending. She has committed attempted bail-jumping. But more important than that, proof of flight from the authority of the court is proof of a guilty conscience. A *criminally* guilty conscience."

"Save it for the court this afternoon," Blackstone said.

"Have a pleasant day, Professor," Hartz said, ending the conversation with an arrogant attitude, and leaving the defense counsel for Vinnie Archmont in a suffocating cloud of pessimism.

Blackstone caught a side-street, put his car into a quick U-turn, and then headed to the federal court building. He needed to confront his client immediately. The question plaguing him now was why she had risked the defense of her entire case in a foolish act that looked very much like an attempt to escape from the jurisdiction of the U.S. District Court.

Blackstone parked his Maserati and hurried into the federal building. After clearing the metal detector and the security guards, he reported to the U.S. marshal's office. The agent there took Blackstone's identification, checked it, and blandly advised him to wait until he could be escorted to the interview room.

Thirty minutes later, the lawyer was taken to the room where Vinnie Archmont was waiting for him, sitting at a metal table. She was still in handcuffs.

Blackstone saw in her face a dark realization. The recognition that both she, and her legal defense, were now in a perilous state.

"Why?"

Blackstone's tone was harsh.

"Are you prepared to believe me?" Vinnie asked, her face anguished and her eyes full of tears.

"It depends."

"On what?" she asked.

"On whether you give me facts worthy of belief," Blackstone replied.

"All right then. What I am going to tell you," Vinnie said, "is the truth."

"Fine," Blackstone said. "Why Canada?"

"Because Magister Dee was on his way to Canada. To Quebec. I heard he was meeting with some members of the Canadian Parliament. I planned on seeing him in Quebec…I just didn't tell him in advance about my plan. You can check with him to verify his trip to Canada."

"Don't worry, I will," Blackstone snapped. "But you haven't answered my question. Why?"

"I intended to meet with Magister."

"To accomplish what?"

"I've been very scared. I needed to talk with him."

"About your case?"

"Of course. Wouldn't you be frightened? Wouldn't you want to be comforted by a close friend if you were facing murder charges and the death penalty?"

"Why now—one week before trial?"

"Because," she said, "as the trial gets closer, I am growing more frightened. Why is that so hard to understand?"

"And why not avoid violating your bail and have Lord Dee come to visit you here?"

"That's obvious, isn't it?" Vinnie shot back, her voice indignant. "Magister Dee is basically an unindicted suspect in the Smithsonian crimes. You know that. So does Magister. While he has never been charged, he understands that the prosecution is eyeing him very closely. If he enters America, he could be seized. Arrested. Charged. As long as he stays out of the United States he knows that as a member of the House of Lords he could fight extradition very effectively. I'm surprised that with all your legal intelligence you couldn't figure that one out. Maybe you are not as brilliant as you think you are."

Vinnie was enraged and insulting.

But Blackstone was unmoved by that.

"So," Blackstone said, "you haven't said anything about the restrictions placed on you by the Court. The Court required you to stay within the continental United States."

"I didn't recall that being the case."

"Vinnie," Blackstone said. "I explicitly instructed you about that."

"I really don't believe you did," Vinnie said coldly. "Besides, the Court took my passport. Which means that I was restricted from leaving the country for any destination that required a passport. I was under the impression that Canada still did not require a passport for entry from the United States."

"Up to now," Blackstone said, "it didn't. Canada is now transitioning to a passport system for Americans. But in a world of security concerns, it wasn't too hard for the border agents to check you out and find out that you had federal murder conspiracy charges pending. And that you were violating bail."

"What happens now?" she asked, with a quaver. Her voice was showing that her initial anger was giving way to fear again.

"A court hearing," Blackstone said. Then he glanced at his watch. "Any minute now."

"What will the judge do?"

"First, he will address your bail. And as much as I hope against it, I see no way that he will *not* revoke your bail and put you in jail until the trial. I know you don't want that. But there is something much more damaging than that."

"What is it?"

"The prosecutor, Henry Hartz, is also asking the court to advise the jury during your trial that you had attempted to flee the country in violation of your bail. And that the jury can, if they want, interpret that act as an admission by you that you were escaping because you know you are criminally guilty."

"That's ridiculous!" she cried out. "I am innocent. If you will simply do your best and do your job I will be acquitted."

"I suggest that you keep that opinion to yourself," Blackstone said. "The judge is in no mood, I'm sure, to get a piece of your mind after you have violated his bail order."

Then Blackstone added his honest assessment.

"You have no idea, Vinnie, how impossible you have made your legal defense."

But she didn't have the chance to respond.

Just then, a U.S. marshal entered the room.

"The judge is calling your case, Counselor," he said. "Ms. Archmont needs to come with me. We'll take her up the prisoner's elevator. She'll meet you in the courtroom."

Then the marshal led her away.

Vinnie did not look back.

Blackstone was studying his client as she left. She was a beautiful yet shadowy enigma in a case full of dark mysteries.

But despite that, the criminal law professor was now starting to see the essence of the case before him more clearly, as if illuminated by a light whose source was still uncertain. And he was beholding the shape of the Smithsonian crimes in ways that he had not disclosed to anyone else. Not to his client, nor the staff at his own law firm. And certainly not to Henry Hartz, the aggressive, career-climbing federal prosecutor.

It would only be a matter of time, now. To see if his theory was proven true. Even though he was not quite sure how such an astonishing state of affairs could have ever taken place.

CHAPTER 53

In court, Henry Hartz made a dispassionate but detailed description of Vinnie Archmont's travel from the District of Columbia to the state of Maine. Where she then rented a car and attempted to enter Canada, with her driver's license and birth certificate as identification. She was stopped for questioning by border agents. After a short computer search and discovery of her pending federal charges and bail restrictions, they took Vinnie into custody. The "clear terms of her bail release required her not to leave the borders of the United States," Hartz told the judge. The court had no other alternative, he argued, but to vacate bail and place her into jail confinement pending her trial date.

Vinnie's face was pale and lifeless as she sat at the counsel table next to Blackstone.

Then her lawyer rose to address the judge.

"Your Honor," Blackstone argued. "Canada has up to now *not* required a passport for American citizen border crossings. This court would have reason to be alarmed if she had attempted to leave the country through the use of a forged passport or through some other illegal means. But that is not the case here."

"That doesn't give me much comfort," the judge shot back. "Her attempt to enter Canada was, itself, illegal. It violated my bail restrictions. My bail order. Professor Blackstone, please...give me one reason why she should not be denied her liberty and locked into a jail cell until trial."

"The purpose of bail, Your Honor, is ultimately, and always, to ensure that the defendant will show up for all required court appearances. And, of course, will show up for trial. Yet there is not one aspect of my client's actions at the Canadian border that indicates that she was intending to avoid showing up for her trial."

"You haven't told me," the judge pointed out, "exactly what she was doing, trying to slip into Canada like that. Why did she do it? Why?"

That was a question that Blackstone could have answered. He could have told the judge that Vinnie wanted to meet with Lord Dee, who was planning on being in Quebec on political business.

But that was a point he could not afford to make. After all, Lord Dee was a person already under suspicion. Vinnie's plans for a rendezvous with Dee might slightly incline the judge to reconsider not revoking her bail, but only if the judge determined that her meeting with Lord Dee was intended to be entirely innocent. On the other hand, that was a risky gamble. What if Hartz then used that intended rendezvous with Dee as further proof of an ongoing conspiracy?

Blackstone couldn't afford to take that chance.

"The defense cannot provide any further details at this time," Blackstone said, "on Ms. Archmont's reasons for wanting to *temporarily* enter Canada."

"Then bail is hereby revoked," the judge announced, "and Vinnie Archmont is remanded to the custody of the U.S. Marshal Service for confinement in a suitable federal facility until the time of trial."

"And my motion," Hartz said, rising quickly and leaning on his cane, "regarding my request to advise the jury of the defendant's attempt to flee the United States jurisdiction? Will the court grant that motion as well?"

The judge eyed Vinnie, then surveyed Blackstone's face for a moment. Then he ruled.

"I will take that under advisement," the judge said. "Until the time of trial. I will announce my decision on that matter at that time, and not before."

Then he gaveled the proceeding to an end.

Vinnie was led away in handcuffs by the marshals. As she was escorted out, she turned her head and quickly threw a confused and anxious look back to J.D. Blackstone. Then the side door to the courtroom was opened by the federal guards, and Vinnie was whisked out and the door slammed behind her.

Henry Hartz had a smug look on his face as he gathered up his file. Blackstone was tempted to fire off a caustic comment to his opponent, but he refrained. He was banking on something else. A chance to have something substantive and ominous to tell Hartz. But that was going to depend on what was waiting for him at his office.

Blackstone hurried into the law office just as Jason was finishing a summary of the comings and goings of the key players who had access to Horace Langley's office before and after his murder.

"I'm just finishing up this list," Jason said over his shoulder. He was at the computer workstation in the law library typing furiously.

"Print it out and bring it into my office when you're done," Blackstone said and then hustled down the hallway toward his office, but he stopped momentarily in front of Julia's office. She was poring over a pile of records.

"I'm going over the statistical data on Vinnie," Julia said, looking up. "And I did have a question on something. Maybe you can answer it—our public record search turned up a petition for name change that she filed. She had her last name changed from Wilson to Archmont...after she was an adult. Just wondering whether you knew about that."

"No," Blackstone said. "I wonder if she was an adopted child...sometimes they change their names after they discover who their natural parents were."

"Could be," Julia said. "Maybe you can ask her when you see her next. Which I am assuming will be soon, judging from what I heard. When I interviewed the apartment manager at Vinnie's apartment complex he mentioned you."

"Oh? By name?"

"No," Julia said, trying to be upbeat. "He said he was pretty sure that Vinnie 'had a boyfriend.' That's how he put it. Nice, huh? You're no longer the defense lawyer, you're the 'boyfriend.' Thought you ought to know."

"Vinnie's in lockup now," Blackstone said bluntly. "They caught her trying to leave the United States at the Canadian border. I'm just coming back from an emergency detention hearing. Judge Templeton revoked bail. He's now considering a motion by the government to inform the jury of all this at trial. If he grants the motion and tells the jury, she's going to be in deep trouble."

"I'm sorry, J.D.," Julia said. "Really, I am."

"On the other hand," Blackstone said, "who knows. Maybe there won't be a trial." He had a strange smile on his face when he said that. Julia gave him a puzzled look and went back to her document review.

When Blackstone was back in his office, he plunked down in his executive chair and dialed Tully. He got his voice mail.

"The minute you get anything more on Langley, please let me know, Tully," he said. "I'm counting on you."

Then his intercom buzzed. It was Frieda.

"Detective Cheski is on the line, from the DC Police Department." Blackstone took the call.

"Professor," Cheski said. "I've got some good news about your shooting out at the equine center."

"Great," Blackstone said. "What do you have?"

"We've gone through literally hundreds of checks on white trucks and vans registered within a fifty-mile radius of the shooting," Detective Cheski said. "You can't imagine how many vehicles with that kind of description there are in Northern Virginia."

"I can take a wild guess," Blackstone replied.

"Then we cross-referenced those owners with registered gun owners,". Cheski continued. "On the happenstance that we might get a match of both a vehicle type that you described and a registration of an AK-47, which we know was the weapon used."

"Sounds like a plan," Blackstone said. "Any luck?"

"Not yet. But we have three suspects in particular who lived less than ten miles from the shooting with similar vehicle types who had various gun registrations—although no known AK-47s. Anyway, we are now checking alibis on where they were and what they were doing at the time of the shooting. I get the feeling that something is going to break soon."

"I bet you're right," Blackstone said.

"Anyway," Cheski said. "I didn't want you to think you were being ignored."

"Don't worry about that," Blackstone said. "In fact, if you want to, you can just skip my shooting case completely and put all your energy into the Vinnie Archmont trial instead."

"Sorry that I can't oblige you on that," Cheski said with a chuckle. "But I will be in the courtroom, at that trial date, as scheduled. Too bad you'll probably be on the losing side."

"Just out of curiosity," Blackstone said, "do any of your three suspects in my shooting seem to have any connection with the Smithsonian crimes?"

"We're checking for that," Cheski said. "I will let you know immediately if we find anything."

"Thanks for calling, Detective," Blackstone said, and then hung up the phone.

Jason strode into Blackstone's office with a printed piece of paper.

"Sit down, Jason," Blackstone said and motioned for his summary. Jason reached over the desk and handed it to him.

"I wanted to review some things with you," Blackstone said. "You've been going through the FBI and police reports, crime lab records, evidence records, almost as much as I have."

Jason nodded.

"Let's go over some things together," Blackstone said. "How many forensic reports do we have?"

"Well," Jason said. "Let's see...there was the report on the drinking glass—that came back negative. Blood splatter analysis. It was all Horace Langley's blood. No one else's. A report on some DNA inadvertently picked up from some of the investigating officers at the scene—one sweat drip from one of the crime lab technicians, Bert Thompson, and the other from Detective Cheski, both of them on the crime scene. There was a report indicating the presence of a partial fingerprint on a doorknob that they figured was from FBI Agent Ralph Johnson when he came in before he put on the gloves. Then there was a report on numerous fingerprints of Horace Langley all over the place—on several areas of the office. Of course there is the ballistics report on the bullets. One shooter, shooting from one direction, directly at Langley's chest. The report dusting for fingerprints on the side door activated by the keypad. No discernible prints were detected. Lastly, the autopsy protocol from the medical examiner. I think that's it."

"Just checking," Blackstone said. Then he picked up Jason's summary. "You sure this is completely accurate?"

"Sure I'm sure," he answered, now a little nervous.

"Okay. I trust you," Blackstone said with a reassuring smile. "Now, how about your research on Savannah, Georgia?"

Jason flipped open his steno pad.

"Okay, here's what I found," he said. "The Solomon's Lodge No. 1 of Savannah is America's oldest continuously operating Freemasons' Lodge."

"Interesting," Blackstone said. "Anything else?"

"Just this," Jason said. "Savannah, in the 1700s was the site of the first appearance of 'speculative Freemasonry' when it arrived here in the colonies from England."

Blackstone smiled.

"Good work," he said. Then he dismissed him.

The criminal law professor reviewed the summary that Jason had prepared.

Then he read it again.

And then a third time. And that is when he was able to break into a smile.

After that, he picked up the telephone and dialed the telephone number of federal prosecutor Henry Hartz.

CHAPTER 54

While Blackstone was waiting for the secretary at the U.S. Attorney's office to transfer the call to Henry Hartz, Blackstone was looking over Jason's summary once again:

CHRONOLOGY REGARDING
HORACE LANGLEY'S OFFICE

11:30 a.m.—Horace Langley arrives at his office
3:45 p.m.—Vinnie Archmont arrives
4:20 p.m.—Vinnie leaves
7:45 p.m.—Security guard William Portley checks in with
   Horace Langley

MIDNIGHT

12:50 a.m.—Probable time of death per medical examiner's
   report
1:15 a.m.—Security guard Jerry Lamont discovers Langley's
   body & calls District of Columbia police dispatch
1:22 a.m.—District of Columbia patrol officers Blunt and Jano-
   vak arrive
1:47 a.m.—FBI Agent Ralph Johnson arrives at scene, with
   Special Agent Bob Vorhees
1:59 a.m.—Crime lab team arrives from the FBI: technicians

Bert Thompson, and Lamar Linney, and crime lab chief
Corbin Anglor. Forensic sweep of the room begins; District
of Columbia police photographer arrives for forensic photos

2:44 a.m.—District of Columbia Detective Victor Cheski
arrives

3:20 a.m.—Following interrogation, security guards Lamont
and Portley are released and allowed to go home

3:30 a.m.—Police photographer leaves the scene

6:12 a.m.—Forensic analysis of crime scene complete; all crime
lab staff from FBI leave

6:13 a.m.—FBI agents Ralph Johnson and Bob Vorhees leave

6:15 a.m.—Detective Cheski secures the scene and leaves

Then he heard Hartz pick up the line.

"Henry," Blackstone said when the Assistant U.S. Attorney answered
the phone.

"What do you want, Blackstone?"

"Just wanted to tell you something."

"What's that?"

"You are going to lose this case."

There was a pause on the other end. Then Henry Hartz sort of guf-
fawed.

But Blackstone was looking down at the summary that Jason had
drafted.

"And when you realize that all is lost—when everything in your legal
career begins to look the darkest and the most dreadful, then, Henry,
that is exactly when, more than anything, you are going to want to talk
with me. And do you know what?"

Hartz didn't respond.

"I am going to stand there with you and look you in the eye—and I
am going to have a talk with you."

"Blackstone," Hartz said, "either you are going a little crazy—and I
wouldn't doubt that a bit—either that, or else you are trying to pull some
really lame psych-out trick on me. Some kind of psychological manipulation. Either way, I really don't care. Blackstone, you can't psych me. So
don't waste my time with pranks like this anymore. You've got a client

facing the death chamber. If I were you, I'd be doing double-time trying to help my client. Not that it's going to help in the end. We *will* get a conviction. But maybe you can mount enough of a legal defense not to embarrass yourself…and save what's left of your legal career."

Then Hartz remembered something.

"By the way, I've sent a courier from my office over to yours. He's bringing you a load of documents."

"Sounds like fun," Blackstone said. "I love being buried alive in useless paperwork. What's this all about?"

"I've decided," Hartz said, "to furnish you with a complete set of records of the FBI's physical evidence inventory room for the last twelve months. Just to prove that we are not covering up anything in this moronic drinking glass evidence you've complained about—we both know that issue is a complete and total red herring. Anyway, when you and I see each other on the first day of trial, I don't want to hear any more whining from you about the missing drinking glass and how you think something sinister is going on just because we can't find it."

"Let's put it this way, Henry," Blackstone said. "When you and I see each other on the first day of trial—I'll guarantee one thing."

"And that would be what?"

"I won't be whining," Blackstone said.

After Hartz hung up the phone, Blackstone buzzed Julia. He asked her for the name and telephone number of Vinnie's apartment manager. He called the number and got his voice mail.

"Yes, this is J.D. Blackstone," he announced in his message for the apartment manager. "I am the lawyer for Vinnie Archmont, one of your tenants. Her apartment is number 101, just down the hall from yours. I know my partner, Julia Robins, has already interviewed you, but I needed just a few minutes of your time. Give me a call."

Blackstone left the apartment manager his home phone and cell phone numbers.

Less than an hour later, the courier arrived with a large package from the U.S. Attorney's Office.

Blackstone opened it up. Inside a box there was a stack of records about ten inches thick. On the top of the stack there was a typed sheet that read *United States of America v. Vinnie Archmont:* "Government

Disclosure of Evidence Room Records for Twelve Month Period—Six Months Prior to Date of Criminal Incident and Six Months Post Criminal Incident."

Then Blackstone strode down to Julia's office. She was clearing off her desk for the day.

"Sorry to do this to you," he said. "But I need your help with some records that just came in on Vinnie's case. More government discovery. This time it's records of their evidence room. You know, because I raised a ruckus about the missing drinking glass that had been at the scene of the crime. I'm sure there's nothing in these documents. But if we both take a pile and start reviewing them, it will go twice as fast."

"Twice as fast for you, you mean," Julia said. Then she nodded and added, "Fine. Let's get to it." She stood up from her desk and started walking down to Blackstone's office, following him.

"How about I order some dinner in for both of us while we're working?" he said over his shoulder.

"Thanks anyway," she said. "But let's just get this over with. I'll save dinner for when I am back in my apartment with my pj's on and my cat curled up next to me."

"Alright. Just asking," Blackstone said.

The two of them sat down in Blackstone's office, with Julia in a chair facing the desk and Blackstone at his desk. They divided the stack of documents into two groups. Julia was to review the stack of records for the six months leading up to the day of the murder, and Blackstone took the records from the day of the crime to the present.

An hour passed with only the sound of flipping pages as they scanned each of the evidence room reports, one by one. After another half-an hour, Julia looked up from her pile.

"You have FBI evidence records, right?" she asked.

Blackstone nodded.

"So do I," Julia said. "All of them records from the federal facility where they keep the physical evidence. FBI records—all except one."

"What do you mean?" Blackstone asked.

Julia pulled a single piece of paper out of her pile and held it in front of her.

"Do you have the criminal incident number for the District of

Columbia investigation into the Langley murder?" she asked. "I don't mean the FBI investigation number—I am talking about the DC police report number."

Blackstone nodded. "I've got it in my notebooks," he said. Then he got up and walked over to the bookcase where he had a line of black notebooks, each with the name and case number of Vinnie's case typed on the label on the spine. He pulled one out of the stack and flipped through it. After a few minutes he called out the case number.

Julia looked down at the piece of paper she was holding.

"It matches," she murmured.

"What did you find?" he asked.

Julia handed Blackstone the single piece of paper.

He looked at the top and noticed the seal of the District of Columbia Police Department at the top. Directly under it, it read, "Evidence Inventory." Then a date. The date was the day after the Langley murder.

And in a line under the category "Description of Item" were the words "one drinking glass."

"A District of Columbia police report tucked away in a huge pile of FBI evidence records," Julia said. "Which is interesting enough in itself. But the bigger deal is the more obvious point...I think we've just found the missing drinking glass you've been looking for."

Julia's eyes were wide and expressive. She had a big smile on her face.

"Hey, this is pretty big news," she said.

"Good work," he said quietly. "And you're right. It is big news. Thanks for finding this." He had a satisfied look on his face.

"You don't seem surprised," Julia said. "What gives?"

"You're correct I'm not surprised," Blackstone said in a contemplative tone. Then he added, "I wish I was."

Then he suggested that Julia head home for the night. Blackstone didn't take any of the Vinnie Archmont file home with him that night, as he usually did.

Blackstone was heating up a microwave dinner in his condo when his phone rang. It was the apartment manager.

"Sorry to call so late," the apartment manager said. "My kid had a baseball game tonight. What's up?"

"I needed to ask you something."

"I thought your partner, the lady lawyer I talked to—I thought she got everything she needed from me."

"Yes," Blackstone said. "She did. But I have one more question for you myself. It's important."

The apartment manager said, "Look, I'm kinda tired here and the wife is waiting for me at the kitchen table. And I got my son here…you sure it's just one question?"

"Yeah, I'm sure," Blackstone said. "Just one."

CHAPTER 55

When Blackstone finished speaking with the apartment manager on the telephone, he collapsed on the couch in his condo to think things over. His mind was reeling.

He was now witnessing the slow, grinding gears of the truth behind the Smithsonian crime begin to fall into place, teeth into teeth, the locking of wheels into wheels. It would be up to him to operate the fearful machinery of justice and then watch what it would reveal.

Blackstone saw what his job was. Just a few more matters of corroboration, final bits of evidence and information, and then the curtain would rise on the final act.

He splashed water on his face. He paced. There was the day's newspaper on the glass-top table. He picked it up and tried to divert his mind for a few moments by catching up on the news. He hurried through the front page, the national news, world news, op-ed page. He tossed them aside and turned to the arts and entertainment section.

There was an advertisement for a play that was showing at the Kennedy Center.

He studied it. Then Blackstone looked at it more closely and shook his head. The irony of it was unmistakable. For a split second he even entertained the thought that it was something more than irony. The odds behind these conjoining events intersecting when they did, as he approached the trial on this particular case, seemed to take it out of the category of pure chance. But just as quickly as he considered the hand of fate—or providence—or other similar explanation, he dismissed it.

He picked up the phone and called Julia's home number.

He knew she wouldn't answer. He was right.

"Julia, this is J.D.," Blackstone said. "You're probably there but not picking up. Don't blame you, really. Listen, there is something I would like to have you see with me tomorrow night. A play at the Kennedy. Don't worry—it's not a date. Consider it another assignment for the Vinnie Archmont case—just a little more entertaining than the other work you've been doing for me. Please come with me, if you would. Let's leave the office about six. We can pick up the dinner over at the Center. Please say yes."

In her apartment, Julia was curled up on her couch, watching TV, in her pajamas. Her cat was asleep next to her.

She listened to the voice-mail message from Blackstone. She heard her answering machine go silent when the message was ended. She wiped her eyes. Then she breathed heavily and shook her head in ambivalent dismay.

When Julia arrived at the firm the next day and clicked on the lights in her office, she saw something sitting on her desk.

She walked over to her desktop and saw a floral arrangement wrapped in paper. She opened up the paper, revealing a vase with six red roses in it.

There was a note attached. It read, "Julia—Please forgive my ham-handed double entendre with the six roses. And please forgive other things too. Hope you can make it tonight. J.D."

Stapled to the note was an advertisement ripped from the newspaper. It announced the "last night, at the Kennedy Center, for Ben Jonson's acerbic and witty satire *The Alchemist*."

Julia took the note and the newspaper ad and walked into Blackstone's office. His desk was covered with several trial notebooks, which he was reviewing as he prepared for the Vinnie Archmont trial. He looked up when he noticed Julia.

"So we leave at six?" Julia said casually.

"Yes," Blackstone said. "They have that convenient dinner spot inside the Kennedy, the Roof Terrace. I thought we'd eat there before the show."

"That makes sense," Julia said. "And I thought the half-dozen roses were clever. Six roses...'rose of 6' and all that."

"I just wanted to set the tone for tonight's theme," Blackstone said.

Julia smiled, nodded, and headed back to her office.

Then Blackstone buzzed Frieda.

"Connect me with Lord Dee's personal secretary over in England, would you?" he asked.

A few minutes later Colin Reading was on the line.

"I need to arrange a private meeting with Lord Dee," Blackstone said.

"Actually," Reading said, "Lord Dee just arrived back from some meetings he had in Quebec. I know he is booked solid."

Blackstone didn't miss that.

"I understand," Blackstone said. "But Vinnie Archmont's criminal trial is just a few days off. There is something I need to speak to him about. It's very urgent."

"All I can do is try to pass the message on to Lord Dee," Reading replied. "No promises are being made, regrettably."

"Agreed," Blackstone said. "I'll be in my office for the rest of the day." After that conversation, Blackstone got up, walked over to the door of his office and shut it.

Two hours later, Blackstone received a call from Lord Dee himself.

It was a short conversation, lasting less than five minutes.

When it was over, Blackstone shot a quick e-mail to Frieda, giving her some instructions for the day and asking that he not be disturbed. Then he sent an e-mail directive to Jason with a short list of additional persons to be subpoenaed, some of them for the first day of Vinnie's trial. Some of them would be required to bring documents and records with them.

As he looked at the subpoena list, he realized he was looking at the pivot point of the entire legal defense for Vinnie's case.

When six o'clock came, he tossed on his sport coat and strode into Julia's office.

She was already standing in the doorway of her office, purse in hand. She had changed into a gorgeous dress. Her glasses were off, and she was wearing her contacts.

"I took the Metro over this morning," she said. "That way we only have to worry about one car."

Blackstone smiled and led her out of the office, holding the door open for her, and the two of them walked to his Maserati.

Less than an hour later, sharing a casual dinner with Blackstone at a corner table in the Roof Terrace Restaurant on the top floor of the Kennedy Center, Julia took a minute to look out through the glass wall and survey the lights of Washington DC. She could see the lights of the Lincoln Monument, and the illuminated outline of the Washington Monument with its blinking light on top of the tall obelisk.

"I checked out Vinnie's petition for name change she had filed," Julia said. "After you and I talked, my interest was piqued."

"What did you find out?" Blackstone asked.

"She filed it recently. Just three years ago."

"That would have been after her parents died in that train accident in England?"

"Yes," Julia said, wondering what connection Blackstone was trying to make.

"What did she give as the reason for wanting to change her name?" Blackstone asked. "Usually there is a requirement that the petition for name change give some explanation."

"She said it would help her in her professional life as an artist."

"What was her name before the change?" Blackstone asked.

"Wilson. That was the name of her parents. The parents who raised her—and who were killed."

"But she didn't allege anything about being adopted and wanting to reclaim the last name of her natural parents? Nothing like that?"

"No," Julia replied.

She pushed her plate aside and with a half-smile asked him a question. "So you said that tonight would have a theme?"

"Yes. I've orchestrated this very tightly," Blackstone said with a smile. "Like a Swiss watch. First, six roses, obviously symbolic on several levels. And now this." And with that, he pulled out the playbill for the performance they were to see.

On the cover of the playbill it said, "The Kennedy Center presents Ben Jonson's *The Alchemist.*"

"I thought Jonson's name was spelled the usual way," she said. "You know, *Johnson*."

"It's actually spelled both ways. I think the playbill's got it right… but I really don't know."

"So," she said with a broadening smile, "there actually *is* something the great J.D. Blackstone, that brilliant and iconoclastic mind, really doesn't have the answer to?"

He chuckled and blushed a little.

"I can't believe it," Julia said. "You're blushing like an adolescent on his first date."

Blackstone fumbled with his silverware.

"Okay, so the question," Julia said, "was about tonight's theme. Which is, what? Alchemy? I wouldn't ever have pegged you for a guy who would give that concept any extra thought, were it not for your uncle's ideas. So, you don't believe that stuff, right?"

"Yes and no," Blackstone answered cautiously.

"Oh, this ought to be good," Julia chided him.

"First," Blackstone said, "no, on a factual basis, I don't accept that stuff—and I also don't go for the crank theories about the 'area 54' alien autopsy, the inside job on the Kennedy assassination, or Loch Ness monster either."

"So, where does the 'yes' part of the 'yes and no' come in?"

"It's like this," he said, looking down at the table that separated them. "I have to shave every morning. As a result, I have to look at myself in the mirror. Every day. As a result I've thought about giving up shaving. But I don't think that's a logical solution. What I mean is this…in terms of my personal life…I think I need a little alchemy, or something. In other words, I need to take the base things in my life and find a way to extract some gold out of them."

The lights blinked overhead, signaling that the play would begin in a few minutes. Blackstone and Julia quickly stood up from the table and hurried down the red-carpeted corridors to their seats.

Elizabethan-era theater was usually not Julia's favorite genre. But it quickly became obvious why Blackstone wanted to see this particular play as she studied the playbill's synopsis of the theater piece.

Satirizing the mores and foibles of London in 1610, Ben Jonson's play showed the work of some scam artists who took over a wealthy house vacated during the plague. One posed as an alchemist who tried to use his magic acumen as a means of bilking others.

In the first act of the play, one of the characters announced boldly, "This is the day I am to perfect for him the magisterium, our great work, the stone."

"The philosopher's stone," Julia murmured as she sat next to Blackstone.

As the play progressed, the theme became even clearer, even stunning. A character looked at the audience and declared, "Do you think I fable you? I assure you, he that has once the flower of the sun, the perfect ruby, which we call elixir…In eight and twenty days, I'll make an old man of fourscore a child."

"'Flower of the sun'—'perfect ruby'—even the reference to the elixir," Julia whispered excitedly to Blackstone next to her. "It's as if old Ben Jonson has heard about the very same 'rose of 6,' the red flower from the 'elixir tree' imbedded in crystal that Horace Langley's note talked about—and that John Wilkes Booth wrote about in his diary. Maybe your uncle's interpretation was right after all."

Blackstone glanced back at Julia and nodded. Even he was impressed.

"Okay, I have to admit," Blackstone whispered back, "the similarities between the 'ruby flower elixir' reference in Ben Jonson's play produced in 1610 and the Langley note that copied the Booth diary…" Blackstone hesitated to say it.

But he finally did.

"The similarities are incredible."

CHAPTER 56

So you're being very quiet," Julia said as they walked to Blackstone's car from the Kennedy Center after the play.

"The premise of *The Alchemist* seemed hauntingly familiar," Blackstone said.

"No question about it," Julia said.

"A few decades after the first production of Jonson's play," Blackstone said, walking slowly next to her, "you then have Elias Ashmole, the Gnostic leader of the speculative Freemasons in England—you will recall my uncle talking about him—Ashmole, tutored by occult followers of alchemy, is then pursuing seriously himself the claims of esoteric alchemy. And his pursuit was obviously continued by Dr. Robert Plot, the professor of chemistry who was the first curator of Ashmole's museum. It is clear that there was a group of these occult believers in the seventeenth century who really did believe they were on the cusp of some titanic discovery. And it is also clear that this wild chase for the key to physical immortality had gone on for centuries before them—perhaps for millennia."

Julia was listening carefully. Then she spoke up.

"What are you saying?" she asked.

"Let me ask you a question," Blackstone said. "What does all this tell you? I mean, in a very personal, private way. What do you feel about all that, in the quiet corners of your brain?"

"Is this a test?" she said laughing.

"Sort of," Blackstone replied.

"Well, at least you're being honest," she replied. "Okay. Well, you know I had religious training in the Catholic Church as a child. I suppose that always has some influence on your view on what you might describe as the ultimate issues."

"So where do you stand on immortality? On life after death—all that," Blackstone shot back.

"Wow," she said with a sigh. "I thought you knew where I stood on that kind of thing, given our prior relationship...and intimacy. I thought we had talked about this."

"We never discussed it," Blackstone said.

"Are you sure?" Julia asked.

"Yes, positive," Blackstone replied firmly. "Believe me, I would have remembered."

"Alright," Julia said, venturing ahead after a moment of hesitation. "I believe there is a God. I do struggle with the faith question. But given that there is a divine force out there somewhere, that would mean there is a spiritual dimension. And if there is a spiritual plane to existence, then immortality...eternal life...those kinds of things would be feasible."

"Sounds logical enough—if we assume your premise, that is. About God."

"And where do you stand on the issue?" Julia asked, as they reached his car in the parking ramp.

Blackstone paused to reflect before he answered. "I think," he responded quietly, "that Ben Jonson's play explained it pretty well. Two main realities. First, there is historical proof of a consistent yearning, from some part of the human psyche, that crosses geography and culture and time, some part of being human that wants to reach out to the eternal—the spiritual—to achieve some kind of immortality. So as a result, we get the alchemists, and the esoteric philosophers, and the Freemasons, as well as the more traditional clergy and religionists."

"Okay, that's your first 'reality,' then. The thirst for the spiritual. The eternal," Julia said. "So, what's the second?"

"The reality of human greed and trickery," Blackstone said. "Jonson's play satirized it as comedy. But he was being very accurate in pointing it out."

Then Blackstone added a thought.

"I think those two forces—immortality and greed—may be closer to us in Vinnie's case then we have any idea," he said.

Julia gave him a funny look. Startled and probing.

"But how do you separate the one from the other? Spiritual truth from trickery," Julia asked, "without mixing them up, or being entirely cynical? How do you do that?"

"That's exactly what I plan on doing on day one of Vinnie Archmont's trial," Blackstone said.

As he walked around to open the door for her on the passenger side of his convertible, Julia added one more thought.

"You know, I wasn't talking about your legal case when I asked that question," she said. "I was talking about your *life*."

As Blackstone drove Julia home, the two of them were quiet.

When he reached her apartment in Bethesda and walked her to the door he told her about his plans for the next day.

"I had Frieda book me a flight to London for tomorrow," Blackstone said. "It's a quick trip. Out and back. There's something I have to ask Lord Dee. And I have to ask it immediately."

"Vinnie's trial is just five days away," Julia said. "I'm surprised you're taking an international trip now. It must be important."

"It is," was all that Blackstone said.

He took Julia's hand and squeezed it, and thanked her for joining him that night.

Julia took her other hand and covered Blackstone's and squeezed back.

"I enjoyed this," she said with a smile. "You know, against all odds… you may be a nice guy after all."

As Blackstone was motoring home he received a call on his cell phone from Tully Tullinger.

"Hey, Professor," Tully said. "Are you sitting down?"

"I better be," Blackstone cracked. "I'm driving."

"Reminds me of a story about the guy who drove his car without sitting down," Tully replied. "But I'll spare you that. Let me get down to brass tacks."

"Please do. You're calling on Horace Langley?"

"Yes," Tully said. "Well, I came up with one thing."

"Shoot."

"The guy was a moderately addicted gambler, it appears."

"How moderately?"

"He visited Atlantic City on a regular basis. Rang up some pretty hefty bills at the casinos."

"How much did he owe?"

"Close to a million bucks," Tully said. "Nine hundred thousand and change."

"I never knew they let guys drive up balances like that," Blackstone said.

"They usually don't," Tully said. "Only if they are regulars and they roll high enough, which he was and he did. But they also ask for some pricey collateral. Which, for some reason, they goofed and didn't get from him."

"So, Secretary Langley owed some big money from gambling. And then there is the problem with the potential stain on his professional reputation as the head of a renowned place like the Smithsonian Institution," Blackstone observed.

"Yeah, I guess you put it right enough," Tully said.

"One more thing," Blackstone asked. "Did you dig up any connection between Langley and the city of Savannah, Georgia?"

"Rings a bell," Tully said. "Give me a second to look over my notes."

After a minute, Tully spoke up.

"Okay, here it is. One of the guys I talked to actually said that Langley mentioned going down to Savannah once—he was heading there, he said, after his gambling junket at one of the casinos."

"Didn't say why he was planning on going to Savannah?" Blackstone said.

"Nope," Tully said. "Anyway, sometimes he went to Atlantic City alone. Sometimes he took a gambling buddy with him. I couldn't get any names, though. I'll type up my notes and send them over to you."

"Fine. Thanks, Tully," Blackstone said. "Now I only have one more job for you on this case. And you will actually have a few days to accomplish it. Do you have ways to access adoption files?"

"Yeah...well, you know, they are closed to the public," he said.

"Of course," Blackstone said. "But Vinnie signed an omnibus authorization and release and power of attorney for all her records at the beginning of this case to give us complete carte blanche."

"True, true," Tully said. "But it's still not that easy. When do you need it?"

"I need Vinnie's adoption records by the first day of trial."

"I think that's doable."

"Now I'm heading home. If I'm lucky I will catch a little sleep tonight before flying out tomorrow."

"Oh, to where?" Tully asked.

"Merry old England," Blackstone said. "The land where time stands still."

CHAPTER 57

A day and an half later, Blackstone was handing some pound notes to an English cabbie. He looked out the window of the cab where it was stopped in downtown London.

"This is it—the address on Great Queen Street?" Blackstone asked.

"It is, sir," the cabbie said. "And that's the very building—rather odious and yet impressive, don't you think? Here, buried in this building, is where they keep all the records and the archives of the United Grand Lodge of England and the Supreme Grand Chapter. Or so they say. But I don't belong. So I couldn't really say for sure."

Blackstone looked at the old, gray stone building, rising up several stories in a pyramid-type series of levels, with tall columns on either side of a massive door that was deeply inset within a portico. The effect was imposing. The placement of the door created the effect of a kaleidoscope. As if the front entrance was beckoning the visitor into a series of deeper and deeper mysteries.

Blackstone stepped out of the cab and strolled up to the front of the building.

He knew it was the right place. Lord Dee had arranged for their meeting at that precise location: the historic Library and Museum of Freemasonry.

There was the sound of a car slowly pulling to a stop at the curb in back of him. Blackstone turned around and saw a long, black Bentley limousine.

Teddy Darrow, Lord Dee's driver, decked out in his black brimmed cap and black coat, scurried around to the curbside passenger's rear of the limo and opened the door.

After a few seconds, Dee, with Teddy assisting, climbed out of the Bentley and onto the sidewalk. Dee looked much the same as he had appeared when Blackstone had last seen him, with his beard flowing down to his chest and hair cascading down to his shoulders. But this time he was sporting a walking stick with an ornate silver knob, and he seemed to be walking slower.

Lord Dee nodded his head as he saw Blackstone.

Then two men exited the limo behind him, both in suits.

"Professor Blackstone," Dee said, reaching out his hand to Blackstone. "You look to be in good health. Pleasant to see you again."

After they shook hands, Dee motioned to the two men in suits standing behind him.

"Professor," Dee said, indicating the two men standing close by, "this is my solicitor, and this is my bodyguard. They have taken to following me around...they say it is for my protection. I won't bother to introduce them—as they will not be joining us today."

With that, Lord Dee gave a slow wave of his hand to the two men who nodded and disappeared back to the interior of the limo.

"Follow me," Lord Dee said, and began making his way across the open terrace to the recessed front door of the building. Then Dee stopped at the door and turned to face Blackstone.

"You said in our telephone conversation you had a question to ask me?"

"That's right," Blackstone said. "I believe what you have to tell me will be essential if I am to be able to unravel the truth behind the Smithsonian crimes."

"So, it is truth that you are after?" Dee asked.

But before Blackstone could respond, Dee continued.

"I told you at our last meeting, as we dined together at my home at Mortland Manor...that...that you...that you." Dee quit talking and now was swallowing hard, bobbing his head a little as he did.

When he was finished swallowing, he continued.

"That you were," Dee said, "you were...were...a skeptic. And as a result, I refused to share the deeper metaphysical concepts of our beliefs...

beliefs…held in common by those of us in the highest echelon, in the elite of the esoteric mysteries."

"I recall that," Blackstone replied.

"Why should I change my mind now, Professor?"

"Because I know what you believe, and what you are after," Blackstone said. "While I don't share your beliefs, I certainly understand them now."

"How can you…you…possibly understand?" Lord Dee sputtered. "How? You of the brash, scientific age…cold…and soulless…how could you know the deep secrets we pursue?"

"Try me. Test me," Blackstone said. "And you will find out, Lord Dee, that I already know the one thing that you've been desperately chasing."

"Then open the door," Lord Dee commanded, pointing with his walking stick to the massive door in front of them. "And we shall see, Professor Blackstone, exactly what it is that you do, and do not, understand."

Blackstone opened the door and the two men entered the front lobby. Lord Dee slowly led the way through a dark, underlighted passageway to a room that opened up into a large library full of ancient floor-to-ceiling bookshelves crammed with books and journals and records. An elderly custodian with a Freemason's badge sat silently on a velvet chair off to the side. There was a musty sense about the place. Here and there around the room there were rows of glass cabinets filled with ancient Masonic artifacts. The room was open in the center with a tiled mosaic on the floor, and historic paintings on the walls.

"Now, Professor," Lord Dee said, "I am the teacher…and you…and… you are…you are the student. The test will now…begin…you…have sixty seconds to show me that you have the least inkling of what I am after… and what it is that I pursue. And if you fail, then you and I will not be speaking again, I would wager."

Lord Dee found a dark leather chair with scrolled armrests, which was close to him, and he sat down on it. He perched his hands on top of the silver knob of his cane, which he held out in front of him.

Then Lord Dee said one final word to Blackstone.

"Proceed," he said.

Blackstone strode into the middle of the room and then quickly began to scan, in a circle, everything in the room—the stacks of books—the museum cases filled with hundreds of years of Masonic history and relics—the pictures—the ornamental scrollwork in the high ceiling and crown moldings.

Then he suddenly stopped. A strange look took over his face. And he closed his eyes and gave out a little chuckle, as if realizing the folly of something, or realizing some private joke.

"Alchemy and geometry," Blackstone whispered to himself.

Blackstone looked over at Lord Dee, who was sitting forward, leaning on his cane with both hands. Dee's eyes were fixed on Blackstone like an audience member watching the act of a magician on stage, straining to discover the flaw, the trick, the illusion.

Raising his right hand up in the air, index pointing up, Blackstone then brought his index finger slowly downward, until it was pointing at the floor beneath him.

Blackstone was standing in the open space in the middle of the Freemason's museum. Then he started speaking.

"What has been lost? What is it that is pursued from the ends of the earth?" Blackstone said as if in a rhythmic chant, paraphrasing the Freemason's ritual.

"The secrets of the Master Mason," he continued. "And how shall they be found? By finding the center—the center that is the point within the circle."

When Blackstone finished those words, he stepped perfectly within the very center of the tiled floor underfoot and then looked down, studying the mosaic designs in equidistance from him. There were figures of ornate cherubim in the floor. But that is not what caught his attention. What he was staring at was something else altogether.

"The four corners," Blackstone announced, and with that he pointed as he pivoted around to four designs within the four quadrants of the open center.

"The symbols of the ancient tree of immortality," Blackstone said as he pointed to each of the four spots, "bordering the entire circle." In each design there was the unmistakable image of the acacia tree leaf in mosaic design.

"I am willing to bet," Blackstone continued, "that you won't find any reference to those leaves in any of the neat little museum signs that are posted around the room."

Lord Dee was silent, waiting.

"You seek an ancient flowering plant, Lord Dee," Blackstone continued. "It carries with it the gift, you believe, of prolonging human life indefinitely. The Freemasons have used the symbol of the acacia tree to hide its meaning. Over the centuries, others have called it the 'rose,' perhaps because the plant allegedly took on a reddish appearance. And in fact, the rose is the truer symbol, which accounts for the fact that in the very earliest Freemason's lodges ever recorded, they had roses painted on the ceilings. The rose came to be known not only as the symbol for the keeping of a great secret—but also as the essence of the secret itself, the search for the means to achieve, through the supposed power of alchemy, the power of an everlasting life.

"The ancient 'rose' you seek," Blackstone went on, "is supposedly imbedded in a crystal, which worked to preserve the potency of the plant—something possessing the power to work miraculous healings, or extended life, to those who simply come close to it. As of 1610, during the heyday of playwright Ben Jonson, the word was out that this was some kind of 'ruby flower' that contained the 'elixir' of life. Elias Ashmole, schooled in the occult arts, picked up the hunt for it in the later part of the 1600s. And he was followed by his curator, the professor of chemistry, Dr. Robert Plot. And that is where the chase seems to have ended—until, in your way of thinking, nearly two hundred years later, when Albert Pike, the American Masonic philosopher and a handful of Confederate members of the Knights of the Golden Circle finally figured it all out—or at least so you believe."

Blackstone stepped over to Lord Dee and gazed down at him, sitting in his chair. Dee was now deep in thought.

"And so," Blackstone concluded, "that is what you believe, Lord Dee. And that is what you seek.

"But there is still one last element I haven't discussed," Blackstone said. "Namely—*why* you seek the rose crystal. It could be simply the esoteric thrill of finding something so fabled throughout the annals of alchemy and occult philosophy. Or maybe the desire to taste immortality—a universal desire, I suppose. Could be. But I don't think that is your motivation."

Now Blackstone was standing directly in front of Lord Dee. He knelt down next to the English lord.

"No, I think your motivation hits much closer to home," Blackstone said. "At first I thought the symptoms you showed evidenced Parkinson's disease. But then I saw the combination of your problem swallowing and verbal blockage with words—then I had a pretty good idea of what it was. Something I had run across in my graduate studies in the subject of neuropsychology.

"I'm very sorry, Lord Dee," the law professor continued. "It looks like you are suffering from corticobasal degeneration. Correct?"

Dee half-smiled and nodded.

"There is no cure. None at all," Dee said. "Not even the Parkinson-slowing medications are successful in treating it," he said glumly. "Gradual death of brain nerve cells in the cerebral cortex and the basal ganglia. In a little while, I will be unable to walk. Unable to feed myself. Not able to talk. Then eventually, no movement at all. Death. Slow, debilitating. Agonizing. In about…oh…prob…probabl…probably two years at most… or maybe less."

"May I ask my question now, Lord Dee?" Blackstone asked quietly. Dee nodded.

"According to press reports," Blackstone said, "you are England's third-wealthiest man. So my question is this—since Vinnie was charged criminally at the very beginning of this case—since that time to the present, have there been any attempts from anyone to sell you the Horace Langley note?"

"Just one."

"When?"

"Recently. A few weeks ago."

"How?"

"A letter I received at my address at the House of Lords."

"What did it say?"

"For forty million dollars, someone would give me an exact copy of the note that Horace Langley wrote when he copied down the Booth diary entry, and then the Booth diary itself."

"Did you try to trace back the letter?"

"It was mailed from a city in America."

"What city?"

"Savannah, Georgia."

"And you understand the historical significance of that city to the Freemasons in particular?"

"Of course, of course," Dee replied quickly.

"What were you required to do?" Blackstone asked.

"If I was interested in pursuing it, I should post an advertisement in the London *Times* on a certain date—which I did—asking for help in finding a 'missing rose garden.'"

"Did the letter indicate what would happen if you didn't?"

"Yes—the letter-writer professed the ability to control the critical documents, and the copies, threatened to destroy the Booth diary pages, as well as Horace Langley's notes and any evidence of both of them."

"So after posting the advertisement, then what?" Blackstone asked.

"The letter said that after I posted the ad in the *Times,* then in 'a little while' I would be told where a rendezvous would be set up. My agent was to pick up the Horace Langley note, which 'will be supplied along with absolute proof of its authenticity.' The sender of the letter indicated I should beware of others who might allege they had true copies of the Horace Langley note because they are all 'frauds.' Well, at the time of my receipt of the Langley note we would simultaneously wire twenty million dollars to a designated offshore account…and following that there would be a separate transaction sometime later where I would be given the actual Booth diary pages and I would wire the final twenty million."

"Anything else?"

"No," Lord Dee said. "I have been waiting for further instructions but haven't received them yet."

And then Dee sighed deeply and added, "So—you think me a fool for believing such a metaphysical tale as this, don't you?"

"I wouldn't call you a fool," Blackstone said.

"Professor, I believe in the mysteries of my ancient predecessors," Dee said. "And I will spend my very last breath pursuing their hidden secrets…until I find them."

As J.D. Blackstone climbed into a cab to leave Great Queen Street in London and head to the airport, he had two thoughts. One was profound, and the other much more practical.

I wish I had something convincing, something tangible, to help Dee face his own mortality, was his first thought.

The second thought dealt with something he had brought with him on the plane flight over to London and had reviewed to help him prepare for his encounter with Dee.

Thank heavens I finally got around to finishing my uncle's book on the Freemasons.

CHAPTER 58

B y the time that Blackstone arrived at the office from the airport it was noon. He had scheduled a final review of the case that afternoon with Julia and Jason.

The subpoenas had all been served on the witnesses who would testify regarding the glass from Horace Langley's office, as well as the other trial witnesses, Jason told his boss. Blackstone asked Jason to research two more court decisions he might need to finish his trial brief.

After the conversation with Jason, Blackstone met with Julia in the conference room. She reviewed the approach she would use during the penalty phase of the case, if the jury were to come in with a conviction on a death-penalty offense. Julia also went over with Blackstone the voir dire questions she thought should be put to the prospective jurors to ferret out their opinions about the death penalty.

Then Blackstone leaned back in the conference-room chair, nodded to Julia in approval, but said nothing.

"Did you get the crucial discovery you wanted from Lord Dee?" Julia asked.

"Yes," Blackstone said. "He verified that someone is now trying to extort money from him. I had figured as much."

"Who are the culprits?"

Blackstone fell silent again. Then after a few moments he finally spoke up.

"I don't want you to be offended," he said, "but I think I'm going to have to keep some things about the guilt phase of Vinnie's case private, even from you."

"I'm a big girl. I'll try not to feel hurt," she said. "But I do find it impossible to understand, frankly. Either we are law partners, or we aren't—at least until I make my decision on a departure date from the law firm. I think that is basically the same point you made to me once. That we still are partners for the present."

"Partnership isn't the issue," Blackstone said. "Nor is it a matter of competence. I know of no one better I would like at counsel table with me on this case than you."

"Then what's the problem?" Julia asked, now a little demanding.

"There are some things about the way I am conducting this case that I need to shield you from," Blackstone replied. "For your own protection. I care about you. Which is why I am trying to protect you."

"So why does that sound so paternalistic and patronizing?" she shot back.

"It probably does sound that way," Blackstone said. "And I'm sorry about that. But I know I'm right."

"You always think you're right," she said, visibly perturbed. "Which means you always have the power to close the debate on any subject."

"The subject right now," Blackstone said, "is Vinnie's defense. On other issues, I am willing to admit mistakes...sometimes grossly erroneous ones. Sometimes idiotic ones. But not here. Not on this one."

"Because of your feelings about Vinnie? Is that it? You have to be right here, on this case, because you care so much about her?" Julia asked, her face hiding an ocean of emotion.

"Let's get back to the facts and the evidence," Blackstone said. "We both have some huge distractions at play that could impair our objectivity. Let's not give in to that. Julia, I need every bit of your brains and talent at work in this defense. And if things work out the way I believe they will, then there will come a time when I will call you into my confidence. And when that happens, then you are going to have to give the best legal advice you can give. I will be depending on it. Is that a deal?"

Julia's expression was mingled hurt and confusion. But she nodded yes nevertheless.

With that, Blackstone began focusing on one of the main players in the Smithsonian crimes, Horace Langley.

"Langley's the silent witness here," Blackstone began.

"Let's not forget the obvious—he's also the victim," Julia said.

"Elaborate," he shot back.

"Well," Julia said somewhat dumbfounded. "It's obvious, isn't it? He was shot twice in the chest. Murdered. No signs of struggle. Not an accident. So it looks like a deliberate assassination of the secretary of one of America's most beloved and revered institutions. Langley was a nationally recognized scholar. Plus, the Booth diary pages and Langley's notes were stolen. So the crime was a murder-theft."

"You're the prosecutor," Blackstone said. "In a few sentences, how do you sell this case to the jury in closing arguments?"

Julia didn't miss a beat.

"Ladies and gentlemen of the jury," she said without taking a breath and staring directly at Blackstone, "this was a crime of cold, deliberate intention and malicious murder. Horace Langley, one of America's most honored scholars, was most certainly the innocent victim here—shot down without pity or hesitation as part of a conspiracy to obtain the John Wilkes Booth diary. But he was not the only victim. His family lost a husband and father. His family was victimized. But even beyond that, the Smithsonian Institution has lost its chief executive officer and has also lost one of the most significant historical documents in post–Civil War American history. For those reasons, all America has been victimized.

"And in a moment I will remind you of all of the evidence that proves beyond a reasonable doubt why Vinnie Archmont was a key member of the conspiracy that assassinated Horace Langley just as surely as another conspiracy assassinated Abraham Lincoln nearly one hundred and fifty years ago and, in a way, victimized America's history similarly."

"Good," Blackstone said. "Well done. Exactly the same way I would have played it too."

"So what was the purpose of that little exercise?" Julia asked with bewilderment. "The point is that Horace Langley is a victim—right?"

Blackstone smiled one of his secret smiles.

"A victim?" he asked. "Clearly. But what kind of a victim? Let's just review some of the facts we now know about Horace Langley. He was a scholar with a specialty in seventeenth-century English history. He also was an avid aficionado regarding the American Civil War. Tully called me the other day and explained that Langley owed some sizable gambling debts. Next, we learn that Langley visited Savannah, Georgia, at some point within the weeks leading up to his death. My guess was that his trip was for the purpose of doing some research. Savannah, Georgia, in Freemasons' lore, was the birthplace of the American brand of speculative Freemasonry."

"Yes," Julia replied, "but we have absolutely no proof that Horace Langley was even a Freemason, do we?"

"Oh, I'm satisfied he was never a Freemason," Blackstone said confidently. "But in any event, it is further interesting to note that the recent extortion letter to Lord Dee was mailed from Savannah, Georgia."

"Not by Langley, obviously," Julia said. "He was dead by then. So who mailed it?"

"The same person, or persons, who masterminded the Smithsonian crimes."

"And that would be—" Julia started to say.

"Exactly what I can't tell you right now," Blackstone said. "You'll just have to trust me."

Julia had several clever retorts to that, but decided not to use them. Instead she simply asked if there was anything else he needed from her.

"Get some rest tonight, and a good sleep," Blackstone said.

"You too," she said as she got up from the conference-room chair.

Fat chance of that happening, Blackstone thought to himself. "See you at the federal courthouse at eight tomorrow morning," he said as she was leaving the conference room. "And please bring Jason along to help carry the files."

Blackstone caught up on a few details on some other cases. Then he sent a memo over to the dean of the law school regarding the fall term, as summer was coming to an end.

By late afternoon, he had left the office and headed over to the federal detention center to meet with Vinnie.

Blackstone had lost track of the number of criminal clients he had met with on the eve of trial. They would handle their anxieties differently. Some retreated into a quiet, reclusive shell. Others became talkative and overblown. A few would manage a sense of bravado. But they all had one thing in common: the ever-present feeling of dread that, by the time that the jury stepped out of the jury room to announce their verdict, their lives might be irrevocably changed.

Vinnie was visibly nervous. When he greeted her in the jail interview room and took her hand, it was ice cold, and she was shaking. She pulled herself into his chest and wrapped her arms around him for nearly a minute. He finally pulled himself away gently and motioned for her to sit down in the plastic chair across the table from him.

"I want to walk you through the process for the trial tomorrow," Blackstone began. With that, he described when the case would begin. How the U.S. marshals would bring her into the courtroom. She said she had a nice outfit to wear for the trial. Blackstone said that was good. He said the large jury panel would report to the courtroom, and then would be sequestered into another room while the lawyers argued about "some preliminaries."

"What kind of preliminaries?" Vinnie asked. "Can you explain that all to me?"

"I've filed a motion with the court that needs to be heard before the trial," Blackstone answered.

"A motion?" she asked.

"Yes," Blackstone replied. "It has to do with a missing piece of evidence. A drinking glass from the crime scene that appears to have been misplaced by the prosecution."

Vinnie nodded at that, and managed a smile.

"Do you have any questions about that—about the missing glass business?" Blackstone probed.

"No, thanks," Vinnie said, responding with another smile.

Blackstone was studying his client very carefully. He didn't miss a thing.

He then described what would happen if his motion was not granted by the trial judge. How the voir dire questioning of the jury would be conducted. After selection of the jury, the prosecution would give its opening statement, followed by the defense opening statement. Then the government would begin presenting its case. When the prosecution rested, the defense would begin its case.

"Will I testify?" Vinnie asked.

"I am thinking not," Blackstone said. "But we can discuss that later, during the trial."

Blackstone described, slowly, in painstaking detail, the process by which the government lawyers and the defense lawyers would submit suggested jury instructions to the judge. The judge would decide which ones to read verbally to the jury. Then would come closing arguments and the government's chance at a final rebuttal argument, and then the case would be in the hands of twelve jurors to deliberate and decide.

"If you are convicted on a charge that carries a capital penalty—in other words, death by execution," Blackstone said, "then we will have to proceed to the death-penalty phase of the case. It is important that you ask me any questions you have on that."

Vinnie's eyes widened and, momentarily, she seemed breathless. When she regained her composure, she answered.

"That's what your partner, Julia, has been talking with me about," Vinnie said.

"Right."

"She seems very sharp. Very capable."

"She is," Blackstone said with a smile.

Then he thought of something.

"Julia has gone over your personal background information with you, I know. But one thing needs to be nailed down."

"Yes?"

"Your name change," Blackstone asked. "What was the reason for that?"

"Well," Vinnie said reluctantly, "I know that on my legal petition for change of my name that I filed with court, I had said it was for 'artistic, professional' purposes. But that wasn't really, totally correct."

"Oh?" Blackstone asked.

"No," she continued. "The fact is...shortly before my parents were killed in that train accident, I had found out I had been adopted. They finally got around to telling me. So after they died, I did some checking and discovered that my biological mother's name was 'Archmont,' so I decided to make that my legal name. Does that help you?"

"Immensely, and it's pretty much what I had thought you'd tell me," Blackstone said. Then he pulled together his notes, stuffed them into his briefcase, and got up from the chair.

Vinnie gave him one more hug.

Then Blackstone gave her a reassuring smile, and called for the jailer to let him out of the locked room.

Just before the jailer unlocked the door, Blackstone turned around to share one more thought with his client. "I am going to make your case all about truth and justice tomorrow," Blackstone said. "So that means you should have nothing to worry about."

Regardless of the effect Blackstone might have wanted to create in his client with that last statement, as her criminal-defense attorney stepped out of the jail interview room, Vinnie's face was betraying a look of dread.

CHAPTER 59

The next day, early in the morning, Blackstone, Julia, and Jason were in the federal courthouse elevator. Crowded around them were several suitcase-sized briefcases and half a dozen banker's boxes of documents. Blackstone and Julia were each carrying the laptops they would use during trial to retrieve detailed information out of the morass of facts, evidence, and records in the case of *United States of America v. Vinnie Archmont.*

They watched the numbers appear consecutively on the elevator screen as they climbed their way to the floor where Judge Templeton's courtroom was located. No one was talking. Finally Julia broke the silence.

"J.D., promise me just one thing," she said.

"What's that?" Blackstone replied.

"Please don't let this case get to the death-penalty phase. Do that for me, will you?"

"That's the plan, my dear friend," he replied, with only a mere trace of a smile on his face.

When the elevator door opened, the small defense team could see that the hallway outside of the courtroom was jammed with reporters. Judge Templeton had already issued a decision barring cameras from the trial. But that didn't prevent print journalists from several dozen newspapers and magazines from showing up. There were also reporters from television stations milling about. They would sit through the case and then do stand-up summaries in front of the camera on the courthouse lawn at the end of each day's proceedings.

Blackstone, Julia, and Jason carted their boxes and briefcases through the crowd and into the courtroom. When the reporters began firing questions at Blackstone in the hall, the law professor simply smiled, kept walking, and said only one thing: "Ladies and gentlemen, hang on tight to your notepads. This is going to be a bumpy ride."

Henry Hartz was already at the prosecution counsel's table, flanked on either side by two other Assistant U.S. Attorneys. Sitting behind him were FBI Special Agent Ralph Johnson and DC detective Victor Cheski. Behind them was a row full of law-enforcement agents and officials.

On the other side of the courtroom, several dozen potential jurors had been seated in the benches by the bailiff.

Blackstone and Julia took their seats at the defense counsel table. Jason was sitting in the bench right behind them. A few minutes later, Tully Tullinger scooted into the courtroom with a leather case, took off his straw panama hat, and sat down next to Jason.

In the far corner of the courtroom, Blackstone's defense expert, Dr. Cutsworth, was seated there with his briefcase in his lap.

Finally, Vinnie was led into the courtroom. She was not manacled, and she was wearing a smart blue pin-striped suit with a bright red silk blouse—probably the most conservative outfit Blackstone had ever seen her wear.

Vinnie took her seat between Blackstone and Julia.

A few tense minutes passed slowly.

Then the clerk called out, "All rise!"

The courtroom thundered with more than a hundred feet as the occupants quickly rose to a stand.

Judge Templeton, without emotion, entered the courtroom in his black robe, nodded to the audience, and sat down at the bench. The courtroom full of people sat down.

The clerk called the case, and Henry Hartz and J.D. Blackstone, each in turn, rose to their feet, entered their appearance, and indicated they were ready to proceed.

"The first order of business is a preliminary matter," Judge Templeton said. "Bailiff, please escort the jury panel to the waiting room until I call for them."

When the group of potential jury members had all filed out of the courtroom, the judge continued.

"Professor Blackstone, your motion is before me," the judge said. "It is a motion to dismiss." Then he turned to Henry Hartz.

"Has the government had a chance to review this motion?" the judge asked.

"We have," Hartz replied. "Honestly, we are astounded at the blatant audacity of Mr. Blackstone, Your Honor."

"Well, you had better get used to that," the judge said, shaking his head. "Apparently, defense counsel Blackstone specializes in audacity." A handful of reporters snickered at that, but Templeton leaned forward and barked out a warning for the press to maintain "total and complete silence—I mean, the only thing I want to hear from the media during this trial is the occasional scratch of a pen on a notepad. Am I making myself clear?"

A small tide of press faces were smiling and nodding.

"What is your response to the motion?" Judge Templeton said to Henry Hartz.

"Defense counsel," Hartz answered, "is seeking total dismissal of this case on the grounds that the government, allegedly, had *failed* to produce missing evidence—namely, the same drinking glass from the scene of the crime that Your Honor has heard about previously. But this isn't a proper basis for dismissal. If Mr. Blackstone wants to introduce evidence relating to the drinking glass during the defense case in this trial, he can certainly try to do that. But not a dismissal *before* trial."

"Professor Blackstone," the judge asked, "why should I entertain this motion at this stage? Why shouldn't I follow the government's suggestion?"

"Because I have a right," Blackstone shot back, "to make an offer of proof, by witness testimony, that the evidence in possession of the government supports my client's innocence. And secondly, that it was concealed by the government."

"This is really outrageous," Hartz said, raising his voice and leaning on his cane at his table. "What evidence could you possibly have for these kinds of irresponsible accusations against the prosecution?"

"The fact that the drinking glass has now been found," Blackstone said.

With eyebrows raised, the judge turned to Henry Hartz.

"Is that true?" the judge asked.

"Well, yes, Judge," Hartz replied. "In fact, after a diligent search, we located it and then promptly advised defense counsel of that fact. We are hiding nothing."

"Henry, you buried the District of Columbia evidence inventory record in a six-inch pile of paperwork," Blackstone countered.

"I don't want any frivolous bickering," the judge barked out. "Professor Blackstone, it is true that the government has given you written notice of the fact they located the drinking glass?"

"Yes, Judge, they did," Blackstone said.

"So then, what is it you want here?"

"A dismissal of these criminal charges."

"But on what factual basis?" the judge asked.

"I have some unimpeachable witnesses," Blackstone replied, "whom I believe will substantiate my request for dismissal."

"Witnesses here, today?" the judge asked.

"Yes, Your Honor," Blackstone replied.

"You are prepared to call them?"

"I am," Blackstone answered.

"May I address another procedural point?" Henry Hartz called out to the Court, but the judge waved him back to his seat.

After considering the matter for a few moments, Templeton turned to J.D. Blackstone. "I will allow you a *limited* opportunity to make an evidentiary offer of proof in support of your motion."

Then the judge asked, "Professor Blackstone, who do you propose to call as your first witness?"

Blackstone smiled, paused, and then turned to Henry Hartz, who was seated at the government's counsel table with a scowl on his face.

"Your Honor," Blackstone announced calmly. "I call the prosecutor, Henry Hartz, Assistant U.S. Attorney, as my first witness."

CHAPTER 60

The jammed courtroom erupted with simultaneous outbursts from reporters, bystanders, lawyers, and law-enforcement officials.

In the middle of the tumult, Henry Hartz was objecting wildly.

"This is ridiculous!" he exclaimed, climbing to his feet again with the aid of his cane. "I object. It is procedurally improper for defense counsel to cross-examine the prosecutor. And I object further because the defense is trying to obstruct this jury trial from taking place. They know we have overwhelming evidence of the defendant's guilt. They know the jury is going to agree with me. There is a death penalty waiting for the defendant's cold-blooded cooperation with a conspiracy to murder the Secretary of the Smithsonian Institution and to steal invaluable historical documents. The defense knows all of that—I've seen this all before, Your Honor. The same old defense tricks—obstruction, obfuscation, avoidance, misrepresentation."

J.D. Blackstone was in control and quiet in his delivery.

"I am afraid," Blackstone countered, "that Mr. Hartz uses much to say little. Boiled down to their essence, his objections are twofold. First, he says that it is, as a point of procedure, wrong for the defense to force a prosecutor to testify in a pending case. But I disagree. If you would like, Your Honor, I would be glad to cite the cases where that very process was permitted. Second, he says we are trying to avoid a jury trial. Well, frankly, that is *exactly* what I am trying to do. We are attempting to show that a trial against Vinnie Archmont, under these circumstances, would be a miscarriage of justice."

"Why call Mr. Hartz as your witness?" the judge snapped.

"Because his signature appears on the cover sheet of the most recent discovery packet he delivered to my office," Blackstone explained. "The one that included an inventory record from the DC Police Department. A document that showed that Horace Langley's drinking glass from the crime scene had been kept, not in the FBI evidence locker, but at the DC Police Department."

"An honest mistake," Hartz said, "in view of the fact that our lead investigator was a detective from the DC Police Department rather than the FBI. The glass was taken to the wrong evidence room in the wrong building, that's all."

"I don't use the term *prosecutorial misconduct* lightly," Blackstone said. "And I would rather not use it at all. In fact, I would wager that the misconduct here in hiding evidence doesn't belong to the prosecutor, but to someone else."

"Those are very disturbing accusations," Judge Templeton intoned to Blackstone. "Counselor, you had better be very, very sure of whom you are accusing of malfeasance in a grave criminal case like this."

"I am sure, Your Honor. Now, please, if you would, let me show you why."

The judge turned his gaze to Henry Hartz.

"Mr. Hartz," the judge said. "I will permit a very limited questioning of you by defense counsel. But I stress—*very* limited." Then the judge turned to Blackstone. "I will not tolerate, Professor Blackstone, some wide-ranging fishing expedition in your questioning. Do you understand?"

Blackstone replied that he did.

Henry Hartz slowly made his way to the front of the courtroom, leaning on his cane. He raised his right hand, was sworn, and sat down in the witness chair. Through that process, Hartz's ice-cold gaze was fixed on J.D. Blackstone like a hunting dog studying its prey.

"Mr. Hartz, were you," Blackstone began, "the member of the prosecution team responsible for assembling the last production of discovery to the defense, comprised of records showing the contents of the FBI's physical evidence inventory for the six months before, and six months after, the crime in this case?"

"Of course I was," Hartz replied with contempt.

"One of those documents, from the DC Police Department, showed a drinking glass had been stored in the police evidence room there?"

"It did."

"Was it the same drinking glass, if you know, that had been bagged and tagged from the crime scene in Horace Langley's office—or was it another?"

"I have reason to believe the glass in question was the one taken from the scene by FBI Special Agent Johnson—so I would have to say that it may be the same glass."

"The same glass that later turned up missing?"

"Please listen carefully," Hartz lectured. "I said it 'may' be the same glass. The bag had the same markings made by Agent Johnson at the crime scene when he bagged and tagged it. That's all I know."

"How did you end up discovering the location of the missing glass?"

"I was informed by a member of the DC Police Department that they had found, supposedly, the missing glass in their evidence room."

"We'll get back to *who* in the DC Police Department informed you in a moment," Blackstone said. "But let's go to the question of *whether* it's the same glass. If the glass was in the same evidence baggie, with the same markings, why would you doubt that it was the same glass—the missing drinking glass obtained from the crime scene?"

"Because the glass was different."

"Looked different?"

"Not to the naked eye, not necessarily."

Blackstone was standing rigid at the podium. He was eyeing Hartz now. Hartz twisted his neck a bit and rotated his shoulders.

He is sitting on a bombshell and he knows it, Blackstone thought to himself. And it only took a second for Blackstone to figure out what it was.

"So," Blackstone continued, "you mean to say that the glass had one or more fingerprint impressions—is that what you mean?"

Hartz cocked his head a little, thinking it over, but didn't answer.

"Did the glass have fingerprints on it? Yes or no," the judge asked loudly.

"The glass was determined to have two latent fingerprints on it, yes," Hartz answered.

"And I am sure, as an officer of the court, and as one sworn to uphold the Constitution to convict the guilty and free the innocent," Blackstone said with a smile, "that you sent that glass to the crime lab to determine that very thing. Right? To conduct what would represent a *second* forensic examination, right?"

"We sent the glass to the crime lab, yes, after we discovered it."

"And what were the results?"

"Objection!" the assistant prosecutor at the counsel's table bellowed out. "Asking for hearsay. Not the best evidence. Failure to authenticate. Assuming facts not in evidence."

"There was only one proper objection, Your Honor, in that entire feeding frenzy," Blackstone said. "And that was the hearsay objection. But I think I can cure it."

Then Blackstone turned back to Hartz. He knew that the prosecutor was scrambling in this chess game to save his piece on the board. But it was just a matter of time before his piece was taken. He knew it, and so did Hartz.

"Do you have the crime lab report with you, Mr. Hartz?"

Hartz paused again before answering. Then he finally replied.

"Yes."

"Do you wish to have us go through the motions of marking the crime lab report as an exhibit, and introducing it? Or are you willing to simply summarize it for us and waive your hearsay objection?"

"The findings of the crime lab in that second evaluation," Hartz said in a defeated tone, "showed two latent prints."

"Neither belonging to the defendant Vinnie Archmont?"

"That's right," Hartz said quickly, hoping that Blackstone would fail to ask the next question. But his hopes were dashed.

"So, whose prints were on the glass—were they Horace Langley's?"

"No, they were not."

"They were someone else's?"

"Yes."

"Whose?"

The courtroom had become frozen in time, like the airless confines of an absolute vacuum. No one moved. No one spoke. Until Henry Hartz spoke. And when he finally did, his voice was almost at a whisper.

"They belonged to Hammel Dietz."

"Who?" the judge bellowed out.

"Hammel Dietz," Hartz replied louder. "His prints were on file with the FBI."

"Why were they on file?" Blackstone asked.

"Because Mr. Dietz had been arrested on multiple occasions for theft. Once resulting in a conviction."

"What kind of thefts?" Blackstone asked.

Hartz squirmed in the witness chair.

Blackstone repeated the question, now in a room-filling staccato. "What—kind—of—thefts?"

"High-end art, historical artifacts, those kinds of things."

"*Historical artifacts,* you said?"

"Yes."

"Was he considered to be a sophisticated, skilled thief?"

"Couldn't say."

"You have no opinion whatsoever?"

Hartz wouldn't answer.

The judge leaned over to Hartz and broke the logjam.

"Did law-enforcement agents," the judge asked, "have an opinion on that, which you were privy to, and which you received in the ordinary course of your work in the federal prosecutor's office?"

"The District of Columbia Police Department apparently considered him a very skilled, sophisticated criminal."

"Where is he now?" Blackstone asked.

"Dead."

"That's convenient," Blackstone muttered.

"No more of that," the judge said, reprimanding the law professor.

"My apologies, Your Honor," Blackstone replied. Then he resumed his questioning.

"How did he die?"

"Dietz was on probation from his prior theft. He encountered customs agents at the southern border of the United States while trying to enter Mexico. There was a warrant out against him for another offense. When border agents learned of this, they tried to stop him. There was a shootout. Mr. Dietz was killed."

"And when was that?"

"About a week after the Smithsonian crimes."

"By the way, when did the drinking glass show up missing at the FBI evidence room?"

Hartz paused. "Let's see—" he started to say.

"Let me guess," Blackstone answered for him, "the same time that Dietz was killed—about a week after the Smithsonian crimes?"

Hartz managed a twisted smile.

"Looks like it, yes."

"And did you find any evidence whatsoever, Mr. Hartz, of any connection in any way, between Hammel Dietz, whose fingerprints were on a glass that appears to have been from the crime scene, and my client, Vinnie Archmont?"

Hartz stared at Blackstone while he struggled to avoid admitting the obvious. Finally he relented.

"No connection."

"None?"

"That's what I said, Mr. Blackstone."

A sea of whispers rippled through the courtroom.

"Last question," Blackstone announced. "Who was the Good Samaritan who told you they had discovered the missing glass?"

"Detective Victor Cheski."

Blackstone said he had no further questions, and sat down at counsel's table.

Julia bent forward and whispered over to Blackstone.

"Looks like Detective Cheski is our hero," Julia said in a hushed tone.

Vinnie was smiling. She had been transfixed by what had just unfolded.

But Blackstone was not smiling. He didn't reply to Julia's observation. Instead, he simply pursed his lips and leaned back in his chair, considering some thought that was very private and, for the time being, belonged only to him.

CHAPTER 61

Blackstone's next witness was the Assistant Attorney General for the Criminal Division in the Department of Justice.

There had been some initial wrangling about the motion that had been filed by the Department of Justice to quash the subpoena served on him.

But after hearing Henry Hartz's testimony, the DOJ attorney decided to withdraw his objection and agreed to testify specifically about the fact that the federal detention center, which housed Vinnie Archmont after her initial arrest, had ceased recording prisoners' phone calls on that same day.

Blackstone took the witness directly to the bottom line.

"You are aware, sir, that a Shelly Hollsaker, a prisoner who was in the same cell with Vinnie Archmont, has come forward and told the government that she overheard my client make several incriminating statements while my client was on the telephone? And that, obviously, any recording of Ms. Archmont's conversations would be of vital importance in either supporting, or destroying, Shelly Hollsaker's story?"

"Yes, I am aware of all of that."

"Prior to the day that Vinnie Archmont made several outgoing calls from a phone in the holding cell, sir, did the federal facility have a policy of recording the phone calls of prisoners?"

"It did, unless they were deemed to be attorney–client telephone contacts, and then they were not recorded."

"Why were the prisoner calls recorded previously?"

"For jail security reasons. There were occasional threats against the safety of our jailers. Some terrorist threats by some inmates. So our internal security people would record the prisoner calls and review them to detect possible threats. The records would be unavailable for any other purpose, unless compelled to be produced by court order."

"Did that policy change, suddenly, on the day that Vinnie Archmont was brought into the facility after her arrest for the Smithsonian crimes?"

"It did."

"Why?"

"We were informed by a DC Police official that a District of Columbia judge had ruled that the recording of such prisoner phone calls was illegal and must be discontinued."

"So as a result, DOJ ordered that the recording be stopped?"

"Yes, we halted it immediately, that same day, pending verification of that court order—it all happened to be on the same day that Vinnie Archmont was brought in."

"Who was the officer with the DC Police Department who called you and informed you that the recording must stop because of a court order?"

"Detective Victor Cheski."

"And have you, ever since, gone back to the old policy of recording calls again?"

"We have."

"Why?"

"We discovered that Detective Cheski was mistaken. Apparently there *was* no court order."

" 'Mistaken,' you said?"

"Detective Cheski called it a 'mistake.' However, we were very disturbed by the incident, to say the least."

When Blackstone returned to the counsel's table to grab his notepad after dismissing the Assistant Attorney General, Julia leaned forward to catch Blackstone's attention.

"Good guy in act one suddenly becomes bad guy in act two?" Julia whispered.

"Wait for act three," Blackstone whispered back.

Then he called Detective Victor Cheski to the stand.

Detective Cheski, in his dark suit and tie, handsome, athletic, and confident, was smiling when he took the oath.

Blackstone led him through an initial series of harmless, innocuous questions about his work with the District of Columbia police and his prior warm relationship with Henry Hartz when Hartz was a DC prosecutor and worked closely with Cheski on a number of criminal cases. That was, Cheski thought, the reason why Hartz had named him the lead investigator in the Smithsonian crimes. That—plus, Cheski noted, "the possibility that the crimes could have been an 'insider' crime, committed by federal employees or even federal agents. So I think he considered me an outsider to the Feds because I worked for the District of Columbia."

Then Blackstone began to bore further down.

"You were the investigating officer in several of the Hammel Dietz thefts, including the one where he was eventually convicted?"

"Yes, that's right."

"Was there physical evidence from that crime of which Mr. Dietz was convicted?"

"I'm sure there was."

"That theft involved what kind of location?"

"An art museum. A painting by Matisse was stolen by Mr. Dietz."

"Let's talk about the physical evidence from that case."

Henry Hartz bellowed out an objection on relevancy grounds.

The judge overruled the objection, but warned Blackstone that he had "better tie this up in a hurry and make it good."

"Was there a drinking glass obtained from the crime scene at the art museum?"

"Gee," Cheski said, "that was a long time ago…"

"Well, then perhaps I should ask the judge to order you to produce all your records from the Hammel Dietz prosecution. Should I do that?"

"There was, I think," Cheski said, "a drinking glass. As well as a rope, I believe, a tool of some kind with no prints on it and, I believe, a footprint from a shoe. May have been some other evidence."

"But the thing that convicted Hammel Dietz—the thing that nailed the case shut against him—was the presence of his two fingerprints on the drinking glass, right?"

Cheski was still managing a smile, but his smile was fading.

"The fingerprint evidence was important."

"Now, let's talk about this case. You had access to the FBI evidence room during the investigation into the Smithsonian crimes?"

"Yes, but so did Special Agent Johnson and—"

"You also had access to the evidence room in the District of Columbia Police Department?"

"Every detective does, and assuming certain procedures are followed, so does any other officer."

"You had access to the Hammel Dietz evidence at the District of Columbia evidence room, including the glass with his fingerprints, and you also had access to the evidence room at the FBI building containing the Smithsonian crime investigation?"

"I had access to a number of different rooms in various buildings."

"Yes or no?" Blackstone bellowed. "Did you have access to *both* evidence rooms from *both* investigations—yes or no?"

Cheski was no longer smiling. His face now bore the steady, determined look of a trained professional who could see the oncoming storm he might have to weather.

"I did have access to both, yes."

"And you were the one to report—no one else, just you—that the 'missing' glass that had mysteriously gone missing now had been mysteriously found. You were the one?"

"I was the one who—"

"You were also the one," Blackstone said, steamrolling ahead, "to know that Hammel Dietz could easily be implicated in the Smithsonian crime if the drinking glass with two of his fingerprints could be substituted in the Smithsonian evidence bag for the actual glass from the Langley murder, a glass that had no fingerprints on it."

"Objection! Objection! Objection!" Henry Hartz was yelling.

"Why would I have done something as stupid as *that?*" Cheski yelled, causing the witness-stand microphone to shriek with feedback.

"I would suggest," Blackstone said, "that you did exactly that, in order to make it look like Hammel Dietz, a convicted criminal now silenced by death, was the real murderer of Horace Langley. Isn't it a fact that you did exactly that to cover up the identity of the real killer?

"This is crazy, so crazy!" Cheski called out.

Hartz was resuming his cadence of one-word objections.

"Objections overruled. Overruled!" the judge proclaimed.

"Do you deny that you wanted to cover up the identity of the real killer?" Blackstone called out.

"Absolutely! That is an idiotic lie!" Cheski shouted.

Blackstone held up the FBI report of the crime-scene investigation.

"Do you stand by the FBI report into the Smithsonian crimes?" Blackstone asked.

"Of course—why not?"

"Your DNA was found at the scene. Right?"

Cheski gave a sardonic laugh. "Yeah, and so was the DNA of other officers too...it was a boiling-hot night, a heat wave...the air-conditioning in the Castle had gone out...we were sweating...a few drops of sweat fell onto the scene...so what...so what?"

"The point is," Blackstone said calmly, "that, according to the FBI report, the other officer arrived at the scene at 1:59 a.m., with the crime-lab team, and his sweat droplet was picked up by his own analysis of the scene thirty minutes later. You do agree with that?"

"Sure, why not?"

"Whereas a sweat droplet containing your DNA was picked up at 2:10 a.m. by the crime-lab team. Right?"

"What of it?"

"Well," Blackstone said, turning to gaze back at FBI Special Agent Ralph Johnson, who was seated motionless in the courtroom, was riveted on the testimony, "I guess it has to do with timing and rats and ships and sailors."

"I don't understand," Cheski was muttering.

"How about this?" Blackstone said loudly and slowly. "Do you understand this—the FBI report says you arrived at the scene of the crime in your official capacity at 2:44 a.m., thirty-four minutes *after* your DNA-verified drop of sweat had been picked up by the crime lab team? Or to put it another way, it would appear you dropped a bead of sweat at the scene of the crime before you ever got there to investigate the scene."

Cheski's face was growing paler, and he was tugging at his upper lip with his lower teeth.

"Do you have an answer?" the judge asked, bending over toward the detective and staring him in the eye.

"Sure. Agent Johnson screwed up again," Cheski muttered. "Put the time down wrong for when I arrived. I must have arrived sooner at the scene of the crime."

"Special Agent Johnson is in the courtroom," Blackstone shot back. "Maybe you're a gambling man, Detective. Are you willing to gamble on Agent Johnson backing you up—and saying he got it all wrong by more than thirty minutes in his report?"

Cheski was silent.

In the back of the courtroom, Special Agent Johnson was trying not to smile.

"Speaking of gambling," Blackstone said, "I have a private investigator here in the courtroom with me. He has information on Horace Langley's gambling habits. Nothing illegal, mind you. Just a little excessive. He also knows whether Secretary Langley traveled with anyone else when he went to Atlantic City to the casinos. How many times, Detective, in the course of your relationship with Horace Langley, did you accompany him on his gambling junkets? And how much did you know about his gambling debts?"

In a rage Cheski was sputtering something unintelligible from the witness stand.

"What is it that you're saying?" the judge asked.

"Confusion..." Cheski said.

"Confusion about what?"

"Confusion, Your Honor."

"What kind of confusion?" the judge barked back.

"Confusion," Cheski said in a low voice, "of the Fifth Amendment kind."

By then, Judge Templeton had heard enough.

"Counsel," the judge announced, "I suggest that the government and the defense have a little chat about this case. I think you know what I am referring to. Detective Cheski, you may step down. But please do not leave the courtroom. I would ask that the U.S. marshals assist Detective Cheski here to his seat and stay with him. The government lawyers are probably going to have some further dealings with the detective."

Henry Hartz slowly rose to his feet on his cane and took a few steps toward J.D. Blackstone. In turn, Blackstone took several steps to the prosecutor. They were standing, nose to nose, in the midpoint of the courtroom.

"This is the moment I told you about," Blackstone began. "Henry, this is the meeting I told you we would have."

They spoke for several moments. Blackstone did most of the talking. At one point, Hartz glanced over at Vinnie Archmont, who had a shocked look on her face and was staring straight ahead.

Then Henry Hartz sat down with his two assistant prosecutors. They talked in hushed tones, in strained voices, for twenty minutes while the judge sat patiently at the bench, waiting.

At the end of the twenty minutes, Hartz stood up and slowly made his way to the podium.

"Your Honor," he announced quietly, "we move for the dismissal without prejudice of the charges against Vinnie Archmont, based on newly discovered evidence."

"Any objections, Professor Blackstone?" the judge asked.

"None," Blackstone replied.

"Case dismissed. The defendant is hereby released from custody. Clerk, you can release the jury panel from duty on this case."

The courtroom erupted in wild chaos.

"All members of the media are ordered to conduct any interviews *outside of my courtroom!*" the judge bellowed. Then he struck his gavel down on the bench, rose quickly, and disappeared through the chambers door.

Vinnie was crying and laughing. Next to her, Julia had her arm around Vinnie. Julia had a huge, beaming smile on her face, and she was shaking her head back and forth in disbelief.

"Thank you, oh thank you, for saving me, for rescuing me, oh thank you," Vinnie was saying to Blackstone when he arrived back at the defense table.

Blackstone bent down to Vinnie.

"Okay, you and I have a few details to finalize," Blackstone said. Then he turned to one of the U.S. marshals and asked, "Can I meet with my client in the conference room inside the courtroom, so we don't have to deal with the media out in the hallway?"

The U.S. marshal smiled and nodded and led them to a door inside the courtroom, which he unlocked and then opened for them.

Blackstone took Vinnie gently by the arm and led her into the conference room and turned on the light switch. Then he ducked back into the courtroom.

He motioned to Tully Tullinger, who quickly strode over to him. Tully pulled a folder of notes out of his leather case and handed it to Blackstone. Julia was standing just behind Tully.

Blackstone took the file from Tully, nodding with a smile. Then he looked over at Julia.

"Please stay close by, okay?" he said.

Then Blackstone stepped into the conference room with Vinnie and closed the door behind him.

CHAPTER 62

Inside the conference room, Vinnie was still laughing and crying. She spent several minutes just emoting. Then she praised Blackstone's performance, extolling the brilliance of her defense attorney.

J.D. Blackstone was taking it so much in stride that it almost appeared he had become strangely dispassionate about the outcome of the whole case.

"J.D., darling, you are being so solemn!" Vinnie said. "We have to celebrate tonight...but, I'm sorry—you had some details you said we needed to wrap up. Oh, my, wait till dear Magister Dee hears the good news."

"Details, yes," Blackstone said. "Well, let's start with your adoption."

With that he pulled out the file Tully had given him, perused it for a few moments, and then looked up at Vinnie.

"You gave me the impression you wanted a relationship with me?" Blackstone asked.

"You know I do," Vinnie said, and she took both of Blackstone's hands in hers.

"Then I think we need to speak the truth—both of us," Blackstone said and deftly removed his hands from hers.

"Of course," Vinnie said passionately. "That's got to be number one. And now that you no longer have to represent me in this terrible criminal case, we can spend time on our relationship, darling."

"You lied to me about being adopted," Blackstone said.

Vinnie recoiled for a moment before she replied.

"I don't know what you mean," she said.

"Don't do that, Vinnie," Blackstone said. "I had the best private investigator in North America check the adoption records of your home state and the national adoption registries. You were not listed anywhere. The fact is, you didn't tell Lord Dee you were adopted until *after* your parents had been killed in the train wreck—making them conveniently inaccessible to contradict your story."

"Why would I do that?"

"So you could create a name that sounded fatefully significant to Lord Dee, the Freemason philosopher and Theosophist."

"Significant?" Vinnie asked wide-eyed.

"Yes," Blackstone said, "your research must have indicated that the word *Arch* has great importance to Freemasons," Blackstone said. "In Masonic lore, the arch is an ancient symbol of strength. In addition, Masonic writing points out that at the very top of the arch there is the keystone, the critical architectural element holding the arch together. Your choice of a name that begins with 'arch' was obviously designed to convey the implication to Lord Dee's occult mind that you, Vinnie, would somehow end up being a keeper of the keystone—the key to the 'philosopher's stone.' That impression would then give you unequaled access to Lord Dee."

Vinnie was shaking her head a little and smiling.

"So, J.D. Blackstone, the great intellect, has got it all figured out," she said with a slight smirk.

"Then there's the 'mont' part of 'Archmont,'" Blackstone explained. "The word *mont* means 'mount.' To the Freemasons, their entire metaphysical myth is built on their interpretation of the building of Solomon's Temple—a temple built on what is now called the Temple Mount. By taking the name 'Archmont' you could not have picked a more clever entrée into Lord Dee's confidence, Vinnie. Superbly done. So the name was perfectly suited to endear you to Dee. That, plus your obvious flirtatious beauty and your resemblance to Vinnie Ream enabled you to play out Dee's fantasy that the two of you were some latter-day version of Vinnie Ream and Albert Pike, simply transplanted spiritually into another century."

Vinnie was smiling and eyeing Blackstone closely.

"But then there's the problem of Detective Victor Cheski," Blackstone said.

"Who would have figured him to be such a villain?" Vinnie said, not taking her eyes off Blackstone.

"Yes," Blackstone said, "the villain. And now, unless you do some fancy, very quick footwork, that villain, Victor Cheski, is going to start pointing the finger directly at *you*."

"Me?" she scoffed.

"Come on, Vinnie," Blackstone said with a chuckle. "He's been your secret boyfriend. I know that now. Your apartment manager gave me a perfect description of 'your boyfriend,' the detective. But I had my suspicions. That was simply the capstone. The ultimate proof. The first overpowering evidence was the mailing label on the back of that crime magazine dealing with the Beltway snipers. As you know, it was addressed to Victor Cheski in care of the DC Police Department. Very sloppy of you, Vinnie, and your boyfriend to leave his magazine in your closet."

"Can't a woman have more than one lover?" Vinnie said with an enticing smile.

"Yeah, but then there's the whole have-your-lover-the-detective-shoot-at-your-lawyer thing. I have a hard time with that."

"I had nothing to do with that," Vinnie said shaking her head. "You have to believe me. When I told him about you going horseback riding, I didn't think he was going to try to kill you."

"Can I really believe that? At that point, the Court of Appeals had just decided I could tell my experts and cocounsel about the Langley note," Blackstone said. "Obviously, you both were concerned that the note was getting leaked out and might find its way to Lord Dee and spoil your whole scheme—oh, by the way, interesting technique, having Cheski use a white truck and an AK-47 to try to get rid of me, so the further distribution of the Langley note would be slowed down as you asked the court for more time to retain a new lawyer, giving you and Cheski enough time to complete your scheme.

"And Cheski's method in doing the whole Beltway-sniper kind of scare all over again using a white box truck in case there were witnesses, that was good...except, as you know, in the John Allen Muhammad and Lee Boyd Malvo sniper shootings in 2002, even though the initial reports mentioned a white box truck, those two killers actually used a blue Chevy Caprice and a Bushmaster XM-15 rifle. But the effect created by Cheski in my shooting certainly kept the focus off him and was neatly calculated to look like just another random, crazy, publicity-seeking, copycat sniper shooting—all over again.

"It's just a good thing for me that Cheski wasn't more proficient with the AK-47, a notoriously inaccurate weapon for long-distance shooting—and a good thing also that I was riding a good horse. But as I thought about it more, in my hospital room, who else but a DC police detective who was actually working in that department in 2002 and remembered those sniper shootings would be a better candidate to cook up a simulated copycat shooting?"

"Alright," she said with a laugh, "let's see how very clever you really are—why would Victor Cheski, if he is my lover, sabotage the recording of my jail-cell phone call? That would mean I would have no way to counter the testimony of this Shelly Hollsaker, who would testify that she overheard me making self-incriminating statements on the phone."

"Simple," Blackstone said. "Cheski figured you would panic and call him when you were arrested. And he was right. So when he heard you had been picked up and were on your way to the federal detention center, he made the call to the DOJ to make sure no recording was done. The fact is, you *did* make incriminating statements—and those statements were made when you called your lover boy, Victor Cheski."

"And our 'scheme' that you keep mentioning," Vinnie said, "that would be what?"

"To bilk Lord Dee out of twenty million dollars. That was the plan all along, I'm sure. From the very beginning, twenty million up front for the Langley note. That part never changed. Even after you were charged criminally in this case, the two of you decided to still pursue the plan, and so Cheski fired off a letter to Lord Dee offering the Langley note and mailing the letter from Savannah, the birthplace of the American version of speculative esoteric Freemasonry, just for dramatic effect. You would be unable to collect on the second twenty million, of course—but then you never figured on getting that second payment anyway, because that would require that you then produce the actual John Wilkes Booth diary pages. And of course, you wouldn't want to do that, would you?"

Vinnie smiled again.

"Maybe not," she said.

"No, obviously not," Blackstone added. "Because the Booth diary never contained anything that Langley wrote in his phony note, *did it?*"

"I guess not," she said.

"No," Blackstone said. "Because that cryptic poem in Langley's note was not copied from the Booth diary at all. It was in fact a construct set up by you and Detective Cheski, but actually authored by Horace Langley himself, the scholar on seventeenth-century English history as well as the American Civil War. You gleaned from Lord Dee the details of his cherished theory on alchemy and the elusive elixir of prolonged life, a theory which was fed by his crazed desire to find some occult, magic cure for his incurable condition of corticobasal degeneration.

"So you passed all that information to Horace Langley, who desperately needed some quick cash to pay off his gambling debts and avoid a scandal. Langley thought up the clever note, supposedly derived from the Booth diary, but which in reality was custom-built to appeal to Lord Dee's esoteric fantasies. With a coded message that Dee would have little problem deciphering. But there was another problem—if anyone read the actual Booth diary pages that had just been discovered, they would realize there was nothing metaphysical about them...nothing whatsoever about alchemy or any golden tree or any rose crystal. By the way, what *was* in the Booth diary, anyway?"

"Oh, just Booth's ranting against the North," she said with a sneer. "And complaints about his own situation. That's about it. Victor has it stashed away somewhere."

"So the plan was," Blackstone continued, "to fake a robbery of the Booth diary so that Horace Langley's note would look like the only evidence of it that was left, right?"

"'The best-laid plans,' as they say..." she said.

"Then someone came up with the very nasty plan of not just faking a robbery," Blackstone explained, "but actually killing Langley, then stealing the Booth pages and upping the shares the two of you would get when it was suggested to Lord Dee that the Langley note was now for sale. After all, Detective Cheski had confidential access to the note in his investigation, and Dee's declining health made it impractical for him to be willing to wait for the note to finally be made public. But then something very unexpected happened—you actually got indicted and charged as a conspirator in the crime."

At that point, it was like a switch had flipped. Vinnie started yelling and swearing about Horace Langley, and in between her string of profanities, complaining about why in the world he had to enter into his journal his dealings with her about the Booth diary, and why he made an entry in his computer log that he had given her the pass code to the side door.

Blackstone nodded, as he was now hearing the same kind of complaints Vinnie had made in her jail cell call to Cheski, statements partially overheard by Shelly Hollsaker.

"Was Langley trying to destroy me from the grave?" she screamed out.

Then she settled down.

"What's done is done," she said. "The point is, where you and I go now from here on. First, I'm a good student. I remember what you told me when I first hired you. Everything we just discussed is protected by attorney–client privilege, right?" she said.

"Right you are," Blackstone said. "Everything up to now. So what happens with Lord Dee from this point on?"

"Well, now that the spotlight is on Victor, I suggest we make hay. As soon as I get processed out of jail and released today, we can get my passport back from the court clerk, and you and I can beat it over to Lord Dee in England. You have a copy of the Horace Langley note we can use, right?"

"Sure," Blackstone said. "Why?"

"So, darling man—with just a few more details to work out in terms of strategy, of course—you and I get the note delivered to Lord Dee and pick up our twenty million dollars before someone leaks the note to the media. What else?"

"Oh—you mean deliver the phony note about the 'rose of 6' and all of that?"

Vinnie laughed and got up and knelt down next to Blackstone, wrapping her arms around him and beginning to kiss him on the neck.

"I still need a good attorney to negotiate this deal with Magister Dee," she purred.

Blackstone took her hands off of him and then stood up.

"No, I don't think you and I are going to be partners."

Vinnie had a stunned look.

"So, you're not going to be part of this?" she asked.

"Nope," he said with finality.

"Well, fine. You've still got to keep your mouth shut, or I'll have your license to practice law revoked."

After thinking about that for a few seconds, Blackstone made a funny face. "Oops!" he cried out.

"What?" Vinnie asked.

"Well, the bit about attorney–client relationship—it only applies to *past* crimes. See, it doesn't apply to your intentions to commit *future* crimes, like delivering the phony note to Lord Dee for twenty million dollars—you know, that stuff you just told me—it doesn't apply to that."

With that, Blackstone pulled out his pocket recorder and showed it to Vinnie.

"In other words," Blackstone said, "the confession you just gave right now, recorded here, about your intent to commit fraud."

"What are you doing?" she screamed.

"The rules of ethics for lawyers permit us to report to the authorities our client's plan to commit a future crime. Which is what I will probably end up doing."

Vinnie picked up a folding chair in the conference room and tried to hit Blackstone with it, but he ducked just in time. She screamed and pounded the table and threatened him for nearly a half an hour.

When she stopped pacing and swearing, Blackstone spoke up.

"Don't be so bummed by all of this," he said. "I've hinted to prosecutor Henry Hartz that I might be able to get your cooperation in testifying against Detective Cheski, in return for immunity from the really serious charges—and that you might be willing to plead guilty to a simple fraud charge…sentence recommendation of about ten years in prison. Not bad, really. I don't think you could get a better deal from any attorney in the world. This terrifically great deal is available to you, of course, because I was successful in getting your charges dismissed this morning. That gave us some bargaining power. I trust you'll accept the deal I've worked out for you."

"Don't bank on it," Vinnie screamed back. "You're fired!"

"Too bad," Blackstone said, not at all disturbed. "Because I think that Hartz will revoke the plea deal I just mentioned to you if you don't take it right now. And right here. And if you don't, he will probably get Cheski to implicate you, and he could then ring up the murder conspiracy charges against you all over again."

"Can't do it!" Vinnie yelled. "My case was dismissed!"

"Oops!" Blackstone said again. "Yeah—well, you see, the dismissal in your case was 'without prejudice.' Which means that, while the judge dismissed the case against you based on what looked like new evidence, the prosecution can still recharge you all over again based on even newer evidence. Funny thing about the law and the legal system—sometimes truth and justice really do get vindicated after all."

After another prolonged tirade, Vinnie started settling down.

At that point Blackstone stepped outside and walked up to Julia. She had been patiently waiting in the courtroom the entire time. Off to the side, Henry Hartz, FBI agent Johnson, and two U.S. marshals were also waiting quietly for the result they expected to emerge from the small conference room.

Blackstone stepped next to Julia and whispered in her ear.

"You were the best partner a lawyer could ever have," he whispered to her. "I am regretfully accepting the termination of our partnership and your resignation immediately. Now, follow me...I am about to introduce you to your first solo client."

Julia walked inside the room with Vinnie and Blackstone, and the conference-room door was closed. Then Julia's mentor and former law professor looked at her and smiled warmly and explained what was about to happen next.

"Julia," Blackstone began, "even though we were successful in obtaining a dismissal without prejudice this morning, my former client, Vinnie Archmont here, has made certain admissions to me just now that give us the full story behind the Smithsonian crimes. However, I think Henry

Hartz may be willing to offer Vinnie a plea negotiation on very favorable terms.

"What I am about to tell you now will be the whole truth behind those crimes—and the terms the government will probably be willing to offer Vinnie in return for her cooperation. After I tell you everything, then I want you to tell Vinnie whether, in your professional opinion, she ought to accept this deal—or reject it. Hold nothing back.

"I had told you that, when the time came, I was going to need your brutally honest, objective assessment of something. Well, Julia, that time is now. I am formally stepping out of the middle of this matter. The client has fired me. Though I would have been forced to withdraw if she hadn't. Vinnie, Julia here, I think, would be willing to represent you if you agree. If not, you are free to hire your own lawyer. Of course that takes time…and there is an excellent chance that by then, Cheski will have cut a deal, and the plea bargain I have suggested to you will have been taken off the table by Henry Hartz."

Then Blackstone turned to Vinnie, who was simmering with anger behind a clenched jaw.

"Vinnie," he said, "when my former partner here gives you her evaluation of your legal situation, I want you to listen to her very carefully. You reject her legal advice at your own peril. They don't come any better or any smarter than her."

CHAPTER 63

Six Months Later

A re you free, J.D., to discuss the final outcome of Vinnie's case?"

"Sure. It's all a matter of public record now," J.D. Blackstone said.

His psychiatrist, Dr. Jim Koesler, was nodding, and then went to his next question.

"So Vinnie accepted the plea bargain, then?"

"Yes. At least initially," Blackstone replied.

"But she came after you legally, is that it?"

"Oh gosh, yeah, you might say that," Blackstone said with a chuckle. "After she accepted the deal and gave evidence against her partner in crime, Victor Cheski, and after Judge Templeton sentenced her to the ten years in prison she was expecting, then she turned on me. She fired my former partner, Julia, who had adroitly led her through the plea negotiation process and sentencing phase.

"Then she hired another attorney and filed a civil suit against me, and also complained to the bar association against me, and finally filed a motion with Judge Templeton saying she should be able to get her ten-year sentence vacated because I had 'violated the attorney–client relationship in ways that shock the conscience and betray my oath as a lawyer.' That choice of language in the paperwork was her lawyer's, of course, not Vinnie's. I'm sure Vinnie would have used a much more colorful set of descriptives."

"The result?"

"She lost. I prevailed. On everything."

"Do you feel vindicated, then?"

"That seems like a very hollow description of my feelings."

"How would you put it?"

" 'Trying not to look back'—how about that?"

"And your former partner, Julia?"

"We're talking about putting the law partnership back together again."

"Sounds promising. And on a personal level?"

"A different kind of partnership may be emerging. I am getting Julia into horseback riding, mountain climbing, and kayaking—and she's getting me into being more human."

"That also sounds promising. And your interactions with your father, and your uncle?"

"Oh, the same. I don't have much contact with Dad, I'm afraid. That is probably more my fault. Maybe I should do something about it. And my uncle—Reverend Lamb—he's the same. He tells me that the human condition has two universal truths—that we are all sinners and we all need a Savior. He still invites me on a regular basis to get down on my knees, confess that I am a sinner, and believe in Jesus as the Son of God."

"He was correct, in a way, about the Langley note, though—wasn't he?"

"In a way, yes. He certainly figured out the word puzzle all right, even though the puzzle ultimately was proven to be a fake."

Blackstone paused and thought about something.

"And I was right too."

"Well, J.D.," Dr. Koesler said, "your handling of Vinnie's defense appears to have been brilliant. Gaining a dismissal of the charges, but then motivating her in the end to own up to the truth behind the crimes and receive some measure of punishment...while making sure that the trigger man, Victor Cheski, caught the full brunt of the punishment."

"No," Blackstone said, pondering it. "I didn't mean that. It's just that at some point I came to realize what Vinnie's case was really about."

"And what is that?"

"Two things, I think. The hunger of human beings for eternal life, and the power of greed."

"Or as your uncle might put it, eternity and sin?"

"Yes, I suppose so," Blackstone said.

"So," Dr. Koesler said changing the subject slightly, "you are here for another refill of your medication?"

"No, actually I am here to get rid of you."

Dr. Koesler laughed. "When I hear that, I often think it can be a good thing—that the patient has progressed."

"I'm not sure about that," Blackstone said. "All I know is that I've decided to give up my membership in the 'Better Living Through Chemistry' club. Your pills give me four hours of sleep, rather than three and a half. It's not worth the trade-off. There's got to be a better way."

"I respect that. But, how about the 'not looking back' part—how does that fit into everything?"

"Well, there is one thing I do need from you, now that you are no longer going to be my psychiatrist."

"What's that?" Koesler asked.

"An honest answer to an honest question."

"Which is?"

"Your professional opinion regarding the cause, the etiology, of my accursed insomnia."

"That's really for you to answer more than me."

"Come on, Jim, I know the drill here. The therapist thinks he needs to have the patient do the self-discovery. I know all that. Just give me your theory."

"I really am hesitant," Koesler protested.

"Okay, Jim, really—what do you have to lose? Look, let's make it a bet, alright? Like the old fraternity days together. I dare you, for the sum of ten bucks, in valid American currency—and I've got it right in my pocket here—I dare you to nail the cause of my insomnia. Explain it to me."

"J.D., you're smarter than I am. I'm sure you've already figured it out."

"Well, let's test your theory. Come on. Lay it on me."

Dr. Koesler looked into the face of his friend. He was tempted to play the clinician. To play it safe. By the book.

But he didn't.

"Alright," Koesler said. "You told me once, in one of our first meetings, about the last thing you remember Marilyn saying to you before she left with your daughter for that music recital. What was it she said?"

Blackstone had been looking at Koesler, but now he looked down at some undetermined and unfixed point in space.

"She said…'Don't forget.'"

"Don't forget what, exactly?"

"'Don't forget,'" Blackstone said, his voice faltering a little, "'*to set your alarm.*' So I wouldn't sleep through Beth's recital."

"You were about to take a nap?"

"I had gone two weeks without a solid night's sleep…handling a very demanding, very complicated trial…grabbing a few hours here or there each night, not much more. The case ended. We won. Wonderful. Great. I was exhausted. It was Beth's recital that day. Rather than driving them to the recital myself, I said I needed to lie down for a few hours. But I would meet them at the recital auditorium…in time."

"In time for Beth's recital."

"Yeah, of course, obviously," Blackstone blurted out. "Jim, look—you're the one with the MD degree, you're the psychiatrist. I'm just the one who never bothered to finish my PhD in psychology. Why don't you simply give me your brilliant psychiatric deduction, then? Just tell me!"

"Well, it seems to me," Koesler said quietly, " that the driving force in your internal struggle now is the fact that you didn't drive them. Marilyn did. The route she took just happened to lead her into the path of an oncoming car. But you, J.D., who believe you are the one who has to be right all the time, you knew a different route. And I am guessing you feel you would have taken them on that different route—your route, a better route, a safer route—maybe even a quicker route, less traffic, that's why you would have preferred it. But there was a problem…the fact that you needed sleep. So Marilyn ended up leaving first, doing the driving. She took her route, not yours. The accident happened. And you haven't forgiven yourself for not being there to take care of your family. Not saving them from disaster. So the enemy of those you loved the most, in your view, ended up being sleep. Sleep—your need for sleep, then, somewhere on a feeling level, has been proven to be your mortal enemy. Or so you believe."

Blackstone had stood up from his chair. His face was red, and his neck veins were bulging. Then he exploded.

"Why did I need sleep that day—why that day? Why? You tell me that! It is an absolute fact, beyond debate, that I would have taken a different route. It is absolutely assured that I would have thereby averted their deaths. It is beyond any reasonable doubt that my selfish desire for sleep was the cause of the catastrophic deaths of my wife and my daughter—and that...and that...is true beyond any scintilla of a shadow of a doubt. Now...you tell me to try and fix that, Jim...because...there is no fixing that."

Blackstone turned to the door, still standing, and covered his face with one hand. He stood there motionless for several moments.

When he had regained his composure, he pulled something out of his pocket and tossed it on Koesler's desk.

It was a twenty-dollar bill.

"Keep the change," Blackstone said as he walked out the door.

CHAPTER 64

In the Staffordshire farmland of England, the sun was just beginning to rim the horizon. In the early light, a group of geologists, engineers, excavators, and botanists were standing in an open field, in a semicircle around a mammoth hole that had been opened in the ground. Off to the side there was a collection of earth-digging equipment and several trucks.

In the middle of the group, leaning on a walker, was Lord Magister Dee.

They were all gazing down into the space, where below, several men were excavating the bottom of the area. The dirt was being hauled up to ground level by a bucket-and-pulley system. They had been working from the day before and through the night.

Lord Dee was clutching an area map and a photocopy of an entry made in a late 1600s journal of Dr. Robert Plot.

Then Dee heard the voice of his chief archaeologist from down in the pit. The voice came over the walkie-talkie that Dee's personal secretary was holding up next to his ear so he could hear.

"Lord Dee, we are now clearing the floor, sir. Trying to be careful… though I must say that this is much too rushed for my liking, frankly. We are dealing with a several-hundred-year-old underground structure—a room of some kind. It could be of great historical significance. But I feel, honestly, that we are being pressed too quickly to clear it."

"As long as I'm the one paying the bills here," Dee yelled back into the walkie-talkie, "you will press ahead with as much speed as…you… can…can…muster."

Then he added, "I bought this field, and I hired all of you. You work for me. Please try...try...try to...remember that."

"I think we are getting close, sir," his personal secretary said enthusiastically.

Dee nodded. He knew he was now very close to completing the task he had been pursuing for decades. He thought back to how he had been brought to this final, consummating chapter.

When he learned how the Vinnie Archmont case had ended, Dee bribed a courthouse official to send him a copy of the Horace Langley note. Dee steadfastly refused to believe that the note was a fake or that its message had been invented by Horace Langley, Vinnie, and Victor Cheski to fool him into buying it for millions, despite the mounting evidence they had been out to defraud him from the beginning.

After Lord Dee had reviewed the Langley note, he quickly deciphered it and gained immediate access to the records in the Ashmolean Library, where he then reviewed every journal and diary written by Dr. Robert Plot, Elias Ashmole's curator and disciple.

In one journal entry, he found that Plot had written down a precise description of a farmer's field for some reason. The page was intriguing because Plot had decorated the page with drawings of roses and crystals.

That was when Dee proceeded to consult an old book he had in his extensive personal library of Masonic literature.

The book was an old, massive volume entitled *History of Freemasonry and Concordant Orders*. It had been written in 1890 and had a thick brown-leather cover with the Freemason's insignia embossed on the front, and it smelled of mustiness and aged paper.

Lord Dee had flipped through it until he got to the very last section of the book. Then, at page 872, he read something that took his breath away.

It was an excerpt from Dr. Plot's *History of Staffordshire*, first published during the reign of King Charles II of England. And it contained the astonishing tale of a "countryman" who happened on a strange structure while digging a trench in his field. As the story went, the man broke through to a staircase that led downward a considerable depth to an underground room.

What Dee read had lit up his mind like a roman candle. Dr. Plot had said of the seventeenth-century discoverer,

> Overcoming his fear and summoning his courage, noisily with his feet he descended the remainder of the stairs; the light grew brighter, until at last, at another turn, he came upon a square chamber, built on large hewn ancient stones. The pavement was flagged, the roof lofty, and in the centre of the groin, was a rose exquisitely carved in some dark stone.

But now a voice broke through into Lord Dee's thoughts. It was the chief archaeologist.

"We've uncovered the floor, sir," he said on the walkie-talkie. "It appears to be a floor made of stone. Large stones. Like huge flagstones."

"Wonderful, wonderful!" Dee exclaimed. "Do you see anything else?"

"Say again?" the archaeologist called back.

"I said...do...you...see...anything...else?"

"Not yet...we are clearing the stone floor."

"To the center!" Dee cried back. "Go to the very center of the room."

"Righto."

Several minutes went by. Dee could hear the sound of brushes sweeping dirt against stone over the walkie-talkie.

Then a voice. Then several voices, talking now very excitedly.

"Lord Dee!" the archaeologist called up. "There is something here."

"What is it, man—speak! Tell me!"

Then a few moments went by and more sounds of sweeping and brushing.

"Lord Dee," the man called up, "there is a design on the stone in the very middle of the room...something carved into the stonework...give me a minute..."

Several agonizing minutes went by. Then his voice again.

"Lord Dee, I have illuminated the design so I can see it clearly."

"Tell me exactly!" Dee called back.

"It appears to be a design of a red flower or a rose, inlaid into a stone tile."

"This is it!" Dee cried out. "Anything else?"

"Just the design in the stone."

"Break the tile—dig under the rose design, man, do it…now…do it now!" Lord Dee cried back.

"You want me to break the tile, sir? Are you sure? This is very old… it could be a Restoration-period structure, Lord Dee."

"Hang the Restoration, man, break the tile!" Lord Dee cried out. "And tell me what is underneath—but carefully…oh, very carefully, find what is hidden there…buried, I am sure of it…buried beneath the rose crystal design."

There was the sound of hammering and shattering and the prying of stone out of the place where it had rested in darkness for hundreds of years.

And then a voice.

"Lord Dee."

"Yes, man, tell all…tell it all to me, hold nothing back," Dee was saying, almost out of breath, gasping.

"I have completely removed the stone tile with the design of the rose."

"Yes? Yes?"

"And have revealed what is under it."

"Tell me now, sir, now, tell me!" Dee exclaimed, clutching his hands together.

"Underneath the rose stone, sir—"

"Yes?"

"There is nothing, Lord Dee. Nothing, I am afraid, but dirt."

✧

J.D. Blackstone had been unaware of the Staffordshire expedition, or that at that very moment, as he drove his Maserati over to the storage unit, Lord Dee, on the other side of the ocean, was receiving the empty news that his decades-old pursuit of esoteric and secret truth had yielded only dirt and stench.

It was early evening on the East Coast. There, at the storage facility in a back alley of the Georgetown area, Blackstone leaned out of the window of his car to punch in the gate code that would give him entrance.

He drove over to the metal storage unit marked 308 and parked his car. He walked to the door and fit a small key into the lock. It had not been opened for years and he had to jiggle the key several times. Then the key turned.

I have to do this, he was thinking to himself.

So he rolled up the steel door, clicked on the flickering fluorescent light overhead, and the dusty contents of the storage unit were revealed.

He did not know exactly what he was doing there or why he felt compelled to come.

Blackstone walked among the stacked boxes, randomly opening them. One was a collection of Marilyn's cooking books. Another contained Beth's school papers and report cards and projects she had done for classes. And her music books.

In another box he found an album of photographs of Marilyn and Beth and himself.

In the far corner were plastic bags of their clothing, carefully packed by him after their deaths.

Here were the accumulated traces of the lives that had once been a part of his but were now gone, the only physical evidence that these people whom he had loved had once actually been, but now were no more.

It was becoming harder for Blackstone to endure as he rummaged through box after box. Until he couldn't do it anymore. So he turned to leave.

He caught sight of the wide-brimmed hat that Marilyn used to wear when she worked in the flower garden.

He lifted it up off a box.

Something appeared from underneath the hat.

It was Marilyn's faded blue Bible.

In one particular page she had inserted a bookmark. Blackstone opened it to that page. It had been placed at the eleventh chapter of the Gospel of John.

He closed up the Bible, and with it in his hand, turned off the light, pulled down the metal door, and locked it. He had decided to take one memento of his wife, and it would be the Bible he had seen her leave with every Sunday morning on her way to church with Beth while he stayed home, drinking coffee and reading the Sunday paper.

When Blackstone got back to his condo, he turned on the lights and checked his voice mail. There was one message. It was from Julia.

"Hey, partner," she said brightly on the message. "So we are set for horseback riding tomorrow. Sounds great. I'll swing by your place at nine. Can't wait! Can't wait to see you! Bye."

Blackstone smiled and looked through his pile of mail quickly.

Then he took his wife's Bible and carried it into his bedroom and plopped down on his bed with it. He flipped it open to the bookmark at John, chapter eleven. He now noticed that the page had some of Marilyn's notes written in the margins.

The notes were next to the part where Jesus had been told that Lazarus had just died a few days before.

Marilyn had underlined, with red ink, the verse that recorded Jesus' response: "Jesus said to her, 'I am the resurrection and the life; he who believes in Me will live even if he dies, and everyone who lives and believes in Me will never die. Do you believe this?'"

"How can I believe that?" Blackstone muttered out loud.

Then he noticed the writing in the margin next to that verse.

It was as if Marilyn were standing next to him, with her gentle smile, reminding him of something deceptively simple. But something said so very truly that Blackstone could not shake the feeling of it, could not hide the sense that until that moment he had been living in a dark, closed room with no windows, no light…and it was just then that a door was cracked open.

The note read, "*Because forgiveness is forever, death isn't.*"

Blackstone read it again. And then again. Then he read through the chapter about the miraculous raising of Lazarus by Jesus in the presence of a crowd of witnesses in broad daylight.

Lying in bed, with his head propped by a pillow, he turned to the very beginning of the Gospel of John.

He would begin reading.

And then he would keep reading.

But before he did, he said something out loud, very quietly, but enough so he could tell it had been said. Was it a prayer, exactly? He couldn't say, not then at least.

If this is truly true, help me find the way to believe so I can know for certain that it is true...so then I can truly believe...

Then he started at the first verse of chapter one of John. He would not stop reading until sometime very close to the end of that Gospel, the time he reached the twenty-first chapter, when his eyes began to close.

That was when Blackstone noticed his eyes growing heavy, and so he kept them shut for just a moment.

An instant after that, he was deeply, and deliciously, and soundly asleep.

And J.D. Blackstone would remain asleep, straight through the night, until the next morning, when finally he would be awakened by the sound of Julia ringing the doorbell.

ABOUT THE AUTHOR

Craig Parshall is Senior Vice President and General Counsel of the National Religious Broadcasters Association. He speaks nationally on legal and Christian worldview issues, is a magazine columnist, and has authored seven legal-suspense novels: the five installments in the Chambers of Justice series, and the stand-alone novels *Trial by Ordeal* and *The Rose Conspiracy.*

TRIAL BY ORDEAL
Craig Parshall

Kevin Hastings is ready to stake out his piece of the good life. The last thing he has in mind is a spot under the Chicago River... courtesy of the local Mafia.

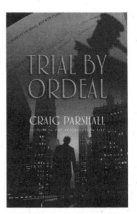

Pursuing a good real-estate investment, the young professor stumbles onto a prime chunk of property in downtown Chicago. It just has an old church building to be cleared away. But the dream deal turns into an ordeal when Kevin discovers he's signed a contract with the Mob—one he can't deliver on.

With death threats coming from the Mob boss and lawsuits piling up, the one bright spot is his new love interest, Tess...until he finds out she's a rabid architectural preservationist.

What else can go wrong? Don't ask. Kevin hires an attorney to untangle the mess, and the guy turns out to be a master of legal intimidation and dirty tricks. When he starts dispensing pain and chaos, Kevin has to run for his life. He ends up finding sanctuary at a local rescue mission.

The lawyers keep ringing the cash register while the bell tolls for Kevin—and he begins to wonder if there's Somebody who can bring justice into all the torment...

"An enjoyable romp for legal thriller aficionados."
Publishers Weekly magazine

To read a sample chapter of this or any other Harvest House book, go to www.harvesthousepublishers.com

CROWN OF FIRE
Craig and Janet Parshall
Book 1 of the Thistle and the Cross series

"There are words in this land as dangerous as black gunpowder."
—St. Andrews, Scotland, 1546—

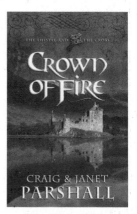

Ransom Mackenzie's life is changed forever when he witnesses one of the Scottish Reformers being burnt at the stake. Soon the young man throws in his lot with the Protestant revolutionaries and John Knox, their spiritual leader.

His dreams of heroism end abruptly when the rebellion is crushed. His father is arrested for printing the Scriptures in the common tongue, and Ransom is forced to hide in the Scottish Highlands. There he meets and starts to fall in love with wild, lovely Margaret.

But his time away from the turmoil is not to last. Knox, facing powerful opposition, summons him to London. Enticed by the glittering surroundings of the Court—and the allure of a young woman of the aristocracy—Ransom finds himself at a crossroads...where a man can burn for his beliefs, and silence is betrayal.

*To read a sample chapter of this or any other Harvest House book,
go to www.harvesthousepublishers.com*

CAPTIVES AND KINGS
Craig and Janet Parshall
Book 2 of the Thistle and the Cross series

London, England, in the year of our Lord 1606

*"You must take Peter with you," Andrew told his brother
in a chilling voice. "Else they will put him to the rack
in place of you. They will torture your son."*

*"No!" cried Philip. "Peter has nothing to do with this. He has a life. He
is in love. I will not ask him to leave England because of my mistakes!"*

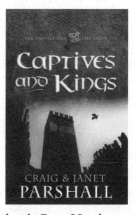

Andrew Mackenzie, an ambitious aide to King James, has little but contempt for his wayward and adventuring brother, Philip... who in turn resents Andrew's high-handedness and superior attitude. The rift is deep, and it seems it will be permanent after Andrew learns of Philip's unwitting involvement in a plot to kill the king—and insists that he and his son, Peter, flee England.

After sailing to the New World with his son—whose heart was left behind with the lovely Rose Heatherton—Philip struggles for survival amid the dangers of Jamestown, Virginia. Back in London, Andrew is the target of a spiritual battle surrounding the King James Bible translation, and of palace intrigues involving yet another plot against the Crown.

Separated by oceans and bitter resentment, will the two brothers survive their own battles to meet on the common ground of forgiveness?

*To read a sample chapter of this or any other Harvest House book,
go to www.harvesthousepublishers.com*

SONS OF GLORY
Craig and Janet Parshall
Book 3 of the Thistle and the Cross series

***When blood is shed,
each man, each woman, must make a decision...***

Boston, Massachusetts—March 5, 1770

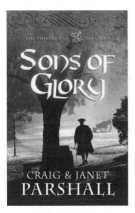

When Nathan Mackenzie, a young lawyer, witnesses the Boston Massacre, he and his mentor John Adams are pulled into defending British soldiers—though both men are pro-independence.

Conflict with fellow patriots and a drama-filled court case follow—and added to this, Nathan struggles with his minister brother, Edward, who remains firmly loyal to what he considers the God-ordained British government.

When the two men's youngest brother, Robby, a radical patriot, is arrested and sentenced to hang, Edward and Nathan must each search heart and soul. How will they act? In dangerous and uncertain times, where does their ultimate loyalty lie? And does ultimate glory rest with a new political order or with something higher and greater?

The Mackenzie family's legacy lives and battles on in colonial America as the turbulent story begun in Crown of Fire *and* Captives and Kings *concludes.*

To read a sample chapter of this or any other Harvest House book, go to www.harvesthousepublishers.com

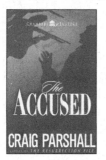

Missing Witness

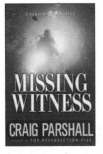

A relaxing North Carolina vacation for attorney Will Chambers? Not likely. When Will investigates a local inheritance case, the long arm of the law reaches out of the distant past to cast a shadow over his client's life…and the life of his own family. As the attorney's legal battle uncovers corruption, piracy, the deadly grip of greed, and the haunting sins of a man's past, the true question must be faced—*Can a person ever really run away from God?*

The Last Judgment

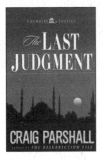

A mysterious religious cult plans to spark an "Armageddon" in the Middle East. Suddenly, a huge explosion blasts the top of the Jerusalem Temple Mount into rubble, with hundreds of Muslim casualties. And attorney Will Chambers' client, Gilead Amahn, a convert to Christianity from Islam, becomes the prime suspect. In his harrowing pursuit of the truth, Will must face the greatest threat yet to his marriage, his family, and his faith, while cataclysmic events plunge the world closer to the Last Judgment.